# FROM DANGER TO DESIRE

## PLEDGED TO PROTECT SERIES
## BOOK 2

## VELLA DAY

Erotic Reads Publishing

**From Danger To Desire**

**Pledged to Protect Series**

**Book 2**

Copyright © 2018 by Vella Day

www.velladay.com

velladayauthor@gmail.com

# ABOUT THE BOOK

**Second chances are great until a killer comes between them.**

Homicide detective, Derek Benally, thought his day couldn't get any worse after he spent all night processing a murder, but he couldn't have been more wrong. The phone call from his nephew telling him Derek's sister is dead unravels him.

Dr. Kelly Rutland is on the verge of a cancer breakthrough when she receives the horrifying news that her sister was in a fatal car accident. The cops ruled it accidental, but Kelly refuses to believe it was anything other than murder. She's determined to do whatever it takes to find the killer.

When Derek learns the woman he had never stopped loving has moved back to town, and that both of their sisters died on the same night, he reconnects with her. Little does he realize that seeing her again will send the killer in Kelly's direction.

# CHAPTER ONE

TAMPA FLORIDA HOMICIDE detective Derek Benally slammed his cruiser's door and scanned the crime scene. Streetlights along the I-275 entrance ramp flooded the main street. He ducked under the tape, his gray police issue, t-shirt plastered against his back. Damned humidity.

Cars honked on the busy thoroughfare and gas fumes mingled with the fishy smell of the bay, adding a measure of unpleasantness to what had already become an unpleasant night.

He halted at the scene and flashed his badge. The two officers guarding the body stepped back. The jumper lay broken on the concrete in front of the thirty-story Waters Edge Condominium. Derek looked up at the surrounding balconies, and his gut soured at the man's violent death.

Loosely covered by a bloodstained sheet, a hand and a foot stuck out at odd angles. Derek knelt next to the victim and studied the blood spatter that extended a good two feet to the street side of the body. Another nine inches and the victim would have soiled the stone fountain. Wouldn't the rich condo owners have had a fit over that desecration?

He shoved his hand in his pocket, squeezed his sage packet, and closed his eyes to center himself, to separate his logical mind from his emotions. He waited to learn if his spiritual guides would send down a hint about what had happened.

A low rumble grumbled in the sky. Could it be them? Anticipation sped up his pulse.

Flashes from the crowd broke his concentration—or had his guides cut the connection? Damn curiosity seekers. He needed help from above.

Did these gawkers actually think a photo of a covered body would satisfy them? Brain matter had oozed out from under the dead man's head, and from the bloody protrusion of the right femur, the victim's leg had been crushed in the fall. If they ever had an up-close look at a real dead body, they'd be sorry. They only looked good on TV.

He swatted away the bugs that landed around his eyes and nose. When one little bugger began feasting on his arm, he flicked the insect away.

Derek lifted the sheet covering the white male, careful not to touch the body. What a waste. Even after nine years on the force, he didn't like seeing the gruesome effect blunt force trauma had on someone.

He studied the building's balconies, trying to figure out why the body had come to rest so far from the condo? Assuming the man stepped off the balcony and hadn't leaped off the railing like a cliff diver, the victim should have landed closer to the entrance, not out by the road.

Given the body's location, suicide didn't seem to be cause of his death. Perhaps the man had been pushed. His pulse sped up at the emotional pain this man must have experienced, and the implication of a possible murder prickled his skin.

Cars honked at the slowdown clogging the Interstate onramp in front of the condo. Damn rubberneckers.

Before Derek could make more mental calculations, Gonzalez, a new recruit, who had been the first on the scene, hovered over him.

Derek stood and looked down at the short, stocky officer. The young cop looked like a puppy dog—eager to please and happy to have to a job. Ah, to be twenty-one again.

"The doorman ID'd him as Carl Vanderwall of condo 2104," the puppy cop said. "Given the location, I called the Captain." He puffed out his chest.

"And?"

The officer's baby-browns shot down to the sidewalk. "The Captain told me to tell you not to hassle the tenants too much." His voice faded at the last few words.

Derek bristled. He wanted to stop any speculation, especially since Gonzalez was new to the force. "I've never strong-armed anyone into talking."

The officer looked up with eyes wide and held up two hands. "Hey, don't shoot the messenger. He also said to remind you the Mayor lives in this high rise."

Like he gave a rat's ass. Derek nodded toward the balcony. "Anyone see him jump?"

Gonzalez motioned toward two teenaged girls sitting in the police car at the side of the building, away from the crowd. "They were leaving the library across the street when they saw him fall, but they couldn't say whether he was pushed or not. They remained calm at first, but then rushed to tell the doorman. They're pretty shaken up."

"Damn." Kids shouldn't be exposed to such horror. "Did the doorman see anything?"

"No, sir. He was attending to something at the desk when the man jumped. The moment he returned to his post, the girls raced up to him."

"Okay. I'll have a word with them. Did you call the medical examiner yet?"

"Sure did. He's on his way."

"Good work." He half expected Gonzalez's tongue to roll out and pant, but instead the new recruit shot Derek a toothy grin.

"And you notified the crime scene unit, right?" He couldn't be sure if procedure was cemented in his brain yet.

"Yes, sir."

Derek nodded, and then made his way to the witnesses. He whipped out his phone and called the precinct a few blocks away. Thinking the girls would feel more comfortable if a woman escorted them home, he asked for a female officer. He'd never been any good at handling females in a time of need.

A cool puff of rotten egg smelling wind pushed through the humid air, relieving the oppressive heat. The bay sure was in a bad mood tonight, belching algae bloom like a smokestack.

Derek stepped over to the cruiser where a beat cop stood watch. The two witnesses were huddled in the backseat—a blonde girl consoling a sobbing brunette. He couldn't be sure under the glare of the streetlights, but he guessed they were no more than sixteen or seventeen.

Derek dropped to his haunches and pulled out his notepad and pen. His pants bunched at his thighs, and he tugged on the fabric to ease the constraint.

The air conditioning poured out from the opened door, providing brief relief.

"Hi, I'm Detective Benally."

The blonde pulled out her iPod earplugs as the brunette sat up and froze, her eyes wide. He knew his six foot seven frame and bald head scared a lot of people, but he didn't know how to make himself look less intimidating other than to crouch down.

"Can you tell me your names?" He used as soft a tone as he could muster.

"I'm Carrie Wilman," the blonde answered.

"I'm Jennifer Mendez," the brunette said wiping the back of her hand under her nose and sniffling.

Derek pulled out a clean handkerchief and handed it to her.

"Thanks. He's really dead, isn't he?" the brunette asked.

"I'm afraid so. Can you girls tell me what you saw?"

The brunette spoke up. "We were crossing the street from the library to go to our car when I happened to look across the street. He was...in midair." She hiccuped a sob. "It was terrible. His arms were flapping and his feet were kicking." She squeezed her eyes shut. "I can't get the sight of him out of my head. When he hit the ground, he made such a loud thunk. Oh, God." She dropped her face into her hands and sobbed once more.

His heart lurched at her pain. She'd never forget the man's shattered body. He could still remember the first time he'd seen a fatal car wreck, and the horrific image had never faded.

Derek turned toward the more composed girl. "Did you happen to look up and see anyone on a balcony?" As in someone who pushed the victim?

"No," the blonde said.

It had been worth asking. "I've called for a policewoman to follow you home.

"Thanks," the brunette said, holding out his handkerchief.

Derek stuffed it in his back pocket, not knowing how else to comfort them. He glanced back at the street. The CSU team had arrived, their flashes lighting up the sidewalk in short bursts.

It was going to be a long, grueling night.

✳✳✳

Seven frigging days of non-stop work and Derek still hadn't made any headway in the Vanderwall case. He had yet to figure out whether Carl had jumped from the high rise or had been pushed. The neighbors had offered no insight into the man's apparent suicide. His coworkers had claimed there was no way he'd take his life. They said he'd only invested a small portion of his money in market, and when it tanked, he'd remained calm, unlike so many of his clients.

Before Derek had a chance to decide his next investigative lead, the phone next to his bed rang. He dropped the dumbbells he'd been hefting and answered, slightly out of breath. "Benally."

"Uncle Derek," his nephew whimpered. "Mom's...Mom's dead. She's really dead. I don't know what to do." Billy's breath hitched. "She...she shot herself in the head."

The fear lacing his voice ripped at Derek's soul. His mind screamed a panic alert as his blood pressure skyrocketed. *Think. I'm a First Responder, dammit*. His nephew was fifteen. He could handle this. "Are you sure she isn't breathing?"

Good. *ABC*. Airway, breathing, circulation. A bullet to the head wasn't an automatic death sentence.

"She's not moving or anything."

His heart nearly jumped out of his chest. Rayne couldn't be gone.

"Call 9-1-1 and hold a towel to the wound, okay? I'll be there as fast as I can."

Anger clenched his gut. Derek grabbed his sage packet and squeezed hard, but his talisman failed to give him any solace.

"Hurry!" Billy cried.

Heart racing, he snatched his wallet, badge, gun, and keys. Once in the car, Derek dialed Billy needing to hear that maybe his nephew had overreacted; that his sister might be only slightly wounded, but the line was busy. Shit, that's right. 9-1-1 kept the caller on the line until help arrived.

Derek tossed his cell on the passenger's seat and sped down the tree-lined street. His fingers gripped the wheel too tight, and he over-corrected on the first bend, nearly clipping an oncoming car. A horn blared.

His sister couldn't be dead. There had to be a mistake. Billy was wrong. He had to be.

Derek turned the truck's AC on high, hoping the cool air would clear his head. After what seemed like an endless drive, he pulled in front of Rayne's house, hoping Billy might be playing a sick joke on him, something he'd done many times before. Unfortunately, the flashing ambulance lights confirmed the worst.

The call was real.

His muscles tightened as adrenaline shot to his heart, and a metallic taste tinged his tongue.

He cut the engine a second before another police car came to a stop behind him. A few neighbors stood outside their doors gawking, apparently not willing to miss out on the chaos.

Derek jumped out of his truck and raced up the drive. Oh, man. There was the pile of lumber he'd placed at the side of her house that he'd promised Rayne he'd build a new porch with. She'd bugged him for weeks to begin the project. This weekend he'd planned to start.

A lump caught in his throat as he swiped a hand across his eyes. She couldn't be gone.

Before he reached the front door, Officer Juan Sosa escorted Derek's nephew outside.

"Billy?" Derek scanned the boy from head to toe to make sure he too hadn't been injured.

His nephew looked up at him, his eyes red, his shoulders slumped. "Mom's d...dead." He hiccuped and his whole body shook, tearing Derek up inside.

Derek rushed forward and drew Billy to his chest, but his nephew didn't hug back, as giant sobs erupted from Billy's thin body.

Darkness clouded his brain as tears trickled down his own cheeks, and Derek grasped onto Billy for support.

His nephew pushed away and wiped the tears from his face. "Why did she do it? Why did she have to kill herself?" His lower lip trembled.

"I-I don't know." Derek's voice faded with the last word. "I need to see her." To make sure there wasn't something he could do.

Officer Sosa placed a hand on Billy's back. "Come on, son. Let's sit in the car. I'd like to ask you some more questions." He nodded to Derek as he escorted Billy to the patrol car.

Derek rushed inside Rayne's house and froze. His sister's lifeless body was on the floor in a pool of blood, and his gaze went to the gun in her hand.

*His* gun. *His* Glock. Suicide: the worse crime he could imagine.

Guilt swamped him. He shouldn't have lent the weapon to her, but she'd insisted.

A paramedic kneeling beside Rayne looked up and shook his head.

Derek nearly lost his morning bagel as a wave of depression, dark and heavy, nearly drowned him. He reached out to grab the table near the entrance to keep from losing his balance, and then fumbled for his sage packet.

*"The child is his mother's son."*

Derek spun around to see who'd spoken, but no one was there. Had his spiritual guides reached out to him? Or had he imagined the unearthly sounding words?

"Sir, are you all right?" the paramedic asked.

Derek turned back to the man kneeling on the floor. "I'm fine."

Like hell he was. It took all he had to keep his voice even. He swallowed hard. "Have you determined time of death?"

"You'll have to wait for the medical examiner."

He knew that.

As if by magic, his long-time friend and Assistant ME, John Ayo, came in with his gear, followed by the CSU team, headed by Carson Stepping. The team, all dressed in white, looked like angels coming to claim their victim.

When both men offered their condolences, all Derek could do was nod at their offered sympathy.

He studied the position of Rayne's body. Despite the evidence before him, no way would she have taken her own life.

Ayo knelt down beside her and examined Rayne with a gentleness and thoroughness Derek appreciated. The doctor wrote detailed notes and took scrapings from her scalp and under her nails. He then helped direct one of the CSU techs taking photos of the body.

Minutes seemed like hours. Wanting to ask him to hurry, Derek nearly bit his tongue. The large black man didn't seem to notice his need to know.

Derek scanned the dining room. Nothing was broken. Nothing had been disturbed. There hadn't been an apparent attack, and his body nearly caved at the lack of foul play.

After what must have been at least half an hour, Derek's impatience got the best of him. "Do you have a fix on the time of death yet?"

Ayo let out a long breath and sat back on his haunches. "If I had to guess from the rigor, I'd say about twelve hours ago. Look here." John pulled Rayne's body toward him and pointed to the back of her neck. "See the lividity pattern? The bruising shows she died here."

Had he expected she'd been killed elsewhere, and then dumped back at her house? He could only hope. Suicide and Rayne were incomprehensible together.

Stepping's team continued to photograph the scene, while another woman he'd never met pulled out her tape measure and took careful measurements of the body's position in relation to the room.

When a hand grabbed his arm, Derek jerked.

"You can't stay here any longer, Derek." It was Sosa. "This is a crime scene."

He was well aware of the rules. He wanted to stay; wanted to make sure the team did everything they could to prove someone had killed his sister.

His friend tugged on his arm again. *Time's up.* Derek took one final look at the tragedy, turned, and followed his fellow cop outside. The sun's rays beat down on his face, and the air was unusually calm, as if nothing sinister had happened inside.

Miraculously, the neighbors had disappeared, almost as if the President has issued a nuclear bomb warning. Billy's face was pressed against the cruiser's window looking lost, and Derek's heart broke. Again.

He wanted to shut his eyes and pretend when he opened them, the nightmare would be over, that Rayne would drive in and laugh at the practical joke, and Billy would race by on his skateboard doing dumb-ass tricks like Derek used to do when he was Billy's age.

But he knew this horror was all too real.

Convinced Billy held the key to Rayne's death, Derek approached the squad car. Before he reached his nephew, the front door opened behind him.

"Benally," the familiar voice called.

Derek turned. Detective Seinkievitz, the primary on the case, motioned him inside. Glancing back at Billy, he held up his hand to indicate he'd be right back and followed the detective inside.

"Did you find something?" Derek clenched his fists at his side.

"Yup."

✳✳✳

Kelly Rutland frowned when her door chimed out the first few beats of *Send My Regards to Broadway*. She'd just arrived home from having breakfast with a friend and wanted nothing more than to get out of her sticky clothes and take a shower.

With one hand on the doorknob, she looked through the peephole and forgot about the shower.

Two policemen stood back from the entrance. Heart pounding, she unlocked the door, and as soon as opened it, warm moist air smacked her in the face.

"Doctor Kelly Rutland?" a female officer asked.

Their cruiser sat in her drive. The officer's rigid stance made her muscles tighten. "Yes?" She swallowed hard.

"I'm Officer Carranza and this is my partner, Officer Oxtal. May we come in?" Both officers showed their badges. The male cop reminded her of Ichabod Crane while the female looked like a much younger version of the cop on that 80's TV show, *Cagney and Lacy.*

"Sure." This must be bad. Really, really bad.

They followed her to the living room. "I think you'd better sit down," Officer Oxtal said, sounding like the funeral director who'd buried her dad.

Kelly's legs nearly buckled. "What's happened?" Ugly, sludgy dread moved through her veins as she dropped into the nearest chair.

The two officers remained standing, backs ramrod straight, and for one hysterical moment, she wondered if they were getting ready for inspection or a firing squad. They said nothing. Jesus, why didn't they answer her? "Tell me what happened."

Finally, the Cagney look-alike took a step forward and twisted her fingers into a knot, her eyes full of sympathy. "I'm really sorry to have to tell you, but your sister, Stefanie –"

Kelly's vision blurred, and her breath caught in her throat. Not Stefanie. No!

"Was in a fatal car wreck last night," the cop finished.

"That can't be!" Kelly shot out of the chair as a giant sob caught in her throat. "I don't believe you. St-Stef can't be—" She couldn't say the word. Couldn't even think it.

These people were lying. Stef would walk through the door any minute now and—

"I'm sorry," Officer Oxtal said.

Kelly grabbed her stomach to calm the sharp jabbing in her abdomen. "How? When?" A gush of tears poured down her cheeks as a low keening sound came out of her mouth. "Nooo. It can't be." Kelly swiped a hand under her eyes, but the flow of tears wouldn't stop.

"The roads were pretty slick last night. From the length of the skid marks on the pavement, she was going close to ninety when her car flipped over a guardrail on the Crosstown Expressway. I'm very sorry."

His eyes spoke the truth—a truth that clawed at her heart. Kelly wanted Stef next to her, warm, happy, alive.

Another piercing stab shot straight to her belly. God, this couldn't be true. She sniffled, but her crying wouldn't cease. "Was she run...run off the road? Was another car involved?" The eyes of the officers never changed. She hadn't misunderstood. "There's no way she'd be speeding unless someone was chasing her." An evil darkness slid down her spine, taking her breath away.

"We're still investigating."

Kelly raced to the kitchen counter and grabbed a handful of tissues. She blew her nose and swiped her cheeks clean, but the ache continued to gnaw at her. With her arms wrapped tightly around her waist, she headed back to the sofa. She stopped short, and then spun toward them. "What time was the accident?" She needed facts. Needed the focus. Needed anything except for this awful biting pain.

She reached up and whipped off her ponytail holder, the band's constraint oppressive.

"The medical examiner put time of death at approximately eight thirty last night."

"Last *night*? Why didn't you notify me earlier?"

His gaze dropped to the floor for a split second. "We couldn't find any ID on her. At least at first. Her cell had wedged under the front seat. Once we located it, we called the last number, but it went to voicemail."

Her mind ceased to function for a moment, the horror too much to bear. Voicemail? Oh, God. She'd turned off her cell right after she spoke with Stef. "I... I did speak with her on the phone around eight. I asked her to go see a movie with me, but she...she said she was on her way to visit a friend who wasn't feeling well." Kelly swallowed the lump in her throat.

The policeman pulled out his pad, and her gaze followed his movements. His fingernails needed cleaning, and his right thumbnail was jagged.

"Do you know the name of this friend?" he asked in a robotic monotone.

Agony squeezed her heart as Kelly shot her gaze to his expressionless face. "No. Yes. I —" God, she couldn't think. Her mind refused to focus. She rubbed her forehead with her palm. Then the name came to her, as it had from Stef's mouth many times. "Rayne Anderson. She's a trial attorney in town."

"Rain? As in R-A-I-N?" His pen hovered above his pad—a gnarly, tooth bitten pen. His brows pointed southward.

"No." She was losing her mind. She never noticed quirky details like dirty, chipped fingernails or chomped-on pens. Maybe she'd entered some alternate reality and Stef wasn't really dead. Maybe all of this was an illusion caused by heat exhaustion.

"Ma'am?"

She looked up at his expectant face. Reality slammed into her again. "No. That's not right."

"Excuse me?" he asked.

*Stick to the facts.* "I think she spells it, R-A-Y-N-E."

He jotted down the information before glancing up. "Perhaps your sister was running late and driving too fast for the wet conditions."

"That's bullshit! My sister would never drive that fast."

"Ma'am—"

"Oh, no." Bile raced up her throat as she fumbled for the chair for support and slid down.

"What is it?" The cop took a slight step forward. This time he sounded less like a robot and more like a human who cared.

# CHAPTER TWO

"I...I just remembered," Kelly said. "Stef called me back a little after eight thirty. She'd already stopped by Rayne's house, but Rayne wasn't feeling up to having visitors, so she left. That was the last time I spoke with her." A giant tear slid down her cheek.

Silence hung between them like a dark, heavy cloud. The female officer knelt down and placed a hand on her shoulder. "Is there someone you can call to be with you?"

Kelly rocked back and forth, her mind unable to put meaning to the woman's question. The officer handed her the box of tissues from the kitchen counter, and Kelly dabbed her eyes and blew her nose again. "What did you ask?"

"Is there someone to stay with you?"

She swallowed. "My sister was my best friend, and my mother...lives in California." Her fists clenched at the agony. The room spun.

"A neighbor perhaps?"

She shook her head, grappling for an answer. Kelly blinked back the tears, forcing herself to answer the woman's question.

***

Derek sat cross-legged on the floor of his darkened bedroom. Two candles flickered on the hand woven straw tray, along with his prized hawk feather and cherished wolf skin. His sister had given him some incense a few years back, but he hadn't burned the sticks because his way of praying was different from hers.

Tonight, he lit the sticks—for Rayne.

Even after eleven hours of solitude, he hadn't figured out squat. Damn. He wouldn't give up—or rather he couldn't give up. There had to be a reason for Rayne's death—and it wasn't because she was pregnant.

An avalanche of injustice slammed into Derek. A giant claw grabbed his insides and twisted. Rayne had wanted another child worse than anything. Now her wish would never come true.

Seinkievitz had found the tossed pregnancy test in her bathroom trashcan and implied she might have been depressed over the results. Unmarried and the sole supporter of her son could have triggered the suicide, he'd said.

Derek didn't buy the scenario. Someone killed her.

Scented smoke curled upward, and the mesmerizing effect of the candles helped him go inward to find his soul.

"Tell me why you took Rayne," he intoned to his spirit guides, even though he didn't expect them to answer. They rarely spoke, but he had to try to reach them.

Derek slowed his breathing and concentrated on his surroundings. His nightstand clock ticked, and the air conditioner hummed a constant buzz. A television show rumbled in a neighbor's apartment.

He closed his eyes and rubbed his hands over the feather and animal skin until he could feel their powers unleash. All noise fused into a static hum. His legs numbed, his shoulders relaxed, his heartbeat slowed. Then his body ceased to exist, and his mind floated above him.

*Don't try to wake the person who is pretending to sleep*, said a voice deep inside his head. At least he thought his mind had conjured up those words.

A shiver pricked every nerve. He kept his eyes shut and his body still. "Who's pretending to sleep?"

His arms turned heavy and a loud shout outside his window

brought him back to his world. He waited for the low voice to return, but the guides were gone.

His eyes flew open and one candle went out. Had the air conditioner killed the flame or had the guides entered his world? His heart beat rapidly, and his hands dampened as he realized he'd successfully linked with them—unless the whole event had been his imagination gone wild.

What the hell good had contacting them done? Derek was no closer to understanding Rayne's last moments than when he'd started the ritual.

More frustrated than ever, he blew out the other candle and stood up. Angry his rare contact with the spirits hadn't told him shit, he flicked on the overhead light.

Fuck it. He didn't need any Indian gods to tell him Rayne would never have taken her own life. Strong people didn't crack, no matter what happened to them. His sister's husband had been killed in Iraq leaving her with a nine year old, and yet she'd gone back to law school. She'd learned to take one day at a time.

He'd have to do the same. Take one day at a time, that is. Even if it killed him, he would find justice for Rayne's death.

Hell, he'd watched men kill time and time again, and he'd managed to stay whole, believing death to be a normal process of nature, but Rayne's dying served no purpose.

His younger sister had always been there for him. Then, in a flash, she was gone, leaving a void so deep he wasn't sure he could climb out. But he had to, for Billy's sake.

Billy.

Guilt grabbed him by the ass and nearly toppled him. He should have been there for his nephew; been a better uncle. He kept telling himself his job came first, but now he could see what a line of crap that had been. He should have taken more spent more time with the kid, shown him how to hunt and fish. Maybe then, his nephew wouldn't have grown up so angry.

Once Sosa finished interrogating his nephew, Derek had asked Billy to stay with him. They needed each other, yet Billy had insisted on returning to the academy where he attended school. Derek still couldn't believe it. The kid said his friends were there, and they'd understand how much he was hurting.

Like he couldn't understand his pain?

Billy's rejection hurt almost as much as Rayne's death.

Damn it. Tomorrow, after his dad returned from hunting, he'd have to tell him his only daughter had blown her brains out.

Tomorrow a little bit more of him would die.

A loud rap on his front door disturbed his introspection. Who the hell could that be at 10p.m.?

He couldn't handle more bad news. Derek strapped on his Glock and strode to the front of the house as the pounding continued.

"Benally, open up," the man yelled.

"I'm coming." What was this guy's problem?

After checking the peephole, he opened the door, surprised to see Rayne's boyfriend standing there. Their paths had only crossed once or twice before. "Justin?"

Justin Bladen's tie was half undone, his shirt untucked, and it looked as if he'd run his fingers through his hair a hundred times.

"Why the fuck didn't you tell me about Rayne?" Justin shouted, as he barged in uninvited. "I had to find out on the goddamn television that the woman I love is dead." His face turned red.

At learning Rayne's suicide made the evening news, a fresh wash of anger blasted him. "I'm sorry. I didn't have your number."

Derek closed the door and studied the wild man, refusing to rise to the bait. Justin's gaze bounced all over the place, clearly not able to focus on one object for more than a few seconds.

"I assumed you knew."

"How could I have known?" Justin spit back, waving a clenched fist. A moment later, his chest deflated. "I called Rayne early this morning, but she didn't answer. I never thought she'd kill herself. How could she have done such a thing?" The last sentence resembled more of a croak than a human voice.

"Come on. Sit down." Derek wondered how Justin had found out where he lived. Maybe he'd looked up his name in Rayne's address book.

Justin tugged on his tie, and then whipped it off as he swayed over to the sofa.

Without prompting, Justin began. "We spent yesterday together with your dad. Rayne was so excited. Did she tell you we were having a baby?" He sniffled and rubbed his eyes with the back of his sleeve.

"Not in person. CSU found her pregnancy test in the trash." Derek forced down his depression and focused on Justin. Could he have killed his sister?

"Oh."

"Did something happen at Dad's?" Derek tried to put the pieces together.

"I'd never met your father in all these months we'd been dating, but Rayne really wanted your father to be the first to know about the baby." He wrapped one end of his tie around his palm, made a fist and tugged on the other end.

That didn't surprise him. Rayne always cared what the old man thought. Derek eased back. "She was excited, huh?" Derek could almost hear her squeal as she announced the news. Deep inside, a part of him smiled.

"I'd never seen her beam like that before."

Her cheerful image didn't mesh with suicide. "Then why would she kill herself?" Like a flicked switch, Derek fought back his rage. Her death wasn't fair; wasn't right.

"I wish I knew." He brought his fists to his mouth, then dropped his hands and looked straight at Derek. "No, that's not true. Maybe her death was my fault."

Derek jumped up from the seat and lunged at him. Justin stiffened and held up his hands. "I didn't hurt her, I swear."

Derek stopped in mid-stride. "Tell me," he threatened.

"Once we returned to her place, we argued. That's all I meant."

Derek studied Justin's face. Justin's hands didn't fidget, and his gaze remained steady. Derek eased back down on the edge of the seat, anxious to hear how their fight might have led to his sister's death. "Keep going."

"Rayne blew everything out of proportion. I think her hormones were on a rampage."

Not this early in the pregnancy, he bet, but what did he know about babies? "What did you argue about?" He wasn't able to keep his voice even.

Justin dropped his head into his hands and sobbed. When he gained control of himself, he looked up. "I wanted to get married right away." He wiped a hand under his nose. "Your sister didn't. She said she wanted to wait until after the baby was born before we tied the knot." He swallowed hard. "I couldn't understand why she didn't want to give the baby my name right away."

"What reason did she give?"

Justin drew his fingers along the corners of his mouth, and his lips distorted. "She wanted to see how I'd handle her pregnancy before she committed to marriage. Does that make any sense?"

Derek tried to put himself in Rayne's shoes. "She practically raised Billy by herself. I guess she thought she could do it again."

"Yeah, that's what she said. But still."

The strain on Justin's face mirrored his own. "Rayne was her own woman." And fiercely private about her background.

"Don't I know it?"

"How upset was she during this argument?" Derek asked, his mind attempting to put the scenario into a neat compartment. Order brought closure.

"Very. I said some awful things to her." His eyes watered, but this time, Justin didn't wipe away the tears. "We, ah, yelled a lot until she refused to talk anymore. I stupidly told her we were through, caput, done." Justin scrubbed a hand over his face and sniffled. "I didn't really mean I'd leave her for good. I only told her that in order to force her to change her mind."

"Yeah, well shit happens." The callous sounding comment came out without any thought.

"I know."

Derek never let his gaze drop from Justin's face. "Then what? There had to have been something more serious than that to have caused her to take her own life. Rayne was no stranger to arguments. She was a goddamn lawyer."

Justin jumped up and stepped behind the chair, acting as though it would protect him from the horror of Rayne's death. He rubbed his hands along the back edge. "My boss, Mr. Davis, was throwing a party I *had* to go to. I couldn't stay and work out our issues."

"You left her?" Derek raised his voice. He wanted to pummel the guy.

"What? You've never walked out on woman who wasn't reasonable?"

Derek took a moment to decide whether he wanted to admit he'd done the same thing. "Yeah, I have." To Kelly. He'd walked out on her when she wanted to break up with him. "Tell me this. Would you have lost your job if you'd told Mr. Davis you were having problems and couldn't go to the party?"

A flash of uncertainty crossed his face. "No, but my boss was counting on me to land a big client that night. The commissions from this guy alone would have paid for all of Billy's tuition this next year."

Derek softened. "If that were the case, why didn't you tell Rayne what was at stake? For Billy, she might have understood." Derek knew the answer, but he wanted to hear Justin's explanation. Once his sister became pissed off, she sulked, and then got even.

"I explained all of that. Rayne grabbed a soda, flicked on the TV, and refused to talk to me. What was I supposed to do? She wanted her space."

A bit of understanding surfaced. "Then you left."

"Yes. I figured she'd fume a little bit, sleep on it, and by morning she'd see my side of things." He wove his tie through his hands as though the feel of silk soothed his pain. He hung his head. "I feel so bad about the way things ended."

So did he. Derek still couldn't imagine Rayne being so unreasonable. "Did she act more despondent than angry by the time you split?"

Justin avoided eye contact and asked instead, "Could I have something cold to drink?" He rubbed his throat. "I'm dry."

His avoidance of the question put Derek on alert. "Sure." He retrieved a cold beer from the fridge, handed Justin a bottle, and sat down. "Mad or sad?"

The bottle froze halfway to Justin's lips, and then he lowered the beer. "What's with the routine questions?" His lips pulled back in a sneer. "This just another case to you, Detective?"

Derek tamped down his anger. If Justin understood Rayne at all, he'd know how close they were. "Hardly. I loved Rayne. The way I ask questions is an old habit. Nothing more."

Justin's shoulders relaxed. He stepped in front of the chair and collapsed back down onto the seat. "I'm sorry. I'm not thinking straight." Justin stroked his fingers through his hair and leaned forward. "Can I be honest with you?"

Derek stilled. "Sure."

"I never expected Rayne to react the way she did. Yes, she argued, being a lawyer and all, but once she quieted, I freaked. I wasn't prepared to deal with the silent treatment. We were in love. At least I thought we were. I've never seen anyone go inward like that before." Justin slammed his palm against his forehead. "The whole discussion was stupid. If I'd agreed to wait longer to get married, she'd be here today."

"It's not your fault."

Or was it? Justin should have stayed with Rayne to make sure she was okay before he left. He studied Justin. If he'd been in Justin's shoes, and the woman had not been his sister, would he have walked out? Derek hoped to hell not.

"I can't believe she's dead." Justin stared ahead, his voice flat. He leaned back against the chair and polished off the beer.

Derek took a swig of his drink, but tonight the cold brew tasted flat.

Something about Justin's story made no sense. When Rayne got mad, she stayed mad until her fuse fizzled. Depression, listlessness, and hopelessness were not words in her vocabulary. She was upbeat, aggressive, and a take-charge kind of woman.

The whole scenario tilted too far to the right, only Derek didn't know how to readjust the playing field.

Justin stood. "I'm glad we had this talk. I'm relieved to find someone who understands what I'm going through."

Relieved? Once he shared his grief, all was well?

Derek stood and offered a hand. "Take care." He showed Justin out and returned to the sofa.

Closing his eyes, Derek reviewed what Justin had said, refusing to eliminate his sister's boyfriend as a suspect.

Derek needed to talk with his father to tell him about the tragedy, but he had no way of reaching him. "He's hunting," was all his dad's friend had said. As soon as his father returned, maybe the two of them could make sense of the horror. Together they could share the grief.

Tomorrow was going to really going to suck—maybe even more than today.

***

After escaping Derek's place, Justin drove over to Rayne's house. He parked one street away from and scoped out the area. Once convinced he wasn't on anybody's radar, he slipped between the two houses behind her home and edged up to the back door.

After wiping his sweaty palms on his pants, he held his breath as he slipped in his key. With a twist, the lock clicked. Yes! Derek hadn't had time to contact a locksmith to change the locks. Once Derek thought about it, he wouldn't want to give Justin free access to the house ever again.

He ducked under the police tape and entered. Justin pulled a small Mag light out of his pocket and flicked it on. The place smelled of death and disinfectant—both final evidence Rayne was gone.

She'd been the perfect woman for him—until he learned she was a goddamn Native American. Why couldn't she have been the full-blooded Irishwoman like she has said she was?

God was he dumb. No wonder she only displayed photos of her now dead husband and son and none of her Seminole Indian father. As for Derek, no wonder he shaved his head. Those blue eyes had sure fooled Justin.

Yesterday's events replayed in his head. As soon as they'd returned from Indian Bob's house, he'd waited until Billy left, and then gone ballistic on her.

If the snoopy neighbor, Mrs. Anton, hadn't yelled at them to keep their argument to a low roar, he could have denied being at the scene of the crime the night Rayne died. Christ. He didn't need the police attention now.

Enough reminiscing. He'd come here for a purpose—to retrieve the file he'd left there by mistake—a file that could doom him for good.

Justin entered the dining room, his flashlight scanning the table. Crap. It wasn't there. He bumped in a side table he didn't remember being there, and something toppled and crashed to the ground. He jumped. "Damn."

His breath rushed out of him, and he froze to see if anyone had heard the noise or seen the light. He twisted off the flashlight and stood still, the blood beating in his head, drowning out all other sounds.

Shit. Now he had to clean up the mess. He'd never met the maid, but he didn't need her reporting to the police someone had broken in after the suicide.

With the Mag Light on, he stepped to the kitchen, careful to avoid anything breakable. After weighing his options, he chose the dustpan and broom over the electric sweeper and then dumped the shards in a trash bag. He'd take the pieces with him. God. He didn't need this aggravation.

When he flashed the light on the pile of rubble, his heart sank. It was Rayne's pottery. One of the few pieces she'd made. Damn it. If Derek ever questioned him, he'd have to say Rayne gave him the piece a few days before she died. He could only hope no one noticed her prize possession was no longer on the table.

Justin couldn't worry about it right now. He had to make sure every piece was picked up. With the dining room light turned on, he scoured the room, making certain no pieces remained.

As an extra precaution, Justin lifted up one heel at a time and inspected the sneaker bottoms. Christ. He'd need tweezers to get out all the pieces, which meant he'd have to toss those puppies. His lousy luck, he'd just bought them.

Once convinced he'd removed all evidence of his being there, he tiptoed into the bedroom, praying he'd find the notebook he'd left behind in there.

A car door slammed outside. Jesus Christ. He'd forgotten to turn off the dining room light. God. What an idiot. Hoping the light from the room didn't spill into the adjoining bedroom, he turned off his Mag Light and peeked from behind the curtains.

It was a squad car. Damn it. Had the neighbor called the cops? Fucking Mrs. Anton.

He had no choice but to get the hell out of there. He sprinted back through the dining room and out through the kitchen back door, remembering at the last second to grab the trash bag on the way out. His foot slipped on the grass, the blades thick with dew, but he quickly regained his balance. Forcing his feet to move, Justin raced back to his car.

# CHAPTER THREE

KELLY CROSSED her legs on the sofa and held the phone in a death grip. "So when do you think you can get here, Mom?" She tried to sound matter-of-fact despite the fear and helplessness that strangled her.

Over the line, her mother sounded as though she'd been crying, tugging once again on Kelly's heart. "I booked the... the redeye from San Diego to Tampa on Thursday. I'm praying I can sleep on the plane."

Her voice wavered. Was she was having trouble breathing again? Kelly didn't want to acknowledge the concern for her mom's health until after she arrived, and they could talk about it.

"You can't get here any earlier?" Kelly hated her tone came out as a whine.

"I wish I could, sweetheart, but this flight was the first one available. I'm wondering if I can even pack by then. I wasn't able to do anything today. My legs are so weak."

Her legs? If she lost her too...*Don't go there.* "Well, bring enough clothes to stay at least a week."

"A week? I can't be away from the shop that long." Her mom's tone turned indignant.

Her mom and her flower shop. "You've got to stay until Stef is buried. I don't know when the funeral will be."

Kelly swallowed her anger. Her mother should have rushed to Florida to be with her only living child, to see to the arrangements for Stefanie's funeral, and not act as though Stef's death created a huge inconvenience.

"I did buy an open-ended ticket."

Kelly let out an audible breath. "That's great, Mom." She didn't want to keep her up longer than necessary. "I love you. I'll see you in a few days."

"I love you too, and don't forget to eat. You're too skinny."

"I promise."

Kelly hung up and dropped her head back against the sofa arm. Depression gripped her hard. Her mom sounded...well, old, and she was only sixty-four, too young to be this frail. Her mother kept repeating that children weren't supposed to die before their parents, and Kelly agreed, though her father's death when she was ten was just as unfair. But cancer never cared about age.

Maybe her mom acted indifferent to spare her the grief of having to console another distraught person. This time she'd give her mom the benefit of the doubt.

Kelly stretched out her legs and adjusted the three chenille pillows behind her head. The added comfort did little though to lessen her growing depression.

The reality of Stefanie's death only now began to sink in. Had her sister been going ninety as the cops implied? If so, there had to have been a good reason.

Kelly blinked away the horrific image of her sister's car tumbling over the rail. When tears streamed down her cheeks and clogged her throat, she pressed her face into the soft pillow.

Kelly sat up. Ohmigod. Had some irate husband who'd been caught cheating on his wife and run her private investigator sister off the road? Surely, the cops would check the car to see if different colored paint scrapings appeared on the side.

After Stef's accident with Michael, her sister had taken a vow to drive carefully, especially in the rain. No way she'd be driving ninety.

Unless she was being chased.

Too wired to sleep, Kelly wrapped her legs under her and turned on the eleven o'clock news, hoping to hear the police had found the person responsible for Stef's accident. The box of cookies called to her once again, but even her favorite desert couldn't convince her to eat.

When she turned the channel to the twenty-four hour a day news station, a picture of Rayne Anderson flashed on the screen. Puzzled, Kelly unfolded her legs, sat up and turned up the volume.

"Rayne Anderson, a prosecuting attorney for *Wildman, Tedesco, and Anthony* was found dead in her home this morning. A suicide is suspected," the announcer said.

Rayne, dead? How could that be? Kelly grabbed a sofa pillow to her beating chest as her stomach threatened to heave. Sure she wasn't a good friend of Rayne's, but Stef was. And besides, she was Derek's sister.

The newscaster skipped to another story, and Kelly muted the screen. Poor Rayne.

No. Poor Derek.

He must be out of him mind with grief. She wondered when he'd heard about his sister's death. Was he handling his sadness in his usual stoic way, or had he softened over the years since she'd last seen him?

Despite their break-up when she headed off to college, a part of her would never stop loving him.

✳✳✳

Early Monday morning Derek pulled in front of his dad's stucco, one-story home. The drive took him close to an hour, whereas it normally took him under forty minutes. The closer to the house, the more his stomach churned, and the slower he drove. How was a man supposed to tell his dad his daughter killed herself? Derek would have to relive the devastation.

After he cut the engine, he sat in his truck with the windows down, almost oblivious to the sweat beading on his head. Interesting. He never noticed the faded exterior paint before. And the lawn? *Jeez, Dad, get a lawn mower.* The place needed a lot of TLC.

Now that he wouldn't be building Rayne's porch for her, he would help his dad touch up the paint and trim some of the bushes. Helping his father was the least he could do. Besides, the manual labor would take his mind off his rage and grief.

Derek stepped out of his truck just as his dad opened the front door. As Derek approached, he could see his dad's shirt was buttoned wrong. Poor dad. He used to take such good care of his appearance.

"Micca? What are you doing here?" he said in a conversational tone.

Micca meant *Chief* in Seminole. The name never did seem to fit.

"Dad."

"Shouldn't you be working?" He flicked his hand as if to dismiss his own question. "Come in, come in. It's too hot to be standing out in the sun, especially with your shaved head."

Always the shaved head. "I guess I should have worn a hat."

"Or grow your hair like a respectable person," his dad mumbled in disgust. His long gray ponytail, neatly braided, whipped across his back.

Derek didn't respond to the barb as he wiped his brow with a clean handkerchief. Telling his father he wanted to fit into the white world and not look like a typical Indian never went over well. Nor would the discussion be appropriate today.

Inside, dad's house was stuffy but cooler than the outside. Still, Derek couldn't stop sweating. "Could I trouble you for a drink of water?"

"Sure. Sit down. I'll get it."

*Stop procrastinating.* Thinking of the painful news he brought, Derek's throat almost closed. He pushed aside a pile of magazines and sat on the edge of the sofa, and then rested his elbows on his thighs. How should he begin?

When he spotted his favorite photo of Rayne smiling at a very young Billy, anger speared his gut. Her death wasn't fair.

"Here." His dad handed him the glass. "What brings you?"

"Did you catch the news last night?" Derek brought the glass to his lips, holding his breath.

"No. I came in late from the hunt and went right to bed. Why?"

Derek twirled the glass in his hand, part to procrastinate, part to check for cleanliness. "I...ah...have some bad news."

His dad sat in his favorite recliner, lit up a pipe, sucked on it several times to draw in the smoke, then exhaled. "You get fired or something?"

His father's wish in life. "No, it's about Rayne."

Concern splashed across his face. "She sick? She looked real good when she stopped by on Saturday." His face fell. "Is the baby okay?"

*Coward. Tell him.* Stalling as long as he could, Derek swiped a finger across the coffee table and picked up a wad of dust.

"What's wrong?" His dad's face went still.

"Dad...Rayne's...dead. The police think she committed suicide." There. He'd told him.

A good thirty seconds later, his dad spoke. "Dead? How could she be dead? I just saw her." His jaw slackened and his eyes turned vacant.

"I can hardly believe she's gone myself. Billy found her lying in the dining room yesterday morning. He's still traumatized."

His dad wet his lips. "How did she, ah, die?" His jaw clenched.

The horrible image of his sister lying on the floor nearly made Derek vomit. Pain came at him from all angles. "She shot herself." No need to say where.

"With the gun you gave her?"

The angry accusation ripped him in half. The guilt already had rendered him near dead inside. "Yes."

His father placed his pipe on the ashtray that was filled with cold ashes. His face relaxed, and his eyes turned glassy, almost as if he wasn't even in his body. He said nothing more about the gun.

Derek almost wanted his dad to yell and tell him how irresponsible he'd been to lend Rayne a weapon. Yes, he'd made sure she'd received lessons, but the bottom line was Rayne was dead because he believed attorneys needed protection.

Derek's knee bounced up and down as he studied his dad. His father's normally healthy skin looked sallow—or had Derek been too busy to notice his father's age before? He had to admit he'd been distracted lately.

With more patience than he thought he possessed, Derek said nothing more as he let his father absorb the news. Slowly his dad's eyes narrowed, and a tear streaked down the old man's cheek. Derek had never seen his father cry—not when his dad had broken his leg, and not when Derek's mom had died.

His father cleared his throat. "There is a saying among our people. *They are not dead who live in the hearts they leave behind.* I know this to be true in my mind, but my heart cannot grasp its meaning." His father picked up his pipe, took another puff, and blew the smoke toward the ceiling, or was it toward his gods.

"The ancestors were wise," Derek said, waiting for his father to break down like he had only hours before.

"Did she tell you she was pregnant?" his father added, his voice distant.

"I found out yesterday. Justin stopped by last night and confirmed it. The guy was pretty shaken up." Derek emptied his glass of water to clear the thickness from his throat.

"Hmm."

What did that mean? "Dad, did Justin seem unhappy about Rayne's pregnancy or something?" He leaned forward.

His father turned and seemed to examine his face almost as if he hadn't seen his son before. "This was the first time I'd met her boyfriend, so I am not a good judge. He reminded me of a stone—smooth and impenetrable. You should ask Billy. He might know the man's soul better than me."

"I will."

"They'd been together for half a year, you know, yet this was the first time I'd met him," his Dad droned, his voice calm yet distant. "There was always a reason why he couldn't join Rayne when she came over. Thought his excuses were kind of... what's the word did Billy use? Fishy."

The world was one big conspiracy to his dad. "Maybe Rayne didn't want Justin to learn about her Indian heritage." That's what she'd told Derek.

His father's gaze shot up. "Rayne was never ashamed about being half Seminole." Finally a spark of life.

*To you, maybe.* "You're probably right." Why anger his dad?

The old man stared ahead again. Then, as if the reality struck, a giant sob erupted, and his dad dropped his head into his hands. His back and shoulders shook as cries of sorrow rent the air.

The two of them rarely hugged. It wasn't done. Yet the pain emanating from his normally stoic dad forced Derek to act. He moved next to his father. His hands wanted to console and just hold him, but he hesitated.

His father raised his head and Derek knew his father needed him. He wrapped an arm around his father's shoulder and drew more comfort than he probably gave.

His father nodded his head, a sign he appreciated the action. Now more in control, his dad sat up and wiped his arm across his face.

Derek retreated to the sofa, unsure of what more he could say to help lessen his grief. Instead Derek looked around. His dad's rifle and a box of shells sat carelessly in the corner stacked next to his mud caked hunting boots. Though he couldn't see into the kitchen, he bet the sink was stacked with dirty dishes. His father was failing. His daughter's death would only aid in his decline, and Derek's heart sunk into despair.

"Why don't you call Tom, Dad?" Derek said, in as soothing a tone as possible. "Ask him to come over and stay with you." His father's best friend loved to straighten things up. "He'd be good company. Better than me."

"You're good company."

"Thank you, but I need to find out who killed Rayne. Clues are freshest right after the murder."

His dad's gaze sharpened. "You said she committed suicide."

"The police said her death was an *apparent* suicide. The forensics evidence hasn't been processed. I don't buy she killed herself, despite what I saw."

The old man ran his hands down the length of his thighs. Back and forth. Back and forth. "Neither do I, neither do I." His voice drifted off. "I told her not to become a prosecuting attorney," he mumbled.

"There were too many criminals out there. Bad ones. They want revenge. I told her, but she wouldn't listen."

Yeah, Derek had told her too. "Criminals are bad, Dad. Even if she'd been a defense attorney, she might have been targeted," he said more to hear the argument for his own sake than to convince his father.

"She followed in your footsteps, you know. If she hadn't, she'd be here today."

Adrenaline flooded his system. "So now it's my fault Rayne's dead?" He didn't wait for his father to respond. "Remember she started law school before I finished my degree. Your arrow isn't flying straight." Never has.

"If you'd come back to the tribe, Rayne would have too."

Derek groaned. They'd been over this argument numerous times. Today, the cut ran deeper.

"Our people wouldn't have harmed her," his dad continued. "An Indian woman in the white world is never safe."

Half Indian, but he didn't correct him. Derek didn't know what else to say. His father was hurting, and Derek was at a loss on to how to soothe him.

"Will you call Tom? Please."

His dad's shoulders slumped. He nodded and picked up the phone. Once Tom agreed to come over, his dad stumbled into the bedroom and came back clutching a photo album. The book was from when he, Rayne, Mom, and Dad all lived in Tallahassee on the reservation. Happy times.

"Do you want me to take care of the funeral arrangements?" Derek asked.

"No. I will. Burying my daughter is the least I can do for her."

Derek understood. A knock sounded on the door a few minutes later. "Must be Tom. I've got to go, Dad. Call me, will you?"

He looked up with red eyes, appearing much older than when he'd arrived. "Sure, Micca. I'll call. But don't you be a stranger either. We've only got each other now."

"There's Billy too."

His father lips lifted a bit. "Yes, there's Billy. He's a good boy."

***

Later that afternoon, Derek slumped down in his truck's driver's seat in the downtown parking garage fifty feet away from Justin's Mercedes. Only because statistics showed those closest to the victim were often guilty, Derek felt obligated to speak with Justin's boss—alone. He saw no need to upset Justin in case he had nothing to do with Rayne's death.

His sister had spoken highly of her baby's father. And she was usually a good judge of character. Her ability to read people was what made her a fine attorney.

At a quarter past five, Justin Bladen and several others poured out of the street level elevator. Close enough now, Derek put down the binoculars. Neatly groomed, Justin looked to be sharing a joke with one of his associates. He was a far cry from the agitated man Derek had seen last night.

Once Justin drove away, Derek took the same elevator up to the brokerage house. He'd called ahead and made an appointment to speak with Mr. Davis, Justin's boss.

A small man, with steel gray hair, Mr. Davis was impeccably dressed, looking every bit like a big time financial advisor.

The wiry money manager held out his hand. "We meet again, Detective. Do you have news about Carl's death? He's sorely missed around here." He motioned Derek to take a seat in his richly paneled office that smelled of new leather.

"No, but hopefully soon." Derek didn't want to discuss the difficulty in determining the cause of death in an apparent suicide of one of his workers. Something about the man's fall from the twentieth floor of a high rise bothered Derek. Like why carry cash and credit cards when you're committing suicide? You can't take it with you.

Winston Davis tugged on his coat jacket and straightened his tie. "Over the phone you asked about Justin being at my party."

"Yes. I trust he told you about his girlfriend's death."

"Yes, such a shame. I told him to take time off, but he said being by himself was too hard."

Derek could relate. "Could you tell me what time Justin arrived at your house?" Pen poised, Derek waited for an answer.

The boss straightened, and his face tightened. "Is Justin a suspect in the girl's death? I thought she committed suicide. Isn't that what the news reported?"

Shit. The man was smart. Derek had no authority to investigate Rayne's death since the Captain had ruled her death a suicide. "Yes, but I'm trying to get a handle on when Rayne died. She was my sister."

Relief flooded Mr. Davis's face. "Oh, I see. I'm sorry for your loss."

"Thank you."

Mr. Davis picked up a silver pen from his desk and twirled the ball-point over his knuckles in a fluid movement. "Well, if I remember correctly, Justin arrived at my house around six or so, though I didn't look at my watch. I do recall it was before diner, because Justin volunteered to put the barbeque sauce on the ribs."

"What was his frame of mind?"

He cocked his brows before drawing them into a pinch. "To be quite honest, he seemed rather agitated. I asked him if there was something on his mind, but all he said was that he'd had a hard day. Nothing more."

"Anything else stand out in your mind about his behavior?" If he'd fought with Rayne, Derek could see why he was upset.

"As a matter of fact, Justin started to drink rather heavily as soon as he walked in the door, which was not his usual M.O." Mr. Davis shot him a small grin. Derek didn't react. "To be frank, he drank so much he passed out."

Derek tried not to let the rush of disappointment show in his body language. If Justin was that drunk, he couldn't have murdered his sister at eight thirty. "What time was this?"

"Seven thirty, eight."

"Then what happened?"

"Dave Crafton and I woke him up from the sofa and half walked, half dragged him to my spare bedroom. We told him to sleep it off."

"And what time did Justin wake up?"

Mr. Davis glanced up to the right as if reenacting the evening. "Most of the guests had left, so I'd have to say around eleven thirty. He looked a little worse for wear when he appeared, but he was sober enough to drive himself home."

Damn. Justin had an airtight alibi. "Thank you for your time."

They shook hands. "If I can be of help, let me know," Mr. Davis said. "And keep me informed of anything you learn about Carl's death. He was a valuable broker."

As Derek located his car in the parking garage, the gas fumes and heat nearly choked him. His hand was on the door handle when his spirit guide's words came back to him: *Don't try to wake the person who is pretending to sleep.*

Holy shit. Could Justin have faked being drunk? He was out of sight for several hours while the party raged on. Perhaps he snuck out of the house, killed Rayne, and then returned.

The *guides* were right. Justin was pretending to sleep. And here Bladen thought he'd created the perfect alibi.

# CHAPTER FOUR

THE NEXT MORNING, Derek needed to see Billy. Like himself, he imagined the poor kid was a mess. Derek never imagined seventy-two hours could change his life so much, but the moment Rayne died, a part of him had died too.

He'd called ahead to Billy's school before crossing the Bay to make sure his nephew would be able to leave class for an hour or so.

"If you'll wait here, Mr. Benally, I'll have someone get your nephew," the gray haired receptionist said with a disapproving glare.

"Thanks."

He guessed he should have explained why he needed to pull Billy from class, but speaking his sister's name to the headmaster had caused enough pain.

Derek studied the waiting area. Scores of photos of skinny recruits, dressed in uniform, lined the walls. Every picture was straight and dust free. They could use a few cadets at his precinct to play maid, especially in Seinkievitz's corner. The guy always left his stacked Krispy Kreme donut boxes next to his desk for days on end, and the man's mess drove Derek crazy.

"Uncle Derek. What are you doing here?" Derek jerked out of his fog. A mixture of worry and embarrassment crossed the kid's face.

"I thought we'd have a little chat." Derek stood and looked down at his nephew who was already close to six feet. Soon, they'd be looking eye-to-eye, and pride swelled.

Billy's eyes turned stormy. "About what?"

"Come on. Your headmaster gave me permission to take you out for some ice cream."

His lips curled. "Ice cream is for babies."

Why was Billy making this so difficult? "Look, I need to talk to you. We can't do it here." Derek gestured to the few cadets who were milling near the office door, not to mention the formidable receptionist.

Defeat seeped out of him. "Okay. How about Wendy's? I could eat a Frosty, I suppose."

"Wendy's it is."

Billy rolled his eyes, not buying his cheery attitude. In silence they strode out to his car.

"Can I drive?" Billy asked with sudden enthusiasm when they reached the truck.

"You're too young. Get in."

Legs straight, lips in a thin line, Billy's hand froze on the handle. "I'm fifteen. I have my permit. Mom let me drive when we were together."

Derek nearly caved. "Maybe on the ride back."

Billy's shoulders relaxed. "Whatever." He dipped his head and slid onto the passenger seat.

Derek started the engine and switched on the AC before pulling out into the heavy traffic. He wasn't good at beating around the bush, so he dove right in. "I need to know about your mom's mindset before you...found her."

Sadness shadowed Billy's face. He turned away and looked out the window. "How should I know? I told you I wasn't home when she shot herself."

"Can you tell me what you do know?" Derek took the first left turn and pulled into the right lane.

"She was going to have a baby." The kid lifted one shoulder as if having a brother or sister wasn't a big deal.

Derek was glad Rayne had confided in Billy. "And how did that make you feel?"

Billy whipped back toward Derek. "What, you some shrink now?"

Derek held his temper. "Billy, listen. I'm just trying to find out if your mother would have killed herself, or rather *could* have killed herself."

"You saw her. She had a gun in her hand. *Your* gun. The one *you* gave her."

His gut soured from the immense guilt. "Billy, I made sure your mom had training." His explanation seemed weak even to him.

Derek relaxed his clenched grip as he pulled to a stop at the light. Needing to explain, he twisted toward his nephew. "Son, there are ways to make murder look like suicide."

"I'm not your son," the kid shot back. His bitterness squeezed Derek's already damaged heart.

"It's a figure of speech." Though Derek wouldn't mind having a son like Billy. "What I'm asking is, do you think your mom was depressed or upset enough to take her own life?" Derek held his breath for the answer.

Billy's brow pinched, as he seemed to consider the question. "Well, she was acting kind of strange."

"Care to elaborate?"

He shrugged, and then braced his feet up on the dashboard. Derek refrained from telling him to sit up straight. Billy dropped his feet leaving sandy smudges on the dash.

"She was being really nice to me for a change."

Hardly a characteristic of the chronically depressed. "In what way?"

"I came home for the weekend because I wanted to go to Chris's birthday party. He's my best friend, you know. Mom said okay. She didn't care I wanted to spend the night."

"And that was unusual?"

The light turned green, and Derek kept to the right, occasionally glancing over at his nephew to get a read on him.

"Yeah. We always argued when I wanted to go out with my friends. But not last Saturday. She was all smiles and stuff." Billy leaned forward and cranked up the air. Derek didn't comment. "Then she told me about the baby. I told her I didn't care if she had a kid as long as I didn't have to take care of it."

It? "Did she act relieved when you didn't put up a fuss?"

"I dunno."

Derek gripped the wheel hard in frustration. Could the boy be any less helpful? Forcing patience into his body, he pulled into a space in the Wendy's' parking lot.

Billy jumped out. "Can we order first?"

"Sure," Derek said. The smell of greasy hamburgers and fries made him hungry. Too bad he'd given up fattening food years ago.

They waited in a short line, ordered two large Frosties and took a seat by the window.

Derek prodded once more, hating to grill his nephew, but knowing he had to try. "Why don't you tell me everything that happened on Saturday?"

Billy rolled his eyes and stuffed a large spoonful of chocolate in his mouth.

"Billy?"

The kid looked petulant. "Do we have to?"

"Yes." This time his tone came out too sharp, but Billy didn't seem to notice.

The kid slumped in his seat. "I don't know what there is to tell. Justin came over around two or so, because Mom wanted to tell Grandpa about the baby. I didn't want to go, but she wouldn't let me stay at the house alone." He looked out the window that opened onto the parking lot. "One minute she's cool, and the next she treats me like I'm a freakin' baby. I'm fifteen for God's sake." Billy turned back to Derek.

"Continue." He took a small spoonful of the Frosty, pretending to eat the ice cream.

"We went to see Grandpa at the casino, and she told him about being pregnant, and then we came home."

He doubted that was all that transpired. "Then what?"

"Mom cooked spaghetti. We ate, and then Justin drove me to Chris's house because mom wasn't feeling so good."

"Did they fight before Justin took you to Chris'?"

"No."

He took another bite of his Frosty. Damn. "Okay. So you spent the night. How did you get home on Sunday morning?"

"Chris's mom drove me." He slammed his cup on the table. "Jeez. What is this? The Inquisition?"

Derek ignored the kid's surliness. "Just trying to get answers."

Billy let out a long breath. He bit the inside of his lip, and then swiped his arm across his teary eyes. "I called home for mom to come pick me up, but there was no answer." His lower lip trembled. "I guess she was dead by then."

Billy dropped his head onto the table. His shoulders shook, but he didn't make a sound. Derek wanted to gather him in his arms, but he knew Billy wouldn't let him.

"Thank you, Billy. I appreciate you answering my questions."

He lifted his head. "So you think someone killed her?" he asked.

"I don't know for sure, but I'll do my damnedest to find out."

Billy sat up, his reddened eyes spearing Derek in the heart.

Once Billy finished his treat, Derek drove his nephew back to school. He was surprised, as well as relieved, Billy didn't mention taking the wheel on the way back. If Billy asked, Derek knew he'd have to let him drive his truck. Right now, he wasn't sure he was up for a teenager's roller coaster emotions, especially when the kid was behind the wheel.

Once at school, Derek slipped out to say goodbye. Billy pressed his lips together and swallowed. Once again the urge to give his nephew a hug and tell him everything would work out, overwhelmed him. Derek walked around to Billy's side and opened his arms. A hot tear streamed down Derek's cheek. Billy took a step forward, and then looked around. A few kids were out by the gym at the end of the parking lot.

"Thanks for the ice cream," Billy said as he slung his backpack over his shoulder and turned away.

Derek dropped his arms, understanding that touching in public was not allowed. Billy had made that abundantly clear in the past.

"Call me, if you need anything," Derek said.

"Yeah." His nephew shuffled off, and then turned around. "Uncle Derek?"

"Yeah?"

"Thanks for trying to find out who hurt Mom."

Derek's throat closed up. All he could do was nod. Before he let his grief hog tie him, he slipped back into the cab.

The sooner he could find his sister's killer, the sooner he and Billy could begin to heal.

***

"What are you doing here?" Captain Vaughn asked as he loomed over Derek's desk.

"Last time I checked I worked here." His Captain had told him to take time off. Derek had tried. He'd failed. The isolation was too much to handle. "My sister didn't kill herself. Someone murdered her," Derek announced with total confidence. He crunched the report he held in his hands.

"I know."

"What?" Derek stood up causing his chair to tumble backward. He stared down at his Captain. "And you didn't fucking tell me?" Derek shouted.

Vaughn took a step back and tried to look unaffected by tugging on his gray, bushy eyebrows, a habit that drove Derek crazy. "I just received the preliminary report back. Your sister had no traces of barium and antimony on her hands."

"No powder burns?"

"Sit down." Vaughn dragged a chair from the next desk and sat. "Now let me ask you something. Was your sister right or left-handed?"

Derek righted the fallen chair and dropped into the seat. "Left."

"The entry wound on the right side of her head implied your sister was right-handed."

His mind reeled. When Derek had walked into Rayne's home after he'd received Billy's call, he'd stood at her feet. He never mirror-imaged the body in his mind or considered the gun was in the wrong hand. Derek looked up at his Captain. "Damn it. How could I have missed such an obvious mistake?"

"Don't be so hard on yourself. You were in shock from seeing your sister."

"No. I should have known. I guess my dyslexia got the best of me."

Lame excuse. His guides had spoken to him the moment he spotted his sister, taking his mind away from the crime scene.

Derek took a sip of lukewarm coffee to wash away the lump in his throat. "Seinkievitz is the primary, right?"

Vaughn's brows pinched hard enough to form a unibrow. "Yes, but stay out of it. You're too close." His Captain stood, sending the chair back with a squeak.

He ignored the Captain's threat. "I already spoke with my sister's boyfriend's boss to see if his alibi held up." Vaughn would find out sooner or later.

His brows furrowed. "And?"

"Justin Bladen, that's the boyfriend, was drunk at a party at his boss's house and slept it off for a few hours before emerging. Rayne was killed during that time."

"So he couldn't have killed your sister."

"I'm not so sure." He relayed his newest theory about Justin faking the drunken routine. He left out the part about his guide's words. Vaughn didn't believe in his spiritual entities.

"We'll do a follow up on Justin. Anyone else you suspect?"

"No, but remember my sister was a prosecuting attorney. Obviously, she's made her share of enemies."

"We'll check out the possibilities with the parole office." Vaughn tapped his fingers on the top of Derek's computer monitor. "Do you have any leads on the jumper case?"

Derek was relieved not to harp on Rayne's death. Talking about his sister's murder caused his gut to cramp with despair, and he certainly didn't need to break down in front of Vaughn.

"I'm still working on the case." Derek cleared his throat. So much for not reacting to the mention of Rayne's name. "Cause of death was from the fall, obviously, but I'm not convinced he jumped without some help."

"Why?" The Captain's slumped shoulders straightened.

"The guy had a great job as a broker and had just moved into his ritzy high rise. Why take a high dive?"

"Maybe the market tanked, and he lost a lot of money. Did he have any family?"

"I don't know. I'm checking out his employment application now to see if he listed a next of kin."

"How did his neighbors and coworkers view him?"

Derek almost enjoyed the usual drill. It gave him routine, and routine brought order. "Friendly guy, driven and obsessed with the stock market. But he was a financial analyst after all. Justin Bladen, the one who dated my sister, worked at the same firm with Vanderwall. He claimed his coworker didn't handle the stress of the changing markets very well. Justin thought Vanderwall either had a gambling problem or was possibly into drugs. Gave me nothing concrete though. Just his hunch."

Vaughn stroked his bushy brows again. "If what the man says is true, drugs or gambling make good motives for suicide. Keep working the angle and let me know how you want to rule his death."

"I will." Suicide was such a waste of life and resources.

Vaughn strode partway to his office, stopped and turned. "Benally?"

"Yeah?"

"Did you hear a friend of your sister's also died Saturday night?"

A chill chased down his spine. "No. Don't tell me she was murdered too."

"Car accident. You remember how wet the roads were on Saturday?"

"Boy, do I. Half of my apartment parking lot was flooded."

"Apparently, her car skidded on an overpass, and she flipped over the guardrail. Landed on the street below."

Derek closed his eyes for a moment. "What was her name?" He didn't know too many of his sister's friends, but he'd met a few.

"Gentry."

Damn, that was the one name he knew only too well.

# CHAPTER FIVE

DEREK SWALLOWED hard at the dropped bomb. "Kelly or Stefanie?"

No way the accident victim could have been Kelly Gentry. Last he'd heard she still lived in North Carolina—not that he'd gone out of his way to find out where she'd lived or anything.

"Stefanie, if my memory serves me right. Do you know her?" Vaughn said.

He relaxed his death grip on the chair handles and sucked in a lung-ful. "Met her once." He wouldn't have been able to survive the blow if Kelly had died. "Who's the primary?"

"Medina is doing the honors."

"Good." Dominic Medina was one of the veteran detectives. He'd even shown Derek a few tricks.

A shout from the other side of the room distracted them, and Vaughn turned to check out the disturbance. Wouldn't you know? Deputy Billadeau was practically dragging some skanky looking guy back to the interrogation room. Two detectives followed on his heels. Bill had a long night in front of him. Sorry sucker.

An earnest young officer, whose name failed to register in Derek's chaotic mind, stepped next to Vaughn and asked him a question. Derek's boss nodded, stood, and walked side-by-side with the rookie toward his office. He guessed that was the end of the discussion about the Gentry girl.

Derek leaned back in his chair and tried to make sense of this world. The image of a seventeen-year old Kelly Gentry—curly red hair, long shapely legs, and a heart bigger than all of Florida—popped into his head.

He sat up abruptly, his chair sending out a groan, forcing her image out of his head. He didn't need any more sad reminders of what could never be.

On his desk sat a pile of folders, all of which needed his immediate attention. In order to be able to attack the paper work, Derek headed to the soda machine. He needed a caffeine hit a lot more than he needed to be thinking about Kelly right now, especially since his head wasn't on straight. Dealing with his sister's death and Billy's angry refusal to accept his mom's loss, not to mention his dad's mental state, already had Derek in a spiral.

The phone on Bob Bronson's desk rang and rang while the man guffawed not ten feet away. He didn't move a damn muscle to answer the call. Knowing him, he was probably enjoying some off color joke, and the man's joy did nothing to help the emptiness in Derek's heart.

Stef was dead? What tough luck. Kelly must be beside herself. Surely, she'd fly into Tampa for the funeral. Should he go for old time's sake?

No. He wasn't ready for a tearful reunion—or rather a crying jag. Derek had no problem touching base with her for old times' sake though. She'd have moved on with her life by now. Probably married with half a dozen kids. Hell, maybe she wouldn't even remember him.

He plunked his quarters into the machine and shrugged. It was better to maintain his distance. When he returned with his drink, Dom Medina was at the coffee machine, pouring a cup of what looked like hot sludge.

"I thought you were a soda man?" Derek asked. The two of them had joked about their mutual addiction.

"Change is nice every once in a while. Tessa kind of converted me to java."

A quick shot of envy filled him. Lucky Dom. He and Tessa were the perfect couple—in love and with a child they both adored. Until he'd seen them together, Derek had never believed a detective's life could coexist with a happy marriage.

Derek refocused on the case. "The Captain tells me you're working the Gentry case. Got anything?" Two good friends dying on the same day had raised his brows.

Medina eased off the lever as the hot liquid rose to the top of the cup. "No foul play as far as I could tell." Dom dumped a load of sugar in his cup, and Derek cringed. "Say, I'm sorry about your sister." He took a long time stirring his coffee. The steam billowed up, filling the air with a cocoa bean aroma. "The Captain mentioned this Gentry woman was one of your sister's friends." The detective looked up from his cup.

"Yes, but I only met her once. Rayne talked about her a lot though."

Rayne's smiling face surfaced. Once she and Stefanie took skydiving lessons. Rayne loved the thrill, but Derek nearly died when he'd found out. Man, had he given her hell.

Medina headed toward his desk, carefully holding the steaming drink in front of him. A thought suddenly struck Derek. "Hey, Dom. How did the Captain know Rayne and Stefanie were friends?"

Medina stopped at his desk. "We dialed the last incoming call from Stefanie's cell phone. It belonged to your sister." He set his coffee cup on his desk and flipped through his notes. "I interviewed her this afternoon as a matter of fact. She said she spoke to Stefanie moments before the accident. Kelly's sister had just come back from visiting Rayne and was heading home when she must have lost control of her car."

"You spoke with Kelly?" Every muscle tensed. "How did she sound?" Broken? Tired? Lonely?

"Sound?"

Why had he asked such a stupid question? He'd just wanted to learn more about the woman who once meant the world to him. "I guess she was all broken up, huh."

Dom Medina raised a brow, looking as though Derek had lost his mind. "Of course, but she held herself together pretty well. A real class act. Pretty too."

His heart nearly jumped out of his chest. "You saw her? How?"

"How? I drove a car to her house." Medina slapped closed his file. "You know her or something?"

How much should he tell? How much dare he give away? "Used to. We went to Hillsborough High together. How could you drive to her house? I thought she worked at Duke University."

Old emotions swamped him. The joy she'd brought when they were together taught him to appreciate the little things in life. And then there was the lust. Lots and lots of lust. They never hooked up though. He respected Kelly too much, but he sure stayed horny his senior year. Each delicate kiss she gave him had driven him wild. He attributed his stellar football career in part to pent up energy.

Medina pulled out his chair, eased into his seat, and motioned Derek do the same. Derek shut off his fantasy and focused on the cop.

"Duke, you say? He whistled. "Not now she doesn't. She does some kind of cancer research for Moffitt Hospital." He took a sip of his steaming coffee and looked over the lip of the cup. "Is something wrong?"

Confusion swirled around him. She'd done it. Kelly was finally a cancer research doctor. Pride for her accomplishment filled him. "No. I guess I wasn't up on my sister's friends' lives as I'd thought. Do you have her address or number?"

"Sure." He ran a finger down the length of his notepad.

Derek was uncertain if he even wanted to see Kelly again, especially under such horrible circumstances, but if Kelly knew anything about Rayne's death, he had to investigate.

Didn't he?

Medina pulled out a Post-it note pad from his drawer and printed Kelly's address in neat block letters. "Here ya go. Let me know if she remembers anything."

"Will do."

Derek stuffed the information in his back pocket and wandered back to his desk, his mind whirring. If Stefanie had visited Rayne before the murder, she might have overheard the fight with Justin.

With Stefanie dead, Kelly was the last link to finding how his sister had died. He refused to admit any of his logic was based on rationalization.

A half an hour later, and only half way through his Vanderwall file, Seinkievitz, the lead detective on Rayne's case, sauntered up to his desk. "Say man, I'm really sorry to hear about your sister."

Derek looked up at Ichabod Crane lookalike. "Thanks. You find any leads on her murder yet?" He held his breath.

"I can't talk to you about the case. You know that." He leaned a skinny hip on the corner of the desk. He glanced behind his shoulder in the direction of the Captain's office. "I just spoke with Vaughn," Seinkievitz said, his voice close to a whisper. "He told me your theory about the boyfriend."

Derek forced casualness into his tone. "It's just that. A theory. No one saw him sneak out of the party." Derek leaned back in his chair. "Say, keep me in the loop, will ya? For old times' sake."

Seinkievitz jumped off the desk as if Derek had some infectious disease. "No can do."

Derek sat back up and casually stacked his files on his desk into a neat pile. "What about the Marcadis case?"

Seinkievitz flinched. "You wouldn't."

Derek propped his feet up on his desk. "I will if I have to." Derek didn't like using threats, but under the circumstance, he had little choice.

The normally cheerful guy turned sullen. "Fine, but if the Captain finds out—"

Derek sprung his chair forward and dropped his feet to the ground. "He won't." Seinkievitz knew he could lose his job if Derek turned him in for sleeping with a witness.

Seinkievitz shouldered a glance again at the Captain's office. "Come over to my desk," Seinkievitz whispered out of the corner of his mouth.

Derek hopped up and followed him away from view of Vaughn's office window. He didn't give a shit about protocol. He needed to be on top of the case even if he couldn't participate.

Seinkievitz plopped down in front of his desk and flipped through a nasty looking manila folder. "I contacted your sister's law firm for a list of her previous clients. Since she was a prosecuting attorney, I figured someone might not have been particularly happy with the outcome of his case."

"I mentioned the same thing to the Captain. I'm surprised he didn't ask you to check with the parole office."

"He did." Some satisfaction surfaced that the Captain took his ideas seriously.

Seinkievitz stuffed a chocolate donut in his mouth, then pulled out a piece of paper from the file folder and slid the document across the desk toward Derek.

A smudge of brown smeared the back. "Seinkievitz! Can't you wash your hands before you read files?"

Brad Seinkievitz swiped a paper napkin over his mouth and acted as though Derek hadn't said anything.

Derek read the document. "Says here, Jose Piloseno did five years for assault, and that he was released two weeks ago."

"You thinking what I'm thinking?" Seinkievitz said with a mouthful of chewed donut in his mouth.

Derek finished reading. "Does he have an alibi for Saturday night?"

"Don't know. His parole officer gave me his address though."

A quick spurt of excitement shot through him. Finally a clue. "Let's go." Derek jumped up.

"No way."

Derek waved a hand. "I'm just along for the ride. Nothing official. Hey, I won't tell if you don't."

"No can do."

He wished the man would stop repeating the annoying phrase. "Seinkievitz. You want me to tell the boys about the time you dressed up in drag?"

"Shh." His face turned whiter than bleached bones. His jaw clenched, and his gaze darted around the room, obviously weighing his options. "Fine, but let me leave first. I'll wait for you outside."

"Thanks." Derek grinned for the first time since hearing of Rayne's death.

Yes, he'd planned on visiting Kelly at some point today, but she probably wouldn't be home from work until at least five. Besides, he needed time to get his thoughts in order before he approached her.

\*\*\*

"Hi, Doc," Kelly's young assistant called as he hustled in through the lab door.

"Hey, yourself. What's the hurry? And what's with the smile?"

"There's someone here to see you," Chip said. His grin widened and his brows wiggled.

Chip, Chip. Normally, his humor about finding the perfect man—for her *and* for him, gave her a boost. But not today. Kelly was convinced some relative of his must own Match.com or something close since he was constantly trying to urge her to find true love online. Please. She had ethics. She also had her share of failures. One lost love and one ruined marriage to the wrong guy was enough for a lifetime.

"He asked to see me?" She spread the culture on the petri dish.

"Yeah, and he's hot with a capital H."

She halted. "Is he really tall by any chance?" Her heart skipped a beat.

"Nope. Just your average Joe, but I wouldn't turn him down." Chip cocked his head back and lifted a brow. She guessed he was attempting to look sexy. He failed.

"Thanks for the review."

She covered her petri dish, placed the experiment in the incubator, and then removed her gloves and goggles, a little embarrassed at her disappointment that Derek hadn't come to console her. But why should he? Just because both of their sisters had died on the same day didn't mean he had to contact her. She did own a phone, which meant she could have called the police department to find him.

She brushed back the errant strands of hair that had escaped her rubber band and headed out of the lab.

A lone gentleman in his mid-thirties, nicely dressed in pinstripes and polished shoes, was standing in the middle of the hall, his hands clutched in front of him. He stepped forward with his hand extended. "Dr. Rutland?"

"Yes." Next time she'd instruct her assistant to let salesmen know she wasn't in charge of buying supplies. She didn't need the interruption, though today, she'd done nothing of any consequence, because her mind hadn't be able to focus.

"I'm Justin Bladen. You're Stefanie's sister, right?"

Her shoulders stiffened. "Yes." Had he come with news of her death?

Justin Bladen. The name sounded familiar.

Two nurses brushed past them, and he looked around. "Do you think we could talk somewhere a little more private?"

"Sure. There's a lounge down the hall."

Had Stefanie dated Justin and forgotten to mention him? Was he looking for closure too?

"Here we are," she said, a fresh wave of sadness hitting her. Could she talk about her sister's death with this stranger and not lose her composure? As it was, she'd broken down twice already in front of Chip.

The lounge wasn't empty, but this space was the best she could find. A little girl squealed as she climbed up on her mother's lap, and a twinge of sadness touched her. If they were here, someone in the family was suffering from cancer. She forced the image of her sick father from her mind.

Justin sat across her and held her gaze. "Well, this is a little awkward." He loosened his tie. "I'm Rayne Anderson's boyfriend, or at least I was until she committed suicide, but I bet you knew that—about the suicide, that is."

Sympathy welled at his loss. "Oh, yes. Now I remember. You're the stockbroker." Something didn't settle well with her, but she figured her own emotions were so out of kilter, she was suspicious of things for no reason. Maybe her sister had mentioned that Rayne and Justin were having troubles. It didn't matter now. "How did you find me?"

"Rayne and I double dated with your sister a few times. They were good friends. Stefanie bragged all night about how you were coming to work at Moffitt for cancer research. A few calls later, here I am."

Stef had bragged about her? Kelly blinked a few times to clear her eyes. "I see."

He leaned forward, his hands twisted in his lap. He wet his lips. "Rayne mentioned your sister planned to stop by the night she, ah, killed herself. Did Stef say what happened?"

The little girl across from them screeched as she fit a long cylinder into a round hole. "They never got together. Rayne wasn't feeling well, so Stef left."

A flash of something crossed his face, and then disappeared so fast she couldn't name his emotion. "Oh. Did your sister tell you why Rayne wanted her to stop by?"

"Not that I recall. Why?" His questions seemed odd for someone who'd lost a loved one.

"I'm trying to get a handle on why she took her life. We'd argued that night, and I can't help but wonder if the fight might have upset her more than I'd imagined. You see she found out she was pregnant. Being unmarried, she was, well, distraught. I begged her to marry me right away, but she said no. We hadn't known each other for very long, she'd claimed." He looked off to the side and shook her head.

"How terrible for her." He hung his head. "And for you too."

He looked up and scoured the ceiling. "Maybe, but now I'll never know the truth." He reached in his jacket pocket, and when he pulled out a business card and handed it to her, their hands briefly touched. His eyes widened, but she dismissed his response. This close, she could smell his woodsy cologne.

"Say, listen," Justin said. "I know how much you must be hurting right now too, so if you ever need to talk, give me a call."

She took his card, even though she knew she'd never contact him. He sounded more like a shrink than another grieving soul. "Thanks."

Justin nodded and stood. She watched him stride down the corridor with a hint of confidence she hadn't seen when he'd first arrived.

"How did the meeting go?" the familiar voice said behind her.

She turned to face Chip. "His girlfriend died the same night Stef did. He wanted someone he could talk to. That's all."

"He can talk to me. I'd listen to him forever." Chip's dreamy gaze followed Justin as he disappeared through the doorway.

"Put your tongue back in your mouth. Did you analyze the culture I gave you?"

"Not yet." He cast his eyes downward, but she could see laughter behind his chagrin.

"Then get going."

Chip saluted and trotted back to the lab. She decided the only way to survive the day would be with coffee. Lots and lots of coffee.

She needed the caffeine hit to get her mind back into her lab work and not think about men, especially men like Derek Benally.

His name alone evoked a kaleidoscope of emotions ranging from sympathy to guilt to depression. She remembered how happy she'd been back in high school, but also how she'd chosen her career over what she thought was love.

In this case, it was best to let the bones stay buried.

# CHAPTER SIX

DETECTIVE SEINKIEVITZ WIGGLED in the driver's seat. "Damn, my butt hurts. What do you say we call this one and return tomorrow?"

Not waiting for Derek's reply, Seinkievitz rolled up the cruiser's windows and cranked up the engine. Two kids on bikes sped down the sidewalk, nearly knocking over an elderly woman.

Derek's fists bunched, his muscles ready to spring into action. Stupid juvies. Just as he was about to help the victim, she steadied and continued to teeter down the street.

Derek returned his attention to his fellow cop's question. "It's your case. Remember, I'm just an interested citizen along for the ride." Right. Finding Rayne's killer was his number one priority. Like he cared if he broke every rule in the police handbook. He'd find Rayne's killer one way or another.

Derek hadn't been able to keep his mind on any of his other cases since Rayne's death, but he needed to close the pesky jumper case before the Captain jumped down his ass.

The problem was that the biting pain of loss kept assaulting him at all the wrong times. And here he prided himself on his control. No more. Derek didn't like how his urge to beat the shit out of someone kept haunting him. Some kind of black ugly sludge had found its way inside his head and was fucking with him.

He rolled his shoulders to loosen his tight neck muscles and to clear his mind. Surveillance always killed him. Give him a clue to track down, and he'd never complain.

Derek slapped the dash. "Dammit. I wanted Piloseno." He was itching for the confrontation, but the guy had been a no-show. Right now, he was their best suspect for who might have harmed his sister.

"Hey, me too." Seinkievitz pulled into traffic and exited the low-class neighborhood.

Good riddance. For now. Derek rubbed his temples to ward off the impending headache that had threatened to erupt all day. He closed his eyes and leaned his head back in an attempt to quell the gnawing at his gut. Something was wrong. He could feel it.

Twenty seconds later, the sweet smell of sugar nearly suffocated him. Derek bolted upright. Seinkievitz was stuffing a fifth donut in his mouth as he shot through a busy intersection. Count 'em, five. How did the man stay so skinny?

A car honked as Seinkievitz nearly clipped a van in the next lane. "Well, in my humble opinion," Seinkievitz said, acting as if no one else existed in the land of autos, "I don't think Piloseno would dare skip town so soon after being released." The cop turned toward Derek.

Derek's muscles tensed. *Look at the damn road.* "He'd better not."

"Wouldn't be the first time a parolee ran though." Seinkievitz returned his attention to the street.

Relaxing a bit, Derek cracked the window to let out the donut stench. He checked his watch for the hundredth time. "I think I'll check out what Stefanie Gentry's sister, Kelly, has to say about her sister's whereabouts the night she died." Given his light tone, he figured Seinkievitz would never pick up on his ulterior motive for wanting to see Kelly.

Derek told himself if he stayed at the station, he'd end up spending the next few hours filling out paperwork. Given his inability to concentrate, he'd do no one any good. No need to short-change the report gods by doing a crappy job.

Seinkievitz passed a motorist going ten miles over the speed limit, and a horn blasted as he cut back across a lane. "Watch it!" Derek shouted. "I want to live for another few days."

The cop didn't slow. Instead, he accelerated and smiled, as if he wanted to test Derek's patience. "You're wasting your time talking to the sister. According to Medina, she knew nada." He licked his sticky fingers than wiped his them on his pant leg.

Gross. Derek shook his head. If only Seinkievitz wasn't in charge of Rayne's case, he'd...

"The dead woman was driving recklessly and crashed. Plain and simple," Seinkievitz ran on, chunks of donut coating his teeth. Disgusting.

"I'll take my chances." Derek still wanted to speak with Kelly—not only about her sister's accident—but about Rayne's death. He didn't dare tell Seinkievitz he planned to investigate on his own time in case the cop spilled the beans to the Captain about Derek's ride-along. It wouldn't help to have the boss on his ass any more than he was already.

After nearly running two traffic lights, his coworker dropped him off at the station. "Thanks, man," Derek said. "I appreciate you letting me come along." *And getting me here in one piece.*

"As if I *let* you." Seinkievitz turned toward Derek, squinted and scrunched up his nose. "I don't like being blackmailed." Derek knew he was only half kidding.

"Then watch what you wear and who you sleep with." The threat in his tone came out too harsh. Tough shit. The man needed discipline.

"Ooooh." He held up two hands, and then laughed. His curled lip told Derek Seinkievitz was still pissed.

Before he met with Kelly, however, Derek needed to shower. Sitting in the car all afternoon probably made him smell like day-old socks, though he sure as hell wasn't about to ask for Seinkievitz's opinion. The man didn't know the definition of hygiene.

As Derek strode back to his truck, two police cars pulled into the lot. Medina rolled out of one unmarked cruiser, waved, and headed inside.

Derek climbed into his cab and eased into traffic, careful to obey all speed limits. Though nearly dusk, the heat of the day hadn't taken a hint and left. When sweat pulled his shirt closer to his chest, he cranked up the AC.

He slowed as he approached the yellow light, nervous about seeing Kelly again—not worried how she'd look, but rather how she'd react to him. Would the lines on his face or his bald head bother her? Would she be cool and cautious or delighted to see him?

*What are you doing?*

This wasn't a date. He was investigating his sister's murder. Shit. How had his priorities become so scrambled? Oh, yeah. The moment he'd heard Kelly Gentry's name, his brain acted like a rat in a maze desperately looking for a way out. Not his dick though. Far from it.

Derek fanned his hand over the AC, hoping the cool air would jerk him back to reality, but it didn't work. His mind refused to stop focusing on her. Would she be happy to see him? Perhaps more importantly, would Kelly accept his comfort?

Before he knew it, his apartment loomed in front of him. Derek parked, but missed the white lines by six inches. Tough. He didn't have time to repark.

He raced upstairs, showered quickly, and then slipped on a clean pair of jeans and a blue buttoned down shirt. Kelly was a doctor who was a class act. She wouldn't appreciate him looking like a slob.

At the last minute, he splashed on cologne. He studied the bottle, and then chuckled without joy. He'd never changed his brand since high school. Would she notice? Hell, he wondered if she was still using Channel No. 5. He shivered, trying to rid himself of his juvenile thoughts.

Needing to keep alert, he grabbed a soda from the fridge on the way out. Shit. He felt like a damn teenager going to his first prom. Why was that?

*Because the witness was Kelly, stupid.* Right.

As Derek pulled out of his parking space, another car shot out from behind him and nearly clipped his bumper. Derek slammed his palm on the horn. Damn it. He needed to concentrate on the meeting, not have to worry about the crazies.

He rolled down his window. "Look where you're going."

The poor woman looked crestfallen. Cripes. He shouldn't have yelled at her. Hell, he hadn't even looked to see it was a woman before he shouted. Seeing Kelly again was messing with his head. She always set his blood pumping and his heart thumping.

Halfway to her house, Derek pulled out the Post-it note with Kelly's name and address on it, but Medina had omitted the phone number. Derek should call the station for the information, but dammit, he needed to see her expression when he quizzed her about Stefanie's last hours in case she had anything to do with her sister's death. A good detective received his clues from eye movement and body language.

He pulled to a stop at a light and opened the paper again with Kelly's address.

Fuck.

Her last name wasn't Gentry any more. It was Rutland. She was married—to someone else. A dart of jealousy flew out of nowhere and pierced his heart. Derek had once loved her; watched her grow into a woman. He'd shared her joys and sorrows, and then watched her leave.

Sick at how things had ended, Derek was tempted to turn the car around. His fingers played the wheel like a piano, debating his choices as he waited for the light to turn green. If he went back now, he'd never learn about Rayne. His sister's smiling face flashed in his mind's eye, and Derek settled into police mode, determined to find her killer. Stowing his emotions into the back recesses of his mind, he took off, anxious to get on with the investigation.

Despite the heavy rush hour traffic heading north on Dale Mabry, the turn off to Kelly's road appeared sooner than he'd wanted. One more turn brought him to her street, and the dead end led to a cozy cul-de-sac, shaded by water oaks and palmetto palms. Nice. Fancy, but not too uppity.

He searched the house numbers, a little surprised the Hyde Park style cottage at the end was hers. He would have guessed a doctor of her stature would own a bigger home. But Kelly came from a poor background, which was probably why they'd gotten along so well. They used to share dreams of having money, of traveling, of making a difference in the world.

She'd succeeded. Had he?

With money? Hell no. Traveling? Not much. To the third question, he hoped so, at least to the victims' families.

A yellow Volkswagen sat in her drive, and he had to smile. Kelly had a fondness for everything yellow, especially sunflowers.

He eased his truck to the edge of the drive and cut the engine. He used the visor to check his appearance. After he pulled back his lip to make sure there was nothing stuck in his teeth, he hauled himself out. Hot air blasted him, constricting his chest. Exhaust fumes from the busy highway a mile away remained in the air.

His muscles were slow to respond. Coward. Move. Meet the husband, meet Kelly, ask her a few questions in a professional manner, and then get the hell out. Stop acting like a high school senior in love.

Though he usually only used his sage when he faced the dead, he removed it from his packet and held the calming scent to his nose, forcing himself to relax, to center himself, to focus.

When he felt ready, he stepped onto her walkway. With a metered stride, Derek headed to her house, careful not to step on the cracks between the pavers. The one superstition his father had passed onto him remained engraved in his brain.

When he'd eaten up all the space between the drive and the door, he knocked.

The scent of the jasmine that clung to the columns on either side of the door let out a sweet smell too strong to ignore. He took a deep breath to prepare to meet the woman who still held his heart in her hand.

# CHAPTER SEVEN

MUNCHING on a stale chocolate chip cookie while sitting at the kitchen counter, Kelly read her emails on her laptop. The day had been disappointing. She'd been convinced the clinical trials of the conjugated linoleic acid isomers were the definitive answer to tumor prevention, but she'd been wrong. Starting all over again put a lump in her stomach.

She kicked off her shoes and sighed with relief from having stood all day. The sandal wedges dropped to the tile kitchen floor with a clunk. Lab work wreaked havoc on the body, but she wouldn't give up her passion for anything. Someday, she'd advance the cure for cancer. And on that day, maybe a little girl wouldn't have to lose her dad.

Not only had the lab results not turned out as she'd hoped, but they'd come right after her unsettling meeting with Justin Bladen.

At first, she'd felt sorry for the guy. He'd lost a woman he loved and the mother of his unborn child. She could relate to the unceasing pain. Okay, fine, his anguish appeared sincere, but when he acted interested in her as a woman, the ick factor had kicked in. Mourning meant you couldn't help but think of that person.

What the heck. Given the horrific week, her mind was probably misinterpreting all the signals. Reading men was not her forte. Oh, well. She'd probably never run into him again and should just be glad someone else understood how death could rip a person in half.

Just as she exited her email account and logged off her computer, a loud knock on the front door made her jump. Were the police here again?

She closed her laptop and rushed to the door, the cold foyer tile helping to cool her hot feet.

She shot a glance through the peephole, and all she could see was the top of a man's chest. A nice, broad chest in a blue chambray shirt. Definitely not the cops.

Confused as to who could be calling, she cracked open the door and wedged her toe behind the door's baseboard to prevent him from busting in. She ran her gaze up to his face. He blinked, and her focus shot straight to his eyes. Only one six-foot six man possessed eyes the color of sapphire and emerald morphed together. Every muscle in her bone-weary body turned to Jell-O.

Derek Benally at *her* door? Interest, excitement, and lust bombarded her, and all coherent thoughts flew out her mind. She opened her mouth to greet him but suddenly turned mute.

She was pretty sure why he'd come. He'd heard about Stef's death and wasn't here to start up where they'd left off. Her initial thrill deflated.

"Hello, Kelly," he said, his voice as rich as Godiva chocolate—her favorite treat.

She swallowed to wet her mouth, hoping she hadn't looked like a gawping fish as she drank in the sight of him. "Derek?"

Of course it was Derek. No length of time could erase his chiseled features or the way his full lips turned up slightly at the edges. And those eyes. Eyes never changed. Especially ones as distinctive as his.

She took in the rest of him. My, oh, my. He was taller, more broad-shouldered than she remembered. But then again, she hadn't seen him since he was eighteen. He'd changed from a teen to a full-grown man. Definite man growth there. Time had been good to him. To his body. To his face.

But he'd shaved his head. Darn. She'd so loved to run her fingers through his long, thick, black hair.

Yet, despite the years since their last meeting, he did unimaginable things to her heart and soul. Always had and probably always would.

"May I come in?" He cocked a brow and focused solely on her eyes. The hard line of his mouth told her all she needed to know.

A slam of hurt blasted her. He wasn't interested in her, which was a dramatic change from high school. He was here about Rayne, she bet.

She forced a calm she didn't feel, plastered on her best cheerleading smile, and stepped out of the way to let him enter. His two long strides brought him into the foyer, and his closeness stole her breath away—again. Her chest tightened along with the pain of their parting. The right words wouldn't form, and all she could do was motion him toward the living room.

Damn Derek Benally. And here she thought she'd moved on.

As Derek walked in front of her toward the sofa, his musky scent trailed behind him, transporting her to a time when they used to kiss behind the football bleachers.

Kelly allowed herself to become lost in the movement of his tight butt, narrow hips, and long muscular legs. And those shoulders. Ooooh. Boy, what he did to her insides.

*Stop fantasizing.* Twelve years was a lifetime ago. *Get a grip.*

Kelly glanced down at her chipped toenail polish and sobered. What was wrong with her? Her sister had just died and here she was acting as if she didn't have a care in the world. She was no better than Justin Bladen.

Recognizing the need for space between them, Kelly hurried behind his powerful form and slipped down into the lone high-back chair across from him. She curled her toes, not having given any thought to her appearance in days.

Wouldn't ya know? She was a mess and today *he* had to show up. Mercury must be in retrograde

Good thing he sat far enough away or else she'd have to inhale his wonderful scent. Remembering how good he always smelled conjured other memories of how he used to hold her with strong arms and kiss her with his full, soft lips. Her mouth went dry as she felt herself lean forward. Suddenly, Stef's face intruded and Kelly straightened, embarrassed by her reaction, especially during her time of mourning.

"You're looking...good," he said, his lips pressed firmly together as if he were holding in a lie.

She knew she looked tired. The bags under eyes were darker than normal because of the sleepless nights since her sister's death. At least she weighed only ten pounds more than she had in high school. Had he meant to say more or hadn't she aged well?

"Thank you." *I think*.

He ran a hand over his bald pate where a dark stubbled shadow threatened to spoil the clean landscape. "I, ah, I wanted to come by and say I'm sorry for your loss."

Just as she'd thought. A sympathy call. Nothing more. Nonetheless, his sentiment touched her deeply. "Thank you. I heard about Rayne's suicide. It was such a shame."

He nodded. Despite the trite conversation, Kelly received comfort from him being there.

"Thanks, but I didn't come here to reminiscence, especially about the dead."

Kelly stiffened at his sudden calloused tone, and she tried not to let her shoulders sag. So what if he hadn't come to give comfort. Disappointment tugged at her belly—or was it closer to hurt?

She leveled him a stare. "Okay. Why *did* you come?" Her hands caressed the nubby chair arm, the fabric soothing her palms, but not her heart.

The planes of his jaw tightened. "Rayne didn't kill herself. Someone murdered her."

She clasped a hand over her mouth. "Oh my God. That's terrible. Do the police know who killed her?" Kelly didn't know whether to be relieved Rayne hadn't taken her own life or angry someone else had. A mixture of the two assaulted her.

"No, but I'm a detective with the Tampa police department now, and I plan to find out."

She knew he was a detective, but not much else. His dream had been to go into law enforcement. Kelly wanted to hear all about his successes and how he liked investigative work, but now was not the time. "Stef had mentioned you worked for the city police."

His eyes widened a smidgen. Had he expected her to call if she knew they lived in the same town? Didn't he know she'd been too embarrassed to make contact?

"Detective Medina stopped by to ask you a few questions about your sister's accident. Did Stefanie mentioned anything about how the meeting with Rayne went the night they both died?"

"Funny. Justin asked me the same thing."

His face hardened, and his fists clenched. "Justin contacted you? Justin Bladen?"

She couldn't understand his sudden anger. "Yes, why?" She curled one leg under her butt, trying to get more comfortable under the weight of his glare.

He snatched the coaster off the coffee table and spun the cork material in his hands, looking as if he wanted to crush it. "He was practically engaged to my sister. Why would he seek out a complete stranger? Or did you know him?"

Taken aback at his continued curt behavior, Kelly spoke with a metered tone. "I only met Justin yesterday. He was looking for some solace, knowing we'd both suffered a loss." She told him as much as she remembered of their conversation, and bit-by-bit Derek relaxed.

"I never pictured him as the sympathetic type," Derek said, his tone tinged with bitterness.

She had no basis to judge Justin and wondered what he'd done to make Derek turn against him. Years past, Derek Benally accepted everyone. Clearly, life hadn't been kind to him. She decided to let the discussion drop.

Instead, she wanted to pass a theory by him. "Given someone murdered your sister, don't you think it odd that Stefanie died on the same night? What are the chances?"

A flash of sympathy crossed his face. "I considered the same thing at first, but Medina and his men have been all over her car. There was no sign of another vehicle or any foul play."

She refused to accept their answer as final. "But couldn't—"

He waved a dismissive hand. "I understand you want to blame someone, believe me I do too, but thinking about the what ifs will only drive you mad if you don't let go."

"I can't...just...give up. I know how bad the weather was the night of the accident, and that she was on the phone to me around that time. It's just—" Kelly bit her inner lip to keep from crying. Guilt hit. If only she'd insisted Stefanie pull over until the rain stopped, her sister might still be alive. "I can't help but think some thing or someone caused her to swerve off the road." She raised her eyes to the ceiling, hoping to stop the flow of tears.

He cocked a brow and waited until her composure returned. "What would be the motive? Rayne mentioned your sister was a private investigator, but did you know if anyone wanted to harm her?"

She grabbed a tissue off the coffee table and blew her nose. "She didn't deal with criminals, if that's what you're asking. Most of the time she was looking for lost relatives or following errant spouses." Kelly wiped the moisture from her eyes. "I was thinking maybe someone she was following didn't want the attention."

He tossed the coaster back onto the coffee table. The cork pinged, rolled, and fell flat. Kind of like her heart. "The police won't investigate without some kind of proof," he said with a soft voice, sounding as if he would have helped if she'd been able to provide some kind of link.

"Oh."

"Look, I'm sorry. My hands are tied." He swiped a palm over his head and cleared his throat. "Back to my original question. Do you know why your sister and Rayne were planning to meet?"

He did the nice-to-harsh switch again, and she took a second to study him. Where was the Derek she'd known and loved?

Apparently gone. Poof.

Had the force made him angry? Or had his sister's death turned him into granite? He leaned forward, no doubt waiting for her answer, and his shirt gapped open at the throat. When he gaze shot to his bulging pecs, she swallowed her intake of breath and answered with amazing calm. "Does there have to be a reason for friends to get together?"

"Maybe not." Derek slapped his thighs and rose.

For some reason, she didn't want him to leave yet. He hadn't been friendly, or warm. Hell, he'd been downright rude, but dammit, they had unfinished business. "Derek?"

"Yes." He sat back down, his gaze locked on her face.

"I need to apologize for the way things ended between us."

There. After all these years, she'd finally said it, and a heavy burden lifted off her shoulders.

His brows drew together as he tilted his chin closer to his chest, looking as if she'd spoken in tongues. "There's nothing to apologize for."

Her mouth dropped open. Here she'd been worried all these years she'd hurt him when she'd left for school. *What a fool I am. What a stupid, stupid fool.* To think she'd wasted all this valuable time on someone who never cared.

"Can I get you something to drink?" she asked, filling the silence with an automatic, if not stupid, question.

His lips firmed. "No. This isn't a social call. I came to find out about Rayne, to see if by chance your sister knew something. Nothing more."

This time when he stood, he looked over her head instead of at her.

His aloofness hurt, damn him. She cleared her throat. "I'm sorry I couldn't have been of more help." She refused to suggest they get together after his rotten attitude.

"If you think of anything, call me." He dropped his card on her coffee table. The corner hit and flipped face down.

Was he afraid their fingers might touch if he handed her the card? He acted as if she was some poisonous snake—get too near and she might bite. *Kelly Lynn, you're pathetic thinking things could be the way they were.*

When he turned to head out the door, Kelly didn't bother to see him out. Her mother would be appalled at her lack of etiquette, but tough darts. Hell, she considered hurling an expletive or two at him for being such a jerk, but that high school attitude would only prove she hadn't changed. And she had. Her ex-husband had taught her a few lessons about the importance of family. Too bad she'd learned them after he left her for someone else.

Derek closed the front door quietly, but once his engine caught a minute later, his tires squealed on the pavement as he raced down the street.

"Asshole!" she yelled to an empty house.

# CHAPTER EIGHT

DEREK PULLED into a parking place at the far end of his apartment complex, killed the engine, and stared straight ahead. He let the sweat drip down his forehead, drop by drop, making no attempt to wipe away the irritation. He didn't give a damn anymore. His Kelly Gentry was now Kelly Rutland. She was married. Taken.

"Let her go," the reasonable, little voice in his head said.

"I wish," he tossed back to the empty cab.

He rolled down his window to let the warm evening air roll over him. The sweet smell of fresh cut grass filled the inside and he sneezed —three times. Stupid allergies.

Nothing had gone right today. Not with Piloseno and not with the meeting with Kelly.

The moment he laid eyes on her, his mind left and his dick had taken over. What a jerk he'd been.

Kelly was more beautiful, more refined, and more incredible than he imagined, yet he'd barely acknowledged her. Instead of finding out how she was doing, he'd turned into super detective, or in his case, super dick.

Granted, he needed to ask questions relating to Rayne's death, but he shouldn't have acted as if Kelly meant nothing to him. Hell, he'd gone to her house in part to learn about her, and to catch up on old times. But had he? No. Did he even think to mention that he'd thought about her twenty-four-seven for twelve years, pining over their lost love? Hell, no. Not jerk face.

How hard would it have been to ask how medical school had gone? How her research was progressing? Was she happily married? Was she trying to have kids?

Kids. His heart took a leap to the dark side. He'd wanted a family worse than anything. They both had, but now they never would—at least not together. He and Kelly had spent hours lying on the grass in summer, staring at the stars, making up names for their children. Did she remember what they'd picked? He did—Alison for the girl and Austin for a boy.

He slapped the steering wheel hard, stinging his palm. Shit. He hadn't even been able to carry on a decent conversation with the woman.

"You're a loser, Benally, with a capital *L*." He never even asked her how long she'd lived in Tampa. From the looks of her place, she'd made a nice home for herself—and for the husband. She looked settled, comfortable, secure.

Not super cop. Oh, no. He'd lived in his apartment for five years and still hadn't fully unpacked. Was he hoping to start a family and move to a real home? Maybe.

He almost laughed. At least her husband hadn't shown up. While Derek didn't consider himself violent, if he'd met the guy, he might have been tempted to beat the crap out of him—for no good reason.

Disgust and loathing caught in his throat. He threw open the truck door and jumped out, royalty pissed at himself. As he jaywalked across the lot to his apartment, a car honked and narrowly missed him in the center of the street.

Derek took the stairs to his apartment two at a time and nearly ran over his next-door neighbor coming out of her place carrying a laundry basket. "Sorry, Sonia." Or was it Sophia?

"Hi, Der-Rick." She stuck out her tits and smiled.

Not interested. "See ya." He ignored her open invitation and rushed inside.

Cool air blasted him. Why hadn't he noticed before that his very white walls were as stark as an endless desert, unlike Kelly's cozy home that begged for long conversations and lots of snuggling in front of her fireplace? Her home was like the old times they'd shared at her mom's.

His sparse, sterile furniture exuded no warmth—a reflection of his heart—cold and dead.

When had he shut himself off from the world? Hell if he knew.

*Kelly. Kelly. Kelly.*

He covered his ears to stop the voices from yelling her name, from taunting him. He dropped down to the sofa's edge and grabbed his head in his hands. She'd offered no additional information on Rayne's case. There was no reason to see her again.

Ever.

Pain whipped through him with hurricane force. *Admit it. She's history.*

***

Dinner tasted like rubber, but Kelly had to eat to keep up her strength. Grief sapped most of her energy and sleep was a distant memory. She tossed the left over salad down the garbage disposal, and then opened a bottle of wine she'd been saving for a special occasion. Without a thought, she grabbed a box of chocolate chip cookies before plopping down in front of the TV.

Stupid Derek.

All these years she'd wondered how he'd fared. And when they'd finally met, he acted as if their years together meant nothing. She took a large gulp of wine to wash away her anger. Though the tangy liquid slid down her throat like velvet and left a wonderful taste on her tongue, she didn't get the usual rush from the rich wine. The jerk even managed to ruin a good glass of Merlot.

If only Stef were here. She'd know what to do. "Forget him," her sister would have said. "Move on."

Kelly let loose a rueful laugh. Too bad Kelly had tried for the last twelve years to do just that but nothing seemed to work—kind of like her addiction to chocolate chip cookies. They were bad for her, but did that make her stop eating them? Noooo.

She was a hopeless mess. Who could deal with the tragic loss of her sister *and* get ignored by her one true love, all in the same week?

No one.

First loves never left one's heart. She could still remember how Derek had been given a job at a feed store, of all places, after school for three whole months, hauling bags of fertilizer to earn enough money to pay for his tux rental and her corsage for their senior prom. And man, did he look amazing. Every girl in the class tried to cut in for a dance, but Derek only had eyes for her.

When a tear slid down her cheek, landing at the corner of her mouth, she wiped away the salty liquid.

Forcing him out of her mind, she yanked her address book from the coffee table's top drawer and flipped to Michael's address. It was time to tie up loose ends. Calling him was the right thing to do. While he and Stefanie had broken up close to a year ago, he had a right to know his ex-girlfriend was dead.

She groaned and slapped the book closed. Calling was so impersonal. She needed to tell him in person. Only God knew how much that man had suffered because of her sister. Maybe she could console Michael, unlike someone else she knew.

Afterward, she'd go for a run. She certainly could use the much-needed endorphins. Maybe a good workout could purge the image of Derek Benally from her mind. Right, and Stef would walk in the front door any minute now.

Kelly changed into her jogging clothes, filled a sports bottle with water, mixed with two teaspoons of an electrolyte mixture, and headed out. The rest of the delicious wine would have to wait until she returned.

As she left her house, the high humidity coated her arms and legs with moisture. Kelly hopped in her car and cranked up the air as she left her safe little neighborhood. Despite the thirty-minute drive to

Michael's, there wasn't enough time to come up with a delicate way to tell him the woman he'd once loved was dead.

Kelly pulled in front of his small West Tampa block home, crammed close to its neighbors. Even though the sun had set, there was enough light to tell the grass needed to be cut and the house badly needed some repair work. Two cars on cinderblocks took up most of the drive.

She slipped out of her VW and straightened her T-shirt. Behind her, neighborhood children raced on their bikes down the narrow road, seeming to enjoy the last few days of summer, but she failed to take in their joy.

Her stomach fluttered, unsure how Michael would take the news. *Here goes nothing.*

She walked toward the front door, and a sudden cool blast of wind blew the hair from her face. The air smelled like rain, which meant she wouldn't get her run in after all.

She knocked once, and then twice. Muted voices came from inside. Michael apparently wasn't alone. A moment later, a small, older woman in an apron answered the door.

"Si?"

Kelly recognized Michael's mom from the Thanksgiving photos Stef had shown her, but she hadn't known his mother lived with him. Maybe he needed help getting around since the accident. "Is Michael home?"

The older woman pulled the door open, stepped to the side and motioned her in. The mom shouted something in Spanish.

Michael clicked off the TV and stood. He used to be so handsome, but a huge scar marred the entire left side of his face. His black hair had traces of gray, and his once friendly gaze was as hard as stone. She studied his right leg. Or rather, where his right leg used to be. In its place was a metal prosthetic, and her heart sank.

"Hi, Michael." Kelly forced herself to sound casual.

"What are you doing here?" His harsh tone surprised her.

Kelly resolved to act civil. "I wanted to talk to you about Stefanie."

"That bitch? What about her?" His bitterness shocked her.

His mother muttered something in Spanish, but she didn't need to be bilingual to understand the chastisement.

Yes, Stefanie had been driving the night their car went off the road, and while her sister had escaped unscathed, Michael had lost his leg. The investigation proved the slick roads had caused the accident.

How ironic, the same event took place again, only this time with a different outcome.

"Let's go outside. I need a smoke." He turned to his mother and said something to her in their native language. She nodded but didn't seem happy.

He limped outside, and Kelly followed. With his back to her, Michael lit his cigarette, and she waved away the acrid smell of tobacco. After a few puffs, his shoulders relaxed.

He turned around. "So, Dr. Rutland. What's so goddamn important that you have to come to my neck of the woods? I never took you for the slumming kind."

Kelly bit back her retort. Slumming indeed. If he'd seen how she used to live, he wouldn't have said that.

He waved his cigarette in the air. "Didn't Stefanie tell you we didn't part on the best of terms?"

She let out a breath. "Yes, she did, and Stefanie never forgave herself for what happened."

"I bet she was sorry. So sorry in fact she dumped me right after she totaled my car."

Anger rushed up her gut so fast, she didn't think. "You pushed her away." Dammit. She'd promised she wouldn't get into a spitting match with him, and here she was pushing his buttons.

"Stefanie had nothing but pity for me. I couldn't stand to see the woman I loved cringe when she came to visit." His eyes narrowed.

Enough. "I'm not here to discuss your broken relationship. I thought you'd want... no, I thought you deserved to know that Stefanie was in a car wreck on Saturday. She's dead." Her throat half closed up as she studied his reaction. Her hands fisted at her side as her stomach threatened to heave, but Kelly forced down her pain.

He laughed. "Well isn't that turn around fair play."

Before Kelly could formulate a good comeback for his cruelty, he tossed the cigarette on the ground, stomped the butt out with his good foot, and stalked back inside.

How dare he walk away? She was tempted to march into his house and demand an apology, but for what purpose?

Throwing her arms into the air in frustration, she stalked to her car, hopped in, and drove off without looking back. She didn't bother to wipe the sweat from her brow as the liquid stung her eyes. Her tears might help wash away the angry pain.

Halfway down the road, his comments sunk in. She pulled the car to a halt on the side of the road, careful not to smash the flowers lining a neighbor's property. *Think.* Could Michael have had anything to do with Stef's death? Could the rainy night have reminded him of another? Had he run Stef off the road?

Reason intruded. No. Killers tried to cover up their deeds, not announce they were pleased the victim was dead. Maybe she should run his name by Derek and have him investigate Mr. Sensitive's whereabouts on Saturday night.

Yes, that's what she'd do.

With a plan in mind, her ability to drive returned, and she headed toward the park to run. She needed an intense workout to clear up the fuzz that marbled her brain. Because the sky had turned darker and more threatening just in the last few minutes, she pressed her foot on the accelerator, wanting to arrive before the rain interfered.

Even though Al Lopez Park had lights, the place became dangerous at night. Relief shot through her when she noticed the lot was half full. Safety in numbers, as they say.

Bicycles and joggers shared the paved path on the south side trail, but the north side was too hidden by trees to chance running this late.

After stretching, she jogged at a moderate pace until her muscles warmed up. Two owners played with their dogs in the enclosed doggie park, and the happy puppy yelps spurred her on.

Anger, frustration, and depression tightened every muscle in her body. Slowly, she increased her pace until she found herself in a near sprint instead of her usual jog. A stitch in her side made her slow, but she knew she'd beaten her nine-minute per mile mark.

After catching her breath, she glanced at her watch. When a shadow moved out from behind a tree, her neck hair prickled. On instinct, Kelly took off in a sprint.

Long fingers grabbed her shoulder, and a scream lodged in her throat.

# CHAPTER NINE

KELLY'S HEART nearly jackknifed out of her chest. On instinct, she jerked away from the grasp and twisted her head to see over her shoulder.

Justin smiled. "Hey, Doc. Fancy meeting you here." His t-shirt was stained with sweat across his chest.

She stopped and let out a sigh of relief. Here, she thought some stalker had caught her—or worse a murderer.

She leaned over and grabbed her knees, gulping in air. "What are you doing here?" She'd never seen him at the park before. "You nearly gave me a heart attack." She stood back up, and a sudden cool breeze across her wet skin gave her goose bumps.

"Sorry. I didn't mean to scare you." He raised his brows, looking innocent. "As to what I'm doing here, I suspect the same as you—trying to let off a little steam after work."

Two joggers and a bicyclist passed them. Her mind was too jumbled to decide if Justin had an ulterior motive for being at the park the same time as her or if he was telling the truth. "Do you come here often?"

He pulled the hem of his shirt up to his forehead and wiped his brow. His rippled abs tightened, and she pulled her gaze back up to his face.

"I like to exercise at least three times a week. I usually get started earlier, but it's been so damn hot, I've been waiting until it's nearly dark before I run."

His explanation made sense. "I know what you mean. I either run at six in the morning or around this time."

"Biker on your left," a man shouted from behind.

They both stepped to the side of the paved path. Justin pointed a finger toward the road. The parking lot was another half mile. He said nothing for a few seconds as she jogged alongside him, swatting away a few bugs that buzzed her ears.

As they rounded the bend on the oval track, Kelly glanced over at Justin, studying his expression. He seemed calm, as if nothing unusual had occurred in the last two days. Hey, maybe he had the right attitude. Denial was easier on the spirit than reality.

He looked over at her and smiled again. Kelly whipped her head back to the path, not wanting him to get the wrong idea. She wasn't interested. Sure he was a nice looking guy with straight white teeth, perfect hair, but he did nothing for her. The moment Derek had shown up at her house, all thoughts of other men had flown out of her brain.

Derek. Derek. Derek. He'd been such a jerk, so why should she still care?

She refused to analyze her feelings. Frustrated at her bad taste in men, she picked up the pace, perhaps hoping to outrun her demons. Justin reached out a hand to slow her down. She'd been so tuned into her own world, she'd forgotten he was even there.

"You going for an Olympic medal?" he asked.

His breathing was even, as if a nine-minute mile was a snail's pace. She hadn't exactly asked him to join her in her workout, but she didn't mind his company either.

"Sorry, I was a little lost in thought." She returned to her usual pace.

Derek's image intruded, again, and she almost smiled at the remembrance of *The Challenge*, as Derek called it. Their senior year she'd bet him she could beat him in the two-twenty. After all, she was on the track team. He was not. Stupid man beat her by a good twenty meters. That ended her challenges.

After Kelly finished her three miles, she stopped next to her car. Sweat covered her body and dripped into her eyes. She usually carried a small towel, but in her rush to see Michael first, she'd forgotten one.

"Well, good seeing you," she said to Justin who'd leaned his butt against the rear of her car. Except for the wet T-shirt and the water beading his forehead, he didn't look like the run had affected him much.

"You too." His gaze shot to the ground. "Say, I know this is probably too soon, and I wouldn't normally ask, but would you be willing to indulge me in something?" He looked up at her through long lashes.

His question registered. "Indulge you how?" Kelly placed two forefingers on her carotid artery to check her pulse.

"Would you mind coming with me to the Casino Royale tonight for some gambling?"

She lowered her arm, too startled to count her heartbeat. The question was so preposterous Kelly couldn't help but laugh. "You like to gamble?"

"What? You never play the slots?" he asked.

"Oh, that kind of gambling." Stupid comment. How many kinds were there?

"Listen. Rayne loved Black Jack. We used to go to the Casino every Tuesday. I know she won't be there, but somehow—you know, given today is Tuesday, I just thought..."

Sympathy coursed through her. "I understand. Stef and I used to go to Starbucks every Sunday morning. Keeping the tradition can help keep her memory alive."

She would not cry—especially in front of Justin.

He looked at her, his gaze almost dreamy. "I'm amazed how much you understand. You don't know what this means to me."

Anger at her big mouth robbed her of depression. "I want to help, but I have so much work to do."

He held up a hand. "I totally understand. We won't stay more than an hour, I promise."

Several cars whipped out of the parking lot, leaving a trace of smelly exhaust, which didn't help after a good run.

*The man is hurting. Help him.* She probably wouldn't be able to concentrate on the lab reports any more than she had when she was at work. "Fine."

Maybe he'd see what a boring date she was and leave her alone after that.

"Great. I'll pick you up in say an hour? I need to change." He plucked his damp shirt off his chest, as if to prove his claim.

"Needless to say, so do I." She pulled open her car door and grabbed a pad of paper and a pen from the console and drew a map to her house. "My house is really easy to find. Here."

Justin looked over the diagram. "See you in an hour."

He'd parked two cars away. She climbed in her Bug, a little ticked she'd forgotten to bring a towel to sit on. Sweat didn't go well with her cloth seats.

As she pulled onto Himes Avenue, regret assaulted her. She had no business going to a casino with a man she hardly knew, or go anywhere with a man she hardly knew for that matter, especially at nine on a work night. And giving a stranger, or a somewhat stranger, directions to her house? What was she thinking?

That was the problem. She wasn't. On top of Stef's death, Derek's visit had scrambled her thought process. Michael's reaction to the accident, coupled with the sudden appearance of Justin, had her fighting to operate on any functional level. If she had to stand trial for some crime, she'd fail the psych test.

Kelly slowed down and edged up to a red light. Casino Royale was a good thirty minutes away from her house. That would put her back home at midnight.

But dammit, if she sat home, she'd probably end up crying all night. She could only hope that being with others would give her a new perspective on Stefanie's accident and on life in general.

A car honked behind her. The light had turned green. Kelly waved, hoping to avoid a road rage fight.

As she turned down her street, she made a mental calendar.

Tomorrow after work she would go over to Stef's and begin the painful act of sorting through her sister's things.

✳✳✳

Derek clicked through the TV stations. Nothing was on but pure drivel, and he turned the damned thing off. Every commercial and every story reminded him in some way of Rayne, or Billy. Or yes, even Kelly.

What the hell was wrong with him? Ever since he'd left her place, a bad feeling had settled over him. At the time, he attributed his foul mood to his father's comment about being indirectly the cause of his sister's death. Now he wasn't so sure Kelly wasn't the source of his crappy attitude.

Only one way to find out. Derek needed to confront the issue with his dad head on. He grabbed a soda from the fridge and settled onto his sofa to call his father.

Drat. The answering machine picked up. Not wanting to leave a message, he hung up. His dad's cell phone yielded the same result. A little worried, he called his father's best friend, Tom.

"Jimmie Williams came down sick," Tom explained. "He asked your dad to take his place at the tables."

Derek took a sip of his soda, relieved nothing bad had happened, and the chilly drink calmed him. "Dad never works at the casino on Tuesday. It's his night to pray."

"I guess he broke his own rule. Don't be hard on him. Every man grieves in his own way."

"Thanks, Tom."

Tom Trueheart—now there was a man who was a throwback to way the Seminoles used to live—simple, spiritual, and down to earth. He hoped his father appreciated his good friend.

Derek polished off the drink, tossed the can in the trashcan, and headed out.

The traffic on I-4 going east was lighter than usual, but then again, at ten thirty, sane folks were home with their families. He exited the

Interstate and turned left toward the Casino Royale. His father should be home relaxing, socializing with his friends once he finished his prayer work, not working. But Dad was Dad. He would never let his grief stand in the way of helping his fellow tribesmen.

When Derek entered the gambling hall, bright strobe lights, cheers from excited customers, and the ca-ching of the slots assaulted him. He'd never liked the place. It was too noisy and had either too much cheer if someone won, or too much misery if he lost.

Derek bought twenty dollars' worth of chips. His father didn't approve of Derek hanging around and not dropping some money for the *cause*, as he called it.

If memory served him, Jimmie worked the roulette wheel, so Derek headed in that direction. He spotted his father and wove his way around the tables toward him. Bells, whistled, and machines clinked. He couldn't wait to get out of there.

If his father had any ill will, he'd start the conversation off about where Billy would live once school let out for the holidays. Derek had already practiced his answer. Did his father think Billy should move in with Derek for the long haul and go to a public school nearby, or would his nephew be better off staying with Dad? His father could teach his grandson to hunt and fish better than he could, and Billy would learn the ancient Seminole customs. It wasn't his own choice of how to grow up, but perhaps he should let Billy decide.

Of course, there was the off chance the local children would treat his nephew as an outsider. Derek would never forget how the Indian kids had treated Rayne and him like lepers when they went to the native school the summer between fourth and fifth grade. Taunting, book stealing, and whispers behind backs happened every day. He hated them; hated the native life.

A cocktail waitress sauntered up to him and asked if he wanted a drink. He waved her away and made a beeline to the roulette wheel.

Once they began discussing Billy, Derek would switch the topic around to what was really bothering him—his father's comment about leading Rayne astray. The statement had cut him to the quick. Derek didn't expect a full-blown conversation this time around. After all, his dad had a job to do.

When Derek reached his dad's table, his father looked up. "Derek?" His dad's brief smiled warmed his heart, and a weight lifted from his shoulders.

"Don't let me interrupt. I can see you're busy."

His father held up a hand for him to stay before turning back to the customers. "Okay, place your bets." He spun the wheel. The little white ball bounced around the grooves, clicking and clacking before eventually settling on a slot. "Red eight. Red eight wins."

After collecting the money from the losers and paying out chips to the winners, he started again. "You playing, son?"

"Sure." Derek dropped two five-dollar chips on black. Any black would do. He wasn't here to gamble.

"You come to see me?" his dad asked. "I can get Ramon to cover."

Yes. "I don't want to interrupt." The lack of anger from his father told him all he needed to know. He'd been forgiven. His dad's outburst had been a reaction to his daughter's death—or so he hoped.

As he waited for the rest of the table to place their bets, Derek looked around, glad to see people were still visiting the place and bringing in the needed revenue to the tribe.

Before he turned back to the game, his gaze caught sight of a woman four tables away that looked a lot like Kelly. The woman shifted toward him. Damn, it was her. And she was with... Justin? An emotion he refused to acknowledge charged up his spine and grabbed hold of his heart.

He took off in their direction, shoving his way through the crowd.

"Derek, your money," his father called after him.

Derek didn't care. "Save it for me," he said over his shoulder. All he wanted was to get to Kelly.

# CHAPTER TEN

DEREK SWALLOWED to keep his anger at bay. What the hell was Kelly doing out on a date? And with Justin no less?

His gaze locked onto the lovely creature in the tight black stretch pants and top so tiny her belly showed. As he pushed through the crowd, the ringing and whistling of the machines appeared to cease. He dodged one cocktail waitress then another to reach his goal.

Kelly looked up and smiled at the father of Rayne's child. Damn. Derek remembered that smile. She used to melt his heart in less time than it took to blink when she looked at him that way.

He invaded her space and halted, glaring down at her. "Kelly?" His voice cracked. Derek wanted to reach out and shake her.

*Control, man. Use control.* He inhaled to steady himself, but her sexy perfume nearly thwarted his effort.

She turned and looked up at him. Her jaw dropped and a full-blown blush raced up her face. "Der...Derek. What are you doing here?" She took a step back and glanced at Justin as if he were her savior.

"I came to speak with my father. He works at the casino. I thought you'd be at home mourning the loss of your sister, not out partying with my sister's boyfriend." Damn it. He'd let his tongue get the best of him.

Kelly's jaw tightened and her lips firmed. When Kelly didn't answer, he faced Justin. Maybe he'd tell him what the hell was going on.

Justin held up his hands in surrender. "Blame me. I ran into her at the park—literally." He threw out a megawatt smile, first toward Derek then at Kelly.

The level of jealousy that raced up Derek's gut took him by surprise. "Is that where you pick up all your women?"

Derek didn't care that his comment made him look like an asshole. When he was pissed, his mouth knew no bounds. He wanted to pummel someone. Anyone. And Justin was the perfect target.

"Didn't Rayne tell you we came here every Tuesday night? Staying away from here was too much for me. The casino reminds me of her." He looked to the ceiling. "I can pretend she's still alive this way." He swiped a finger under his eye.

Crocodile tears, for sure.

Giving Justin the benefit of the doubt, Derek's tamped down his anger. He looked back at Kelly. He had no right to quiz her, but an overwhelming need to protect her took over. "And you? When did you develop the urge to gamble?"

She planted her hands on her hips. The tension in her face told him he'd stepped over the line—way over. "Since when did you become my caretaker?" She didn't wait for an answer and rushed on. "For your information, I needed to get away from my house. When I'm by myself all I can do is think of Stefanie. I can't eat. I can't sleep. Justin is hurting too. If I can console someone, I will," she shot back.

Like throwing water on hot coals, Derek cooled down. "I'm sorry. I'm just surprised your husband would allow you to go out with a stranger."

Her lip curled up at one corner. "Husband? What husband? I'm divorced. I have been for four years."

She could have slugged him, and he wouldn't have been more shocked. "Divorced? Why didn't you tell me?"

He took a step closer and got another whiff of that spicy perfume, and lust shot to his groin. He certainly didn't need her as a distraction. Not now. Not ever again. She messed with his head.

"You never asked." Anger colored her statement.

*Touché.* Derek's senses started to level. The clinking of glasses, the pulling of levers, the shouts of joy, and sighs of defeat finally filtered through the rush of blood in his ears. He glanced around and realized they'd drawn a small crowd.

"Ah, I think we've become part of the entertainment."

Kelly looked around too. If possible, she turned an even prettier shade of red than her gorgeous mass of curls. She leaned closer to Justin. "Would you mind taking me home?"

Justin had the nerve to smile at Derek, and then wink at Kelly. "My pleasure." He took hold of Kelly's arm and led her away before Derek could stop them.

*Do something, dumb ass.* But what? He had no right to interfere in Kelly's life. She didn't belong to him anymore—as if she ever did.

Justin plastered Kelly by his side. She fit snuggly, almost as if they were made for each other, but something seemed out of whack.

Anger snaked up his gut and nearly choked him, as he lost his visual on the two when they ducked into the crowd. He didn't like them together. Not one bit.

✳✳✳

Derek had woken up the next morning with a pounding headache. Seeing Kelly with Justin had kept him up most of the night. Those two, acting like a couple really pissed him off. She didn't belong with a stockbroker. At least not one who'd supposedly lost the love of his life three days ago.

His anger festered as he rode along with Seinkievitz on another hunt for Pileseno. If Kelly needed comforting, why hadn't she called him? Oh, right. He'd been a jerk—twice as a matter of fact. Why had he been? Fear of rejection? Hell if he knew.

Seinkievitz raced up to the light, and then slammed on his brakes when the signal turned red, fast-forwarding Derek to the present.

"Damn, Brad. Watch the head. I'm suffering here." Why did he let himself get talked into coming with this maniac?

"My heart bleeds for you, Benally. Take my advice. Don't drink." Just as Derek was about to deny the allegation, Brad Seinkievitz cut a ripe one.

Derek rolled down the window to get a fresh breath. "You are a disgrace to the human race."

Seinkievitz smiled. "You didn't have to come with me."

"You bastard. You farted on purpose."

"I plead the fifth. So, you gonna kiss my ass when Piloseno turns out to be guilty?"

Derek went along with the change of subject. Seinkievitz was convinced the ex-con had offed Rayne for the pure pleasure of killing. Derek wasn't as cynical. Piloseno was capable of robbing Rayne or even beating her, but murder? He wasn't so sure.

Derek rubbed the bridge of his nose. "Piloseno's last stint was for armed robbery, not murder, you know."

"Doesn't mean he's an angel."

"I'm not saying he is, but felons don't usually change their M.O. I'm not buying he's our man, but I won't rule him out on that alone."

Seinkievitz took off down the road, then leaned forward and flipped up the AC, sending a shot of cool air to Derek's face. "We still need to talk to him."

"Fine." Derek rolled up the window. Piloseno was as good a lead as any.

Seinkievitz stuffed another chocolate donut down his throat with one hand while holding onto the wheel with the other. "Sure you don't want a one?"

"No, thanks."

"You look like shit, you know."

So he hadn't felt like shaving this morning. To be honest, he hadn't felt like doing much of anything. Just like Kelly, he couldn't sleep and he couldn't eat. Seinkievitz was right. He was a mess.

"You're no bed of roses either my friend. That day old chocolate on your chin?"

"Say what?" The cop did a quick swipe of his face and removed most of it off.

"Is that all you eat for breakfast?" Derek asked nodding to the donut.

Seinkievitz looked affronted. "Hell, no. Sometimes I have glazed."

"I don't know how come you're not fat." Derek had to work at keeping in shape.

"Lucky, I guess."

Derek took a large gulp of his soda, hoping the caffeine would help the ache behind his eyes. Too bad there wasn't a drink to salve his heart.

Without warning, the maniac jerked the cruiser to a stop again, only this time he stopped in front of Piloseno's bright turquoise duplex. Seinkievitz yanked the key from the ignition and oozed out of the car one skinny leg at a time.

Derek dropped his sunglasses to the bridge of his nose and stepped out. The sun aggravated his headache, and the heat made his stomach turn, but he needed answers.

"Let's hope we're more successful this time and find him home," Derek said.

As they marched toward the left half of the duplex, anger bubbled up inside Derek. Given his sister had put him away, this man had good cause to kill his sister, but had he? Except for some circumstantial evidence placing Piloseno near his sister's house the night of her death, the police had squat.

Seinkievitz pounded on the screen door. "Tampa PD. Open up."

Curses emanated from inside. A moment later, a medium height Latino answered. He didn't look like he'd shaved or washed in weeks, and his lips reminded Derek of a pig—overblown and pink with dirt stains where a mustache might have been.

"Yeah?" Piloseno tucked his sleeveless T-shirt into his jeans, which didn't help his looks one bit. "What d'you want?"

Derek and Seinkievitz held up their badges. "Can we come in?" Seinkievitz asked.

"Hell, no. I don't want no cops in here."

Derek thought he could detect the scent of pot inside. "We'd like to ask you some questions about your trial." Derek hoped to catch the man's interest.

"What about it? I did my time. Now I'm free."

"Rayne Anderson prosecuted, right?"

Piloseno's lip curled up. "What is this? If you know so goddamn much, why ask me? I don't remember the bitch's name." He grimaced, exposing coffee stained teeth.

Derek held in his anger at the name-calling. "Have you tried to contact her since your release?"

"Why should I?" Piloseno picked his teeth with a dirty thumbnail.

Seinkievitz took a step closer to the ex-con. "Mind telling us where you were Saturday night around ten p.m.?"

Piloseno stopped his hygiene action. "Yeah, I mind."

"Would you like to come down to the station to answer our questions?" Brad asked.

"You can't make me go nowhere. I've done nothing wrong. Ask my parole officer." Piloseno belched, and then slammed the door in their faces.

Seinkievitz shrugged then turned away. "That went well."

"Now what?"

"I say we look into who else has motive. In the meantime, I'll keep digging into Piloseno's background. I'm betting he's the type who likes revenge," Brad said.

"You said Piloseno was the only one recently released, right?"

Seinkievitz slipped into the cruiser's driver side. "Cons aren't the only ones who kill."

"True."

"Don't worry. I'm going to ask the Captain to put a detail on Piloseno. The guy's hiding something, and I aim to find out what."

Derek smiled for the first time all morning. "I like the way you think."

This time Seinkievitz's driving didn't give him a heart attack. Maybe there was hope for the guy.

Once his temporary partner dropped him off at the station, Derek wanted to stop by Rayne's house. He needed to check her answering machine to see if Justin had called her on Sunday as he'd claimed.

Justin gave off some strange vibes. The night he'd come over, angry he'd learned about Rayne's death on the nightly news, his eye movement had troubled Derek. Not that he knew the guy's habits, but Derek read people.

He climbed in his truck and took off. The twenty-minute drive to his sister's house calmed him somewhat, and the pain behind his eyes even began to subside. Perhaps the anticipation of seeing his sister's possessions helped bring him a step closer to accepting his loss.

As he drove down her street, he checked the neighboring houses. At this hour, with the kids were in school, all the garage doors were down, and no one was wandering the streets.

What had he expected? Some creep would come back to the scene of the crime three days later?

He must be losing his edge since desperation was eating away at his common sense. While here, Derek wanted to question the next-door neighbor, Mrs. Anton, hoping she saw someone.

Derek parked in Rayne's drive and slid out, sunglasses firmly in place. Though the police tape had disappeared, he bet no one had entered his sister's house in days. Derek unlocked the house with a spare key and let himself in.

With the AC set to the high eighties, Rayne's place smelled bad—musty and slightly warmed over. As he walked to the kitchen past the dining room where Derek had last seen his dead sister, he squeezed his eyes shut for a moment. He pulled a soda from the fridge and forced down the bile.

She always stocked his favorite drinks for him. To think he'd never see Rayne here again, never eat her lasagna, or drink her homemade wine.

He tried to stay calm, to detach his emotions from the job, but it was damned hard. He had to remain strong for Rayne though. He was her best hope of finding out who'd killed her.

Derek believed his spirit guides had tried to help, but the messages they'd sent meant crap to him. *Strangers sleeping and sons of mothers?* What the hell did that mean? Sounded more mysterious than serious.

He shrugged and took another swig of cola. Derek stepped over to the answering machine and pressed the button where black fingerprint powder marred the surface.

"You have two messages. Message one: Sunday, ten fifteen a.m.

*Mom, I'm at Chris's. I thought you were going to pick me up at ten. Where are you?*; Message two, Sunday, ten thirty: *Mom, Chris's mom is going to drive me home. Bye.* End of messages."

Derek chugged the rest of his soda and enjoyed the bite that followed the cold liquid trailing down his throat. Apparently Justin hadn't called to apologize. He knew that guy was trouble the minute he met him. According to Billy, Justin had promised to take the kid water skiing on several occasions but had cancelled because of some big meeting he'd had to attend. Broken promises and forgotten presents; the man was not trustworthy. Only Rayne appeared smitten.

He shook his head, annoyed by the vision of Kelly that suddenly invaded his head. Women. He never understood them. Probably never would.

# CHAPTER ELEVEN

BECAUSE DEREK WAS NOT OFFICIALLY on the case, he stuffed his badge in his pocket. On the way out, he took one last look around. The table near front door stood empty where Rayne's vase had been.

What the—?

He stepped closer and ran his fingers across the shiny tabletop. Clean. He tried to remember the last time he'd seen her prized possession.

Had Billy broken Rayne's vase? The loss of the irreplaceable item choked him up. Rayne would never create again.

*Aw, Rayne. Why did you have to die?*

Swallowing to clear his throat, he locked up her house and headed next door to the world's nosiest neighbor. If anything had gone down the night of Rayne's death, Mrs. Anton would know. He'd bet his badge on it.

He stomped over to her place, circling past the hedge that separated the two properties. The old lady's lawn was brown with intermittent tufts of green that looked like a bad case of chink bugs. Several pots of wilted flowers stood by the front door.

He knocked on the wobbly screen.

"I'm coming," Mrs. Anton shouted from inside. A moment later the front door opened. "Yes?" She squinted her eyes and ran her hands down the front of her stained apron. "Say, aren't you a friend of Rayne's?"

Given she'd forgotten his identity, he wondered about her reliability as a witness. "I'm Rayne's brother, Derek Benally, remember?"

Her face crinkled into a smile. "Oh, yes. You're that police detective. I saw you go into her house the day she died. Why, I don't know how I could have confused you with anyone else, you being so tall and all."

The sun burned his head as sweat trickled down his back. "Could I come in and talk?"

"Oh, my, of course. Where are my manners?" She ushered him in. "Can I get you anything to drink?"

"No. I'm fine." He patted his forehead with his handkerchief to stop the sweat from dripping into his eyes.

"Do you mind if I make myself a cup of tea? I always have tea when I have company."

Hot tea? She had to be kidding. "Sure. Go right ahead."

"Make yourself at home," she said as she headed into her small kitchen off the entryway.

Derek only had to walk a few feet before reaching the edge of the living room.

Whoa. Dolls sat everywhere—dolls on bookcases, dolls on the sofa cushions and on top of the sofa, and dolls on the mantle.

Half had fallen over as if an earthquake had shaken the house, and most were so dusty he wouldn't be surprised to find nests of spiders inside their bodies.

To reach the sofa he had to step around a pile of books. Something gnarly clogged the fibers of the brown shag carpet and he stepped around the stain. He didn't want to guess what the mess might be.

"I'll be right out," Mrs. Anton shouted from the kitchen. The teapot whistled, then china clinked together. A moment later, Mrs. Anton waddled out, holding her teacup with one hand and dunking the teabag with the other. "Have a seat." She motioned to the sofa. "Oh, don't mind Jeanette. Just push her aside."

Jeanette? She'd named her dolls?

Derek gingerly moved the foot tall doll to the right, along with a stack of fashion and food magazines spread over the seat and sat down, making sure the spot he picked wasn't caked with gum or something.

Before the dolls came to life and attacked him, he figured he better get down to business. "Were you home the night Rayne was shot?"

She set her tea on the nearby coffee table and dropped down into the chair with an "Umph." She blew out a breath as if making the tea had winded her. "Yes. Yes, I was home watching television. Why?" Her eyes widened. "You don't think I'd harm that nice girl?"

He held up a hand. "Mrs. Anton. Don't worry, you're not a suspect."

"Suspect? Why would I be a suspect? Didn't the poor girl kill herself?" she shouted. She clasped a hand over her mouth, and then let go. "I'm sorry. I should have been more delicate."

Apparently, the woman was quite hard of hearing. He made sure to talk louder. "I appreciate your sentiment, but being blunt cuts to the chase. As to my sister's death, the forensic evidence confirms she didn't die by her own hand, but we don't think you were involved in any way."

Her shoulders visibly dropped and her cheeks sagged. Mrs. Anton picked up a Raggedy Ann doll that was squished next to her on the seat and kissed her head. Then she carefully placed Raggedy Ann on her lap. "You had me worried, young man."

"Back to Saturday. Did you hear or see anything that night?"

She bit her lower lip and looked off to the side. "They were having this big tiff." She hugged the doll to her chest.

"They?"

"Your sister and that man of hers."

He sat up straighter and pulled out his pad and pen. "Do know the time they fought?"

"Do you think I watch the clock all day long? I have better things to do." She picked up her cup of tea and took a sip.

For a split second he was afraid she'd offer a drink to Raggedy Ann.

He ground his teeth and inhaled through his nose to force himself to relax. "Could the argument have been around ten?"

Mrs. Anton shook her head so hard, the doll fell over, but she didn't seem to notice. "Oh, no. At ten he was long gone."

"How can you be so sure?" She just said she didn't watch the clock.

"A rerun of Monk was on. I love Monk." She patted the doll's head. "It's Raggedy Ann's favorite show. She loves how he always finds the killer. Have you ever—"

"No, but, thank you, Mrs. Anton." Derek stood. If Justin had already gone by then, he didn't kill Rayne—unless he snuck back into the house while he professed to be sleeping off a hangover.

"You didn't ask me what they were fighting about."

He knew the argument was about their potential marriage but decided to placate her. "And what did they fight about?" He questioned whether she could even hear the conversation giving the decibel range of her speaking voice.

"Well, I wasn't eavesdropping or anything, mind you, but I had my window open, and I couldn't help but hear a few words, you know."

He bet she probably stepped outside to listen to the whole conversation. "What was the gist of the fight?"

"Please sit down. It strains my neck to look up at you." He sat. "I'm a little embarrassed since the topic had to do with her pregnancy." She covered her mouth again and her brows pinched. "Maybe I shouldn't have told you about the baby."

"I knew she was pregnant. Go on." Derek refused to dwell on what would never be.

"Wait a minute. Let me get my hearing aids. I don't wear them when I'm alone. That way, I won't have to strain to hear you."

That would explain a lot. She put down her cup, made Raggedy Ann comfortable first, and then stood. A moment later she returned, her finger in her ear, adjusting the volume. "There. Now we can talk better. Okay, where were we?" Her speaking voice came out at a normal level.

"The fight."

"Oh yes. Rayne, your sister, wanted to get married, but that boyfriend of hers—what was his name?"

"Justin."

"Yes, Justin. Well, he wanted her to have an abortion."

Every muscle tensed. "Are you sure you understood correctly? Could Justin have wanted to get married, but my sister didn't?"

"Oh, I'm quite sure." She tapped her ear. "I know what you're thinking. I heard them all right, loud and clear. I have to wear these hearing aids when I watch TV. Anyway, he, Justin, called her all sorts of bad names. Why, I had to shut my window. I've never heard such filth."

This didn't make any sense. "What kind of names?"

She blushed, drained the tea from her cup, and then took a deep breath. "Indian slut." She immediately covered Raggedy Ann's ears.

His heart pounded. "Are you sure he said, *Indian* slut?"

"Yes." She clamped her mouth together, acting as if she wanted to wash her mouth out with soap.

This changed everything. Rayne and Justin had fought bitterly, but the argument wasn't about what Justin claimed. Still Mrs. Anton's explanation didn't put Justin at Rayne's at the time of the murder either.

He was back to square one.

"I can't thank you enough, Mrs. Anton. You've been very helpful."

The shame on her face seemed to disappear with his compliment.

Mrs. Anton walked him to the door, and then followed him outside. "Oh, Detective, I just remembered something else."

Derek stopped and turned. "Yes?" He shielded his eyes against the sun.

"You asked if Justin was here at ten, and I said no. But there were two other people outside her house at that time." She tilted her chin in a rather defiant pose. "I know I'm right because my show had just ended, and I'd gotten up for a drink."

He swallowed hard. "Did you recognize these people?"

Her gaze shot to Rayne's house. "No. I really didn't pay any mind to them. I was still thinking about the terrible fight Rayne had and how hurt she must be. I even debated going over to comfort her, but I decided that ten at night was too late for a social call." She pushed her glasses up on her nose. "Her boyfriend wasn't one of them if that's what you want to know. He was long gone by then."

His heart sped up at the new information. "Could you tell if these people were two men or two women?"

"One was a woman, but I couldn't see the other person. My hedge blocks some of the view to your sister's place," she said, nodding to the four-foot tall treed wall.

Her hedge? That's why Rayne had erected the damn thing—to keep out the nosy neighbor.

"Do you know what kind of car they were driving?" he asked. *Please let her I.D. the vehicle.*

"I'm seventy-five years old and know nothing about cars. It had four wheels. That's all I can tell you."

"Just one car?"

"Yes."

"What color was it?"

"I didn't pay attention." She sniffed, acting as if his questions were uncalled for.

"Okay. Do you have any idea of the person's age?" If she couldn't remember the color of the car, he doubted she'd be able to identify a person.

Derek pulled out his handkerchief and swiped the cloth across his head. His dad was right. He needed to wear a hat.

"The woman was young, Rayne's age maybe, with blonde hair, I think. Those streetlights don't give out much light, you know. Besides, I only glanced out the window before closing the blinds. I didn't want them to see me, and to be perfectly honest, I wasn't in the mood for any more arguing."

Her I.D. might come in handy. "Is there anything else you remember?"

She looked down at the ground for a moment. "No. I do hope you find who murdered your sister. She was such a sweet, young thing. Her son, however, was quite the tear."

Derek wasn't in the mood to hear about his nephew's small acts of terrorism.

"Thank you, Mrs. Anton. Detective Seinkievitz might be stopping by to ask you these questions again. Is that okay?"

"Why certainly. I always like to help the police."

He handed her his card. "Call if you think of anything."

\*\*\*

What a bitch. Thank God the old biddy was too stupid to recognize one car from another or tell whom Stefanie was talking with. But memories had a way of coming back—memories that could be damning. That wouldn't do. Loose ends had to be clipped.

The problem would be to find a way to kill her in such a way that wouldn't tie her death to that of Rayne's or Stefanie's. The cops were too stupid to connect an apparent suicide to a car crash, but if a neighbor was shot to death, they might make a connection.

Leaving no trace was an art. And art took time, planning, and precise execution.

Hmm. Maybe poison would be the way to go. Certain toxins were slow and could be quite painful. Slow and painful was good, but getting Mrs. Anton to ingest the poison would be the difficult part.

Maybe suffocation would be better.

So many choices, so little time.

# CHAPTER TWELVE

KELLY LEFT the University Square mall with a new romantic comedy—a book she'd planned to buy for weeks. She needed to get her mind off the constant pain of her sister's death, even if only for a few hours.

Oh, how Stef loved to read. Science fiction, mysteries, thrillers; you name it, she read them all. The only ones she couldn't handle were ones that made her cry.

Serial killers? No problem. But child molesters? No way. She wouldn't touch 'em for anything.

Her sister used to pass down all her reading material, but Kelly could only stomach the uplifting stories.

Wrapped in a crinkly, plastic bag, Kelly pressed her purchase to her lips to keep from bursting out in tears in public. Each step she took became more difficult as grief slowed her pace.

*Don't do this to yourself. Think of something pleasant—like Derek.*

Or not.

The man's verbal attack at the Casino still stung. What had he been thinking? She was merely accompanying Justin, doing him a favor and being nice. And yet Derek concluded she was dating his sister's boyfriend. The man needed a life.

Date Justin? Yuk. His lame attempt to kiss her by her front door left a bad taste in her mouth—literally. Once she saw Derek, she'd been in no mood to kiss another man, especially a stranger.

A car honked behind her, and she scooted closer to the line of parked cars. Enough. She didn't want to use even one more brain cell thinking about Justin Bladen.

Instead, she needed to use her time to find a killer. Kelly refused to accept Stef's death was an accident. Of all people, her sister drove carefully, especially after the crash that maimed Michael.

Sure, Stef could get distracted if she talked on her cell while driving, but she never exceeded the speed limit. Not ever. And when it rained, Stef took extra precaution, like staying in the right lane at all times.

Michael, however, was a different story. His belligerent reaction to the news of her sister's death haunted her. Most likely the man didn't have a hand in her murder, but he certainly had motive for wanting her sister dead. His baseball career had ended before it ever began because of Stef's poor decision to drive during a downpour.

Lost in thought, Kelly wasn't paying much attention where she was walking. She stopped in the middle of the mall's parking lot and look around, searching for her car. The lot was surprisingly full for a weekday night. Could she have parked in the back this time? Hmm.

Ah, there was her Bug. Whew.

Kelly raced to her car and jumped in, locked the doors, and fired up the engine. Safely inside, she sat there, her mind returning to Stef's former boyfriend. Perhaps he'd wanted to maim her sister like she'd maimed him. Tit for tat so to speak.

Nah. Michael wasn't like that. At least he hadn't been when he'd started dating Stefanie. She'd always thought he'd complemented her sister well, but tragedy had a way of changing things, changing people.

The police were convinced Stef ran off the road while talking on the phone and not because someone wanted her dead. Without any evidence of foul play, they said they couldn't investigate.

Fine. Her sister had only died three days ago, but it seemed like a lifetime. Grief blasted her in the pit of her stomach, and Kelly dropped her head to the steering wheel and sobbed—sobbed for the fun they'd never again share, sobbed for the loss of her best friend, and sobbed because life seemed so unfair.

Kelly hiccupped as she tried to recall their last conversation, to savor her sister's last words, to store them in her mind forever. Stef had sounded worried on the phone. She said her friend was feeling so bad she couldn't even come to the front door.

At the time, Kelly hadn't questioned her. But if Rayne had been so incapacitated, how had Stefanie learned of Rayne's condition?

Ohmigod. Kelly sat up straight. Had Justin been at Rayne's house when Stef stopped by? Maybe he killed Rayne and Stef saw him. She shook her head. No. Her P.I. sister would have called the police immediately.

Kelly leaned back against the headrest and closed her eyes to block out any distraction. If Stef could place Justin at the scene of the crime, he might have decided to get rid of her. A chill grabbed her whole body and stole her breath away.

A woman's laughter outside her car door jolted her out of her daydream. Kelly cleared her throat and pulled out of her space, determine to find some clue to convince the police to investigate.

Once on the road, a raw ache built in her belly as her determination grew. She would not let the cause of her sister's death go unknown.

On the way to the Interstate, she passed Chuckie Cheese, the kid restaurant where Stef took underprivileged kids to lunch once a week, and a new wave of pain slammed into her. Stef's death had been so senseless. She donated her time and money to help the poor. Who'd want to harm a person as good as her?

Kelly grabbed a tissue from the glove compartment and wiped her eyes and nose, refusing to give up on the idea that Stef was murdered.

Maybe she could sift through her sister's files and interview her clients. Someone Stef was tailing could have decided the private investigator would be better off dead. The problem was that a search would take too much time, and Kelly needed action now.

An eyewitness! That was the key. At ten on a Saturday night, the toll road would have cars—and cameras. Someone had to have seen something. Maybe a person living nearby had witnessed the crash. At that thought, a small burst of hope calmed her.

Kelly came to a halt at a red light and turned on the radio to a soft rock station hoping the music would help get her thoughts straight. Kenny G began to sing. Oh, God. *Every Time I Close My Eyes* was Stef's favorite song. Kelly turned up the volume and pretended her sister was singing along, but then like a rock sinking to the bottom of the ocean, despair dragged her down.

The light changed, and she forced herself to stay focused. Kelly jumped on I-275 toward the Crosstown, where Stef had died. Kelly hadn't been willing to visit the site before now for fear some evidence might remain. Seeing any signs of the devastation would be hard, but she had to search for a clue—for Stef's sake.

Kelly shoved down her queasiness and rolled down her windows to feel some warmth on her face. The smell of gas filtered in, but at the moment, Kelly didn't care. Noise from the passing cars drowned out the music reminiscent of her loving sister, but that was just as well.

After battling downtown traffic twenty minutes, she entered the ramp to the Crosstown Expressway, and her stomach threatened to heave. Stef had died on this very road. She wiped away the hot, salty tears that trickled down her cheek.

*Don't you dare fall apart, Kelly Lynn. Stef needs you.*

The elevated highway took her through a rich neighborhood, and then through the seedier part of town. As she rounded a bend, she spotted a dented guardrail on the left hand side of the road, cordoned off by orange cones and barricades. The area jumped out at her like a squirrel racing across the road, and a rush of agony stabbed at her heart once more.

Workmen had begun to fix the crumpled mess, but there was no doubt this was where the accident had occurred. Stefanie's car must have bounced off the metal railing before careening over the edge.

Kelly pulled onto the emergency lane past the accident site and swallowed hard to keep from falling apart. With her emergency lights flashing, cars slowed as they passed her by. Kelly took one last look behind her. Dear God. A car would have to have been doing a hundred or more to flip over the two-foot high barrier.

Her stomach lurched again, and bile rushed up her throat as she thought of the horror her sister must have experienced seconds before her car plummeted onto the lane below. Ready to vomit, Kelly had to leave—had to get away from the horror.

She drove a few hundred feet to the next exit and doubled back on the road below. Two prostitutes resembling stuffed sausages stood on the street corner looking for business.

Kelly shuddered as she drove under the overpass near Stef's fatal accident. She pulled off to the side to gain control. Her legs shook so hard, she didn't have the strength to find a witness.

*I have to do this. I can't wimp out now.*

When she calmed down enough to think straight, she looked over to where the vehicle must have landed. The last rays of the day hit the road, illuminating sparkles. Were they shards of glass from Stef's car? Kelly grabbed her stomach and took deep cleansing breaths. Needing to think, the noise from the traffic overhead forced her to close her windows.

Finding someone who might have seen the accident was key, but the neighborhood didn't appear safe. The few houses off to the side had boarded up windows. Weeds grew tall along the edge of the road, and two For Sale signs sat prominently in the yards. Her heart sank. No one would have been here to witness the crash or its aftermath.

With her hand on the gearshift, ready to pull out onto the road, she glanced in her rear view mirror. Bedding sat high on the incline up under the overpass, along with some clothing and two garbage bags stuffed to the gills with who knows what. Her heart sped up. Could a homeless person have witnessed the accident? She scoured the area, but saw no one. Surely, he or she wouldn't have abandoned his possessions.

Kelly made a decision to stay put. When the person returned, she'd try to make some small talk, and maybe ask some questions.

Or would that be foolish?

Whoever lived up there could be mentally unstable, drugged, drunk, or dangerous.

Kelly pulled out her cell, along with Derek's card and called him. It was better to be safe than sorry.

Derek answered. "Benally."

She refused to let the sound of his sexy voice affect her and had to place a hand over her heart stomach to calm the fluttery excitement. Why did the man still affect her so?

"Derek. It's me, Kelly. I need your help." She flicked on the AC to stop from sweating.

"What's wrong?" His urgency spurred her on.

"I know you'll think I'm crazy, but I can't stop thinking about Stefanie. I think someone tried to run her off the road."

He didn't say anything for a minute. "You mentioned that before. Have you found some evidence?"

"Not exactly, but there's a mattress and some possessions under the overpass near the spot of her supposed accident. I'm hoping whoever is living there saw or heard something the night Stef died."

"Like what?" Derek sounded interested in her theory. "There wasn't any paint on your sister's car to indicate someone rammed her side. It's not as if—never mind. Tell me your location."

She was now used to his abrupt behavior and told him the cross streets.

"I'll be there as soon as I can. And Kelly?"

"Yes."

"Stay in your car until I get there. The neighborhood's not the best. Promise?"

"Yes, yes, I promise. Now hurry."

She checked her watch. Seven thirty. She glanced at the mattress again. How long before this person returned to his home?

Kelly kept a constant vigilance to see if anyone approached. Five minutes later, a group of four youths on dirt bikes came barreling down the sidewalk to her right. As they passed, one kicked her car—hard, and anger rushed up her belly. Two gave high fives, laughed, and continued on their way. Jerks. Kelly was tempted to chase after them, but the last thing she needed was to get in the middle of some gang fight.

Once they disappeared down a side street, the streetlights began to glow, casting parts of the area in heavy shadows. A large vacant lot to her right held an abandoned grocery cart and a microwave oven in the middle of the uncut field.

Headlights flashed in her rearview mirror and a horn honked. She jumped in her seat as adrenaline zipped through her veins. Her gaze shot to the side view mirror as she clasped her chest. Boxed in, fear ripped her so hard she nearly screamed.

Someone tapped on the passenger's side window, and she whipped to her right. Her shoulders sagged in relief. Man, was she a mess.

She rolled down the window. "Jesus Christ. Thank you for coming so quickly, but you scared the shit out of me."

He cocked his brow. She'd never used such colorful language when she was eighteen. Too bad. She'd grown up.

"The station's not far," Derek said.

Kelly undid her seat belt needing some air. Glad her knees didn't buckle, she stepped around her car to the sidewalk, keeping her gaze away from where Stef's vehicle had landed. She didn't want the image burned into her brain.

With her back to the road, she faced his mile-wide chest and corded neck. Her gaze lifted to his deep, rich, blue-green eyes. That was a big mistake.

Either the hot air was making it difficult to breathe or it was being close to Derek. Jeans snug over his muscular thighs, Derek's blue button down shirt emphasized his comforting chest. Right now though, she'd like nothing more than to unbutton that top button— and a few more—and snuggle against him, if only to forget the world and all the bad people. But she couldn't—at least not now.

Or maybe never.

"So where is this eyewitness?" he asked, gazing down at her with dreamy eyes.

Kelly blinked to erase the effect he was having on her. She took a step back and when she glanced at the embankment, a rush of warm, stale air, tinged with the smell of urine made her wrinkle her nose. "I'm waiting for him. Or her."

Derek took a step toward her, and Kelly backed up again until her butt hit the passenger side door. He ran his hand down her arm, slow and gentle. His lips parted, and her heart melted. This close, his cologne sweetened the air, and every memory of their past rushed in. Lust, love, excitement took her breath away.

"Kelly, look, about last night at the Casino. I'm—"

She held up a palm not needing an apology and steeled her heart. "Don't worry about it."

Derek's image had intruded too often as it was, and now wasn't the time for her to soften toward him, not when she should be mourning Stefanie.

His shoulders stiffened, his face turned hard. "Fine."

The shattering of glass made her spin around again. A homeless man stood across the street, directly below the mattress, looking down at the broken bottle wrapped in a brown paper bag. He shrugged and took a step up the incline to his home.

*Here goes nothing.* "Come on." She hoped this interview turned out better than the one with Michael.

Kelly reached into the front passenger seat and grabbed her purse, not wanting to leave anything valuable in the car.

# CHAPTER THIRTEEN

THE HOMELESS MAN, puffing away on a cigarette, was halfway up the cement embankment by the time they crossed the street. Two cars whizzed behind them, kicking up dirt from the road, and a pebble nailed her in the calf. "Ouch."

Derek looked down at her with concern, and when he pressed a palm to the small of her back, his touch sent a shot of intimacy through her, reminding her of what they'd once shared.

Once shared, she repeated to herself—not currently shared. *Remember that, Kelly Lynn.*

"You okay?"

"I'll be fine." She took a step up the incline ignoring the sting from the pebble, trying to put some distance between her and Derek's reach.

"Sir, can we have a word with you?" Derek called out, apparently oblivious to the effect he was having on her.

The man stopped, turned, and hobbled toward them. Kelly couldn't state his age with much certainty, but if she had to guess, she'd say around fifty. His shoulders were rounded and his beard long was matted. His dirt-stained clothes were stretched taut over his rounded belly, and she had to work hard not to wrinkle her nose at the stench of whiskey.

"You wanna talk to me? About what?" Even though his words weren't belligerent, they were slurred, and her hope of finding lucid answers slipped away.

Derek flashed a couple of one-dollar bills in front of the man's face. "We want to ask you about an accident the other night."

The unkempt man came closer and grabbed at the bills, but Derek held them out of his reach.

"What accident?" the man asked, his lips forming a thin line.

She jumped in. "On Saturday, around ten at night, a black Land Rover flipped over the guardrail above you and landed over there." She turned and pointed to a spot fifty feet away. Her heart squeezed, forcing Kelly to hold her breath to keep everything down. Derek ran a soft hand down her back, giving her the strength to continue. "I'm sorry. My sister died in the wreck. Do you remember the crash?"

Derek handed the money to the man. He stuffed the bills into his pants pocket. "Yeah, I remember. Couldn't forget that noise." He took a drag on the cigarette and blew smoke in her direction.

She moved back to get away from the acrid smell. "What can you tell me?" Her nails bit into her palms.

"Hmmm. Let me think." He stroked his tangled beard.

Derek waited a minute, and then pulled out a five-dollar bill.

The vagrant shot them a grin and grabbed the cash. "Well I did have a little to drink the other night and was sleepin' when I heard tires squealin'. Then came this loud crash. I thought the Crosstown was coming down on me."

"Did you see the car land?" Kelly clasped her hands together and held her breath. She pushed back the image of the anguish and paralyzing fear Stef must have experienced as her car flipped before speeding through the air to the ground.

"It was dark, and as I said, I'd had a little bit too much to drink. I heard the crash, all right, but I fell asleep after I realized I was safe. Besides, what could I do? I don't got a cell phone, you know."

She exchanged a sideways glance with Derek. She shoved her hands in her pockets to stop the trembling. "Then what happened?" Tears spilled over her lashes, but she didn't wipe them away.

He looked to the overpass and started to whistle. Impatient, Kelly dragged her purse from her shoulder and pulled out a twenty. "Here. That's all I have."

The man crushed the money in his hand, nodded, and scratched his chest with his other hand. "You know, I do remember hearing a car door slam above me right after that big, black SUV landed on the road. It's a lot louder below the road here, you see. Reverberation noise, I think it's called." He pointed to the roadway above him. "Anyway, I thought it was," he shifted around on his feet, "you know, kind of odd."

She took a step toward him, wanting to study his eyes, to see if he was telling the truth. "What was so odd about another car stopping? People rubberneck all the time."

"There wasn't no shouting or nothing. I knew the person had stopped and gotten out of the car 'cause I heard the door slam."

He'd said that already. "How long did this person stop?"

He stared at the ground, mumbled something to himself, and then faced them again. "Geez. A good minute or two, but time has a way of slowing down when I drink." The old guy dropped his cigarette butt and stomped it out with his faded sneaker.

She turned to Derek. "Do you think someone stopped, saw the mangled car, and then drove off realizing the person must be dead?" She wiped the salty tears from her cheek. "How could someone at least not call for help?" Maybe if Stefanie had received immediate care, she'd be alive.

Kelly prayed Stef hadn't been trapped in her car bleeding to death with no means of escape. *Don't even go there.*

Derek ran a gentle hand down her arm. "It's possible," he said with the gentlest tone. "There are folks who don't want to get involved." Derek faced the informant. "Mr., ah –"

"Reynolds. Joseph Phillips Reynolds at your service." The man gave a little bow at the waist.

"Mr. Reynolds, did any other motorists stop or pass by on this road after the crash?" Derek asked.

"Well, like I said, I fell back to sleep, being out of it some. I woke up when someone started making a big racket. The sirens came a little bit later."

"Did the police ask you if you saw anything?" Derek asked.

"I, ah, left once the cops came. No need to draw attention to myself."

A deepening sense of dread filled her. "Thank you, Mr. Reynolds, for your time."

He patted his pocket. "Any time."

Her step unsteady, Kelly followed Derek across the dark street to their cars with more questions than answers.

She opened her mouth to ask Derek what he thought, when he turned and faced her. "Kelly, I have an appointment to meet with someone about my sister's case." He tapped his watch. "I'm late. Sorry." Derek looked genuinely unhappy to leave her.

"Oh, sure, you go ahead." She couldn't remove the disappointment from her tone.

A rush of warm air pushed past her. She wiped her face with the back of her sleeve and couldn't wait to crank up the car's A.C. She stood on the curb waiting for a break in the traffic before jumping in her car.

Halfway to his cruiser, Derek stopped and jogged back. "I know you want to talk about this. Can I stop by your house in an hour?"

Her spirits lifted at his concern. How was he able to read her mind so easily? Just like old times. "I'd like that."

She smiled, and then drew her lips down. How was she ever going to keep her heart in check if he acted like the Derek she used to know and love?

\*\*\*

Derek didn't like leaving Kelly in her fragile state, but he'd set up a meeting with Justin at eight, a meeting he couldn't cancel. Not willing to tip him off as to the reason for the visit, Derek told him there was new evidence in Rayne's case. What he didn't say was that this new evidence pointed a finger at him.

True, Rayne's next-door neighbor's story seemed to corroborate Justin's alibi, but there was always the possibility he'd come back later and shot Rayne.

Derek pulled up to Justin's house, followed the lit sidewalk to his door, and rang the bell. The bugs that had gathered at the front light flew in his face, forcing him to swat them away.

Justin opened the door. "Come in." He stroked his tie, as if it were a lifeline.

Derek followed Justin into the modern living room and took a seat on the sofa across from him.

Justin continued to fiddle with his tie. "So? What's up?"

"The lab report came back. Rayne didn't kill herself. She was murdered." He watched Justin's body language.

His sister's boyfriend blew out a long breath. "Murdered? Oh, my God. Do the police have any leads?"

Disappointed Justin showed no signs of guilt, Derek decided to try a more direct tack. "You don't look too upset."

"Well, I have to admit I'm actually a little relieved that I didn't cause her death. I'm still grieving, but to know I didn't push her over the edge, makes me..."

Bitterness tinged his mouth. "What? Happy?"

Justin's jaw clenched. "No. Less guilty."

Derek leaned back on the sofa and spread his arms along the top, trying not to look threatening. "When you called Rayne Sunday morning, what did you say in your message?"

Justin didn't blink. "I didn't leave a message. After the third ring, I hung up. I figured she was picking up Billy or else she wasn't ready to talk to me."

His comment had validity. Now for the hard part. "A neighbor heard you and Rayne fighting."

His gaze shot off to the side. "I'm not surprised. We were a little loud."

"She said you called Rayne an Indian slut." Derek's fists balled.

Justin shot up from the chair. "That's a goddamn lie. I loved Rayne. I would never call her a filthy name like that."

Derek forced himself to remain seated, to control his need to hammer the guy. "Had Rayne ever told you our Dad was Seminole?"

Justin slipped behind his chair, a habit that was beginning to annoy Derek. "Honestly, no, but I didn't care what her nationality was. Hell, I like to gamble at their casino. You know that. And they asked me to invest their funds. If you think I don't like Indians, you're full of shit."

Native American, but now was the time to correct him. His angry sincerity convinced Derek he was barking up the wrong tree, but the warning from his spirit guides still preyed on his mind.

"Did Rayne talk about anyone who might have wanted to harm her?" Derek motioned for Justin to sit down.

Justin took a moment to think. His shoulders relaxed as he dropped back down into his Lazy Boy. "No one specifically, but we didn't talk much about her work."

When Justin said nothing more, Derek stood to leave, frustrated at the dead end. "Listen, I didn't mean to imply anything by my comment. I'm sorry to have bothered you. I just wanted you to know the findings."

Justin relaxed. "Thanks. I appreciate it."

Back in his car, Derek headed toward Kelly's, his fingers tightening on the steering wheel. He wasn't done grilling Justin, but he needed to find more evidence to nail the guy. And he would. He had no doubt about it.

✳✳✳

By the time Kelly arrived home, her thoughts were so scattered she didn't know what to make of her eyewitness. On the one hand, the person who'd stopped right after the wreck may have seen the bent guardrail and stopped out of curiosity. If that were the case, why not call for help? Didn't this person have a cell phone?

If they didn't, why not flag someone down? Or didn't they see Stef's car because they didn't want to chance stepping near the damaged railing? The possibility shook her.

She dropped onto the comfortable sofa, but right now the cushiness did nothing to lessen the mounting realization the police might have been right—it had been an accident. When Kelly was talking to Stef on the phone had her sister become distracted and sped up? Had the slick roads caused her to swerve and flip? Or had she blown a tire and gone out of control?

Kelly dropped her hands in her head needing some guidance. Deep inside she believed someone meant to harm Stef. Despair claimed her body, and she gave into more tears.

After the fresh wave of doubt passed, she trudged to the kitchen and grabbed her box of cookies. Once her sweet tooth was satisfied, maybe the answers would come.

In any case, Kelly was glad Derek planned to stop over tonight. If the homeless man provided no direction, there was always Michael as a suspect. She bet Derek wouldn't toss out her theory about the ex-boyfriend as quickly.

She looked at the clock on the kitchen wall. A half hour had zipped by. She took a deep breath, put away what was left of the cookies, and rushed to the bedroom. Derek would be here soon.

She jumped in the shower and poured a handful of lemon shampoo in the palm of her hand and scrubbed until her hair was light with foam. She then squeezed her eyes shut and, for a brief moment of escapism, pictured Derek's hands on her naked skin.

She had to make up her fantasy since all Derek had ever done in the two years they'd dated was kiss her. He'd told her he wanted to wait until marriage before they made love. Ah, high school innocence.

The steam fogged the shower door and her fingers pruned. She had to hurry. Once she toweled dried her body and hair, she pulled on a pair of jeans, a tank top, and a pair of sandals that had yellow daisies on them.

A quick dash of make-up to cover her freckles and smooth out her complexion, and she was ready to meet him and his stoic attitude.

NO SOONER HAD SHE FINISHED SPRITZING ON A BIT OF PERFUME THAN THE DOORBELL RANG. EXCITEMENT WARRED WITH TREPIDATION AS SHE RACED TO ANSWER IT.

SHE OPENED UP AND SWALLOWED TO STEADY HER VOICE. "HI."

KELLY ALMOST SMILED UNTIL SHE REMEMBERED HE WASN'T HERE FOR A DATE. STILL, HER HEART POUNDED AT THE SIGHT OF HIM. DAMN HIM FOR PITTING HER HEART AND BODY AGAINST HER MIND.

"You ready?" he asked.

Derek fiddled with his top shirt button. Was he nervous? He couldn't be. Not the smooth, unflappable, Derek Benally.

"For what?" She'd almost forgotten to answer.

"I'm starving. I thought we could do some dinner and discuss the cases."

She tried to act nonchalant. His willingness to talk about what happened to Stef didn't mean he believed someone had harmed her, but she couldn't ask for a better chance to share her suspicions. "Sure. Let me grab my purse."

After locking up, they walked side-by-side down the front walk, just like old times. She opened her mouth to reminisce about their high school dates but then thought better of it. Detective Benally was only interested in finding a killer, not in rekindling what they'd once shared.

There was that word again. Shared. Kelly needed to exorcise it from her vocabulary.

She'd better start thinking about something other than how handsome he looked or how her pulse fluttered every time he came near, or she'd be in trouble.

Okay. Breathe. The jasmine clinging to the front post sent out a sweet smell that helped put more pep in her step.

"So how long have you been divorced?" he asked, catching her off guard.

She tried to read the level of his interest but couldn't. Maybe her marital status had been the cause for his standoffish attitude. "Four years."

She'd already told him that statistic at the Casino. Did he think she'd made up a husband? Surely he wasn't trying to trick her into some kind of confession about how miserable she'd been since their breakup.

Derek opened the passenger side to his truck without a follow-up comment. Guess not. The stifling heat just walking to the vehicle caused a quick sheen to form on her forehead. A lot of good her shower did.

Derek jumped in and started the engine. Putting aside her adolescent fantasy, she refocused on the subject at hand. "So what did you think of the homeless man's observations?" She lifted her hair off her neck to cool off.

"That he made an unreliable witness," he answered. Before she voiced a comeback, he continued. "Okay, listen. I'll grant you that someone could have stopped to check out the bent guardrail. It was dark by ten, and there was no reason for him to get close enough to look at the street below."

"I know." Defeat nearly drowned her in despair. They had zip, zilch, zero.

"You know?"

She twisted in her seat to see him. "At first I thought if someone saw the railing, they'd stop and look over the edge, but I realize that whoever did stop might have been afraid to move to close and took off."

"So you're giving up?" She appreciated his incredulity.

"No. You know me better than that. There's one person who had reason to harm her."

He whipped his head to look at her for a second. "Who?"

"Michael, her ex-boyfriend." She told him about the meeting.

His jaw tightened. "What do you know about this man, other than he probably has a right to be bitter?"

"I don't know much about his background. I liked the guy when he and Stef were dating. He was a risk taker. He raced cars. If he wasn't dreaming of driving at Daytona, he was playing baseball. He played college ball and had been drafted into the Devil Rays minor league teams until…"

"The accident happened," he finished. "That's tough to have your life turned upside down, but it's not necessarily a motive for murder."

Derek stared ahead. Kelly was at a loss for words. How could he defend a man he'd never met when they were talking about her sister! Sure he was a cop and that's what cops did, but their history together should have made him a little nicer.

"He could have chased her off the road," she said.

"Could have isn't the same as he did."

Jerk. It didn't matter if he had a point or not.

Twenty minutes later they pulled into the International Plaza parking lot. "I figured we'll have lots of food choices here," he said, acting as if they'd been talking about the Tampa Bay Buccaneers recent game and not her sister's death. "Are you still into Asian?"

Suddenly, he sounded like the Derek of old. Pleasure that he remembered her food preferences interrupted her gloom. "I am."

She didn't like the way she forgave him so easily, and she didn't like the way she was in the depths of depression one minute, and then flying high the moment Derek appeared. She acted like the ball in a pinball machine. *Get a grip*.

Hell, maybe it was nature's way of helping her heal.

Diners strolled past the restaurants, looking at their choices, and scented flowers lined the small courtyard as hostesses smiled at potential customers.

Because it wasn't a weekend, they were seated right away at the Asian restaurant.

His easy dismissal of Michael as a suspect left her at a loss for conversation. For some reason it seemed weird to bring up friends from the past or make small talk. After all, this wasn't a date.

To avoid any more of his deadly glares, she decided to stick to the case. "How's your sister's son handling his mom's death?" She watched his eyes.

His body tensed. "Not good. He found her, you know."

Her stomach churned. "No, I didn't. How terrible."

"Yeah, it was."

His cell rang, and he pulled it out of his shirt pocket. His brows pinched together. "Excuse me." He glanced off to the side. "Hello? ... When?..." His face went pale. "Are you sure? Thank you."

He swallowed as he clicked his phone shut.

# CHAPTER FOURTEEN

"W HAT'S WRONG?" Kelly asked.

Her question took a moment to register. "Billy's run away from boarding school." Derek shoved back his chair barely able to contain his rage and fear.

Her eyes widened and her jaw tensed. "When?"

"That was the Headmaster on the phone. The best he can guess, about four hours ago. Come on."

Her brows pinched together. "You think he ran away because his mother's death is only now hitting him?" she asked gathering her purse.

"I have no idea, but his timing sucks." He didn't need to be worrying about Billy when he should be finding Rayne's killer. "You'd think he'd call me if he planned to split."

She stood up as Derek tossed a ten-dollar bill on the table to cover the water. As he rushed out, he dialed Billy's number. Damn voice mail. He tightened his grip on the phone. "This is your uncle. Please call me the second you get this message. It's urgent." Derek pressed the Off button.

"Where do you think he'd go?" she asked slightly out of breath as she caught up to him.

"It's hard to say where a kid his age would disappear to. His best friend lives about ten minutes from his house." He raked a hand over his head. "I'm making the assumption he left the boarding school voluntarily."

She grabbed his arm. "You think someone might have kidnapped him?"

He refused to go there. Couldn't go there. Billy and his dad were all that were left of his family. If anything happened to either one, he wasn't sure how he'd survive. "I don't know what to think anymore."

He glanced upward and then right, hoping his spirit guides would help. They seemed to disappear whenever he needed them the most.

"Maybe he's headed to your place as we speak, looking for your support."

Derek ground his teeth to keep from losing it. "I doubt that. The last time we spoke, he wasn't receptive to me. Why should he want my comfort now?" Billy's rejection still stung.

They pushed their way through the crowd of people milling outside one of the popular restaurants where loud music was blaring from inside.

"Not everyone absorbs loss in the same way," she said sounding like a shrink, but the compassion in her voice gave him hope. "Some people don't grieve for weeks or months."

Not him. Rayne's death hit him hard the second he saw her—and the pain kept coming.

When they reached his truck, he opened the passenger door for her. "I don't think I handled him well. I drilled him about his mom's death instead of trying to console him."

She climbed in the seat. As soon as he was behind the wheel, she spoke up. "I'm sure he understands. As to him acting distance, kids never act like they care about any adult, when in fact they do."

She hadn't seen Billy. "Did I mention *my* gun killed Rayne?" He started the engine and peeled out of the lot. "I think the kid thinks I'm responsible for his mom's death. My dad sure does."

"Oh, Derek, they can't possibly blame you."

"Wanna bet?"

She sat in silence for a moment. "How did the killer get a hold of your gun?" Alarm sounded in her tone.

"I lent Rayne my old revolver. I wanted her to be safe." He honked as a car in front of him took its sweet time turning. "I had her take lessons and everything to make sure she could use the damn thing. She wouldn't have brought out the weapon unless she felt threatened by an intruder." Guilt and remorse chased down his spine.

"Or someone close to her knew where she hid the gun and wanted to make her death look like a suicide. You said the police proved she was murdered."

He glanced over at Kelly, not believing he hadn't thought of the possibility. "You're right. I assumed a strange noise must have scared Rayne, and she grabbed the gun for protection. The intruder overpowered her and took the weapon away from her. But if someone she knew found the gun from her hiding place…" His thoughts raced back to Justin. Or could Billy have accidentally shot Rayne? No. That could never have happened.

"Do you know where to look for Billy?" she asked, as he turned left out of the lot toward Dale Mabry.

"No, but first I'm taking you home."

"Oh no you don't." Aggressive Kelly on the move again.

"Listen, I need to do this alone." *Please let her understand.*

She grabbed his arm. "I want to help."

"I don't need your help." He shrugged out of her grasp.

"Stef was my sister."

He pulled up to a red light and faced her. "What does that have to do with anything?"

She rolled her eyes as if he didn't have a clue. "Stef's and Rayne's death, now Billy's disappearance, might all be re-lat-ed."

"They aren't."

She shook her head. "You don't know that."

Someone behind him honked. He pressed too hard on the accelerator and Kelly grabbed the dashboard to steady herself. "Derek, please."

"Sorry." He knew she meant he needed to drive more carefully, but her angst made him reconsider. "All right, you can come with me, but it won't be any picnic." Why did he cave so easily? *Be a man, Benally. Just say no.*

"I'm not looking for a glory date." She sounded somewhat mollified.

He pulled out his phone as a new thought struck. "I'm such a dumb ass. Billy adores Dad. I wouldn't be surprised if he went there. Hell, I wouldn't put it past Dad to drive down to St. Pete and pick him up."

"Without telling you?"

"Yeah. Remember, Dad thinks if I hadn't given my gun to Rayne she wouldn't be dead."

She placed a light hand on his arm. "Maybe your father didn't let you know because he was trying to spare you more hurt feelings by not telling you Billy would rather spend time with his grandfather."

There goes Miss Sunshine again, always looking at the positive side

"Maybe." Derek didn't want to get into his family's long dysfunctional history. He pressed his father's number and let it ring and ring. "Pick up, dammit." Derek disconnected. "He's not answering."

"Maybe he's on his way to pick up Billy."

"No, Billy went missing over four hours ago, and Dad always keeps his cell phone on unless he's in the woods."

"So now what?" Kelly asked.

"Billy was at his friend Chris's birthday party the night Rayne died. I'm thinking maybe he's there now."

"Why don't you just call this Chris kid and ask him?"

He bit back his impatience. "I don't keep the kid's number in my cell."

She said nothing more as he took a few wrong turns trying to find Billy's friend's house. Eventually, he located the home and pulled in front. The lights blazed from inside. Good. Someone was home.

Derek slid out of the front seat and hurried to the passenger side to open her door, but Kelly beat him to it. Shoulders straight, she marched to the front door, and he hurried alongside her. Boy, was she pissed. Why? He'd let her come. *Women. Can't live with 'em, can't – forget it.*

Night blooming jasmine filled the air, replacing the scent from

Kelly's perfume—a blessing in disguise. The oppressive heat from earlier today seemed to have gone off to sea.

Deb, Chris's mom, answered the door. "Detective. What a surprise." Deb nodded to Kelly, obviously wanting for an introduction. There wasn't time for niceties.

"Sorry for stopping by so late. I'm looking for Billy. Is he here by any chance?" His fists clenched by his side.

"No. Didn't he go back to school?" Lines of worry creased her forehead.

He tried not to let his disappointment show. "Yes, but the school called and said he missed evening study hall. They searched the campus but couldn't find him anywhere."

Chris popped out from behind his mom. "Hey, Derek." His gaze shot to Kelly, then straight to the ground. The kid was hiding something, or someone.

Derek turned to Deb. "Do you mind if Chris and I chat? Alone?"

"No. Come in. I'll be in the den if you need me." She pulled her lips into a thin, grim line.

He'd been meaning to speak with Chris about the night Rayne died, but he hadn't had the time. Once Deb disappeared, Derek motioned they sit in the living room. The furniture looked worn but comfortable.

Chris sat on the edge of the chair, his gaze not focused in any one spot for long.

"When was the last time you saw Billy, Chris?"

Kelly sat down next to Derek. Her leg touched his thigh, sending his thoughts to the wrong place. He cleared his throat.

Chris shifted in his seat. "At my party." He turned his focus to his hands.

"What's wrong?"

He swallowed. His chin trembled. "It's been eating me up."

"What has? Tell me." Derek leaned forward, his hands clasped in his lap.

"Billy wasn't at my party the whole night. He left for a little while to go back to his house." His gaze caught the rug and stayed there.

Derek couldn't move. The room seemed to darken as if an evil spirit had entered and was strangling the breath out of him. "What time was this?"

"About ten."

"Ten?" Derek couldn't breathe. He wanted to unbutton the top button to give him more room the breath but found it already open. "Go on."

"We'd just finished watching a movie and the guys thought it would be cool to have some..." Chris's gaze caught the ceiling.

"Some what?"

"Beer. My mom doesn't let us drink, of course, and Billy said his mom had a ton of the stuff in the fridge." He finally looked at Derek.

Rayne always kept a six-pack for him, not for her son. Every nerve ending sharpened. "How did Billy get to his house?" It was too far to walk. The dread building inside almost stopped the blood flow to his brain.

"I, ah, let him use Mom's car." He looked past the hallway, to where his mom had disappeared. "She didn't know anything about it. You're not gonna tell her, are you?" His eyes pleaded with Derek.

Derek didn't care that Billy drove without a license, nor did he care he'd stolen his Mom's beer. He struggled with the fact his nephew was at his house at the time Rayne died. "I'm a cop. What do you think?"

Chris paled. "Mom will kill me. She'll ground me for life."

Now wasn't the time to give the kid a lecture about morals or breaking the law, though he did wonder where Deb had been when the party was going on, but he'd address that issue her another time. "What time did Billy return to the party?" His gut went into a spasm waiting for an answer.

"Ah, gee, I don't know. He couldn't have been gone longer than twenty or thirty minutes." He slumped back in the chair, defeated. "I know it was wrong, but it seemed so cool at the time. I didn't think."

No shit. "Did Billy act strange when he arrived with the beer?"

Sweat appeared on Chris's forehead. "Strange? How do you mean?"

"Did he mention anything about his mom?"

His eyes brightened. "Yeah. He said when he snuck in the back door he almost blew it 'cause the damn door banged real loud." He looked at Kelly. "Sorry."

"That's okay," she said, in a quiet voice.

Chris continued. "He said his mom must have been asleep or something because she didn't catch him. He ran out as fast as he could." His eyes widened and his mouth contorted. "Was she dead, and he didn't see her?" He shook his head. "That would be gross."

Derek searched Chris's eyes but found no deceit. "I don't know." His voice cracked. "When I find him, I'll ask."

The fear lifted off the kid's face. He looked anxious to help. "Did you try his cell?"

"I did, but he didn't answer."

"Did you try Megan's cell?"

Derek straightened. "Who's Megan?" Kelly's hand grabbed his thigh, and he tried to ignore her touch.

Chris firmed his lips.

Kelly leaned forward. "Chris, we don't care if he's with someone you think his mom wouldn't have approved of. All we care about is finding him. We want him safe, that's all."

Her soft approach seemed to work. A moment later, Chris pulled out his phone. "Her number is 555-6981. She's, ah, older. She goes to Plant High School. I guess he never told you."

"No." Derek put her number in his cell. He'd try it as soon as he left. "Anywhere else he'd go?"

"Just to his grandpa's place."

A touch of jealousy surfaced. He should be happy the older and younger generation bonded so well, but he wanted to be the person Billy turned to for help. "Thanks, Chris. Promise me one thing."

He glanced to the den where his mom was watching television again. "Sure."

"Call me if Billy contacts you."

He bit the inside of his lip. "Okay."

Derek wouldn't count on it. "Tell your mom goodbye." Chris nodded.

Once in the car, Derek called this Megan girl. Unfortunately, she was no help in locating Billy. She claimed they never really dated, that they only sat together at the Plant High School football games. Given her concern about his disappearance, Derek believed Billy hadn't contacted her.

"Now what?" Kelly asked.

"I'm out of options, which means we wait for either Dad or Billy to call us."

# CHAPTER FIFTEEN

WITH THE LIGHTS OUT and two candles lit, Derek sat cross-legged on the hardwood floor in his bedroom, his feather and wolf skin in front of him. Images of Rayne's body, Billy's stoic reaction to his mom's death, and his own steely-hearted attitude toward Kelly, nearly drowned him in despair.

His world was majorly fucked up, and he'd caused most of it. If only he hadn't lent Rayne the gun; if only he'd been around more for Billy; if only he'd been able to talk to Kelly about how upset he was. *If, if, if.*

He detested that word.

He alone needed to take responsibility for the events in his life. Who knew what other disasters might befall him if he didn't get his shit together?

He took a gut filling, chest enlarging breath. The smoke from the sage curled upward, helping to calm his inner turmoil. As he pushed out the air from his lungs, he began to feel his spirit lift from his body. All outside noise faded to a dull hum as the sound of his inhalations reached his ears. Derek grabbed his sacred animal skin and concentrated on reaching his spiritual guides. He needed them to lead him in the right direction, to tell him if he'd ever crawl out of his tunnel of darkness.

"Can you tell me where Billy is?" Derek intoned.

He closed his eyes awaiting some phrase that would give him a clue.

Nothing.

Desperation clawed at him. He had nowhere else to turn and needed his spiritual guides. His pulse sped, and his palms moistened. Derek swore they'd spoken when he was standing over Rayne's body, and then poof, they'd abandoned him. He'd heard from them what? Five times in his life?

*Let's try for six.*

He tried to relax his shoulders, his spine, and then his ribcage. Patience. All he needed was patience. The guides would speak if he waited long enough.

The scented smoke surrounded his face, entered his nose, and spiraled into his lungs. His body seemed to hover above the floor as if his soul were trying to escape his mortal flesh. Derek wanted to hear their words and ponder their shrewd advice, but the guides seem to be ignoring him. Maybe he wasn't fit to receive wisdom from the great ones.

He yearned to call his guides fakes, to rid his mind of the dependence, but he knew their power was strong. He'd grown to rely on them—perhaps too much. They'd contacted him in the past—or had he imagined the voices and imagined their clues?

If nothing else, his father had taught him to respect that which he could not see. As much as he wanted to rebel against his native heritage, he believed in a higher power than the self.

"Come," came their command with such force, it startled him.

Before he could ask his question again, his guides whisked his soul away. Fear shot to his heart as he glanced downward and saw his head bowed, and his fingers slowly stroking the soft feather.

What the—?

Wind rushed past him as if he were being pulled through a sci-fi wormhole. "Where are you taking me?" His voice cracked.

"Don't ask questions," came the reply. The voice from beyond was different from the one who usually issued the spirit guide's commands.

In a flash, he was on a horse in a harsh, hot environment, the sun blinding him. Shielding his eyes, a vast desert stretched before him with no end in sight. No telephone poles, no homes, no highway, no people. Just an empty, hot desert.

Heat burned his flesh, and the dust from the galloping horses clogged his nostrils. Derek grabbed onto the mane, desperate not to lose his balance.

He looked around, his thighs straining against the magnificent animal's flanks. What kind of place contained no evidence of life other than the horse beneath him and the men by his side? Could they have hurtled him into the past? Or perhaps the future? Or into a different universe?

Six Indian chiefs, sitting tall in their saddles, flanked him. Faces painted, they stared ahead as if he didn't exist. Had he been thrust into a war between the Indian nations in some kind of parallel universe?

"Where are we going?" Derek asked again, desperate for some sense of where he was, his heart speeding faster than the horses' hooves.

No one responded or acknowledged his words. The stallion underneath him zigzagged to the right, almost throwing him off the horse. Derek hadn't ridden in so long, he'd lost the ability to balance. He squeezed his legs tighter, but the animal responded by galloping faster.

"Can we stop?" he pleaded, trying not to sound like a wimp.

"Keep riding," said the chief next to him, his headdress flapping in the wind. "No more questions."

He must be kidding. They needed to explain so much. All they'd ever done was talk to him. Never before had they taken him anywhere or shown themselves.

Derek swallowed a yelp as his balls smashed against the saddle. Now he knew why he'd never make Chief if riding were a prerequisite.

Thundering hooves continued to eat up the sand. If they didn't want to tell him squat, they wouldn't. Damn their powers.

Derek would be able to concentrate on his situation if his brain stopped bouncing against his skull. He couldn't tell if the chiefs were all Seminoles or if they'd come from different tribes. Each wore his own distinct headdress, almost as if each were from another time and place.

A chief on a large Palomino nudged between Derek and another chief next to him. Derek's horse shied to the side, then reared up, throwing Derek high into the air.

He landed hard, waiting for the pain, but none came.

When he opened his eyes, he was back in his room, the sage a faint pile of ash and the candle extinguished. The clock read two in the morning.

Shit. Dazed, he looked around, half expecting to see the warriors sitting on his bed. "Hello?"

He held his breath awaiting further instructions. His arms throbbed and his full weight pressed onto the floor. What the fuck had just happened?

Had he really been through a desert? Like on a horse with no name? Thank you, Neil Young.

Head spinning, he picked up his artifacts and stumbled to the kitchen. Derek poured a glass of water, spilling half of it on the counter, but he didn't bother cleaning up the mess. Drinking the cold liquid quenched his dry throat but not his heart. He ran a hand over the spill. Wet. At least he wasn't imagining things anymore.

A slow burning in his elbow caught his attention, and he rolled up his sleeve.

"Blood?"

Derek checked out the rest of his arm. Scrape marks ran from his shoulder to his wrist.

"What the hell?"

He looked at the ground, and then knelt to check out the material caught in the cuff of his pants.

"That can't be sand," he mumbled.

Both gave credence the vision had been real. But how was that possible? All he'd ever heard were one-line sayings he'd tried to morph into clues. He'd certainly never been abducted before. At least not that he remembered. Given the headdresses, he assumed they weren't some aliens from a foreign planet dragging him through some kind of Star-gate system.

Was it some kind of time travel? Forget it. Derek didn't have time for this nonsense.

Unable to make sense of the mysterious experience, he drank two full glasses of water to clear his head. Hell, maybe he'd fallen asleep and dreamt the trip in the desert. But then how had he bloodied his elbow and scraped his side if he hadn't fallen from a horse? And where had the sand come from?

He and Kelly hadn't eaten before he received the call about Billy's disappearance, so perhaps hunger had caused the hallucinations. If that were the case though, how could his imagination create blood?

He didn't dare ask his father about the mysterious event. The vision, or trip, would only serve to drive another wedge between them when he expressed his skepticism. Anytime he brought up the power of the gods vs. the one and only God, they argued. It was tough being raised by a Catholic and a Seminole shaman at the same time.

Maybe it was time to put away the sage.

✳✳✳

Kelly finished writing up her research findings and said goodbye to Chip, who promised to clean up the lab.

She hadn't been able to keep her mind on work all day. Little wonder. She was up half the night worrying about Billy, worrying about Derek, and wondering if her sister's death would ever be resolved.

Two nurses entered the building for the evening shift as she was leaving. They waved at her, and Kelly managed to smile, pretty sure they hadn't heard of Stef's death yet. She wasn't ready to deal with any more sympathy from well-wishers since the pain was still too raw.

Cars whizzed by on the road bordering the college campus. She hurried to her VW, frustration strangling her. Once she and Derek left Chris's, he'd turned sullen and distant. He'd driven her straight home without a word—not one sentence. True, his politeness extended to walking her to her door, but he left without a thank you or anything. She still couldn't believe his attitude.

She clicked open her car and jumped in. Sweat claimed her face and hands. When would the heat end? She stabbed the key in the ignition and started up the car.

Derek, Derek, Derek. She should delete him from her mind's hard drive. Right. That would never happen if her heart kept making excuses for his bad behavior.

She ached from his pain. Billy was his last link to his sister, and now he'd disappeared. Kelly would have given Derek comfort, but he kept pushing her away, claiming he could find his nephew better alone. Fine. Couldn't he see she cared? Everyone—even the most stoic—needed compassion.

Lost in thought, Kelly pulled out of the lot and turned left toward Fowler Avenue. An eerie feeling spiraled down her neck, and she checked the rear view mirror. Was someone following her?

When the car behind her passed on her right, her shoulders relaxed. She needed a chill pill. The recent pressures had made her lose her appetite and prevented her from sleeping. She would have to find a solution soon before she crumbled into something Chip might smear on a petri dish.

Derek wasn't good for her health, plain and simple.

Forcing her mind off Derek for a moment, Kelly concentrated on her sister's case once more. If Derek dismissed Michael as a suspect, and no one saw anything on the road below the crash site, she'd have to find some other clue.

Though exhausted, Kelly decided to take one last look at the guardrail, assuming the workmen hadn't fixed it already. She slugged through the lines of traffic heading to downtown. Once on the Crosstown, she was thankful the large amount of cars made traveling below the speed limit possible. She safely pulled over to the right once she passed the dented railing. Kelly breathed a sigh of relief the repair work remained unfinished.

She parked and stood on the shoulder, staring at the bent metal, sick that Stef had bounced over the short rail. The hot fumes from the passing cars made her stomach queasy.

Damn. She needed evidence. As Kelly turned to go back to her car, she caught site of a dark rusty spot at the end of the metal rail. She stopped in her tracks. Seeing no police cars, she stepped around the cones and hurried to the railing. A car honked, but she ignored the intrusive sound.

Kelly loomed over the splotch. She might not be a forensic scientist, but she knew dried blood when she saw it. Why hadn't the police found this evidence before? Did it belong to Stef? Had her sister been thrown from the car only to hit her head on the railing just as her car careened over the side? Or was this from a different accident? A more recent one?

Aaargh! Something didn't make sense. As much as she didn't want to bother Derek again, she needed answers.

He answered on the first ring. "Benally."

"Hi, it's me." Kelly walked back to her car, cell phone clutched tightly, fearful someone would stop and arrest her for trespassing.

"What's up?" He blew out an audible breath. She might be the last person he wanted to talk to, but too damn bad.

"I'm on the overpass again where Stef had her accident. I found blood on the guardrail."

"Are you sure it's blood?"

She could tell his interest was piqued. "As sure as I can be without testing it. I deal with blood in my work."

"Go back in your car and get off the Crosstown. I'll meet you below the overpass. And Kelly?"

"I know. Don't do anything stupid."

"Yeah."

She heard the familiar levity and smiled. Maybe the old Derek wasn't dead after all.

Heeding his warning, Kelly exited the freeway and parked beyond the overpass. Not only had the man who resided under the bridge disappeared, no prostitutes were on the corner either.

A few cars passed, but no one seemed to pay any attention to her. Kelly straightened in her seat when an older woman in a frumpy housedress limped down the sidewalk toward Kelly's car. She double-checked the door locks just in case the woman was dangerous.

Dangerous. Right. Her imagination was definitely out of control. As if a sixty-year old woman would be some kind of serial killer. The lady slowed as she neared. When the woman was parallel to the passenger's side door, she stopped and knocked on Kelly's window.

Not wanting to be rude, Kelly rolled down her window a few inches.

"Yes?"

"Can you help me?" the older lady said.

Heat poured inside the open window. Kelly expected the woman to hold out her hand and ask for money. "What do you need?"

"I'm trying to find Bayshore Boulevard."

Kelly sighed, relieved she only wanted directions. "Keep on this street. It dead ends on Bayshore."

"Thank you," the woman said with a too white smile.

Strange. Bayshore was a good seven miles long from one end to the other. Given the road held the most exclusive homes in this end of town, she wondered what business the woman had there. Maybe she was a maid and not the bag lady Kelly had first assumed.

Before she could speculate further, Derek pulled up behind her. A blanket of safety wrapped around her as she stepped out of the car.

Tension lined his face. "So where's this blood?" He was all business today.

"Above us on the end of the guardrail," she said.

"You stay here while I check it out." He scratched his head. "I can't believe we didn't catch this."

"Why would the police have checked? They never suspected any foul play."

"Could be." He didn't look convinced.

Derek wheeled around and headed to his cruiser.

She didn't want to be alone, not with bag ladies, homeless people, and hoods on bikes. "I want to come with you." He turned back to face her and quirked a brow. "It's kind of creepy staying here alone."

"Fine. Lock your doors, and we'll take my car."

Driving in a cruiser lent more authority to her being there. "Okay."

It only took a few minutes to return to the entrance ramp. When they reached the accident spot, Derek pulled over, and she jumped out.

"It's at the end of the rail," Kelly said, pointing to the broken metal.

Derek stepped around the cones. He crouched down to come eye-to-eye with the railing. A short phone call later, he strode back to her. "CSU will be here shortly. If it's blood that hasn't been contaminated, I want proof."

"That's why I called you."

He turned to her. "What were you doing up here? This is a crime scene."

"No it's not. You said it wasn't a crime but an unfortunate accident."

He nodded, but she could tell he wasn't happy with her flawless logic. "Let's go. Once the lab analyzes it, I'll let you know."

Mr. Not-so-friendly took her back to her car. What was eating him?

"Have you heard from Billy yet?" she asked.

His shoulders relaxed. "As a matter of fact, I have."

A surge of relief lowered her pulse. "Where was he?"

"With Dad."

From his terse tone, she guessed Billy staying with his dad was a bad thing. "But he's all right, isn't he?"

"Yeah. Dad figured the kid needed some R & R so he picked him up at school to go hunting—and told no one." He wiped a drop of sweat from his brow. "The bad thing is, when they're in the woods, Dad's cell doesn't work. I lit into Billy about calling me when I finally spoke to him." He scrubbed a hand over his head. "Bad move. I think the kid hates me now." Pain and worry creased his face.

For a moment, Kelly was tempted to wrap her arms around him and tell him everything would be all right, but after all these years, any display of affection might not be welcome.

"In the morning, he'll rethink things. Billy knows you care. That's all that matters to kids in the end."

"I hope so. Rayne would be so upset if she thought we couldn't have a good relationship." He pulled open her door. "I promised Dad I'd have dinner with the two of them."

"Sure, go ahead."

"Hey." He took a step closer and her heart sped up. "Be careful, okay?"

"I will."

"And no more snooping."

"Someone has to."

Derek frowned and gently placed his hands on her shoulders. "If the blood turns out to be something, I promise we'll investigate."

"Thank you."

"Kelly, listen." His eyes glanced to the sky for a moment. "It's hard enough dealing with two deaths, I couldn't handle it if anything happened to you, okay?"

With his tender words, Kelly forgave him everything. Again. "If you promise to let me know as soon as you learn about the blood, I'll keep my nose clean."

"It's a promise."

# CHAPTER SIXTEEN

WHAT THE HELL was that woman doing here again, snooping around at the crash site like that? Didn't she know that stirring up such a fuss could get a person killed? If the police believed it was an accident, then it was an accident. If the bitch couldn't keep her nose out of their business, she too would have to die.

Wasn't it bad enough she'd already brought in Rayne's brother? Another stupid mistake on her part. Her snooping was gonna get him killed also.

Damn, but this killing was getting dangerous. All these loose ends were beginning to make a mess of things. The bleeding had better stop soon or the police might get wise about Rayne and Stefanie's real killer. Jail was not a place for the faint of heart.

Shit. Back to the drawing board.

\*\*\*

"Are you sure?" Derek's throat suddenly went dry. He leaned back in his chair, his mind reeling with possibilities.

"There it is in black and white." Medina tossed the report on

Derek's desk. The papers landed with a slap. "The blood belonged to your sister."

Trying to cover his shock, Derek watched as one sheet escaped the folder and floated to the ground, but he ignored it. The tip of the report peeked out from the edge, and Derek jerked on the page, scanning the information. "This can't be."

Medina took a sip of his soda just as Derek looked up. His mouth watered. He could use an icy cold one right about now.

"Pole axed me too," Medina said, swallowing. "Ms. Gentry was inside the car with the windows up when she went over the guardrail, so she didn't leave Rayne's blood there."

"Never thought she did."

"Here's a possibility, though it has too many holes. Ms. Gentry might have stopped by the side of the road on a bridge, wiped her bloody hands on the rail to get rid of the evidence after killing Rayne, and then returned to her car and drove over the edge. Guilt can be a strange motivator."

Derek mentally replayed the possible scenario. "She couldn't have accelerated fast enough to flip over the rail—not unless Einstein's laws have changed."

Medina scrubbed a hand down his jaw. "You're right." He set down his drink and opened another folder. "The autopsy didn't show any blood on Gentry other than her own."

"You have any ideas how my sister's blood ended up on the railing?"

"The killer left it there."

Derek sat up straight, adrenaline jump-starting his heart like ten downed sodas. Could Kelly have been right? "Maybe the front door to Rayne's house had been open and Stefanie walked in on the killer. She ran. He followed. With the roads wet, her car swerved out of control."

Medina arched a brow. "She would have called the police from her car. She did have a cell phone, remember?"

He was losing it. "You're right. Maybe the killer understood that Stefanie could place him at the scene. When she left, he followed her. When she realized the danger, she sped up and lost control."

"Go on."

He snapped his fingers. "How could I have forgotten? According to

Rayne's next door neighbor, there was a woman about Stefanie's age at Rayne's house near the time of the murder." The words of the homeless man came back. "Kelly and I talked to some man who lived under the bridge where the accident occurred. He claimed to have heard a car door slam right after Stefanie's car went off the overpass long before the ambulance arrived."

"And you think it was the killer checking out his handiwork?"

"You have a better idea?" Derek asked.

"No, but explain how under the wet conditions that night, Rayne's blood didn't wash away."

A strange sense of excitement sent his mind into rapid-fire mode. "I checked with the weather bureau regarding the night they both died. It rained hard for no more than thirty minutes. You know how the weather is around here. Torrential one minute, dry the next. Hell, it can rain on one side of the street and not the other."

Medina slipped a hip on Derek's desk and grabbed the soda can. "So where do we take it from here?"

"We find the killer."

✳✳✳

The next few days were hectic. Her mom flew in the day before Stefanie's funeral and complained the whole time.

"My cat misses me so much," her mom had said. "Why, I wouldn't be surprised if his fur falls out from the stress." Or, "What do you bet all the flowers in the shop are dead, no thanks to the useless girl I call my assistant. I swear, she has the blackest thumb." But the best was, "I can feel it in my bones that my house won't be there when I return home. Surely, some unnamed tsunami has washed it away."

The visit should have helped soothe her sorrow. Instead, Kelly was more depressed than before. At least the ceremony yesterday had been wonderful. So many of Stefanie's friends had come and told wonderful stories about how many lives Stephanie had touched.

The biggest surprise was that Derek had shown up. As much as she wanted to speak with him, there was rarely a moment when she wasn't surrounded by Stef's friends. That, or her mom was clinging to her.

No sooner had she taken her home, than her mother announced she'd be flying out the next day. Kelly thought about arguing with her, but she recognized it wouldn't do any good. Beside, Kelly had a case to help solve.

After she escorted her mom to the airside, Kelly left. Exhausted, she dashed home. Derek had said the result of the blood test would be back soon, and she couldn't wait to check her answering machine in case he'd called about the blood results.

Why, oh why, hadn't she checked to see if her cell was charged before she left to take her mom to the airport after burying Stef? Nerves, she guessed.

She hated being away from her house for so many hours, but she couldn't just dump her mom in a cab, not when she lived only fifteen minutes away from the airport.

Wouldn't you know, the one time she needed the plane to be on time, the flight was delayed for two hours. What a nightmare.

Kelly fumbled through her purse for her front door key. So much junk, so little time to find anything. She needed to clean out the dang thing. Tomorrow would be soon enough.

Her neighbor drove down the street and honked. Kelly waved, anxious to be inside. Key in hand, she let herself in. The cool inside air helped calm her but couldn't take her mind off the last few days.

Despite the strong front, Kelly could tell her mom hadn't handled Stef's death well. If only her mom had cried, Kelly could have consoled her.

She stepped into the kitchen to check the phone. There'd better be a message from you-know-who.

Kelly halted. Damn. No blinking light. Frustrated, she poured a glass of cold water to quench her parched throat. How long did a blood test take anyway? She'd waited over a week already. Her lab didn't deal directly with DNA or else she would have run the test herself.

She placed the empty glass in the sink, turned toward the living room and stopped. Dammit. She needed answers now—not next week. She picked up the phone and called Derek's cell.

"Benally."

His voice released the tension in her neck and delivered warm, liquid sensations to other parts of her anatomy. She dropped down onto the living room sofa and kicked off her shoes, almost pretending they were sweethearts again. "Hi, it's me."

"Hey, I was just about to call you."

His flat tone extinguished her momentary bit of happiness. He'd received the results. Nothing more. From the strain in his voice, something was wrong. "What did they find?"

He cleared his throat and took forever to answer. "The blood on the rail belonged to Rayne."

Her heart raced at the implication. Kelly jumped up from her seat and paced in front of the sofa. "Ohmigod, Derek. How could it be Rayne's blood?"

She could picture him running a hand over his shiny head.

"We're thinking Rayne's killer might have followed your sister after she left Rayne's house. Stef probably spotted the killer in the house or nearby. In a rush to escape, your sister hit a wet spot, which caused her car to careen over the rail."

Her jaw slackened and her legs weakened. She stepped over to the kitchen island and pulled out a stool, her mind replaying the scene. Horrified, her stomach almost revolted, and she had to swallow to keep down the bile. "You're thinking that the killer had some trace of Rayne's blood on him. After Stef's car went over the railing, he leaned over to see that the deed was done? It was dark outside, you know. He probably didn't even see the red stain."

"It looks like that may be the case. I guess you were right." The softness and concern in his voice helped ease her pain. "Your homeless man might have been right too."

Relief, or perhaps validation, rippled through her. "Will the police investigate Stef's death?" She tightened her grip on the phone.

"They will now. Given the two crimes are most likely related."

He didn't sound happy in any way. "What's wrong?"

"I'm no longer on the case. Not that I was ever really on it. Shit. I wanted to be the one to find Rayne's killer."

His bitter disappointment saddened her further. "I'm sorry."

"You and me both. Officer Medina and Detective Seinkievitz are the principals. They'll do a good job."

"What can I do?"

"Nothing," he said without a pause.

She shot back a quick retort. "That's not my style, in case you forgot."

She thought she heard a rueful chuckle. "Oh, I remember your style all right. Once something gets in your head, you were a bulldog about achieving it. But not this time, Kelly. Let the police do their job."

She wasn't taking no for an answer. "I can't sit around holding my breath for weeks or months, waiting for your people to find another clue. I have to stay active."

"I understand, believe me, but civilians do not get involved in police work."

"Maybe not directly, but ten bucks says Stef's files might give us a clue."

He let out an audible breath. "Kelly, Stefanie might have been an innocent bystander. Her job might have had nothing to do with this case."

Anger at his easy dismissal made her clench her teeth. "But you don't know that."

"No, I don't."

She pushed her hair from her face. "I haven't had the desire to go through my sister's things, but I think now would be a good time." Kelly wasn't sure why she wanted Derek's help, but she did. "We may not be able to work directly on the case, but if by chance she wasn't an innocent bystander—"

"You want me to help?"

His eagerness gave her a small boost. He must be chomping at the bit to find a clue too. "Yes."

Kelly wasn't sure they'd find anything though, but if nothing else, it might bring them closer together.

Is that what she wanted? Really wanted? Or would he push her away if she got too close? Hell, maybe this time she would send him packing, like she had before—but that was when they were both eighteen. She'd had to go to school—and he'd heard voices.

"Give me her address," he said. "I can meet you there if you like—unless you have to be back to work. Or is your mom still in town?"

"No, she's gone, and I have a few more days of leave." Kelly gave him Stefanie's address. "How about meeting me at three?"

"Fine."

After Kelly hung up, her spirit lifted, partly from believing she was helping to find her sister's killer and partly because she'd see Derek again.

After changing into a pair of shorts and a tank top, she hopped in her car to buy some packing material. Kelly didn't look forward to gathering her sister's things, knowing that once all her possessions were stored or given away, her sister would truly be gone.

To her surprise, Derek's car sat in front of the apartment when Kelly drove up, and her pulse raced. She took a few deep breaths to push aside her...what? Nervousness? Frustration? Excitement? *Please don't let it be excitement.* She'd just buried her sister, for goodness sake.

Okay, truth be told, it was excitement—and lust. What was it she'd told her mother? Denying the truth would only delay the healing process? In this case, denying the truth was only delaying the inevitable.

"Hi," Derek said, with sympathy welling in his eyes. "Let me help you with the boxes."

"Thanks." Her hands sweated from pulling the stack of cardboard from her Bug.

Just having Derek nearby gave her solace. His shoulders looked strong enough to carry both of their burdens.

"Do you really think we'll find anything that can help us?" he asked, nodding toward the apartment building.

"I don't know, but I can't stop thinking about some of her cases. She mostly looked for lost relatives. Occasionally, she followed husbands and wives who cheated on their spouses. I suppose one of them could have come after her, but she never mentioned believing she was ever in danger."

"Did Stefanie screen the cases she took?"

"Yes. She claimed she never became involved in anything she thought was too dangerous. She was the Internet search queen. She could find dirt on anyone, anything, anytime."

Kelly unlocked the front door.

Derek motioned she enter first. Despite the air conditioner running full blast, it smelled musty inside.

Kelly's step faltered, and her eyes began to well with tears. Every chair, every pot and pan, and every photo on the wall reminded her of her sister.

"She wasn't the neat one, was she?" Derek said, but his tone held no judgment.

"No. Stef and I are...were almost complete opposites. Maybe that's why we got along so well."

Derek set down the cardboard and hooked his thumbs in his jeans. "Where do you want to start?"

The comfortable way he asked took her back twelve years. They'd done everything together back then. "She did most of her work in the back bedroom. I can start with her computer files if you want to go through those folders over there." She nodded to the stack on the dining room table. "Her place may look a mess, but her filing system was fairly orderly."

"It looks like we'll be here for a while. I haven't eaten lunch. Mind if I order in a pizza while I work?"

Derek and his pizza. "Sure."

"You still like veggie?"

He remembered, and her heart warmed. "Yes, but remember—"

"I know, no olives."

Wow. Of course, they'd spent many a Saturday night at his mom's house watching television and eating pizza with no olives. Those were happy times until he began to hear voices. She wondered if he still did.

Kelly retreated to the back bedroom and fired up the computer. She started with Stefanie's newest cases and worked her way backward.

"Pizza's here."

"How?" She looked at her watch. "I must have lost track of time."

She went out to the dining room where Derek had set out the

pizza, two sodas, and paper napkins on the table. Warm cheese with tomato sauce made her stomach grumble.

His sleeves were rolled up, exposing an ugly scrape on his elbow. "What happened?" Kelly asked, pointing to his injury.

Absently, he rubbed the area. "Nothing. Bumped it or something."

Kelly took a closer look. "There's sand encrusted in the wound. You need to clean it with some Povidone Iodine."

"Thanks Doc, I will."

He smiled at her, acting as if the injury was commonplace. Men. They had no common sense when it came to taking care of bumps and scrapes.

Derek sat down and had placed the file folders in neat stacks on the floor.

"Did you find anything in her files?" she asked as she picked up a piece of the mouthwatering pizza.

"Not yet, but I'm not giving up. I'm guessing your sister had a camera. Know where it is?"

"Sure. She used a really nice digital camera. Eleven mega-pixels. The zoom was better than on her phone."

"Nice." Kelly started to get up, but he waved a hand for her to sit. "Eat first. It'll still be there after we finish."

After one slice, Kelly didn't want any more. She was still struggling with the wave of depression she'd felt ever since walking in the front door, and the pizza started tasting like one of the cardboard boxes.

She watched Derek for a minute, knowing it was sappy to think he looked great even when he was chewing his food. Disgusted with herself, she pushed back her from the table. "I'll look for the camera."

It took a moment to find Stefanie's prize possession. She brought it into the living room and clicked the On button. The camera chirped to life.

She sat next to Derek and flipped through the images, holding the camera so they both could see. Their shoulders touched and once again, she was reminded of the comfort and reassurance he'd given her all those years ago. If only she could help him in return. Knowing he was hurting, her heart ached to talk to him about his life and his family. Now didn't seem the time though.

Derek slid the camera from her fingers. "What the hell?"

Her heart stepped up a notch. "What is it?" She leaned near him. Her gaze shot to the screen.

"It's Rayne," he said.

She studied the small picture. "Is that Justin with her?"

"It sure as hell is."

"Justin told me he and Rayne had double dated with Stefanie on occasion. Perhaps these were fun photos and not related to her business."

He clicked through a series of other shots. All were of Justin. Justin at lunch. Justin at Starbucks. Justin at the casino.

He tilted the camera back to her. "You recognize this guy?"

Confused, she stared at the four square inch screen for a moment. "No. It's too dark to see anything. I can tell the man on the left is Justin, but the other man's features aren't clear."

"I agree, but they're standing in front of The Waters Edge Condominium."

"So?"

Derek let out a long breath. "A few weeks ago, a man Justin worked with, named Carl Vanderwall, dove off his balcony. He lived at the Waters Edge."

She sucked in a breath. "I remember reading about that case. You don't think Justin had anything to do with it, do you?"

"I don't know, but I intend to find out. The immediate question is why would your sister be following Justin?"

She had to admit, the photos were taken without Justin's knowledge. "Someone hired her is my guess. Would Rayne have?"

"I can't imagine why. She trusted him. Hell, I suspected she even loved the guy."

"Let me see something." Kelly took the camera back, her fingers brushing his. *Not now. Damn out-of-control hormones.* "It gives the dates of each photo. Maybe knowing when they were taken will help identify her employer." Kelly clicked through the menu. "Here it is: August 29$^{\text{th}}$."

Derek leaned over and picked up a stack of files from the floor. He flipped through them. "Here is her August file. I hadn't gotten this far."

He sat in silence as he read through the report. His eyes widened and narrowed, and his jaw tightened the further he read.

"What does it say?" Kelly asked.

"Holy shit." He leaned forward. "Vanderwall hired her."

She leaned close enough to read over his shoulder. "The jumper?"

"Yeah."

"Do you think that's him in the photo?" She looked up and gazed into his azure eyes.

He cleared his throat. "I can't tell. When I saw him, his face had been rearranged by the cement. It should be easy to find out once I return to the station, though. I think we have a photo of him from his work."

"Talking to someone who then kills himself isn't a crime," she said. "Maybe Justin could tell the man was depressed, and he wanted to see he arrived home safely." She saw no reason to condemn Justin.

"Maybe." He lowered his head and looked at her with raised brows. "I'm the principal on the Vanderwall case. I think it's time Justin and I had a little talk."

He stood.

"You're going now?" she asked. "What about helping me pack?" *Without making sure I don't fall apart when I touch my sister's belongings? Without giving me a hug?*

Derek looked torn. "This won't take long. I can be at his office in twenty minutes, tops. I'll be gone no longer than an hour. Then I'll come back. Okay?"

"Why don't you just call him?" *And stay here with me? You're pathetic, Kelly Lynn. You don't need anyone to lean on.*

"I don't want to tip him off. Hey, do you think you could print a copy of this for me? I want to see Justin's reaction to the photo."

"Sure." Happy to have something tangible to do, she rushed into the bedroom.

After a few failed attempts at getting the picture to the printer, she succeeded.

Kelly marched back into the living room holding the photo in front of her. "It's kind of grainy."

Derek studied the picture. "Doesn't matter. It's clearly Justin. This should make him sweat if he did have anything to do with Vanderwall's death."

"You're coming back, right?"

He smiled and a little bit of her melted. "Wouldn't consider otherwise."

# CHAPTER SEVENTEEN

DEREK RAPPED a little too hard on Stefanie's door, but his frustration level had been escalating since the moment he'd left Justin's office. "It's me."

Kelly pulled the door open wide. Her eyes were red, and she looked as if a one hundred pound weight sat on her shoulders. Guilt swamped him. He should have stayed to help her get through the emotional ordeal of packing her sister's things. Crap. He didn't seem to be able to do anything right where Kelly was concerned.

"Hey, what did you find out?" She looked as if she were fighting more tears and another breakdown.

His arms itched to hold her and tell her everything would be all right.

"He wasn't there. Justin was a no show at work this morning too. His boss didn't have a clue where he was."

She turned and walked back to the dining room table acting as if it didn't matter that their prime suspect had disappeared. She finished wrapping a plate in newspaper, the sound of the crinkling paper louder than it needed to be.

"Did you try his cell?" she asked. Her tone sounded casual, but he could hear her fighting for control.

"His boss called his home and his cell. No answer."

She placed the plate carefully in a box. "He could be sick and not answering." He couldn't tell if there was hope in her voice or not.

"I thought of that too, so I went to his house, but he wasn't there."

She whipped around, worry creasing her brows. Finally, there was a reaction. "Are you going to put out an APB on him or something?"

He took a step toward her, his hands extended. He waited a second before answering, hoping she'd step into his arms.

She didn't move. Damn. "If only it were that simple. Without evidence to back up the request, I can't issue an APB."

"Oh."

Her disappointment sent a flood of concern through him. Kelly was strong, but how much more could she take? Damn it. He should have made up some story about Justin being away on business.

He took another step, closing the gap between them. When she looked up at him with those deep green eyes, he lost control. Almost as if they were positive and negative magnets, he pulled her to his chest. Damn the consequences to his heart. He didn't care if she told him to go to hell. He needed to hold her, touch her, feel her silky skin against his. Every curve of her body molded against his in perfect proportion. Like always.

He liked how the top of her curly hair tickled his chin, and for a moment, he let himself enjoy the lemon scent of her shampoo. Her body relaxed in his arms, as if she'd been waiting all day to have a shoulder to lean on.

Kelly leaned back and looked up. The temptation to kiss her rattled him. He stepped away. "Let me help you pack."

She shook her head and looked down at the carpet. "I think I've done all the packing today I can handle. It's hard boxing up Stef's possessions."

He didn't want to think about having to do the same for Rayne's things. "What will you do with all of the files?" He motioned toward the stack of folders in neat piles on the table. Speaking of cardboard and paper was a lot easier than discussing emotions.

She bit the inside of her cheek. "I guess I'll keep them for the time being. I'll never know when they'll give us a clue." She swiped a tear from her cheek. "I've called Goodwill to come for her furniture and clothes, but I'm keeping a few things. To, ah, help me remember."

He cupped her chin and ran his thumb along her cheek. "I know what you mean. I have to clean out Rayne's place pretty soon, but I want Billy to be there to help."

She swallowed. Hard. "I gather he's not ready."

"No."

Kelly straightened. When her gaze shot right and then left, Derek clasped her shoulders. "What's wrong?" he asked.

She dropped her head and nibbled on her lip. "I...I found a folder on Justin." Derek's body went on full alert. "Did you know he was arrested for murder when he lived in Utah?"

His heart sped up. "And you didn't tell me right away?"

She lifted one shoulder. "Do you think Justin killed Stef?"

She'd reached her emotional limit, which meant he had to be careful. "Maybe, maybe not. Let me see what you found." Derek kept his voice as soft as possible.

Kelly stepped over to the table, picked up several yellowed and somewhat tattered newspaper articles and handed them to him.

Derek scanned them quickly. The first one dated back some twenty years. He decided to read the first one out loud as he paced the small living room. "Bobby Novaro was killed Thursday night in Silverton from a gunshot wound to his chest. Justin Bladen was arrested for the murder. Holy shit." He looked up at her. "That wasn't in there. The holy shit part." He thought he caught a quick smile. "While a blood-stained jacket with Novaro's blood was found in the trashcan next to the Bladen's house, the case was dismissed after Bladen proved he was elsewhere during the commission of the crime." Derek scanned the rest of the article, but nothing of interest appeared.

Alibis. The man seemed full of them.

"I can't remember. Does it say if the murderer was ever found?" Kelly asked, running a finger under her nose.

"No."

She wrung her hands. "Do you think Justin is guilty of killing Stef and Rayne?"

"Not if we believe he was asleep at his boss's house when they were murdered."

"I never believe in ironclad alibis. Too many people cover for guilty people."

Derek raised a brow. "Since when did you become a detective? Or a cynic for that matter?"

A red blotch stained her cheeks. "I'm a big CSI fan."

He couldn't help but raise his eyes to the heavens and groan. "Isn't everyone?" Though, truth be told, he enjoyed seeing some life come to her face.

She drew back her shoulders. "So what do we do now?"

He wasn't ready to deal with the look of aggression in her eyes. "*We* don't do anything. I'm going to Utah to see if I can get any dirt on Justin. I remember Rayne mentioning that Justin's mother was still alive. Even though the two don't speak anymore, she might provide a clue as to his whereabouts. His mom could still live in Silverton. I want to pay her a visit."

"I'll go with you," she said.

"No way. It's too dangerous." He held her shoulders lightly. "This isn't a vacation, Kelly."

Her jaw clenched. "I think it's a hell of lot more dangerous staying here, don't you think? There's a killer on the loose, or did you forget?"

She pushed away. Derek wanted to shake her and kiss her at the same time. "It never leaves my mind."

Her body relaxed. "If Justin finds out you've gone to investigate his past, and he really is in Tampa, he might come after me."

"That's not his style. He's a careful man."

"Careful, as in careful not to get caught, maybe."

She had a point. When Kelly wanted something, Kelly went after it. Like her medical degree. Like her research. Knowing her, she'd jump on a plane and follow him the moment he took off.

"Fine. We'll take the first flight out I can book, but you have to promise me one thing."

She nodded. "I know, I have to promise not to do anything stupid and do everything you say."

She strode up to him, and when she fingered the buttons on his shirt, fire shot straight to his groin, and he inwardly groaned. "Something like that. Come on. Let's get out of here."

If he didn't get away from her, he'd give into temptation.

And that would cause some real danger.

*\*\*\**

Justin reread the text message on his phone from his boss. "Police after U. Think U killed girlfriend –Winston."

He had to get some place safe. Damn Benally. Why couldn't the man believe that Rayne had killed herself?

Justin checked his rear view mirror for the tenth time. "Shit." Why now? He didn't need the scrutiny. He'd been so confident he'd gotten away with it.

He thought about calling Kelly and telling her he had nothing to do with her sister's murder—or Rayne's for that matter, but how could he convince her? Apparently, Benally didn't think his alibi of being at Winston's party was good enough.

It was time to disappear. He'd done it often enough, but what a pain in the ass that was. He liked his job, liked the money he received. Now all of that would be gone. Fuck.

The only safe place he could think of hiding was at his home in Odessa—the home he kept for his secret trysts. Not even his closest friends knew about it. Yes, it was expensive to rent a second home, but it was far enough out of Tampa that he could do whatever he wanted. Thank God there weren't any nosy neighbors to complain if the noise became out of control either.

After circling the block to make sure the police weren't at his house, he pulled into the carport. A garage would have been nice, but this old heap didn't have one and the owner was a stingy old bastard.

Arriving in daylight wasn't particularly smart, but he needed to shower and change.

And to plan. He hadn't been there in over a month and dreaded the stale air inside. As he put his key in the lock, the door nudged open.

Justin froze. Had someone broken in? Why? There was nothing of value to take.

He rushed inside and halted, straining to hear sounds of glass breaking or furniture cracking.

Silence.

The stack of books he'd tossed on the coffee table before he'd left the last time wasn't there. He rushed toward his bedroom. The pile of laundry in the hallway? Gone too.

"Hello?" Blood pounded in his ears.

He didn't expect anyone to answer, but if a burglar had been hiding, he wanted to give him a chance to escape. The last thing he needed was a mugging or a police report.

Stepping softly into the kitchen from the hallway, Justin paused. While he remembered having washed the dishes, he'd stacked them in the drying rack. Now the counter was clean, and the drying rack gone.

He checked the cupboards. The dishes were there. "Fuck."

Then he spotted a single piece of paper on the dining room table, neatly folded. Dread and hatred filled him until he nearly choked on his bile.

"Noooo. It couldn't be." That bitch.

He picked up the note. "They're after you, and they'll find you." It was written in small, neat letters—letters he despised. He continued reading. "Or will you run away like you did before? Turn yourself in or I'll take care of that girl you like." An evil darkness crept down his spine.

It wasn't signed, but he knew who'd written the threat.

✳✳✳

*Silverton, Utah*

"We appreciate you meeting with us," Derek said, as he shook Officer Mariani's plump hand. The deputy worked for the Sheriff's department in Silverton, a small suburb an hour outside of Salt Lake City, Utah.

Mariani motioned to the two chairs in front of his worn desk. A large evidence box sat on top, the frayed edges and many markings testifying to its age.

"After I received your fax, I pulled the Novaro case. It's been closed for almost twelve years." He tapped the box.

Derek nodded. "When we spoke on the phone, you mentioned Justin Bladen had been arrested for the murder."

"That's right. The murder occurred before my time, mind you, and before DNA testing. We weren't very sophisticated back then, but we did our best."

No apology in his eyes. Good. "What can you tell me?"

Mariani twisted the ends of his long, black mustache, then glanced up as if reading the report off the ceiling. "We knew that Justin's daddy had hanged himself the week before the murder. The suicide note said he lost his promotion to Novaro. Naturally, we suspected revenge from the Bladen family."

Neither Justin nor Rayne had mentioned his troubled background. Derek did some quick math. "Wouldn't that put Justin at around seventeen or eighteen?"

Mariani tapped the first page of the report. "Just had just turned eighteen. Such a shame for a boy that young to be involved in such a messy affair."

How true. "The department must have found some evidence to make the arrest."

"We found evidence all right—his high school letter jacket, but Justin had an airtight alibi. He was at a party that night. The Mayor's daughter happened to be there too, though I don't know why. She normally didn't hang out with his crowd. She confirmed he was there all night."

The airtight alibi sounded too familiar. "Is his jacket in the box?"

Mariani pulled out his desk drawer and gloved both hands. He lifted the lid on the cardboard box that sat like a Christmas present on his desk. Extracting the jacket from a paper bag, he placed it face up on the lid. "Look here. The blood has faded over time, but the victim's blood was spattered all over the letters." He tilted the evidence to give Derek a better view.

"I read about that. You sure this jacket belonged to Justin?"

"Yup. His name was embroidered on the back." Mariani flipped over the jacket. "We found it in the garbage can outside his trailer. Lucky for us the trash man hadn't picked up yet."

Derek leaned forward to get a good look at the item, but he didn't touch the evidence. "Rather careless don't you think to leave something so incriminating next to his own house?"

"No one said murderers had to be smart."

Derek smiled. "You have a point. I trust you've done a DNA test on the jacket since then."

"Yes, a few years back. The blood belonged to Novaro all right, but we couldn't get any other evidence off the jacket. We spoke with the mom who swears no one came near their place either before the murder or afterward."

Derek found her willingness to throw her son to the wolves a little strange. Mothers usually became mute when their child was in question. "You find any other evidence?"

"Sure did." Mariani dipped his hand into the magic box and withdrew a 9mm pistol with a tag dangling from the trigger. "This is the murder weapon. The bullet we extracted from Novaro's body matched the gun."

"And I suppose you found the gun in the trash too."

He held up a finger. "According to the report, the gun was found in Justin Bladen's gym bag—inside the house."

Derek studied Kelly. Her fingers were clenched on the arm of the chair. He bet she believed Justin killed Novaro, although he wouldn't put it past the guy. How had his sister fallen for him? Or was he the innocent bystander he claimed?

"How did he get off?" Kelly asked, her tone bitter.

"Ma'am, the jacket and gun are circumstantial. We arrested the boy, but the girl, Courtney, swore he was at the party the whole time. She was a credible witness. We had no reason to suspect she lied."

Kelly looked up at Derek, silently pleading for him to interfere.

"Does Courtney have a last name?" Derek asked.

"March, but she's Courtney Wolfendon now."

They might get a lead off her. "Does she still live around here?"

"As a matter of fact, she does."

Finally, he had a break. He waited for Mariani to offer up the information, but the officer leaned back in his chair and seemed to study Derek.

"Do you have her address by any chance?" Derek asked.

Mariani glanced over his shoulder. "Say Carrie, can you get me the address of Courtney Wolfendon? Thanks."

Derek needed more. "Does it say how many other witnesses the officers spoke to at the party? Courtney could have been covering for him," Derek said.

Mariani cocked a brow. "We may be a small force, but the Sheriff's Department always does a good job."

Now he'd done it. Pissing off Mariani would get him nowhere. "Sorry. I wasn't implying incompetence. I often forget to confirm alibis."

Like with Justin's recent case. Damn it. Why had he taken the word of Justin's boss? For all he knew, the two were in cahoots.

Mariani twirled his mustache once more as if he needed time to chew on Derek's apology. He picked up the report. "I understand. From what I could gather, back then the Mayor's daughter was a good girl, not that she isn't now, but she was class valedictorian and all. I don't suppose the investigating officer suspected those two were a couple. Apparently he bought her story and didn't look any further. Like I said, she had no reason to lie for him." He ran a finger down the page. "It didn't say if the officer, Ralph Winters, talked to anyone else, but I suspect he didn't."

"Is Winters currently on the force?"

Mariani shook his head. "No. He passed away about five years ago. Cancer."

"Sorry."

"You here to find Justin Bladen?"

"Hopefully. He's a suspect in a murder in Tampa."

"In Tampa, huh? And you think he's in Silverton?"

"Just a hunch."

Mariani cocked a brow. "Well, if I hear anything, I'll let you know."

Derek suspected Mariani knew more than he was telling. "What kind of kid was Justin Bladen?"

Mariani shrugged. "Never met the kid. I only know what I've read in the report. He left town before I moved here."

Carrie stepped over to Mariani's desk and handed him a piece of paper. "I attached a map so they could find their way to Courtney's." She turned to Derek. "It's not far from here."

"I appreciate you going to all the trouble," Derek said, and Carrie smiled.

"I suggest you call her first," Mariani said. "Courtney's a bit touchy about the murder."

After twelve years? A red flag waved in his mind's eye. "I appreciate the heads up. Do you have the home address of Justin Bladen's mom by any chance?"

Mariani flipped to the back page. "This might be old information, but they used live at 1342 West Sanders Road." He pulled out a piece a paper from his drawer. "I'll draw you a map to her place. I'm not as neat as Carrie here in the map-making department. The last time I ran into Mrs. Bladen must have been, oh, I'd have to say a year ago. People like her usually stay in one place though."

"People like her?"

"Poor, low income job. You know. She keeps to herself."

"Thanks."

Once outside, Kelly tugged her lapels closer to her chest. Derek, for one, loved the cool breeze. It was a nice relief from sticky Tampa.

"I didn't like him much," Kelly said.

"Hmm. Seemed like an upstanding guy to me."

"You cops always stick together."

He figured it best to let the conversation drop.

When they reached the rental car, Derek held open the door for Kelly.

"Now where to?" she asked as she buckled her seatbelt.

"I'd like to hear what Courtney Wolfendon has to say about the night in question."

"Do people really remember what happened twelve years ago?"

"If it's traumatic or memorable enough, they might."

# CHAPTER EIGHTEEN

"LIKE I TOLD you over the phone, the murder happened a long time ago," Courtney Wolfendon said, as she ushered them in.

Trying not to look too obvious, Derek checked out her house. Nice and upscale. Hell, the atrium ceiling almost made him feel small. She'd done well for herself, which wasn't too surprising, considering she was the ex-Mayor's daughter.

Her gaze locked onto the hard wood floor as she led them over to the plush leather sofa. Mrs. Wolfendon sat opposite them on the edge of a chair and wove her fingers together. Lips pinched, she appeared to debate whether or not to spill the beans.

Derek threw out a prompt. "You told the police that Justin Bladen was at the party the night of the Novaro murder. Were you with him the whole night, or could he have snuck out and then returned without your knowledge?" Like he had, perhaps, the night of Rayne's murder.

She looked off to the side, inhaled, and held her breath. Worry shot through Derek. Maybe she'd forgotten the details. Twelve years was a long time.

She wagged a finger and opened her mouth. Before she got out a word, the front door flew open and a flabby man, with curly red hair barged in.

"Courtney, what's going on?" The guy looked royally pissed as he marched straight for her.

Mrs. Wolfendon's eyes widened, and she grabbed the chair's seat cushion. "This man is a police detective. From Florida. They've come about Justin."

Just Justin? No full name? He must be a common topic of conversation in this household.

The newcomer stepped in front of her and faced Derek. From the way his eyes shifted from side to side, the guy had something to hide. "You talking about that prick, Justin Bladen?"

Derek stood, straightened his shoulders and looked down at the pudgy man. He put on his most sincere face. "Yes, sir."

"Justin Bladen was a no good, sleazy asshole. That's all you need to know."

Mrs. Wolfendon tugged on the man's sleeve. "Please George, don't. We were just kids back then."

He spun around and loomed over her. "If I ever see him near you, I'll kill him, I swear." He stomped off into a back room. Mrs. Wolfendon's face reddened as her shoulders sagged. There didn't seem to be much love in that marriage.

Derek looked at Kelly, and warmth spread through him. They'd always treated each other with respect. Even after she'd dumped him she'd been nice about leaving.

"I'm sorry," Mrs. Wolfendon said, obviously shaken. "Justin and I had a thing for each other in high school." She crooked her fingers around the words. "I know we came from the opposite sides of the tracks, so to speak, but there was something about Justin that appealed to me."

"Like what?" Kelly asked in a soft, reassuring tone.

"Well, for one, he was smart and driven. He wanted to get out of this go-nowhere town and make something of himself." Her gaze turned almost dreamy, like she was reliving her high school crush.

Kelly leaned forward. "So what happened between you two?"

Smart girl. Women talk was not his forte. Derek sat back, letting the two bond.

Mrs. Wolfendon looked behind her, her brows pinched in fear. "It was our high school graduation party. His dad had killed himself a few days before, and all I wanted to do was console Justin, but he refused any kind of sympathy. The next day, when the police came around asking questions about the murder, Justin kind of freaked and moved out of his house. He told me he couldn't handle his mom, but if you ask me, I think he was just in a funk because of his dad's death. The suicide really tore him up. My father didn't like Justin, but we had a shed in the back where my father kept his tools. I told Justin he could hole up there for a few days."

More information than Derek had hoped for.

"How long did he stay with you?" Kelly continued.

She bit down on her lip. "Maybe a week. Once his name was cleared, he left town."

"Did he ever see his mom again?"

"No."

Derek schooled his features. So Justin and Mrs. Wolfendon had quite a history. "Did your folks know he was staying on their property?" From the way Mariani described her dad, he wouldn't have put up with the likes of Justin.

"Oh, no. Daddy was the Mayor at the time and very strict. Maybe that's why I was attracted to Justin in the first place." She glanced over at Kelly. "You know, the bad boy thing."

Kelly glanced at Derek with a twinkle in her eye. "I sure do."

Derek didn't need the conversation to wander. He nodded toward the room where her husband had disappeared. "Your husband certainly doesn't like Justin."

She glanced over her shoulder. "You're right. He wanted to date me our senior year, but I wanted Justin." Her voice came out a mere whisper. "George knew that. I only agreed to go out with him after Justin left for good."

Kelly tilted her head to the side and let out an audible breath. "I understand. When Justin left, you felt alone and vulnerable. George stepped up and was there for you."

She barely smiled. "I guess so."

"Did Justin ever contact you again?" Derek asked, his fists clenched.

Her eyes widened. "No. It was like he disappeared from the face of the earth."

Eighteen-year old boys didn't leave their gym bags if they planned to split, nor did they throw their jackets away in houses where they no longer lived. If DNA testing had been available twenty years ago, Justin might never have been arrested.

As much as he wanted Justin Bladen to be guilty, it didn't look like the guy had committed the Novaro murder. The pieces fit too nicely—as if the poor son of a bitch had been framed—or else Justin wanted it to look that way.

"Can you give me a list of some other people who were at the party that night?" Derek asked.

She rolled her eyes. "Oh, boy. You're asking me to think back really far."

"Try, please."

"Well, William McKee was there. He's my cousin. Then there was Megan Hornstrom, my best friend and a ton of others." Her eyes squinted nearly shut. "Why?"

He jotted their names in his pad. "We'd like to corroborate your story."

She sat up straighter. "It isn't a story. I was with Justin most of the night. If you think he had time to leave, kill that man, and then come back, you're wrong. I'd have known if he'd left."

"I hope so," Derek said. And he meant it. "I wasn't implying you were lying. Sometimes other people notice things you might have missed. It's possible you were talking to someone and lost track of time."

She chewed her thumbnail—what there was left of it. "I guess it's possible. I didn't want my father to find out we were dating, so we never talked in public for long. We tried to keep our relationship a secret. Parties were the only time we really saw each other."

It was time for a different tack. "Besides driven and smart, what kind of boy was Justin?" Derek kept his tone non-threatening.

"Why all the interest in Justin? Has he done something?" She grabbed the lapels of her jacket and tugged them tight across her chest. Clearly, it was a nervous habit. What was she afraid of? Her husband or Derek's questions?

"Justin was engaged to my sister. Now she's dead."

Mrs. Wolfendon clasped a hand over her mouth, and then dropped her hand to her lap. "And you think Justin killed her?"

"I don't know what to think, but he fled Tampa a few days ago. I thought he might have come here."

"Poor Justin. No, he wouldn't come back home. He and his mom never got along, and I heard he knew I had married George."

"Maybe he wanted to see his mom again to make things right after all these years."

Her gaze raced around the room. "I don't think so. As I said, they hated each other. Not that I blame him. His mom was strange." She gulped down a breath. "Have you spoken with her yet?"

"No."

"Oh, boy. Are you in for a treat. She's distant and angry, and I have to admit, downright odd. I haven't had much contact with her these last few years, thank goodness. I doubt she has changed though."

Derek leaned forward and steepled his fingers, interested in her assessment of Justin's mom. "Odd how?"

Mrs. Wolfendon checked behind her. The husband remained out of sight. "Justin told me she belonged to some white supremacist group."

Derek felt the blood drain from his face. He inhaled to keep his blood pressure from falling further. "Go on."

She gripped her hands on her lap. "Justin tried not to hate the Navajos because he played ball with some of them, but both his parents taught him the Indians were out to get you. His folks became obsessed with purifying the race. It was no wonder Justin learned to hate."

Before Derek had a chance to absorb the information, the door behind her slammed open, and her husband stomped back into the room. "You want to know about Bladen? Well, I'll tell you. He was a bigot, just like his old lady—a real despicable kid." He turned to his wife. "I can't believe you fell for him."

So the man had been eavesdropping. He hoped Mrs. Wolfendon

wouldn't feel the brunt of her husband's wrath after they left. She opened her mouth but then quickly closed it.

Rayne mentioned she'd never told Justin she was half-Seminole. Deep inside, maybe she suspected his bigotry. When she and Justin visited Dad, perhaps finding out she'd misled him had set him off. Maybe he had killed her. That though made his stomach sicken.

Derek forced down his temper and looked up at the husband. "Have you spotted Justin around town?"

George's eyes narrowed. "No, but if I ever do see him, the prick'll be sorry."

Derek grabbed Kelly's hand and stood. "If you hear from him, call me." He placed his card on the coffee table. "You've been very helpful, Mrs. Wolfendon. Thank you. We'll see ourselves out."

Kelly said nothing until they piled into the car. "I'm sorry."

He closed the driver's side door and started the engine. "About what?"

"Knowing that the man Rayne might have married hated your race. She bit her lower lip. "Do you think Justin could have killed her?"

Derek backed out of the drive, thinking about her question. "I don't know. I'm sure some shrink would say it wasn't Justin's fault if he had committed a hate crime. Hell, what do I know? My dad preached everyone was responsible for his own actions. Background plays a role, sure, but we make our own destiny, and I have to agree."

"I guess our next step is to meet this infamous mother?"

"If we can find her." Like mother, like son?

"She has no way of knowing we're even in town, so it's not like she'd run."

"We can only hope." He handed her the paper. "See if you can make any sense of these directions."

Kelly studied the hand-drawn map and then looked out the window as they headed down the empty two-lane road out of town. "I hope your appearance doesn't scare Mrs. Bladen," she said under her breath.

Huh? Kelly never seemed to be bothered by his size before. Or was it his coloring she thought might upset Justin's mom? "You act as if I should get skin whitening cream or something. Kelly, I'm not afraid of prejudiced people. I've dealt with them my whole life."

She stared down at the paper. Dammit. He hadn't meant to upset her. *Good going, Benally.*

✳✳✳

Kelly broke the silence only to give Derek directions. She understood his anger. Finding out someone could hate you for your race was enough to upset anyone. The strain around his eyes and the way his lips pressed together told her he was fighting for control, but he didn't have to be sharp with her.

"This is the place," he said.

Derek pulled up in front of a rundown trailer in the middle of nowhere. She double-checked the address. "I can't believe Justin was brought up in such poverty. The home sure could use some new siding, or whatever they do to trailers to fix them up." No landscaping of any kind, other than dirt, covered the ground between the trailer and the street.

"Rayne never mentioned Justin grew up poor."

"Maybe he never told her."

"I'm learning there was a lot she didn't know about him." He slapped the wheel. "Come on. Let's get this over with."

He slid out of the car, and Kelly followed him to the front door. He rapped on the screen that looked ready to come off its hinges. Kelly drew her jacket tighter around her chest not anticipating Utah would be this cool in October.

Derek tried again, but got the same response. "I guess she's not home."

"Now what?" Kelly glanced at him. He squared his shoulders and unwanted and unexpected lust shot straight to her groin. She cast her gaze downward and turned toward the car.

He reached out and gently stopped her. Startled, she turned and looked up at him. He nodded to the neighbor's trailer. "Maybe we can find out what we need to know another way."

She glanced in the direction he'd motioned. A similar sized trailer sat a hundred feet down the road. The place looked worn, but at least it had a lawn and a few shrubs.

As they drew closer to the neighbor's place, an elderly woman peeked her head out the door. "You lookin' for Lilly?" She pulled the shawl over her shoulders.

"Yes," Derek said.

"Well, you won't find her. She's been gone for a bit."

"Let me speak with her," Kelly said so only Derek could hear. "I think you might scare her." Back in high school Derek received a lot of measured, dark looks.

Kelly stepped a little closer to the neighbor's trailer. "Hi, I'm Kelly Rutland. We're friends of Mrs. Bladen's son. Do you know when she'll be back?"

"Lilly don't got no son." She seemed to shrink back as her gaze zeroed in on Derek.

The woman looked too thin, as if she hadn't have enough to eat or else was ill. Her sallow skin coloring gave a good case for the latter.

Derek placed a hand on Kelly's lower back and the sense of familiarity overwhelmed her. She took a cool, deep breath to steady her nerves. Why did his mere touch send her into a tizzy? It's not as if she'd never been with a man. She'd been married for two years for God's sake.

"Your neighbor's last name is Bladen, right?" he asked.

"Yes."

"How long have you lived here?" Derek asked, walking slowly toward her with Kelly by his side. The woman didn't budge. If anything, her shoulders straightened.

"Six, seven years maybe. Why?"

"Just wondering."

"Can you tell us a little something about Lilly?" Kelly asked.

"Why?"

She could tell the woman was nearing the end of her patience. "Justin spoke so much about his mom, we wanted to meet her. We're passing through and thought we'd say, hi."

"Then you got the wrong woman. Lilly isn't the kind people want to meet."

"Really?"

"I'm losing heat here." The woman pulled the door closer to her. "You ever been in jail, mister?"

Kelly swallowed a smile at her question.

"Nope," Derek answered.

She ran her gaze up and down him a few times. "You don't have any weapons on you, do you?"

Derek patted down his chest. "No, ma'am."

"All right. Come in. Can't afford to heat the outside."

Kelly let out a long held breath. Despite the brisk air, her under-arms had started to sweat. Playing detective took more nerve than she'd anticipated. Lying was not her game, but if Justin had killed Stefanie, she owed it to her sister to find out as much as possible about the man. And the best way to learn about someone was to know his mother.

The older woman led them to a cramped space Kelly guessed acted as the living room.

"Excuse the mess," the woman said.

That was an understatement. A large sofa and two chairs surrounding a coffee table took up half the narrow trailer. Pictures, books, piled newspapers, and assorted junk made her place look like a yard sale gone bad. And it smelled like the trash needed to be taken out.

"What do you want to know about Lilly?" the woman said as she plopped down on one of the worn chairs. "Sit, please."

They did as she directed. "For starters, how long has she been gone?" Kelly asked, half wondering if Derek intended for her to do the entire interview.

She shrugged. "I'm not her keeper. We don't talk much, but if I had to guess, I'd say a few months."

That must have taken some cash. "Do you know where she went?"

"Nope, but she's always disappearing. No wonder the front of her place is nothing but a pile of dirt. I got to say the inside is neat as a pin. Go figure."

The neighbor would do well to follow in Mrs. Bladen's footsteps. "I didn't catch your name," Derek said.

"Madeline Cohen."

Derek stuck out his hand and introduced himself. The handshake was brief.

"Lilly's son, Justin, is engaged to my sister," he said with a cheerfulness Kelly never remembered hearing before.

"I told you, she don't have no son. Maybe you got the wrong Lilly Bladen."

"Okay, maybe we do, but can you tell us a little about your neighbor?" Derek's voice came out so gentle, Kelly had to strain to hear him.

"Well," Madeline began. "She's a strange one, if you know what I mean."

This was the second time someone had used that phrase. Kelly leaned forward thinking the woman might respond better to her questions. "Could you be more specific?"

"She belongs to this group. I'm not sure exactly what they do or what they're called, but the best I can figure, it has something to do with purifying the world."

Mrs. Wolfendon had been right.

"Purifying the world?" Derek said just as Kelly opened her mouth to ask the same question.

"Well, you know, like Hitler tried to do." Madeline's lips pressed together so hard they turned white.

Given Madeline's last name was Cohen, Kelly wondered if Lilly and she didn't see eye to eye because of religious differences.

"Do you know where I could contact someone from this organization?" Derek asked.

Madeline's hand raced to her chest. "Of course not. I don't want to know anything about them." She pressed her hands on the sofa and stood. "Now if you'll excuse me, I have work to do."

Hopefully, the work included cleaning. *Kelly Lynn. That's mean.* Too bad. She wasn't in a good mood. Derek stood up and Kelly followed.

He placed his card on the table. "If you see Lilly Bladen, could you give me a call?"

Madeline cocked a brow. "Is she in some sort of trouble?"

"No, she's not."

"Oh." The woman sounded disappointed.

Derek grabbed Kelly's hand and practically dragged her out of the trailer. The moment they were out of earshot, she took a deep breath to clear her head.

"That didn't go very well, did it?" she asked.

"Never does in an investigation."

She looked to the clear sky. "We've got a lot of daylight left. What's next?"

"We find this white supremacist cult."

# CHAPTER NINETEEN

DEREK DISCONNECTED as he pulled up to the stoplight, his mind racing faster than the engine.

"What did Mariani say?" Kelly asked.

He didn't feel right blurting out his disappointment, but getting this mess off his chest might do him a world of good. Derek needed to share—wanted to share, actually. He hoped like hell he wasn't creating more problems between them by telling her.

"The white supremacist group Lilly Bladen supposedly belonged to no longer exists, or so Mariani believes." He glanced over at her and then the wheel. "Damn it. We were so close. If only I could have talked to Justin's mom, I might have figured out why he freaked and killed Rayne."

"Aren't you jumping to conclusions?"

He wasn't in the mood to address her accusation. It was easier to avoid the issue than deal with it. "Mariani did say one of the leaders of the group was a guy by the name of Elton McDermitt."

"Was? As in dead was?"

A horn blared behind him. Green light meant go. Derek pressed too hard on the gas pedal, and Kelly slammed back against the headrest.

"Sorry." Too bad his frustration didn't make his apology sound sincere.

She brushed the hair from her face. "Don't try to stall, Derek Benally. You can't fool me."

He never could, so why did he try? Shit, he didn't know. "Okay. To answer your question, no, the guy's not dead, only the group is, or they've gone underground."

"Time out. Aren't we here to find Justin?"

"Yes."

Derek turned left onto what might be mistaken for the main road. Though in this town, nothing looked particularly main about it. When his stomach grumbled, he decided the hunt could wait.

"Then how does unearthing all this stuff about his mom help?" she asked.

He gave up. "We find the group, we find his mom, who hopefully will lead us to Justin."

Kelly leaned her head back against the seat, looking exhausted. He never should have let her come, but he was weak around her, way too weak.

"Are you planning to drive up to this pervert's house and ask if he belonged, or belongs, to some kind of Nazi skinhead group? And then ask where Lilly Bladen is?"

Derek glanced over at her and smiled for the first time in days. Or was it weeks? For a second, she sounded seventeen again, asking sweet, innocent questions. "In this case, I don't think the direct approach will work. Mariani told me about a bar where some of the more self-righteous people hang out, if you get my drift. I'm hoping to get some background on this guy."

"And you want us to go where they'd just as soon run over an animal or kill a person of color than change their clothes?"

The hint of fear in her tone made him feel guilty. Not that he blamed her, but did she think he'd actually take her someplace unsafe?

He searched the strip mall they were passing, looking for a food joint. He'd even take fast food if the place had a McDonalds.

"I want to get a bite to eat first, and then find a room for the night.

While you're snuggled in the bed watching TV, *I'll* go to Dave's Place and see what I can learn."

Derek kept watch for a place to eat while he waited for her wave of anger to hit.

"Not on your life," Kelly said right on cue, sitting up straight. "We're in this together in case you've forgotten. Where you go, I go. Besides, you don't exactly look all-American." She took a deep breath. "If you walk into a bar where people only like lily-white people, no pun intended, they might beat the crap out of you." She rushed on before he could set her straight. "Those blue eyes may fool some people, but your dark skin won't be mistaken for the English gentry."

He bristled. "Few people mistake me for being Native American. I just look tan, not dark-skinned, as you say. Remember, I'm part Irish."

"Regardless, you'll look less out of place if I'm along."

"We'll see." Not on his life. "Hey, there's a Denny's. I can't believe this town even has a chain restaurant."

"You act as though you've never been to one before."

His initial enthusiasm had been faked for her sake, but then nostalgia bit him. "Don't you remember how the whole football team and their dates took up most of the restaurant on Saturday nights?" Good times. Boy, had his life changed.

"Of course," Kelly said.

Why did she sound so sad? Was she thinking of how much fun they used to have? Or did she regret wasting time with him when she could have been with a different crowd?

He shook his head to rid his mind of past mistakes and pulled into the mostly empty restaurant lot. No doubt about it. He shouldn't have allowed her to come. Kelly was too much of a distraction, and Utah was turning out to be a worse place than he'd expected.

\*\*\*

Derek knocked on the door connecting their motel rooms. Given this cheap one-story had less than twenty rooms, Kelly was surprised they had what the desk clerk called a suite.

"Just a sec," she called out as she stuffed her underwear in the drawer. She twisted the lock on her side and pulled.

"I want to keep this doors unlocked," Derek said as he stepped past her. "Not that I expect anything to happen, but I want to be able to come in if you receive an unexpected visitor."

A small chill rippled through her stomach, but the trail of his after-shave helped calm her. "What do you mean an unexpected visitor?"

He walked to the window and looked out to the parking lot but didn't answer.

God, did he look good. Powerful, hot, secure. *Stop it, Kelly*. Not the time, not the place, not the circumstance. "A visitor? Who do you expect?"

"No one in particular, but word spreads in a small town. If Justin is here, he might try something." He closed the curtain and faced her. "I'm heading to the bar now."

"So soon?" She looked a mess. "Give me sec to freshen up."

"Kelly, you aren't going." His firm tone made her bristle.

"Now wait a minute. We had an agreement." Her hands seemed to plant themselves on her hips.

"*You* had an agreement. Bars like Dave's Place aren't safe for women, especially good looking women."

She should have been pleased with the compliment, but her anger overshadowed the emotion. "I am too going."

"No!"

"Yes. I'm not staying here alone. What if Justin comes and tries to kill me?" Not that she believed it, but Derek had dropped his name.

His face turned to stone and his gaze shot through her. "If you lock your door, you'll be safe."

He turned and walked out of her room. No tenderness, no apology. No nothing.

She couldn't believe it.

*So, snap out of it. Do something.*

Kelly raced to the dresser and pulled out her purse. As she shot through the front door, Derek was backing out of the parking space. She sprinted after him as he eased down the road and shook her hand in the air. Dumb jerk didn't even slow down. Of course, he might not have seen her.

Shoulders sagging, she trudged back to the room—to think, to plan, and to plot.

\*\*\*

"Yes?"

"You told me to call you if anyone showed up asking questions?" the informant said.

"Who came?"

"There were two of them. A real tall guy, kind of dark skinned, built –"

"Derek Benally. He's a cop from Tampa. And the other one?"

"A hot little number. Red curly hair and a bod ready for action."

"That would be Kelly Rutland. Dr. Kelly Rutland. Here's what I want you to do."

"As long as I get to sample her when I'm done, I'll do what you say."

"Suit yourself."

The bitch needed to suffer, to realize that stirring up old messes would have dire consequences.

\*\*\*

Kelly was tired of waiting around. The TV was mostly static, and the stations that came in clear held no interest for her. And then there was the smell. The place was a dump. Between the smoke and mildew, she was convinced she'd have a full-blown sinus infection by morning.

What was taking Derek so long? How long did it take to ask a few questions? She was no psychic, but the creepy feeling that had invaded her body about an hour ago wouldn't go away.

She didn't know where the bar was, but given the size of the town, it couldn't be that far away. Derek was either lying in a ditch with a bloodied face or enjoying himself, playing pool.

In either case, she couldn't just sit and twiddle her thumbs any longer. Though she wasn't a trained professional, she had her ways of extracting information. Someone had to know something about Justin Bladen.

Headlights flashed in her motel window, and she pulled open the shades and spotted the yellow cab she'd called. She checked the mirror once more. The fairly low cut top gave a hint of cleavage, but wasn't so low as to invite disaster.

With her purse slung over her shoulder, she stepped outside, and cool, clean air filled her lungs.

A quick burst of indecision grabbed her. Was this stupid? No, came the answer roaring back. She planned to honor her promise to Derek to stay out of trouble. If she found him safe, she'd turn around and return to the motel. That's all. No heroics on her part.

"Where to?" the cab driver asked as she slid into the back seat.

"Dave's Place."

He glanced into the rear view mirror and raised a brow. "You sure? You ever been there?"

She inhaled to steel her nerves. What smelled like beer assaulted her nose.

"Lady?" the cabbie asked again.

If she stayed, she'd become more agitated. It would be better to check out the place and learn if Derek needed her. "No I haven't, but I'm meeting a friend there."

He shrugged. "It's your dollar."

The trip took less than ten minutes, which was almost close enough to have walked. But she wouldn't have chanced it—not at night in a strange, little town with more motorcycles than cars. And with Justin possibly out to get her.

"Do you want me to wait?" he asked in a bored tone.

"If you wouldn't mind." Kelly glanced at the man's license when she opened the door. John Miller.

She got out and handed John Miller the fare. "This shouldn't take long."

Motorcycles littered the dirt packed parking lot along with a lot of pickups. A brisk breeze rushed past her, and Kelly rubbed her arms to ward off goose bumps.

Off to the side of the drinking establishment sat their rental car, and a quick shot of relief surged through her. Thank goodness Derek hadn't left—or been chased out of town.

An overhead light, mounted above the door, was aimed straight at her, forcing her to shield her eyes from the glare. Atop the roof a blue neon sign announced Dave's Place, except the P and L weren't lit so it read, Dave's ace.

Noise masquerading as country music shook the small wooden structure. Taking a deep breath, Kelly marched toward the door with one hand in her pocket, grasping a small tube of mace.

As she took a step inside, smoke blasted her. The stench of beer was so strong she almost gagged, but Kelly refrained from slapping a hand over her nose. Whoa. Wall-to-wall bodies either gyrated to the music in the middle of the dance floor or were crammed into little booths or onto stools. Peanut shells crunched under her feet as she moved further inside.

"Howdy," said a scruffy-looking, chinless man with coffee-stained teeth. Hands in his pockets, he materialized in front of her, standing too close for comfort.

Kelly stopped inhaling until the smell of his breath dissipated. She took a step backward. "Maybe you can help me. I'm looking for my husband. He's a real big guy."

His eyes widened. "You married?"

Could she have a husband without being married? Maybe he thought she meant an ex-husband. "Yes."

"Bald guy?"

"Yes, again."

"He's dancin' with Nancy." Chinless pointed to a section of the room that disappeared behind the bar.

"Thank you."

Dancing with Nancy? Kelly wanted to rush over and grab Derek, but her legs turned heavy as lead. After taking a deep breath, and not choking, she pushed her way through a cast of thousands until she could see Derek and a petite blonde looking up adoringly at him.

Men grabbed at Kelly and whistled as she made her way toward the side of the bar. She ignored all of them, her focus solely on the man she'd come half across the country with.

Derek whirled Nancy around and smiled down at his partner. Smiled. Like he wanted her. And this would get them closer to finding her sister's killer, how?

Furious, Kelly spun around to flee. The music stopped for a mere second before changing to the Billy Cyrus song, "Some Gave All." She liked some country songs, but not enough to stop and listen. Almost to the door, a hand reached up and grabbed her arm.

"Hey, sweetie, what's the hurry?"

Kelly looked down and had a hard time distinguishing between the carved design on the table and the man's tattoos. "I think I'm going to be sick."

He let go quicker than if a snake had bitten him. Wimp. Keeping her gaze focused on the front door, she raced outside. No one stopped her this time.

Thankfully, Mr. Miller was still in his cab. Windows down, he was smoking up a storm. She jumped in the back seat and nearly gagged from the tobacco's disgusting odor. "Take me back to the motel."

"Your guy's not there?"

"No."

Kelly's mind spun. Furious at Derek, she wanted to strangle him. He'd come here to do a job, and he'd ended up having a little fling with a local floozy. Good thing he meant nothing to her or she'd be really hurt.

After paying the cab fare, Kelly jumped out when they reached the hotel. John Miller took off so fast gravel kicked up from his tires and nailed her in the legs. "Hey, watch it, jerk face!" she shouted.

She didn't care if she woke up the whole place. Stupid Silverton. Nothing was working out as planned.

As Kelly strode toward her room, she fumbled for her key in her purse. Why the hell had Derek put the thought into her head that someone might come after her? Now she'd never sleep.

Kelly opened the door into pure darkness and froze. Could someone have gotten inside and was waiting for her? Nonsense. Stuff like that only happened in movies, right?

Not wanting to be labeled too-stupid-to-live, she stayed in the doorframe, ready to bolt as she ran her hand along the side of the door, not recalling if the lone light on the nightstand had a wall switch.

She couldn't find one. Damn.

She listened for breathing or any movement inside the room. Only the hum of the lights outside her door filled the silence.

*Stop being paranoid. You're safe.*

Kelly crept inside the room, leaving the door ajar where the light from the walkway spilled into the room. Careful not to knock into the bed, she fumbled for the light switch on the lamp. Click. The yellowed light shone brighter than a beacon, and Kelly's tight muscles relaxed.

Whoa. The bed was turned down and a bottle of wine sat next to a plastic glass on the nightstand. Now that was a surprise.

Exhaling loudly, Kelly rushed back to the door and locked it. She twisted the deadbolt, and as an added measure, secured the door with the chain.

Safe at last, she slumped against the door.

What a minute. This dump had maid service at night? Not likely. And where had the wine come from?

She stepped over to the nightstand where a note sat neatly folded next to the bottle.

She picked up the heavy stock card and read it. "Enjoy—Derek."

Perhaps he'd been guilty at leaving her in the room all night, prompting him to have the bottle delivered. The note wasn't in his handwriting, but unless he'd gone to a wine shop first and signed it, it wouldn't be. When had he had the time to order the bottle?

Was it from Dave's Place? Maybe. He probably paid someone to deliver it. The clerk in the office would have let a local into her room.

Good. With a logical explanation in hand, she plopped down on the bed, ready to relax.

What better way to calm her nerves than with a glass of wine? No use waiting for Derek to come back. He was probably having too much fun with Nancy, or Ninnie, or whatever her name was. Had he forgotten they were here to find the white supremacist guy? And Justin?

Kelly shucked off her shoes and clothes, pulled on her nightgown and crawled into bed. Tomorrow morning she'd shower to get rid of the bar smoke that clung to her skin. Right now, all she wanted to do was relax. She'd find some comedy on TV and put Justin, Derek, and what's her name out of her mind.

She flipped on the television. No surprise the reception sucked. She poured some wine and toasted to a good outcome of the trip.

✳✳✳

"Come on, sweetie, one more dance." Nancy leaned closer to his ear.

Derek had a headache from the loud music and the smell of B.O. "I've got to go." Derek tried to pull her arms from around his waist, but Nancy seemed determined to keep him in her grasp. "It's getting late, but I'm going to see you tomorrow, right?"

She thrust out her bottom lip and pressed her crotch to his. Irritation snaked through him as he moved out of reach. Now, if Kelly were standing in front of him that would be a different story.

"Yes, but when we're at Granddaddy's, we have to behave. He doesn't believe people should express their emotional side in public, if you get my drift." She lifted her hand to his cheek. Before her finger reached its destination, Derek grabbed her hand.

"Tomorrow at seven."

She pulled her arm down, attempting to look coy. He stepped back and patted his front pocket where he'd placed the directions to her grandfather's house. "Got the directions right here."

"Do ya think afterwards we can go back to my place?"

Not in this lifetime he wanted to say, but of course, he didn't. "We'll see."

She smiled. "So you're the hard-to-get type, huh?"

Derek smiled and winked. His father always did claim he could make a fortune at poker. With a slow, even stride, he left the sleazy bar.

He'd heard enough racial slurs to last a lifetime. Fortunately, none seemed to have been aimed at him.

There was a nip in the air, but without the dampness he was accustomed to in Tampa, the coolness helped rejuvenate rather than chill.

The rental car started without a hitch, and he was thankful no one had sabotaged the engine. That meant he'd fooled everyone inside in no small part due to Nancy's acceptance. Once she'd latched onto him, the elbow jabs had stopped.

He prayed when he returned to the hotel, Kelly would be safe. And asleep.

Derek pulled up to the motel and ducked into his room, needing a shower. Bad. The smoke had dug deep into his pores. Two men had spilled beer on him, and it had been no an accident either. Until he'd convinced Nancy to dance with him, he'd received nothing less than cold stares. Outsiders were not welcome in Silverton. That much they'd made clear.

He closed the bathroom door, just in case Kelly heard him come in and wanted to hear every detail of his evening.

No use worrying her now about what he'd uncovered.

After he showered, he slipped into bed, hoping for a good night's sleep, forcing his mind to relax. Unfortunately, visions of Kelly intruded. Damn. He took long, slow breaths, counting backward, hoping to stop the erotic dreams.

Frustrated he couldn't sleep, Derek tried to sit up, but some white light blinded him, and horses galloped beside him. Heat, heavier than a wet blanket, sat on his shoulders. Derek pulled on the reins to stop the jarring movement. What the fuck was going on? He'd been given no warning this time before the spirit guides sucked him to a place he didn't want to go.

"Keep going. We shall rest soon," came a strong, powerful voice next to him.

Derek looked over. The same Chief from before rode by his side. "Where are we going?" he asked, knowing full well he wouldn't get a satisfactory answer.

No surprise, the chief remained silent. Derek's throat was parched and his skin prickled from the sun beating down on his unprotected skin. He studied the landscape, hoping for some clues as to the time and place.

An abandoned, rusted car sat next to two small trees. Delighted he'd narrowed down the century, Derek relaxed into the saddle. Suddenly, a covered wagon edged over a hill in the distance. Huh?

Some type of Native American village appeared out of the blue, sheltered under a copse of trees, where none had been before. This dream made no sense.

His horse halted, nearly throwing Derek to the ground again, and anger rushed up his gut. "What's going on?" he asked.

"Get down."

# CHAPTER TWENTY

Miffed and anxious, Derek dismounted, understanding that now wasn't the time to piss off the Chief.

Derek ran his hands down soft, hand pounded animal skin, and then looked down and what he was wearing. When the hell had he changed into tribal dress? And how had his guides known where he was or how to contact him when he hadn't even brought his sage to Utah?

"Come."

There was too much to think about. Right now he needed to figure out what was going on. The retreating back of his tormentor forced Derek to move his feet.

Finally he'd get to see what all these trips were about.

The rocky ground bit into his thin moccasins, but he ignored the discomfort. A tall bald man in blue jeans wearing the same shirt Derek had worn to Dave's Place stood with his back to the village. The man didn't move when a white man kicked one of the young native boys. When Derek tried to rush forward, an arm shot out and stopped him.

"Watch and learn."

Watch and learn what? "Do something," Derek shouted to the bald man, then glared at the chief.

"He can't hear or see you."

"Is that me?" Though how the bald man who dressed like him could actually be him, he didn't know.

"Have patience."

"What is this place?" Sweat dripped down his back and bugs nipped at his bare arms. This dream felt real enough.

"It is who you are."

Anger walloped him in the gut, but he tamped down the urge to fight. "What's that supposed to mean?"

"Your prejudices have become your guide. You cannot move on until you free yourself."

Free himself? What bullshit. "I'm not prejudiced."

As Derek waited for an explanation that made sense, the scene disappeared and his body returned to the soft mattress of his bed, cushioning his body. Damn it. Just when he was on the precipice of learning something important, the spirit guides split.

Derek flicked on the light by the nightstand, hoping for a clue, but nothing in the room had changed, other than the fact the clock showed he'd lost an hour.

He checked his clothing, finding no moccasins and no buckskin, only good old-fashioned boxers. Twenty-first century stuff.

His arm itched where several welts dotted his arms.

"Damn. Mosquitoes."

He shot out of bed to check to check if he'd left the window open. The insects must have gotten in somehow or else the sheets were infested.

The blur between reality and his dreams was starting to eat at him. Had his imagination caused the images? Now he wasn't so sure.

He could use a dose of the real world. Derek glanced at the closed door between his room and Kelly's. Sound from her television seemed louder, as though she hadn't changed the volume when a new show had come on.

Derek headed over to check on her, to see her, to know something in his life was tangible.

As slowly as possible, Derek opened the door, and for once it didn't squeak. Lights on, Kelly was still. Her eyes were closed, and she looked like an angel, her red glossy hair rippling across the white pillowcase. A bottle of wine sat next to her bed on the nightstand.

He took a step closer. The bottle was nearly full. Hmm. She hadn't had much to drink.

Hey. How had a bottle of the alcohol gotten there? The room didn't have a mini bar. Had she ordered it? From where? Silverton must be more sophisticated than he'd thought.

At least no danger had come to her while he'd been at Dave's. He slipped back into his room, determined to get some sleep.

***

"Kelly?" Derek shook her shoulder but received no response.

A strong shot of light speared through the partially closed drapes. She hadn't responded to his pounding on the door either.

Thinking a blast of light would rouse her, he threw open the curtains to flood the room, and dust motes swam in the air. He coughed from the intense particle storm. She moaned and his relief surprised him.

He expected her to open her eyes, only she didn't. Her breaths came in shorts puffs, but the steady rise and fall of her chest convinced him she was okay. Just in case, he placed a palm on her forehead, and the heat nearly singed his skin.

Derek dropped down onto the bed and grabbed her hand.

"Kelly, can you hear me?" He waited a moment. "Squeeze my hand if you can hear me."

No response.

Fear rushed into every vein. Derek whipped out his phone and called 9-1-1.

***

"Mr. Benally?"

Derek looked up from the magazine. A tired looking doctor with the Salt Lake City Hospital insignia partially covered by his nameplate with kind eyes approached. The doc was small in stature—at least compared to him and was dressed in starched whites. He flipped through his charts before making eye contact.

"How is she?" Derek closed the magazine, his mouth dry. He hadn't finished reading even one article in the three hours he'd been waiting to hear of Kelly's progress. He looked down at his nails. Damn. His fingernails were bitten to the quick, but Derek didn't remember chewing them. He never bit his nails.

The doctor sat down next to him in the nearly empty waiting room. "She's going to be fine."

His shoulders sagged as he let out a long held breath. "That's great. What happened to her?"

"She was poisoned with Ketamine. Well, maybe poison isn't the right word."

"As in Special-K?"

"Yes, I see you've heard of it. Kids use it to get high. In small doses, it can be as benign as nitrous oxide, but Kelly had over 100 mg in her system. If she'd had more than one glass of wine, the combination could have killed her."

A shudder raced through him. The thought of losing Kelly almost made him fold. "I don't know where she got the wine," he said more to himself.

"When your young woman is more oriented, we'll ask her. She's still groggy from the drug."

"May I see her?"

He hesitated. "Yes, but only for a little while. I don't want to tire her."

"Of course not."

Derek followed the doctor into Kelly's room, anxiety racing through him. Her red hair was matted with sweat, and dark shadows under her closed eyes made her appear as if she'd seen death and not yet fully returned.

"I'll be back to check on her," the doctor said as he headed out.

"Thanks, Doc." Derek pulled up the heavy, padded chair next to the bed and took Kelly's hand in his. Her fine fingers lay limp in his palm.

"Kelly?" His voice cracked. If anything happened to her... *Don't even go there.*

Her eyelids fluttered. Two of her fingers pressed down on his palm.

A slow fury made its way up his body. He wouldn't leave here until he found out who'd harmed Kelly. Obviously, they'd touched a nerve by coming to Utah.

Was this a signal from someone in the bar to beware or had leaving Tampa for Salt Lake set off the alarm?

She cleared her throat. "Derek?" Her faint voice jerked his attention back to her face, and he had to bend down hear her.

"I'm here." Derek wound one of her red curls around his finger. Bound together, as one. He let the thought slip away like a petal floating on a lake.

She opened her eyes and looked around. "I'm in a hospital? What happened?"

"You ingested Ketamine."

"Ketamine? How?" She closed her eyes for a moment then opened them. "Oh my God. I thought the wine tasted funny." She licked her cracked lips. "Someone must have tampered with the bottle."

At least one piece of the puzzle was solved. "I'll have Mariani do a lab sample."

"I do appreciate you sending it though."

She wasn't making any sense. "What are you talking about? I didn't order any wine."

"But the note said you sent the bottle."

A chill raced down his spine and grabbed his gut. "Kelly, I had nothing to do with the wine. What exactly did the note say?"

"From Derek. It wasn't in your handwriting, but I figured you'd called it in, or something." Her eyes closed for a moment. He shouldn't push her, but he needed answers.

"I didn't send anything. Are you sure it said my name?"

Her eyelids fluttered open. "Yes. I thought it was sweet. I only had one glass though. I must have fallen asleep right away."

His mind went into cop mode. It was easier than thinking Kelly had almost died. "Who delivered the wine?"

"It was in my room when I returned."

A fresh wave of anger hit so hard it stunned him. "What do you mean when you returned? Where did you go?" He hadn't meant to yell, but where Kelly was concerned, he lacked restraint.

"I went to find you at... at Dave's Place." She swallowed hard.

"You went to Dave's Place?"

Her eyelids fluttered. "Why are you repeating everything? And stop shouting. It hurts my head, which is already throbbing." She dragged her hands over her eyes, and then pressed the tips of her fingers to her temples.

Compassion swamped him. "I'm sorry. Now start from the beginning. Tell me everything."

Derek tried not to lose his cool when she explained why she'd gone to the bar. It took her several minutes to get the whole story out, and he had to force himself not to interrupt.

"You see I had a good reason to go," she said with a smile that no doubt took what was left of her waning energy.

"The ends don't justify the means. You disobeyed a direct order."

She groaned. "I'm not a police officer. I don't take orders from you." She licked her lips, looking like she could use a drink.

He didn't want to fight. "Can't you see something bad might have happened to you at the bar? Those men are the kind who take what they want and don't ask for permission." He wanted to shake her, hold her, comfort her.

"Something bad did happen to me. But you. You got to take what you wanted. I saw you dancing with that girl and having a good old time."

"Nancy? Blonde, short, kind of cute."

"Is that her name?"

Derek poured her a cup of water and handed it to her. She drank most of the liquid. Then it dawned on him. "You're jealous."

She set the Styrofoam cup on the side table. "Jealous? Are you kidding?"

"Truth?"

He'd heard that edgy tone in her voice only once before when he'd tossed the winning football to Brianna Perkins instead of to her their senior year. Maybe someday he'd tell her it was for Brianna's little brother who was recovering from a major illness and not for Brianna.

She rubbed her stomach. "Okay, maybe a little. But only at first. You were having fun, and I was stuck in a motel room in a strange town."

"Is that it?" Sympathy for her plight got the best of him. "The woman you saw me with was Elton McDermitt's granddaughter."

She took another sip of water. "Who's Elton McDermitt?"

Maybe the drug had affected her more than he thought. He wondered if he should even answer. Knowing her stubborn streak, Kelly might find a way to follow him when he went to the old man's house for dinner.

"Someone who might know where to find Lilly Bladen."

Her gaze shot to the left. "McDermitt. Isn't he the guy Mariani said might be linked to the white supremacist group?"

Cat's out. "Yes. In fact, I have a meeting with him tonight."

"Really?" She tried to sit up but fell back down, letting out a long breath. "Let's hope the doctor releases me so I can meet him too."

Damn. He couldn't lie. "I have to go alone. I finagled a dinner date with ole granddad and Nancy. She has supper with him every Sunday. I'm hoping to pry information out of him about Lilly and Justin."

Her face fell. "I guess my presence won't help the situation."

"No. But Kelly, you'll be safer here." Or so he hoped. He rubbed her hand, and she seemed to perk up. "Someone tried to murder you once. They may try again." Not wanting to scare her, he kept his voice as soft as he could, but the stubborn woman needed a dose of reality.

She looked up at him, fear in her eyes. "You think so?" Her tone came out sarcastic.

*Way to go, Benally.* He should have kept his trap shut. "You and I have been asking questions, and we've obviously struck some kind of nerve here."

"More like a vein, but why would someone poison me? I'm nobody."

Not to him she wasn't. She was more important than he cared to admit. "Perhaps to get at me. Someone doesn't like us snooping." He glanced at his watch. "I want to stop at the Sheriff's office back in Silverton to report the attempted murder before I meet Nancy at her grandfather's."

She shivered. "Attempted murder sounds so ominous.'"

"It is what it is."

"Will you stop by after your big dinner?"

"It's a promise. But McDermitt lives back in Silverton. The commute between Salt Lake and there will take me over an hour."

"Oh."

"Why?"

"Having someone to talk to takes my mind off this wicked headache."

Now he felt bad leaving her, but he had to make contact with the one person who could help them. "Can't the doctors give you anything for it?"

"Not with this drug still in my system."

Kelly looked so forlorn, he was tempted to lean over and kiss her, but he wouldn't. Right now, they needed all their senses focused on finding Justin Bladen.

\*\*\*

Nancy was waiting by her car when Derek drove up to her grandfather's home. He was happy she'd agreed to meet at him there instead of having to pick her up.

She smiled, and while he hated to deceive her, he had a job to do. Kelly needed protecting, and he needed answers.

Nancy wrapped an arm around his waist when he stepped up next to her. Her possessiveness made him uncomfortable, but he couldn't afford to anger off.

"Let's not keep your grandfather waiting," Derek said, hoping she took the hint.

"Fine."

McDermitt didn't stand when Nancy and he came in. The blanket over his legs implied he might be infirmed.

Instead, he smiled and waved them both in. "Nancy told me she'd met a nice young man," he said to Derek as they shook hands.

"Hi, Granddaddy," Nancy said in a cheerful voice.

No hug, no kiss, just a friendly hello. Maybe the old man wasn't the fuzzy type.

Derek wasn't sure what a white supremacist should look like, but this wasn't it. Perhaps Mariani's intel had been wrong. Frail and nearly bald, Elton McDermitt looked like someone's kindly grandfather. At least looking like he did, he could move in any circle and no one would suspect his bigotry.

"Have a seat and tell me about yourself," he said, his gaze steady on Derek. Straight to the point. Derek had to respect him for that. Derek looked for some indication the old man guessed his Native American heritage but found none.

Nancy and he sat next to each other on a plaid sofa across from McDermitt's wooden chair. Telling the truth, peppered with a few lies, was easier to navigate than out-and-out lies. "I'm in town to speak with Lilly Bladen."

McDermitt cocked a thinning, gray brow. "Is that so?" The old man picked up a cigar and lit it, his face suddenly shuttered. "You don't mind if I smoke, do you? So many people today claim they're allergic to it. In truth, they want to flaunt they've stopped smoking."

"No problem." It was his house.

"So why do you want to see Lilly?"

Derek noted the use of her first name. "My sister is engaged to her son. Justin's been living in Florida for the last five years, and my sister wants his mom to come to the wedding, but Mrs. Bladen won't answer Justin's phone calls. Guess they've been estranged for a while." He watched McDermitt to see if he knew of Rayne's death, but he gave no indication. Good. He'd bought the story. Too bad his own gut twisted with grief at her memory.

"Justin's engaged to be married? Hmm. Lilly never mentioned it. Or else she didn't know."

Either he was familiar with the family, or McDermitt knew

everyone in the small town. "Given Mrs. Bladen will be my sister's mother-in-law, I said I'd try to convince her to break the estrangement. I was planning on doing a little gambling in Las Vegas and Silverton wasn't too far out of the way."

The old man took a few puffs then set down his cigar, his eyes searching the floor. "You must love your sister."

Derek swallowed hard. "I do."

McDermitt's eyes slightly glazed over. "Justin's getting married. Hmm. Why, I haven't seen that boy in I don't know how long. Were you successful in convincing Lilly to make the trip?"

At least someone was willing to admit she had a son. "I stopped by her place, but apparently she's out of town. I know I should have called before I came, but I didn't want to tip my hand."

At the mention of a hand, Nancy slid hers onto his thigh and looked up at Derek. "I remember Justin." She too had that dreamy quality to her face. "Of course, he was three years older than me." She turned back to her grandfather. "Don't you remember when he came over that one time for the meeting? He was so gung-ho."

It was as though a wall dropped in front of the old man. "No."

"Sir, do you know how I might contact Mrs. Bladen?"

As if the old man remembered he was in the company of a stranger, he smiled. "I'd like to help, but I haven't a clue. Once my legs gave out, I stopped going out." He turned to Nancy. "How about heating up the dinner Mrs. Johnson cooked for us?"

"Sure." She squeezed his thigh. "Why don't you help me in the kitchen?"

He couldn't exactly say no and not appear rude. There'd be time during dinner to question McDermitt about the elusive Bladen family.

Thirty minutes later, the three on them were seated around an oval, lace covered dining table. If the man did head a racist group, he knew how to act down-to-earth.

Once the food was passed around, McDermitt stared at Derek as he chewed. "So what nationality are you?"

"Irish," Derek said without hesitation. His mother had been Irish, and her mom British. Hence the blue eyes. He left out his father's heritage.

"Hmm. Rayne doesn't sound like an Irish name."

Because it wasn't. "It's Celtic. She was named after some ancestor." Weak, but it was the best he could do on a moment's notice.

"You look a little dark for Irish."

"Granddad, you don't have to put him through the inquisition. He's a visitor for God's sake."

Apparently, all of Nancy's dates had to be checked out.

"I'm from Florida. We get lots of sunshine there." Not that he had time to sunbath or had the inclination.

"Which part?"

"Woodlands, Florida." Derek doubted the town existed, which would slow McDermitt's research. It might even delay the old man running him out of town once he found out about his police background.

"Is that near Miami or Fort Lauderdale?"

"Tampa."

"Oh. Sorry I had to ask, but we have a lot of Navajos around here. You can't be too careful." He wagged a finger. "Watch out for them. They cheat and steal. They'll kill you just as soon as talk to you."

Derek clenched his fists to keep from jumping up and beating the shit out of the guy. Old or not, he wouldn't mind giving him what he deserved, but he held in his temper.

The bigot glanced at Nancy. "Why don't you clear the table and bring out the dessert that Mrs. Leopold made just for you."

"Thanks." Nancy sashayed her way into the kitchen. Derek turned back to McDermitt. Trying not to grit his teeth, he addressed the issue of the Navajos. "We've got the same problem in Florida. Only we have the Seminoles. Useless race. I can't believe we gave them land. They even had the nerve to buy the Casino Royale franchise."

McDermitt's eyes sparkled at the racial slur. "What do you do for a living?"

"I teach."

"Teach? That's a noble profession. You know, Silverton could use more good teachers. I think you'd like it here, except for the Indians, that is. We do have an exclusive private school though." McDermitt's gaze studied him.

"I'm happy in Florida."

The old man stroked his chin. "In any case, I'd like you to meet some friends of mine. I think they might be able to convince you this is a good place to raise a family." He shot a glance at Nancy as she entered with a pumpkin pie.

"Granddad, he just arrived. Besides, he's not here to stay so stop trying to control my life. Or his."

McDermitt smiled, the gentle, kind smile an elder bestowed on an ignorant child. "This has nothing to do with you, dear. I think this nice young man should spend a few days checking out our town. Besides, it will give me time to ask around about when Lilly might be coming back."

Derek nearly groaned. "You don't have to go to all the trouble. I can stop back on my way home." He yawned before glancing at his watch. "I really should be going."

"But you haven't eaten your pie," Nancy protested.

Derek stood and held out his hand to her grandfather. "Nice meeting you, sir." He nearly choked on the last word. "I'm staying at—"

"Rustin's motel," the old man answered with arrogance.

# CHAPTER TWENTY-ONE

A SINKING feeling shot down Derek's throat and landed in the pit of his stomach. If McDermitt knew where he and Kelly were staying, could he be responsible for harming her? "How did you—?"

"There's only one motel in town."

Derek slowly expelled his breath, and then smiled—for real this time. He turned to Nancy. "I guess I'll be seeing you around."

"I'll walk you out." Her lip jutted out, making her look twelve instead of twenty-six.

Thank goodness they'd driven separately. Past nine, he wanted to stop at the hospital before Kelly fell asleep. He'd promised her.

Nancy slipped her hands around his waist, and he almost choked on her heavy perfume. "Do you want to come back to my place?" she asked.

Her invitation held a lot of promise. Too bad he wasn't interested. "Some other time." He couldn't afford to make her nervous or suspicious.

She frowned. "Tomorrow night at Dave's is Ladies Night. I'll be there." She dragged a finger down his chest. "Stop on by."

Part for show and part because she expected it, Derek leaned down and placed a chaste kiss on her lips. "Tomorrow then."

He yanked open his door and jumped in the car. He couldn't wait to get away from the negative energy that permeated the house. Hell, he wouldn't have been surprised if a burning cross sprang up on the front lawn. The whole area gave him the creeps.

He was also worried sick about Kelly. If only he knew Justin Bladen's whereabouts he'd feel a hell of a lot better.

For the next hour, he kept an eye on the rear view mirror to make sure no one followed him. Close to Silverton, he spotted a convenience store and pulled in. His muscles relaxed for a moment when he spotted no other cars in the lot.

Inside, he strode up and down each aisle looking for something to cheer up Kelly. Nothing but cleaning supplies, car accessories, and outdated cookies lined the shelves. He grabbed a soda and headed to the cash register. A fake rose, its petal covered in a layer of dust, sat in a plastic tube. Tacky, sure, but he hoped the phrase: It's the thought that counts, would apply.

A pimply teenager with a tattoo on his shoulder rang him up. Two beefy thugs strolled in, sized him up, and then walked to the hotdog counter in the back.

Derek paid and got the hell out of there.

It was a little past ten thirty by the time he pulled into the hospital parking lot, an hour later than he'd planned. Kelly would probably be asleep, but he wanted to make sure she wasn't suffering any side effects from the drug. He'd been told persistent vomiting was common.

If the staff let him, he'd spend the night.

The corridors were mostly deserted until he made his way to the wards. Nurses scurried down the halls with purpose, and the scent of cleaning solution helped but didn't completely mask the smell of illness.

"I'm sorry, sir," a soft-spoken nurse said as she popped out of a patient's room. "Visiting hours are over."

Relatives would be allowed. "I'm visiting my wife." The word, *wife* struck a chord he hadn't expected. Being married to Kelly would be a challenge and a hell of a ride.

She shot a glance at the rose and smiled. "Oh, in that case, go ahead. Do you know her room number?"

"Yes."

Derek spot-checked the rooms with opened doors. Most patients were asleep. He didn't notice any sinister looking creep ready to do Kelly in. Best of all, he didn't see Justin Bladen.

Thankful she had a private room, he tiptoed in. A nightlight above her bed showed her beautiful sleeping form. When he moved the chair to beside her bed, he froze when his wooden chair leg creaked across the floor. Damn, the slight noise was enough to wake her.

"Sorry," Derek said, happy to see her pallor had disappeared.

"Hey. How did it go?"

"Fine." He pressed the plastic rose toward her. "It's not much, but I—"

She smiled and his heart warmed. "Thank you." Kelly pressed the button on the side rail, and her bed elevated. Derek shot to his feet and fluffed the pillow behind her. "So tell me."

How much should he tell? The truth? Or only part? The question was how much could she handle?

"If his attitude was any indication, McDermitt seemed to have been involved with hate crimes. There's no doubt in my mind he despises Native Americans of all kind. I could barely keep my lasagna down I was so mad."

"That's good." Her eyes shut, and she leaned her head back against the pillow.

"Good? There was nothing good about the man except the town's insidious nature became clearer. Did the doctor give you something to help you sleep?"

"I've had enough sleeping aids to knock me out for a...for a month."

"I'll tell you about him tomorrow."

"I'm fine. I've been forcing myself to stay awake so I could hear every—." Her lips parted slightly.

She'd fallen asleep. It was just as well. Exhaustion had nearly made him doze off at the wheel.

Derek awoke with a start. Light streamed in through the window, and he jerked forward. Whoa. He'd fallen asleep in the chair.

Kelly raised her head up from the pillow and smiled. "I think you slept more than I did."

Derek raked a hand over his stubbly head. He needed a shave. A quick glance at his watch told him she was right. "I guess I did."

A knock sounded behind him, and he turned. Kelly's doctor strode in with a clipboard in hand. "We tested the blood sample we took last night, and it looks like your body has eliminated the tranquilizer."

"Great. When can I leave?"

"As soon as you get dressed."

Excited for her, Derek stood up. "I'll wait outside."

By the time the hospital checked her out, it was close to ten.

"Are you hungry?" he asked. "I'm starving."

"Yes, but could we stop back at the motel first? I really want to shower, change, and most of all, brush my teeth."

"No problem."

Because the trip to the motel took a little over an hour, they stopped at a drive through for some coffee, and the caffeine hit the spot.

Derek kept a constant vigil on who traveled the road. As much as he expected to have a tail, no one seemed interested in them. When they arrived back at the hotel, only a few cars sprinkled the lot. The maid's cart waited outside an open door at the end of the hall. He couldn't guess if she'd finished their rooms or was working her way toward them.

"I don't have my key since it's still in my purse in the room."

"Just come through my room, Kel."

She smiled. "You haven't called me that in a long time."

A slip of the tongue. "I guess I haven't."

He opened his door and let her step in ahead of him. She halted, and he nearly ran into her.

"Ohmigod. Who would do this?" Kelly asked as she scanned the mess.

The dresser drawers were pulled out and his suitcase and clothes were dumped upside down on the floor. The bed was still unmade, implying the maid hadn't been there yet.

"Probably the same person who put the poison in your wine."

Derek flicked open his cell and called 9-1-1. He was routed to the police station a moment later.

"Mariani here."

Excellent. Derek relayed the crime.

"I'm heading out now. Don't touch anything." Derek almost threw back a retort. "Never mind," Mariani added quickly. "Force of habit. You know better than I do what not to touch."

"I won't let the maid come in and clean if that's what worrying you."

"I'm worried you'll try to find the perpetrator. Please leave the investigation to my staff."

"No problem."

Derek shoved the phone into his top pocket and turned back to Kelly. "He'll be over shortly. Don't touch anything."

"I won't. I watch enough crime shows to know what not to do." Derek couldn't help but roll his eyes. "While you're waiting for the police, I want to shower and change. I'm gross."

He could sympathize. "No can do. We have to wait for the crime lab people."

"Oh. Can I at least sit on the chair?"

Kelly looked miserable. "Sure. I'm going to speak with the maid. Stay right here."

Without waiting for her retort, he strode outside and immediately spotted the maid's cart six rooms down.

He knocked on the opened door.

"Yes?" the maid said. The pretty girl with dark skin was not much more than twenty. She looked too heavy with child to be doing grunt work, and his heart went out to her. "I'm in room 113. While I was gone, someone broke into my room and disturbed my suitcase and chest of drawers."

"Oh, I'm so sorry." Her eyes contained a world of worry, as if she'd be accused of the incident.

He waved a hand. "Relax. I know you're not responsible. Did you happen to see anyone enter my room this morning?"

"No, sir. Each day different people come and go. I'm busy working and not paying attention to each and every guest."

"I understand." He smiled. "Thank you. If you hear anyone bragging about messing up my room, could you let me know? I'll make it worth your while."

She nodded, looking more scared than happy with the new assignment.

As Derek headed back to his room, a Silverton Sheriff's Department vehicle pulled up in front of his room and Mariani slid out. That sure was quick. With him was another deputy, young, white, and thin. Derek led them inside.

Mariani whistled. "Someone was pissed." He turned to his young officer. "See if you can get prints off anything." He turned to Derek. "We'll need yours, of course, for elimination purposes." He turned to Kelly. "And yours too, Ms. Rutland."

"Sure." Derek said. "I haven't had a chance to look through my things to see what was taken."

"Give Al a sec. There will be time enough to check your possessions when he's done. So why do you think someone did this?"

"Beats me."

"You must have pissed off someone."

"Apparently," Derek said, keeping a close eye on the deputy who seemed to be doing a thorough job.

Mariani withdrew a folded sheet of paper from his front pocket. "I almost forgot. I became curious about the Novaro case and did a search on Justin Bladen. Came up with this. It's dated nine years ago." He handed the paper to Derek.

"John LaBelle, stock analyst for Kreplick & Deland, was shot to death today." Stymied how this related to Justin, he read on. "Police have Justin Bladen in custody. Shit." Derek looked up when he finished the article.

"I did a little more research," Mariani said. "They had to let Bladen go when the evidence couldn't be linked directly to him."

"What kind of evidence?"

"The police had a search warrant for his apartment. They found a shirt with LaBelle's blood on it, but Justin—"

"I know—had an airtight alibi."

"Yeah." Mariani cocked a brow. "How'd you know?"

"This isn't the first time he could prove he wasn't near a crime scene."

"Like with Novaro."

"Exactly." Derek didn't fill him in on Rayne's case.

"Looks like we need to find this Justin Bladen fellow. God help Silverton if he's here. We don't need the trouble."

"I hear ya."

The technician closed his case. "I'm finished in here. I'll check the other room now."

Kelly stood and came over to Derek. "Do you think I could shower in your bathroom now that it's been cleared?"

Before he could answer, Al returned. "I can't find the wine bottle."

"That's not possible." Derek stormed into Kelly's room. Al said something about not messing with a crime scene, but he didn't care. This was the last straw. He stood in the middle and surveyed the room, hoping the technician had missed the obvious.

Mariani strode in behind him. "Who took the bottle?"

"Damned if I know."

"Why don't you look through your things to see what else is missing." Mariani turned to Al. "Fingerprint the place anyway. Someone was in here."

# CHAPTER TWENTY-TWO

"HOW LONG WILL it take for Mariani to get the fingerprint information back?" Kelly asked.

Derek tapped his spoon on the table. "Could be weeks. He has to send the prints to Salt Lake to be processed."

"Not very efficient system, is it?"

"Processing crimes takes a long time. If only we could solve a crime in an hour like they do on CSI, life for the homicide detective would be sweet."

"Well, I hope they match the prints to someone."

"I agree." He stuffed a French fry into his mouth. "I think we should leave." Derek took a drink of his soda.

"We're not done with lunch." Though, it didn't matter. Her appetite had basically disappeared. Even the juicy hamburger in front of her didn't tempt her, but Kelly understood the need to keep up her strength.

"No, I mean leave Utah."

The fork she'd been holding dropped to the table with a loud clatter. "You can't be serious. What about finding Justin?" And learned who'd killed her sister?

"I'm not sure he's even in the state."

Now she was royally pissed. "We came all the way—"

"I know, I'm sorry."

She tossed her napkin on the table. "Well someone tried to poison me. I can't just forget about it."

"Poison isn't the signature of a man like Justin. He'd be more subtle if he wanted to harm you."

"More subtle? What? Like shoot me or run me off the road?"

Derek winced. "Bad word choice. Statistics show poison is more of a women's crime."

"A woman? You mean like Nancy?"

His brows shot downward. "No. I don't think Nancy has any interest in, or even any knowledge of you. Besides, she was with me when the wine was delivered."

"Okay. Maybe not Nancy, but I spoke with one of the men at the bar and mentioned I was there looking for my husband. Who knows who he told?"

Derek smiled. "You told the person at the bar that I was your husband?"

"Don't flatter yourself. I would have said the bar was on fire if it would have found you any sooner."

His dimples creased his cheek, and then disappeared a moment later when he looked up at her. "You were worried about me?"

Did he really think the hanged dog look would work? Okay, it kind of did. "Worried, yes," she said. "If anything had happened to you, what would I have done?" She couldn't admit how much she cared for her, needed him, lov—*Don't go there.*

"You are one of the most resourceful women I know. I'm sure you would have found a way home."

The compliment caught her off guard, and her ego jumped up a notch. Kelly took another bite of her hamburger while she composed her thoughts. When she finished chewing, she washed her food down with her iced tea. "Was there any other woman you were friendly with at the bar?"

His eyes turned steely blue. "No. I only danced with Nancy to get close to her grandfather. But what about Lilly Bladen, herself?"

It appeared as if he wasn't interested in any local color. Good. "She isn't even in town."

"Not that we know of." Derek picked up his spoon and banged it on the table.

"Can you not do that?"

"Oh, sorry. I say we let Mariani do the detective work to figure out who poisoned you. He's welcome here. We're not. I'll see about getting us on a flight tomorrow." He finished off his soda.

"That's it?" She jabbed her fork into the pile of fries on her plate. "We're leaving because you say so? Doesn't my opinion count?"

"Yes, your opinion is very important, but you saw what happened when I left you alone for a few hours."

Oh, that was rich. "Maybe they weren't after *me*, but after *you*," she said, leaning forward again. "You're one of those despised *Indians*."

"Shh. Keep your voice down." He looked around. "I don't trust people. Especially around here." Derek shoved aside his plate and its half-eaten sandwich.

She lowered her voice, making sure no one but Derek could hear. "Have you considered Mariani could be the culprit? He knew you were looking for Justin as well as for his mom. Could he have notified whoever poisoned me?"

Derek took a moment before answering. "I don't see it. He wouldn't have told us about the murder in St. Louis, nor would he have led us to Courtney Wolfendon."

Deflated, she dropped back against her seat. "You have a point. So now what?"

"I'm going to call the Tampa precinct to see if anyone has spotted Justin while we were away. I'll have Seinkievitz investigate both the Novaro murder and the one in St. Louis. If the same person committed both crimes, we might be able to bring in the FBI."

She shivered. "Do you think the person will come after us again?"

Derek didn't answer. Instead he waved to the waitress and signaled for the bill.

\*\*\*

The phone by Kelly's nightstand rang, interrupting the first pleasant dream she'd had in days. Damn. Cobwebs clouded her mind until reason intruded. Someone wanted to speak with her.

"Okay, already." Her mouth was dry.

She opened her eyes and swung her arm over to the nightstand next to her bed to turn on the light. Was the lab calling? Or was it a prank call?

Wait. She wasn't home in Tampa, but in a strange little town where they ate hate for breakfast. The cops insisted she and Derek move to two different rooms as their old rooms were still being processed, and the nightstand in her new room was on a different side.

Her hand finally connected to the switch on the base of the lamp. She sat up and flicked on the light, squinting at the sudden change in brightness. The annoying ringing made her head pound.

She picked up the receiver, swallowed, and then answered. "Hello?" She glanced at the clock. It was just past one in the morning. Something bad must have happened. Her heart pounded.

"Kelly?"

The masculine voice wasn't Derek's. "Yes?"

"I like your pink nightgown."

She glanced down to see what she was wearing. Pink fabric clung to her body. Her skin crawled. "Who is this?"

"Just someone who wants to let you know I can see-eee you. I know your ev-ery move." His voice came out breathy, like a drag queen trying to be seductive.

Her gaze shot to the window, but the drapes were closed. "You can't see me." Or could he? She looked up at the ceiling but didn't spot any hidden cameras. Well, duh, that's because the lens might be hidden.

As if the phone was a deadly virus, she slammed the receiver back onto the cradle, her hand shaking as adrenaline sped through her system. Fear coursed through her as she tried to imagine what kind of sicko would call her. And watch her. And taunt her.

The phone rang again. She jerked. No way would she talk to that creep again. She didn't want to hear his lecherous voice. Even after she pressed her hands over her ears, the sound still filtered in. The ringing wouldn't stop.

She grabbed the phone and shouted, "Why are you doing this?"

"Go home. You and your Indian lover aren't welcome here." His tone had turned deadly.

Then he hung up on her.

A car alarm right outside her window went off, jerking her gaze to the drawn curtains. She had to get out of there, but her body wouldn't respond to the move command. The sound ramped up to a siren and then died before whooping up to a screech again. The outside door in the next room squeaked opened. "Derek, is that you?" she croaked, her throat too dry to make a clear sentence.

Forcing herself to move, Kelly jumped out of bed and raced to the adjoining door. Not bothering to knock, she whipped it open. Derek's bed was empty and the door to the outside ajar. Believing the jerk who'd called had set off the alarm, she raced to the window and peeked out.

The outside lamps in between the rooms cast enough light into the parking lot to see Derek checking the area. She scanned the lot too but found no one.

Afraid the pervert could somehow see her, she closed the adjoining door, and then flung herself onto Derek's bed and covered herself, taking comfort from the heat left by his body. She'd be dammed if she let that filthy caller watch her again.

She pressed her face onto Derek's pillow, and his scent calmed her and his warm sheets comforted her.

The car siren shut off. "Thank God," she mumbled, as she rolled over.

"Kelly?"

Derek! She leaned over and turned on the lamp. Wearing nothing but his boxers, an unbuttoned shirt and sneakers, he closed and locked the door. At the sight of him, her heart did a double take at his bare chest and broad shoulders.

Her raced to her side. "What's the matter? Are you okay? Did the alarm wake you up?"

"No. I'm mean yes, but that's not what woke me." Her teeth chattered.

He wrapped his arms around her. His warmth, his caring, and his presence brought her amazing relief.

"What happened?" he said in a soft, kind voice.

"Some weirdo just called me."

His body went rigid. "Start from the beginning and tell me what he said. Include everything from the tone of his voice to any background noise you heard." His abrupt comment sounded like his cop tone.

"He said he could, ah, see me." Her voice cracked as shivers of disgust washed over her. "I was too scared to pay attention to any background noise."

Derek nodded and focused on her face. "When did he call?" He wiped a tear off her cheek she hadn't even known she'd shed.

"Right before the car alarm went off. Derek, he knew my name and told me what I was wearing." Her voice trembled.

Derek hugged her again, and Kelly sank into him, letting herself believe she was safe—at least for the moment.

"Did you recognize his voice? Could it have been Justin?"

"I don't think so." Kelly repeated as much as she could, but fear must have blocked some of his phrases. "That's all I can recall. I was in shock. Maybe he was one of the men I met at the bar."

"Oh, Kelly, I'm sorry I got you into this mess."

She looked up to him, his lips inches from hers. "It's not your fault. I insisted on coming. You warned me it might be dangerous."

"I promise I won't let you out of my sight from now on. Nothing will happen to you."

"Oh, Derek."

His soft breath caressed her face. She lifted her lips up to his and the next moment he was kissing her. Hard. Not the soft tentative kisses he used to bestow when they were kids, but hard, needy kisses from a man who knew how to kiss.

As if she were drowning, she grabbed his shoulders. When he hugged her tight, a blanket of safety enveloped her.

Derek leaned her back onto the bed and trailed kisses down her throat. "I've wanted to do this for years." His voice came out a mere whisper. Sexy, desperate, needy.

"I was a fool not to make love to you before." Admitting her feelings liberated her.

"You got that right."

It didn't matter that Derek had been the one to stop from consummating their love. He wouldn't stop now. She wouldn't let him.

He lifted off her nightgown and tossed the cotton shift on the carpet. "You're so beautiful. More incredible than I remember."

As he traced the outline of her breast, need pricked her nipple and her heart nearly exploded. Derek explored her body as if each square inch was more precious than the last drop of water in the desert. Kelly moaned as she ran her hands down the muscular planes of his back. She didn't want to think of the horrors of the call or why they were here. She wanted Derek.

Only Derek.

His musky scent filled her senses with wonder, and she relaxed in his arms. Ever so gently, Derek grabbed a nipple with his teeth and when he sucked on her nub, the tugging sent shivers down her spine. Her long ago fantasies were finally coming true.

"More," she said with a pant, not caring that she sounded wanton. Cupping his head in her hands, she dragged his face to hers. "I want to kiss you. No. I need to feel your lips on mine again." Her desperation embarrassed her, but she wouldn't stop now.

He smiled. "It will be my pleasure."

He opened his mouth to let her in, and he tasted of mint toothpaste. Their tongues danced to an aged old ritual. Familiarity blended with the added excitement of experience, heightened the incredible kiss.

They must have heated up the room, for the air conditioner clicked on. Kelly couldn't get enough of him and lifted her hips to meet his groin. "It's huge," she said with a laugh, the second she contacted his erection.

"Don't worry. I won't hurt you. I'd never hurt you." One at a time, he kissed her eyelids.

"I know you won't." Kelly let the euphoria bathe her in wonder.

"I want to make love to you. No, I need to make love to you."

"I want that too, but first, we need to get you out of those boxers and shoes."

"Can do." In a second, he was naked—oh so, gloriously naked. His erection was huge with a capital H. My, oh, my. She mentally tried to decide if she could even handle someone his size.

Derek crawled next her again and gently kissed her lips, her chin, her eyes, and her nose. She reached up and ran her hands over his head, enjoying the short stubble covering his scalp. He placed his hands on either side of her head and arched his chest, depriving her of the pleasure of his warm, wonderful kisses.

"Why did you stop?" she asked, as he stared down at her.

"I want to look at you. To drink in your beauty."

"I didn't know you were so romantic." She couldn't help but smile.

"There's a lot you don't know about me."

His smile disappeared for a moment, and then it returned before she could name the expression on his face.

Derek kneeled back and began to explore the rest of her. Kelly let herself enjoy his hands on her breasts, on her belly, and between her legs. She loved the texture of his sinewy body, the sparse hair sprinkling his chest, and the gentle way his hands touched her sensitive skin.

When his tongue dipped into her folds, she sucked in a breath, almost believing she'd shot into space, as glorious waves of desire washed over her. Derek plunged his tongue in and out, and then drove a finger into her. Kelly arched, wanting more than one slim forefinger.

"I need more," she panted. Just as Kelly was about to lose her mind, Derek rolled off her and jumped off the bed. Hey. "Where are you doing?"

"I need to some protection." Derek grabbed his jeans, shoved a hand in the pocket, and took out his wallet.

Protection. His concern for her safety warmed her insides. Then it dawned on her. "Did you hope to have sex with me?"

From his wallet he took out the condom. "I think I've been hoping to make love to you for the last twelve years."

At his words, every part of her being melted. Did he love her? He'd never said the words, but did it really matter? Actions were what counted. A woman would be crazy not to want to be with a man so good and so kind, and who was so remarkably sexy. She held out her hands. "Let me do the honors."

When Derek handed her the rolled up condom, she turned it sideways. "Will this even fit?"

He chuckled. "I hope so or you'll have one pissed off lover on your hands."

She laughed. "Just to make sure it goes over you completely, let me lubricate you first." She loved flirting with him again.

"Kelly?" His voice cracked.

She leaned over and ran her tongue down the throbbing vein of his cock then looked up. Derek's eyes were closed and his mouth gapped open as if he'd been transported to heaven.

After she finished moistening him, she ran her fingers up and down his hard shaft.

Keeping his eyes shut, he groaned. "Take too much time and you might have a mess on your hands."

Her whole body heated up. "Party pooper." She sheathed him, excited about her soon-to-be E-ticket ride—one that was twelve years coming.

Kelly rolled on top of him and kissed him silly, wanting to drive him crazy like he was doing to her.

"Oh no you don't. I can't last must longer. Have mercy on my soul." Derek wrapped his arms around her and flipped her on her back. He then lowered himself onto her and parted her thighs with his knees. "I want you so much." His voice came out in a strangled cry.

As he fit his tip into her, she wrapped her legs around his waist. As he eased his way in, Kelly gasped from the size. When heat pooled between her thighs, she was able to take all of him inside her. Closing her eyes, she let the moment send her toward ecstasy. Sweet sex filled the air as he thrust into her. My God, he was more amazing than she ever imagined. All those nights in the backseat of his Chevy was nothing compared to this amazing experience. Derek was powerful, yet gentle at the same time. Could this be love?

Derek moaned. Blood thrummed through her veins as he pumped

harder and harder until his cock grew and throbbed. A second later he climaxed. Her mind blown, Kelly let herself go and reached her orgasm seconds after him.

Exhausted, Kelly dropped her arms to the bed. "That was incredible."

Derek kissed her lips tenderly, like he had so many years ago. "Amazing, was more like it."

"Yeah, that too."

He rolled over and gently kissed her. She couldn't remember when she'd felt so needed, so appreciated, or so adored. Dare she hope there could be something between them? While she might have been foolish to leave him so long ago, was now the time for them to start again?

Derek caressed her face and ran her hair through his fingers. "Everything about you is amazing."

Kelly smiled.

She hadn't realized she'd dozed off until Derek's body rocked the bed. He'd draped the sheet and blanket over her. Rolling over to her side, she placed her head on his chest.

If she died tomorrow, she would die happy.

# CHAPTER TWENTY-THREE

LIGHT BLINDED DEREK, and he shielded his eyes with one hand, managing to hang onto the galloping horse with the other. Squinting, he looked around to see if the landscape had changed from the last time he'd been taken.

No.

Shit. He'd just spent the most incredible night of his life with Kelly, and these chieftains decide now was the time to yank him away from a wonderful sleep? What the hell had he done wrong? Something must have pissed them off.

"Hurry," the man next to Derek shouted over the pounding of the hooves.

"Are you taking me back to the village?"

"Yes."

At least they were predictable. Derek hunkered down and let the horse have his way. Throat-clogging dirt swirled upward and nearly choked him. How had the people long ago handled these poor conditions?

He wouldn't see the village in the distance; it would just appear out of thin air, like a sudden mirage. Maybe if he concentrated on Kelly, he could jettison himself back to the motel room with her warm body snuggled up against him.

"Halt."

Without warning, his horse obeyed the Chief's command, nearly throwing Derek out of the saddle. "Quit that."

"Silence."

The commanding tone was becoming tiresome. He didn't need to hear what these men had to tell him. He had a killer to find and a woman to protect.

"Get down." Another command.

"Happy to oblige," Derek said as he slid off the horse. His thighs were grateful for the respite.

"Come."

Terse lot. At least they were letting him participate instead of standing back and watching.

"Go into the teepee with the gold and white feathers above the opening," stone-face motioned.

Derek jogged to the destination believing the sooner he arrived, the sooner he'd be returned to Kelly.

Indian women were preparing meals over an open fire, and children were laughing and screeching nearby, yet no one seemed to notice him. Was he invisible or didn't they realize he wasn't one of them?

Before he could decide on whether they could see him, he arrived at the teepee. He didn't think knocking on the cowhide flap was appropriate, so he pushed aside the material and entered.

Derek refrained from rolling his eyes at the clichéd setting. A man, with long, stringy gray hair sat on the dirt floor smoking a pipe. The cloying, sweet smell made Derek cough.

Couldn't his spiritual guides have come up with something more original?

"Sit."

More one word commands. He obeyed and sat cross-legged like the man opposite him.

"You want to know why we brought you here," the old man said.

Derek swallowed his impatience. "You could say that."

The man inhaled on his pipe and blew out a long string of circles. "We could have set up this meeting in an office, complete with a Power Point presentation, but we felt you could relate better to this setting."

Dumbfounded, Derek straightened and stared at the old man. What kind of place had they brought him to?

"Okay, we will begin," the shaman said. "You are a great warrior, Derek Benally."

Hardly. Tempted to leave this scene that seemed to come from a bad B movie, Derek figured it might be best to give the guy a chance. Besides, he didn't think the chieftains outside would be pleased if he split so soon.

"Fine, I'm a great warrior. I kill buffalo to support my family, and I slay many white men."

"You don't need to take that tone with me. I'm trying to help you."

"Fine. Go on. I'm listening."

"We are pained you do not embrace your heritage." He held up a hand. "Just hear me out. Yes, your father wanted you to follow in his footsteps, but you have bigger ideas, better ideas."

Derek jumped to his feet. "My father is behind all of this hocus pocus?"

"Sit down and stop acting like a petulant child."

Breathing heavily, Derek dropped back to the ground, not pleased with this whole charade. "Now what?"

"Now, you listen. You have chosen to use your talents in the white world. You need to accept that what you are doing is for the good of all men, not just for Native Americans or for the Whites. Because you help bring justice to the world, we want to help you."

He laughed. "If you want to help me, then tell me where Justin Bladen is."

The old man laughed briefly. "You don't need our help. In time, you will find the person who killed your sister."

"So why did you bring me here?" Fury raced through him as sweat dripped down his back and arms. This whole dream was bullshit, if it was a dream.

"To give you permission to accept who you are."

He had to be kidding. "I do accept who I am."

The old man waved a hand, and the tassels on his buckskin shirt wiggled back and forth. "You do not. If you truly understood who you were, you'd be able to accept others for who they are. You expect others to change because of your choices, not theirs."

That's bullshit. He didn't need platitudes and lectures at his age. "I'm not some controlling maniac."

"You judge others. You judge your father because he chooses the way of his tribe. You even judged your sister on how she led her life. And you wanted Billie to be like you, not your dad." He blew more smoke rings. "Let each soul determine what is best for himself."

\*\*\*

"Derek?"

When he opened his eyes, Kelly was sitting on the chair across from the bed and faint light was streaming through the curtains. It was morning. How was that possible? He'd just fallen asleep.

"Why are you over there?" he asked, not understanding how she'd slipped away from him.

Her arms were wrapped around her knees. "I don't know who you are anymore." She looked off to the side, acting as if the weight of the world had crashed down on her.

"Come over here." He held out her arms.

She shook her head. "Where were you just now?"

Oh, shit. "Was I staring or something?" A giant claw twisted his gut.

"Staring or something? Good Lord. You've been sitting cross-legged on the bed, not moving a muscle for an hour—a whole hour. I tried to rouse you, but you wouldn't respond."

Kelly blinked and swiped a hand across her eyes. Had she been crying? He couldn't handle tears. Here he thought they'd finally connected both physically and perhaps even emotionally, and he'd fucked everything up by taking a trip to another world. Would she understand what he'd been through? Or rather could she understand? The last time he tried to describe the voices he'd heard, Kelly had run away.

To college.

And out of his life.

He couldn't let that happen again. But should he lie? His spirit guides kept saying he needed to accept himself for who he was. A little voice in his head, who he was positive had nothing to do with any spiritual guides, told him to go for it. If she left him, then she was not the woman he knew and lov—.

"They why didn't you call 9-1-1?" he asked.

"I thought about it, but you were breathing just fine. I figured you were in some trance."

"I was." He scooted to the edge of the bed to be nearer to her. Ever since Rayne died, I've been having these...these, what I can best describe as out of body experiences." He held his breath, waiting for her laughter or worse, derision.

"Out of body?" Her brows knitted together as if the concept repulsed her—or was it a look of confusion?

He had to push on and make her understand. "I can't control these sessions. One minute I'm either lying in bed sound asleep or meditating, and the next moment this band of chiefs, from all different tribes, sweep me away to who knows where."

She opened her mouth and shook her head. "So you're telling me men with big feathers abduct you to the great place in the sky?"

Derek couldn't blame her for her attitude, but he knew if he could make her understand, she'd accept what happened as part of his nature. "I know it sounds farfetched. Hell, it is to me too. Each time they've taken me, something different happens. It's not like a recurring dream."

"How many times has this happened?" Now she sounded scared, as though each experience had altered him in some molecular way.

"I...I don't know." He mentally went through the list of abductions, if that's what they were. "Maybe three, four times in all."

"Weren't you scared? I know I'd be petrified."

She believed him? "I kind of was after the fact."

Kelly pursed her lips. "As a scientist I don't believe in the hereafter, Gods, or spiritual guides, but I'm game to hear what they had to say." The animosity in her tone lessened a bit.

"You sure?" He couldn't believe how hard his heart beat. He had to reach her. Every cell in his body vibrated with a need to connect.

"I won't laugh if that's what you're afraid of."

"Laughter is the least of my worries." Try running away? He took a deep breath. "Here goes. Each time they took me, I was able to see a glimpse of myself."

"Like you were looking in the mirror?" There was a hint of interest in her tone.

Derek leaned forward, anxious to share. "Not quite. It wasn't a reflection. It was more like I was watching a movie where I was the star. At least the first time or two that was what happened. In this last trip, I met with a wise man, a shaman of some sort. I wasn't watching anyone portray me. I was myself."

"And what did this sage tell you?"

Dare he share? Her gaze focused hard on him. "He told me to accept my heritage, and to stop fighting my father and what he represents. I should seek out evil to benefit all mankind."

"That's powerful stuff."

He couldn't tell if she was being sincere or mocking him. "I thought the same thing."

"And did they tell you how you were supposed to conquer the world?"

As if she flipped a switch, Kelly changed gears. He refused to let her fear deter him from continuing. "Not the whole world, just my world. He said to trust my instincts."

"That's it? Just trust your instincts?" She rolled her eyes. "I'm disappointed in their lack of intellectual depth. Did they tell you anything else?"

Clearly she didn't believe him. As if he'd plunged off the edge of a cliff into a black hole, his heart tore in half. "Not really, but I figured as long as I had their attention, I'd ask if they knew where I could find Justin."

Interest sparked in her eyes. Finally. "So what did they say?"

For a moment he debated whether to tell her. She looked so eager and so sexy that he caved. "The spirit guide had every confidence in my abilities to find the person who killed my sister on my own. I no longer needed his help, he said."

She collapsed back against the chair. "They weren't of any help then."

Derek sank back onto the pillow. "No." He tried to ignore the ache in his heart.

*Stupid move, Benally.* Why had he bared his soul to her? It wasn't as if there was any hope she'd want to rekindle what they once had, despite the mind-blowing sex they'd shared.

Kelly always thought his voices made him different—too different to be around. Fine. If Kelly didn't want to accept him for who he was, he'd have to move on.

Right. And the world hunger would disappear tomorrow.

She stood up. "Can we eat now?"

From the brittle way she held herself, she acted as if he'd personally betrayed her, and nothing he could say would change her mind.

End of discussion. End of any chance of them being together.

Derek swallowed hard. "Sure, but first, you need to pack. I'll call the airport to see if we can get on the next flight back." He kept his tone professional, impersonal, and to the point. Good.

She spun toward him. "What? And not find the jerk who tried to intimidate me? No way in hell am I leaving here without learning who he is. I want justice."

He almost smiled at her feisty attitude. He could handle feisty. It was the scared Kelly he had a hard time dealing with.

Not wanting to rile her further, Derek kept his tone even. "Let's leave the policing to the sheriff's department."

"Them? What if they're part of the problem?"

"We've been over this. We have no facts to support Mariani is the bad guy. Besides, he's all we have. We came here to find Justin. That's all. Let Mariani deal with the drugging and the stalking. We can't let what happened make us lose focus on the real issue."

She closed the gap between them, grabbed his arms, and lasered him a stare. "I want to know who's trying to scare me, or worse, kill me. Or don't you care?"

Derek couldn't help but run a finger down her cheek and inhale her delicious flowery scent. He had to keep her safe—even if it meant she'd hate him for it. "It's too dangerous to stay here. The person who's harassing you could come back again. There's no guarantee I can protect you. I won't chance it."

She stepped out of his grasp, turned her back to him, and wrapped her arms around her waist. Kelly dropped her head back. "I wish I knew what to do."

"Leave town."

Spinning around to face him, she stepped within arm's reach. "If we leave, this person will have won."

She infuriated him, while at the same time made him want to kiss her, hold her, and have her more than anything. "Kelly, if we find our sisters' murderer, I think we'll find the person who is trying to harm you." She looked so lost that it took all his strength not to clasp her to his chest and give her comfort.

Kelly took one step closer and dropped her head forward onto his chest. "Derek. I'm so sc-scared."

At the sound of her wavering voice, Derek gave in and held her tight. She might not accept his religious beliefs, which meant she'd never truly be his, but he could make certain nothing else happened to her.

From instinct, Derek leaned down and kissed the top of her head. The fresh smell of her shampoo sent a jolt of desire through him, but he pushed the thought away. They were through—over.

Kelly stepped back again, and his heart ached at her renewed rejection.

"What's going to happen with this McDermitt fellow?" she asked. "Will Mariani watch him too? He's practically a criminal, and yet Mariani hasn't done anything to him yet. Maybe McDermitt's the one who wants you out of town and believed that if he scared me, I'd make you leave."

Kelly sounded like the analytical woman he remembered. He thought back to the end of the conversation he had with the old man.

Talking about the case would help calm his lust and put a cage around his heart.

"No. As a matter of fact, he asked me to stay. Besides, he has no idea you exist."

As Kelly paced the small room, Derek watched, helpless to calm her.

"How can you be so sure I'm this invisible commodity? How do you know McDermitt doesn't know I exist, or that Nancy doesn't know I exist? Remember, I told that jerk at the bar you were my husband. Maybe he talked." Kelly's hands gestured like a deaf person. "And that caller was watching me. Somebody knows I'm here!" Her brows furrowed.

He stepped around the bed and cupped her cheek. "Kelly, I'm not the enemy here. I want what's best for you."

His logic must have gotten through to her because her shoulders sagged. She took two steps over to the bed, sat, leaned back, and draped an arm over her eyes.

Her breaths came out fast. Helpless as to how to ease her fears, he sat down next to her. "What do you want me to do?"

She lowered her arm and stared up at the ceiling. "I don't know, Derek. I'm confused. I'm confused about who would want to hurt my sister. I'm confused about my feelings for you. I'm confused because I don't know which way to turn."

Derek moved a strand of hair covering her eye. He didn't want to ask, but he had to. "What about us has you confused?"

Dare he hope? Had he misunderstood her rejection?

She sat up and faced him. "I'm tired, I'm disappointed, and I think I want to go home."

He couldn't figure out which part of her sentence related to their relationship, but there was no doubt, Kelly had had it.

"I'll call Mariani and see if he can trace the call to your room. Then I'll make the reservations. You pack. Once we're back in Tampa, we can sort everything out."

"Fine." She closed her eyes and lowered her chin to her chest.

Without giving any thought to his actions, he wrapped his arms around her again, but she squirmed out of his arms. "Derek, please."

Hurt, he moved away. Kelly needed space to digest what had happened—most notably his visions. She'd been through a lot.

He had one purpose in the next twenty-four hours. Get Kelly safely home. As long as he wasn't wrenched from the present by his guides, he'd make sure nothing happened to her.

# CHAPTER TWENTY-FOUR

"OH, HELLO." Mrs. Anton's eyes widened as she pulled open her door. "I didn't expect to see you again. Come in."

"With Rayne's death and all, there was no reason to come back." Until now, you old biddy. "I needed to pick up some things I had at the house, but I wanted to stop by and say goodbye."

"Well, that's so nice of you. Can I get you anything to drink?"

"I'll have whatever you're having."

The sofa was littered with dolls—dirty, nasty dolls. Cobwebs collected on the shelves above the sofa, and that velvet painting of the two Cockatiels kissing was disgusting. What was wrong with this woman?

The cramped living room was suffocating with its too many sofas and chairs—and dust—lots and lots of dust.

"I was just brewing some tea. Is that okay?" Mrs. Anton chirped from the kitchen.

"Perfect." Too bad the bitch wouldn't live long enough to drink it.

Once the old lady began fixing the tea, out came the rope. The teapot whistled and the china cup clinked against the saucer.

The time to kill had arrived.

The bitch would never know why she had to die today, but it didn't matter. Couldn't have her talking to the police. Given time, she might remember who was outside Rayne's house the night she died.

Better make this quick.

Mrs. Anton's loose neck begged to be taken. With a quick flick of the wrist, the rope wrapped around her throat, and the pathetic woman's hands grappled at the noose. One jerk, and fifteen seconds later, she was on the ground. Dead.

Snap. Crackle. Pop. Easy. Too easy in fact.

Killing boosted the immune system, sending endorphins through the system. The power of taking a life intoxicated one's whole body. There was nothing like it.

Enough enjoyment for one day. Now to make sure all trace evidence disappeared.

Cups were left in the sink piled high with dishes, which meant the cops wouldn't be able to tell which cups had recently been left and which had been there a week. There was no time to deal with the mess though. The living room was a different matter. God, her place was a disaster, but a quick swipe of the dust cloth and a little straightening of those stupid dolls, and Mrs. Anton wouldn't have to be embarrassed when her friends and family came to say goodbye.

A car door slammed outside. Shit.

Voices.

Cops.

The only way out was through the back door. Not to worry, they'd never suspect who'd killed the old lady.

Next up. Snoopy Dr. Kelly.

\*\*\*

The smell of day old coffee swirling around him, Derek leaned back in his desk chair, unable to concentrate. He'd been back in Tampa a week already, and he hadn't heard from Kelly or located Justin.

He'd begged her to let him keep watch over her, but she'd been adamant he stay away. She didn't want or need a protection detail. Damn, stubborn woman.

Nothing was going right. Hell, even the jumper case had stalled. Derek either needed luck to fall from the sky or his spirit guides to drop the moratorium on pertinent clues.

His cell phone rang, and his pulsed revved. Was it Kelly? Not likely. His spirit guides? *Get a grip, buddy. They're not going to contact me by office phone.* He grabbed the receiver. "Benally."

"It's me, Seinkievitz."

Derek relaxed back in his chair. "Why are you whispering?"

"I don't want the Captain or anyone else to hear me."

Derek whipped around and saw Seinkievitz hunkered down over the desk not more than fifteen feet away. "Just come over here and talk to me."

"You know the Captain will have my head if he sees me with you. He'll assume you're pumping me for information," Seinkievitz said.

"Fine. What did you learn?"

"You won't believe it. A neighbor of Rayne's called in a while ago and said she spotted Justin Bladen going into your sister's house." He picked up the paper. "A Mrs. Anton."

Every bone in his body turned rigid. "When exactly did she call?" That would mean Justin might still be at Rayne's.

"I don't know. I just walked in and found the note on my desk. It's not time stamped, but I'm heading over there too. Thought you'd like to know."

Derek ignored the sarcasm, pushed aside his stack of never-ending papers, and leaned forward on his desk. "Thanks, I owe you one."

Derek hung up and raced out of the station before Seinkievitz even left his desk.

Rayne's house was a good twenty minutes away. Justin would be long gone but just knowing he was in town boosted Derek's energy. He'd find the bastard no matter what it took.

Derek sped down Rayne's street. As he rounded the corner, he pulled over and had to park two houses from hers. An ambulance, three police cars, and two civilian cars were parked in front of Mrs. Anton's house.

"Shit."

He jumped out and raced to the neighbor's place. Heat blasted

him, but he ignored the discomfort. Just as Derek made it to the front
door, the paramedics came out with a sheet-covered body on a gurney.

"Is it Mrs. Anton?" he asked, knowing full well the answer.

"Yes."

Anger socked him in the gut. Why now? Had Justin become more
blatant in his killing? He needed answers before he went nuts.

As Derek entered Mrs. Anton's house, Steppings and his crew were
busy at work gathering forensic clues. Steppings looked up from his
crouched position near the doorway. "Derek."

"What happened?" Derek asked.

The CSU lead rose to his feet slowly. Arthritis maybe? "Someone
strangled Mrs. Anton with what I'm guessing is a 10 mm thick rope."

"Like a climbing rope?"

"That's as good a guess as any."

Was Justin a climber? He'd never heard Rayne talk about his love of
the outdoors.

"Hey," Seinkievitz said a little out of breath as he stepped next to
Derek. "Yikes. This place looks like a Toys-R-Us sale."

"That's an understatement." Derek moved further into the living
room. Whoa. What had happened? The dolls were neatly lined up on
the shelves and free from cobwebs. The large couch doll sat up straight
in the middle of the sofa—alone. Gone were the magazines and other
paraphernalia he'd moved when he'd visited Mrs. Anton.

"Someone cleaned up."

Steppings eyed him from beneath his bushy brows. "Maybe Mrs.
Anton was feeling energetic or spring cleaning came really late this
year."

"I was here maybe a week or two ago, and the house looked like it'd
been collecting dust for years. The dolls were tossed on the shelves, on
the chairs, and on the sofas. Not in neat little rows like they are now."

Steppings' gaze swept the room. "Someone cleaned up then."

"Maybe she hired a maid," Seinkievitz put in.

"I doubt it," Derek said. "Not on her fixed income."

Derek walked back to the kitchen where another one of Steppings'
team was taking measurements. "I don't see any evidence of a strug-

gle," Derek said over his shoulder, hoping to learn their take on the murder.

"You're right." Steppings joined him. "And no forced entry either. Buscemi is canvassing the neighbors to see if anyone noticed someone entering the premises."

Steppings seemed to have everything under control. "I'm going to check my sister's house. She reported seeing Justin next door. I want to see if he touched anything."

"Good idea. If you find anything, let us know."

Derek nodded at Seinkievitz and stepped outside. Frustration gripped him. When would this killing stop? Justin was on the loose again, and Derek had no more evidence than the night Rayne died. Dammit. Would Kelly be next? Or his father? Or Billy for that matter? After all, Billy had Seminole blood in him too.

Or was there some master plan he was missing?

A neighbor on the other side of Rayne's was mowing the lawn, causing Derek to sneeze. He loved the smell of fresh cut grass, but the allergens wreaked havoc with his sinuses.

As he stepped up to his sister's door, negative energy poured from her house. Had losing Rayne had cast a pall over the property—or had Justin's presence ionized the air?

Using the key she'd given him, Derek let himself in. Although he'd set the air to eighty-four, the place smelled of mildew. He had to find the time to clean out her place before the task became too overwhelming. Touching her possessions would tear out his heart.

Nothing looked disturbed, but then again, Justin was a careful man.

*＊*

Kelly needed to run, needed the boost from the endorphins. She hadn't spoken with Derek since their return. She might have overreacted when she told him she needed her space, but the man complicated her life. However, she needed to talk to him. Questions about Justin, questions about Lilly, and questions about Derek cobwebbed her mind to a point where she'd become ineffective at work. That's why she needed the run.

Outside, the night sky was covered in clouds, threatening rain. Even if she were caught in a downpour, she wouldn't melt. She'd take her mace and phone just in case something happened.

Once dressed, she jetted outside, careful to lock the door behind her. Despite it being October, the humidity slapped her in the face. A clap of thunder sounded off in the distance, but Kelly didn't care if she came home drenched in sweat or just plain drenched. The exertion would do her good. Her tree-covered street would provide some shelter from the elements.

She'd run no more than a mile when her phone buzzed, startling her. Keeping her gaze on the road, she flicked a glance at the caller I.D. "Private number." Curious, she answered. "Hello?"

"Please don't hang up on me. I need to talk to you. Thank God I reached you."

The man's panicked voice didn't sound familiar. "Who is this?" She rounded the bend in the road and stepped further into the roadway, away from the shoulder that was covered in slippery gravel.

"It's Justin."

Kelly halted, and her breath gushed out. Her pulse jumped to warp speed. "Justin?"

If only she knew how to notify Derek that he was on the line. It wasn't as if she could exactly flag down a car and tell them to call 9-1-1 while she was on the line with a murderer.

"What are you doing?" he asked.

What an odd question, until she realized her rapid breath must sound like a freight train. "I'm jogging."

"Sounds like it. Kelly, I need to talk to you. I...I don't know where else to turn."

His desperate plea caused sympathy to well up, until she realized he was acting, trying to elicit sympathy. She refused to fall for his line. For a second, she debated telling him guilt would follow him for the rest of his life if he didn't turn himself in. Instead she tried to sound casual. "You could try talking to the police. I bet they'd listen."

What sounded like a laugh came over the line. "They won't believe me. They think I killed the woman I loved. I know you think I had something to do with your sister's murder as well, but I swear to God I didn't kill either of them."

His sincere tone was coupled with what she decided was fear. "Why should I believe you?" A car barreled down the road, and Kelly stepped off to the side, her pulse spiking.

"When we were together, did I act like a murderer?"

A crack of thunder sounded closer.

When they were together? They'd spent one evening and had one run in the park. "Not really." Drops of rain splattered on her nose, so she turned around and began to walk back to her house.

"Kelly, I don't know what to say that would convince you I'm innocent. How does anyone prove innocence?"

"I don't know. You tell me." If she could keep him talking, maybe there would be some way to trace his call.

"Okay. For starters, I really was at my boss's house the night of Rayne's murder, passed out in the downstairs spare bedroom. I was so shit faced, I could barely see, let alone drive. I couldn't have—"

Kelly slapped the phone. "You're breaking up."

"Sorry." His voice came in clearer. "Is this better?"

"Yes," she said, relieved not to lose the connection.

"I took it off speaker phone. Anyway, my boss told me some cops came by the office and actually calculated how long it would take to drive to Rayne's house, kill her and return, assuming I faked being drunk."

Derek had thought the same thing. "What did they find?" She was pleased her tone sounded even and not jittery like her stomach.

"That's not the point."

"I beg to differ. If the time frame works, then your alibi doesn't hold up."

He groaned. "You see why I don't want to go to the police? Have you talked to Derek?"

That came out of the blue. "Not in the last couple of days." It wasn't a lie.

"It doesn't matter. Tell me. Did he ever say if the police had any physical evidence to tie me to the murders?"

"Like fingerprints or something?"

"Yes."

She tried to think. Justin had two prior murder convictions on the books, her sister was tailing him for some client, which didn't look good, and he and according to Derek, Rayne had had a bad argument with Justin the night she died. But hard evidence? "I don't think so."

"See there?"

"That doesn't mean you didn't kill Rayne or my sister."

"How about if I tell you who did kill them?"

Kelly's throat went dry. "You know who murdered them?"

"Yes."

# CHAPTER TWENTY-FIVE

"WHO?" The word came out as a croak. A dog started barking in the neighborhood, and Kelly hoped it was just a passerby.

Kelly looked behind her and gripped the phone hard. When heat lightning lit up the sky, she held her breath waiting for Justin to reveal the name of the killer.

"My mother." He sounded like an ill-tempered child.

His mom? "That's rich. You're going to tell me your mother killed two women? She must be in her, what, sixties?"

"Yes, but what's age got to do with it?"

Killers weren't typical people. "Right."

Headlights came around the bend behind her and slowed. She whipped around, grabbed the mace from her pocket with her free hand and jumped off the pavement. Swallowing the lump in her throat, she forced herself to stay calm.

"I know I'm repeating myself," she said, "but tell me again why I should believe you?" The car passed, and her shoulders relaxed a bit.

"Because I'm innocent!"

Suddenly nervous being alone on the road, she picked up her pace, imagining Justin nearby with a gun trained on her head. She shuddered. "Even if you didn't commit the crimes, that doesn't mean your mother killed my sister and Rayne. Besides, doesn't she live in Utah?"

"Rayne tell you that? Never mind. I did grow up in Utah. I had no reason to believe my mom wasn't there until she showed up at my house today."

That might explain Lilly Bladen' empty trailer. Kelly's legs weakened, but she pushed to reach the safety of her house. "If your mother confessed, why not turn her in?"

"I didn't actually see her. She left a note with no signature, but I know she wrote it. No one could duplicate her chicken scratch handwriting."

"Why are you calling me?" The whole conversation sent creepy prickles across her skin.

"I needed to tell someone." The sound of shuffling papers rustled through the line. "Let me read this to you and I quote: If you don't turn yourself into the police and confess to the murders, I'll come after that new girlfriend of yours, Kelly Rutland.'"

Kelly's blood pressure shot up and she began to sprint, acting as if Justin's mom were right behind her with a gun trained on her back. Her road was less than a tenth of a mile away. She could make it.

"She wants to come after me? I don't even know her. And I sure as hell am not your girlfriend." Nor did she ever want to be. Shades of Utah returned, and a raw, biting jab punched her in the pit of her stomach.

"Somehow she knows I've talked to you about Rayne, but don't ask me how. I'm totally confused about why she would even come to Florida. We haven't talked in years. We don't exactly get along." He let out a groan. "And that's putting it mildly. She hates me. Begrudges me for running away when my dad died and for not staying and working in town in order to share the living expenses."

His story matched Courtney Wolfendon's, but was he telling the truth about the note? Kelly turned down her road, keeping up her pace, staying in the middle of the lane. *Think, Kelly, think.*

"Can you make a copy of the note and email it to me? Or better yet, fax a copy to the cops?" Her level headedness made her legs lighter.

His laugh came out rueful. "I can't prove I didn't write the note myself, even though it's not in my handwriting. And don't suggest I have the crime lab analyze the document. My fingerprints are all over the damned note. Even if they did go to the expense of checking out the paper and do a handwriting analysis, it could be months before they came up with an answer. By then my mom might have killed again."

"Give it a try. I believe—"

"You believe? You haven't believed anything I've said, have you? I thought you wanted to find out who killed your sister. This conversation is total bullshit. You don't care anything about me." The line went dead.

Kelly pulled the phone from her ear, and then listened again, but he was gone. "Damn it." What the hell was that about? He didn't trust cops so what could he hope in telling her? Maybe he secretly wanted her to go to the police for him. That was so like a man not to express his true feelings.

Close to her drive, she stopped and looked around. Where was Justin calling from? Close by?

Looking right and then left, Kelly dashed to her door. Her hands shook so much it took a minute to get the damn door opened. Once inside, she twisted the lock and pressed her back to the solid structure. Justin Bladen had called her. Oh my God.

Damn it. Why hadn't she asked him to explain the murders in Utah and Missouri? She clutched a hand to her chest. Maybe it was a good thing she hadn't revealed what she knew about his past. If she had, she'd have more than his mom to worry about.

Kelly pulled out her phone and called Derek. Trembling with outrage and fear she paced in the small tiled foyer, waiting for him to pick up.

Four rings later he answered. "Yes, Kelly?"

"Justin just called me."

"Justin? When?"

"I just hung up with him. Or rather he hung up on me."

"What's his number?"

Derek didn't ask her: What did he say? Where is he? or Are you okay?

"I don't know," she said, disappointed he seemed so focused on the case and not on how she was handling the call.

"Don't you have caller I.D.?" She could hear his anger and frustration.

"Yes, but it said the number was private."

"Are you home?" he asked.

"Yes."

"Stay there. I'm coming over."

Derek hung up before Kelly could answer. What was with these men?

Full of edgy energy, Kelly closed all the drapes in the house. Could Justin have been the one in Utah looking in on her?

Oh God. She stepped over to the living room window and peered through an opening in the drapes. A white Mercedes drove slowly down her dead end street, and her stomach churned. When she caught sight of a bobbing ponytail in the driver's side as the car passed, she let out a sigh of relief. She had to calm down or she'd start imagining evil under every bush.

Kelly checked her watch, calculating when Derek would arrive. She needed something to calm her nerves. From the refrigerator she pulled out a beer and drank straight from the bottle. Wouldn't her mom be horrified?

Sweat was caked on her skin from her run. From his station, it would take Derek a good twenty minutes, which meant she had time for a quick shower.

*** 

Derek's worry for Kelly forced him to drive over the speed limit. Why the hell had Justin contacted her? Had he asked her to help him in some way? Derek sure as hell hoped not. Then again, she was an easy mark for the down trodden. Even in high school, she tutored what were known as the social rejects—a horribly unfair name, for sure.

Derek sped around the corner and zipped down her street. Seeing Kelly's yellow Bug in the drive shot some relief through him. In a hurry to make certain she was safe, the front wheel rode up on the sidewalk. It was a bad parking job, but he had more important things to worry about.

Derek jumped out and raced to her front door. This time he didn't care if he stepped on the cracks. It was a stupid superstition anyway.

He knocked. "Kelly, it's me. Open up."

No answer.

He pounded on the door—harder this time.

Still no answer.

Like a snake crawling up his leg, fear struck his gut. He jogged to the side of the house. Damn, all the shades were drawn. Fearing Justin had decided to visit her, Derek sprinted around back. The kitchen window's shade was partly open, and he looked inside. Nothing appeared disturbed, and his fear lessened somewhat, but his insides were still clenched.

A light off to his right caught his attention. Not making a sound, he crept along the side of the house. A bolt of thunder crackled in the sky, and then the rain came down in earnest, but he ignored the discomfort.

Derek sidled closer to the window. The cracked drapes gave him a view of ...holy shit. Kelly.

Alone.

Naked.

Except for white lacy panties. He went rock hard. He should turn around and not peek, but some primal instinct made him stare. Having tasted her once and made love to her so sweetly, he wanted her and needed her. Too bad, she'd never accept him.

He grunted. She looked more beautiful than in Utah, if that was possible.

Not wanting her to catch him, he raced around to the front. By the time he ducked under the porch overhang, his shirt was soaked and his jeans were wet through and through. He readjusted his pants and rang the bell.

Kelly shouted something from inside, and a moment later she

pulled back the door, all fresh faced and wearing a tight tank top and shorts. His groin ached.

Derek stepped in and grabbed her arms. "Are you okay?"

She smiled and his heart did something funny. "Yes." She ran her gaze up and down him. "Eww, you're all wet."

"It's raining."

"Let me get you a towel before you ruin the hard wood floors." Despite her laugh, her face held a lot of tension. Derek wanted to question her about the phone call, but decided she'd tell him when she was ready.

Embarrassed, he stepped back to the tiled foyer. She returned with a white, fluffy bath towel. Thinking of Kelly showering made him hard again. Jeez. He had to pull himself together or he wouldn't be able to concentrate on Justin's all-important call.

He wiped down his face and dragged the towel over his shirt, but it didn't help much. His clothes still dripped.

"Why don't you take off your shirt?" she suggested.

Derek studied her face to see if there was any sexual implication. When he followed her gaze to the puddle beneath him, he decided she was being practical. He did as she asked, balled the shirt in the towel, and handed the mess back to her. His wet pants were staying put. Boxers or no boxers.

She glanced up at his chest. "Uh, why don't I get you another towel? I don't own anything big enough to fit you."

"That would be great."

Kelly took away the shirt and returned moments later with a flowery beach towel. He wiped his pants the best he could, and then wrapped the towel around his shoulders.

He followed her into the living room, enjoying the way her hips swayed. *Concentrate*. He forced himself into cop mode. "Tell me what Justin said—his tone, his stress level, and anything else you can remember."

"Would you mind sitting on the towel?" Her casual tone didn't fool him. She was still scared.

Kelly sat across from him and relayed what she remembered of the conversation, but some bits and pieces seem to be missing.

"Are you sure he said his mother killed Rayne?" This didn't fit with all the evidence.

"Yes."

"And you believed him?" Derek wanted to understand Justin's level of conviction. He wasn't ready to take what he said at face value.

She leaned back on the sofa and closed her eyes. "I don't know. He sounded sincere. And scared." Her lashes fluttered open. "What do you think?"

"I've wanted the killer to be Justin for so long I'm blind to his cause. As a cop, I've yet to see any proof."

"Did you believe Justin loved Rayne?" she asked, leaning forward.

The top of her breasts peeked above her shirt and distracted him for a moment. He searched the ceiling for the answer long enough for her image to disappear. "When you love a woman, you don't call her a slut." His jaw clenched as a renewed rush of anger soared through him.

Kelly's mouth dropped open. "How do you know he said that? Did Rayne tell you?"

"No. Mrs. Anton overheard their fight the night Rayne was killed. And speaking of which..." Kelly had had enough of bad news, but she needed to know. "Someone killed Mrs. Anton this afternoon."

Her face lost its color. "Ohmigod. How?" She waved a hand as if to erase her comment. "No, don't tell me. I never met her, but I know you said she was elderly. Do you think Justin killed her?"

His lips thinned, and he tried to squash the fury that blasted him. "I wish I knew. Mrs. Anton called the police and said Justin was next door. She'd heard on the news we were looking for him, so we know he was nearby moments before she died."

"Would she have let him into her house knowing he was a potential killer?"

"I'd wondered the same thing, but I wouldn't be surprised if she did. The woman seemed desperate for company. Plus, there was no sign of forced entry."

Kelly grabbed a sofa pillow and hugged the green chenille square. "Could she have confronted him about the night of Rayne's murder? Didn't you say she was a snoop?"

"Quite a snoop." A box of chocolate chip cookies sat on the coffee table. "May I?"

"Sure. He must not have pointed a gun at her to get inside or she would have slammed the door in his face," Kelly said.

"Or tried to. He could have easily barged in. Here's the thing. Given the position of the tea pot on the stove along with the discarded little packet covers, she was in the process of making tea when the perp strangled her."

He stuffed two small cookies into his mouth. They tasted good—almost as sweet as Kelly.

She drew the pillow up to her chin and rested her head on the cushion. "When I'm nervous, I want something to do with my hands." Kelly patted the pillow she was holding. "Perhaps Mrs. Anton thought she could stall Justin, hoping the police would arrive in time. After all, she'd called you guys already."

She had a point. "Could be, but the tea set implied a social visit."

"Maybe Justin wasn't the murderer. Maybe the killer was a woman."

"Why? Because Mrs. Anton offered tea to this person?"

"Because Justin planted the idea in my mind about the killer being his mom."

He grabbed another handful of cookies. "I don't know. Strangulation is not the usual act of a female. At first I thought it odd she'd offer tea to Justin, but then I remembered she offered me tea when I stopped over. I had the impression she'd offer tea to a stray dog if he came around."

Kelly rolled her eyes. "Is there any way Mrs. Anton would know Justin's mom?"

Kelly didn't seem able to get off the killer-mom scenario, so he went with it. "Not that I'm aware. Remember, until recently, Lilly Bladen was in Utah."

"Mrs. Cohen said Lilly had been gone a few months though." Kelly shifted on the sofa. "Okay, how's this? Maybe Lilly stopped by Mrs. Anton's house pretending to sell something, like cosmetics or health insurance, and the gullible Mrs. Anton let her in."

"It's possible." He scanned her face. "Technically we shouldn't be discussing this case. This information is not public knowledge, so please—"

Kelly held up a hand. "I won't say a word. Speaking of tea, can I get you something to drink?"

"Anything—as long as it's not tea." He cracked a thin smile, and then spotted the beer bottle on the table and nodded. "If you have another beer, I could use one."

"Sure." Kelly strode to the kitchen, all nervous energy and tension. She returned a moment later with his drink.

Derek grabbed the cold bottle and took a hit. Ah, the beer was smooth. "Tell me again about the letter Justin found at his house."

"Like I said before, he told me it was from his mom. It said if he didn't turn himself in for the two murders, she'd harm me." Kelly took a long drink.

He watched the tension build around her eyes. "I don't like the sound of that. If Lilly Bladen really did leave a note, you can't stay here anymore."

She squeezed the bottle until her fingers turned white. "You want me to leave so she won't find me?"

He expected nothing less than a confrontation. "Yes."

Her features turned rigid. "I'm not leaving my house. Besides, the word *harm* could mean all sorts of things."

He wanted to hold her, kiss her, and then shake some sense into her. "Kelly, three people are dead. He, or she, won't stop because you're too stubborn to hide. I don't think harm, here, means keying your car."

She bit her lower lip, and his thoughts shot downward. Christ. He needed all the blood to stay in his brain.

"I can't just up and leave town. I have a job."

The desperation in her tone made him open his arms. "Come here."

She paused, as if debating her choice to seek comfort.

"It's only a hug," he added.

She stepped around the coffee table to the sofa and nestled in his arms. The spring scent of her freshly washed hair filled his senses, and Derek held on tight and closed his eyes. Having Kelly in his arms felt right.

On instinct, he lowered his lips and kissed the top of her head. She looked up, and her watery eyes made his gut clench.

"I'm scared," she said.

"Me too."

As if his spiritual guides led him, he dragged his lips from her forehead to her mouth. Her eyes squinted shut as she pressed her breasts to his chest, and all rational thought raced out.

He wanted her to set the pace, to ease her need.

"Oh, Derek," she panted, and then opened her mouth.

The invitation sent both his pulse and his dick skyward. Their tongues did the ancient ritual that brought the past colliding with the present.

She grabbed his face and pulled him toward her. Gone was the ice princess, gone was the shaken woman, and gone was the shy girl he once knew. She acted like she had in the Utah hotel—hot, sexy, and wanton.

Derek disengaged his arms, stood up, and then scooped her into his arms. He dipped his head and placed the lightest kiss possible on her lips, showing her he'd be gentle.

As if he'd dumped her in an ice-cold ocean, her eyes sprang open, and her body went rigid. "Derek, I can't."

He froze. "I thought—"

"Wrong," she finished. "It's my fault. I started it. I'm sorry."

He lowered her legs to the ground and stepped away. "Me too, but it doesn't solve your immediate problem." Derek had no idea what had just happened, but then again, he never understood women.

# CHAPTER TWENTY-SIX

DEREK DROVE MORE AGGRESSIVELY than usual, as frustration pushed the pedal to the metal.

Stubborn woman. It had been a dumb idea to suggest she move in with him as a way to keep her safe. Once she pulled out of his embrace, Derek knew his chances of convincing her would fall on deaf ears.

Sure, Kelly said she'd think about the new arrangement, but he knew better. Yes, she admitted she wanted the protection, but staying with Derek brought back too many memories.

Bullshit.

He might as well forget about the whole arrangement. Once Kelly Rutland set her mind to doing something, it was as good as done.

It didn't matter that he promised to sleep on the sofa and let her have the bedroom. He knew what her problem was. He'd spooked her back in Utah when his damn spirit guides had taken him. Now she wanted as little to do with him on a personal level as possible. For once he wished she'd see him as a police officer and not as a former lover who had paranormal issues.

He slapped the wheel. Stupid, stupid. He should have insisted she pack immediately, but the hands on the hips thing she did so well and the squaring of her shoulders told him that anything short of hoisting her over his shoulder wasn't going to get her out of her house.

At least she let him check that all of the doors and windows were locked and the shades were drawn. He'd debated called Seinkievitz and asking him to stand watch, but if Kelly spotted him, she'd never speak to him again.

Shit.

If anything happened to her, he'd never forgive himself.

Derek could only hope in time Kelly would see reason. For now he needed to check on his dad and warn him a nutcase was on the loose. Thank goodness Billy would be staying there for the weekend. That would kill two birds at once, so to speak. While he was there, Derek might as well set a time for them to pack up Rayne's house too. Delaying any longer would only cause more grief.

Then there was the discussion about where Billy would live once school let out. Did he want to continue going to the military academy or move in with Derek and attend public school? Or did he prefer staying with his grandfather? His fingers clenched the wheel just thinking about that dreaded the confrontation.

Derek turned down his dad's road. The front porch light was burned out, but even in the dim moonlight, he could see the two missing shutters. The place probably could do with a new roof too. As soon as he was free, he'd help his dad fix up the house.

Guilt plowed through him. Derek had made that promise before and hadn't followed through. He made a vow right then and there to reconnect with his father no matter what happened with his caseload.

After he parked, Derek rushed up to the house and knocked. "Dad?" Derek twisted the knob. It was unlocked, and a fresh flush of frustration poured into his gut.

"Coming." His father sounded weak.

Derek pushed open the door. One low-watt bulb burned in the hall. The T.V. was blaring from the living room and the smell of...bleach? nearly knocked him over. "Hey, Dad."

"Derek, what brings you here?"

Worry laced the planes on his dad's face. His color was lighter than usual, but Derek decided he'd wait before he'd address his father's health.

"Is that Uncle Derek?" Billy said in an angry tone from the sofa, not bothering to look up from the TV. Billy had his feet propped up on the coffee table and a remote in his hand. Kids.

Derek moved into the living room and looked around. "Something's different," he said.

His father glanced at Billy. "I hired a maid. Figured with Billy here, us two bachelors needed someone to cook and clean for us. Right, Billy?"

"Right."

His cheap dad never spent money frivolously. "What's going on? Did you find someone from the reservation to help?"

Someone around his dad's age? Maybe he was finally coming out of his shell. After all, it had been twelve years since Mom died and eighteen since they'd divorced.

Billy put down the TV remote. "It's Mrs. Lupold. She was our maid before mom..." He looked away for a moment and cleared his throat. "Grandpa said he needed help and I thought of her. She's real neat."

The name Lupold rang a bell, but he couldn't place it. "Well, I have to say, the place looks better. How's her cooking?"

"Fine," they both said in unison. The expression on their faces so similar, a feeling of comfort grabbed him.

Derek sat down and motioned for his father to return to his seat. The TV blared and Derek shot Billy a glance. He lowered the volume a bit.

"I have some disturbing news. Rayne's neighbor spotted Justin lurking around the house."

Billy sat up and muted the TV. "That creep? Why was he allowed near our place?"

Derek forced his tone to come off as unbiased. "He still has a key. I'll ask him for it as soon as I find him. I checked inside but nothing seemed disturbed."

His dad took a puff on his pipe. "You still think he killed Rayne?"

His dad's eyes widened right before a coughing fit overtook him.

Derek started to rise, to see if he could help, but his father waved him down before dabbing a handkerchief to his mouth.

"You okay?" Derek asked.

"It's the stress, I think. I haven't been feeling my old self. I'll be okay though. Now tell me about your theories."

"Are you sure you're up for this?"

"Yes."

"Rayne's neighbor, the one who reported seeing Justin, was murdered today. She was strangled."

"Mrs. Anton?" Billy's face contained a mixture of curiosity and fear. Poor kid. He'd been through so much.

"I'm afraid so."

Derek expected him to add a comment, but he didn't. "Kelly Rutland received a call from Justin about an hour ago, claiming his mom was the one who killed Rayne and Kelly's sister, Stefanie."

"Who's Kelly?" Billy asked, his mouth in a frown.

Derek didn't want to get into their complicated relationship. "Her sister was Stefanie Gentry. She was a friend of Rayne's. I don't know if you ever met her."

"Stefanie? A couple of times, I think."

"Well, she died the same night as your mom, and we believe the two deaths are related."

"Oh."

Derek turned back toward his dad, checking to see if his breathing had improved. It hadn't. "Justin told Kelly his mom was on the warpath, and that she was next on her list of victims. If what he says is true, I think his mom might target you two."

"She doesn't know us," Billy piped up.

Derek didn't want to discuss the hate group issue with Billy. It was hard enough for Derek to deal with. "I know, but if she killed Rayne because of who she was, this insane woman might want to wipe out the whole family—including me." Anger rushed up his gut.

His father sat still, looking off in the distance.

A moment later his dad spoke up. "I'll keep my gun handy." He stood up. "I have something for you."

The tension seeped out of Derek's pores, because he'd expected an argument.

"Who's Justin's mom?" Billy piped up.

"Her name is Lilly Bladen. She used to live in Utah. Other than that, I don't know much about her."

"She old?" Billy asked.

"I'm guessing in her sixties."

His dad returned carrying a parcel wrapped in a worn cotton cloth. He stepped over to Derek and slowly unfolded the material. Billy shot up from the sofa, apparently interested in the item.

"It's the Chanupa pipe," his father announced with pride, as he unwrapped it.

It couldn't be. This was the sacred pipe. The chimney part, or receiver, was made out of ornately carved wood and was covered in green stones and multi colored crystals. The stem was less decorated but hollowed out to hold tobacco.

Derek's hands stilled. He knew the legend. The pipe was passed down from one generation to the next and represented the highest honor a man could receive. He'd seen his father use the pipe many times but had never even held it.

"I'm sure you realize," his dad continued, "that this pipe is the most sacred tool used by our people. Do you remember the ceremony when I received this?"

How could he forget? "Of course, but you're a shaman. I'm not." His voice came out breathless.

"You are deserving."

Did his father really believe that? Derek didn't dare let his hopes lift that he'd been forgiven for leaving the tribe. "I can't accept this gift. What about the ceremony where we pass the pipe around in a circle?"

His father shrugged, and then handed the sacred object to him. "Time is of the essence. There is a black cloud over us all."

That was an understatement. "I don't deserve this." He looked deeply into her father's eyes. "You said so yourself." Nonetheless, Derek examined the peace pipe, his heart pounding in his chest at the gift. Heat seemed to emanate from the cloth.

"I was wrong," his dad announced with more vigor than he'd shown since Derek's arrival. "Rayne was a grown woman. She made her own choices. I know I've pushed you hard to stay with the tribe, to help them instead of being true to what your mother taught you, but I'm proud of your achievements."

His dad's words meant the world to him and sounded a lot like his dream. "Thank you, but I still don't see why you're giving this to me."

He'd done little to be considered a part of the Seminole Tribe. He'd shunned them his whole life, but deep inside, he knew his soul belonged to his spirit guides.

"Evil spirits hover above us, and I am too weak now to pray as I should. When time permits, we will have the circle and drum ceremony. Your people will welcome you with open arms, but with this gift comes responsibility."

Derek knew he'd have to pray when others needed hope in their life. Could he be receptive? He didn't know. "I understand."

"If you smoke the pipe, remember what you wish for will come true."

Derek said nothing, not certain if he believed in its great power like his father did.

His dad cleared his throat. "It's getting late, and I'm tired. Goodnight."

With that, his dad shuffled back toward his bedroom. Derek could tell Billy wanted to inspect the pipe, perhaps even give it a try, but his time had not come. With care, Derek rewrapped the sacred item, his hands shaking from awe.

The honor bestowed on him by his father had yet to sink in. His whole life he'd learned of the mysterious pipe, learned of its powers, and learned how it could help a person find his way.

Now was not the time to tell Billy about the momentous event. Derek wanted to savor the moment.

Alone.

"We have a lot to discuss," Derek said to his nephew.

Billy eagerly leaned forward. "Like what you can do with the pipe?"

"No. Like packing up and selling your mom's house."

A flash of disappointment crossed his face. "Oh."

Now came the hard question. "Have you given any thought where you'd like to live when you're not at school?"

Billy trudged back to the sofa and collapsed down onto the seat. For a second, Derek thought he wouldn't answer.

"With Grandpa. He's cool. Besides, he said I could go to the reservation school. I want to learn about my heritage." Billy didn't look at Derek.

Derek bit back his retort that the reservation school system might not be as strong academically as what he'd get at the Academy. "I think you should know you might meet some resistance from the other kids." Derek certainly had when he had spent time with Dad one year.

"I've warned him," his father said, suddenly appearing from the bedroom door.

"I'm a Seminole," Billy said with the look of a fierce warrior. "Why would the kids not accept me?"

The air left Derek's lungs. "You're only one-fourth Seminole. That's a far cry from being full-blooded."

There were a hundred reasons why Billy shouldn't stay here. Derek wanted the best for his nephew, and he wanted to respect the wishes of his sister who never wanted her son to stay on the reservation.

Billy turned back to the TV apparently not willing to discuss the situation. "Whatever."

Derek stood. "We'll discuss this later."

Billy jerked back toward Derek. "How come I always have to do everything your way?" His anger was palpable.

Derek glanced up at his father who shrugged as if to say he wanted nothing to do with the argument.

What had his spiritual guides told him? Be tolerant. Embrace your heritage. Maybe they were right. If Billy wanted to make his own choice about how he wanted to live, perhaps Derek should give Billy the same opportunity.

"Be careful what you wish for," he said over the blare of MTV.

\*\*\*

Working on Saturday was not Derek's usual MO, but his obsession with the jumper case prevented him from staying home. He pushed aside the stack of folders and began to fill out the paperwork. Keeping his mind on the task remained difficult as his thoughts drifted to the other two cases.

When he'd awoken at four in the morning, he'd tried reading and even worked out, but the image of Kelly being threatened by Justin's phone call remained in his head. He'd called to see if she was okay, but apparently he'd woken her. She sounded a bit unhappy with his over protectiveness. Tough.

In all good conscience, he couldn't sit home and do nothing. He needed to be at work, needed to be involved, and needed to stay focused.

"Benally," one of the young officers said. "You have a visitor."

Derek looked up. A woman in her late twenties with pierced eyebrows and three, count 'em, three nose rings, dressed in too tight jeans, approached.

She held out her hand. "I'm Carl Vanderwall's sister."

Derek held in his surprise. No relative had shown up on the search. "Have a seat, Miss..."

"Lemón. Shirley Lemón." She stressed the second syllable.

"How can I help?"

Her features hardened, as if she didn't want to share information. "Every October I visit Carl on his birthday. Only this time when I arrived, the doorman told me he was dead." No emotion passed over her face. "I convinced him to let me in since I had nowhere else to stay. I hope that was okay since it was a crime scene and all."

Hard woman. "Yes. Thank you for being considerate." She didn't even blink. "I'm sorry for your loss. If I'd been able to find you, I would have called."

Now her eyes shimmered with a hint of a tear. "That's okay. Carl was my stepbrother. Anyway, I was looking through his things and found this envelope. I think you should read it." She handed him a number ten envelope. "It says a guy by the name of Justin Bladen probably killed him."

Derek's heart nearly stopped. He dragged on a pair of latex gloves and lifted the flap on the envelope. He doubted there'd be viable latent prints, but he didn't want to take any chances.

He read the contents. Twice. "Your brother claims to have proof that Justin cheated the Seminoles with their financial holdings. Did you find the evidence?" The ramification of the act lodged a rock in his throat.

Shirley pulled a large, brown envelope out from an equally large, red sequined bag. "Here. I looked at the stuff, but I don't understand any of it. Stock and bonds are foreign to me."

Derek scanned the material, understanding enough to see Justin had been cheating his father's people—or rather his people—and he swallowed hard. "May I keep this for evidence?"

"Sure." She slouched back in her seat. "Do you think this guy really killed my brother?"

"It's possible. I'm going to have to send the crime lab over to his place again." With the new evidence, he would insist on a more thorough approach.

She shrugged. "Okay."

Derek waved the file. "I appreciate this. I know you probably want to start packing his things, but could you wait until my men are done?"

"Sure."

Once Miss Lemón left, Derek assembled a CSU team to go over the condo with a fine-toothed comb. Even if they found Justin's prints at the place, it wouldn't prove he'd killed Carl. Coupled with the photo of Justin standing in front of the Waters Edge with the victim, however, he might have enough to hold him.

If they ever found the elusive SOB.

Kelly said Justin had claimed his mom left a note on his dining room table, which meant his surveillance team should have spotted her going into his place. So why hadn't they?

✳✳✳

Derek's team finished dusting every surface in Carl Vanderwall's place and came up with one palm print on the sliding glass door. Now all they needed was Justin to see if it matched.

"Hey Detective," one of the crime lab men said. "Look at this."

Derek stepped out onto the six by ten patio. Sun blasted him in the face, but the view commanded his attention for a brief moment. Nestled between hotels and high-rises, Tampa Bay's inlets were flanked by palm trees and dotted with boats. It was pretty as a picture. Too bad he couldn't enjoy the view right now.

He turned back to the tech. "What did you find?"

"Someone moved this plant, and I'd wondered why. I moved it and found a bloodstain. I'll test it back at the lab, but I'm guessing it belongs to either Mr. Vanderwall or the killer."

Derek stepped closer and did a quick scan of the area. "You find any evidence of a struggle?"

"Yeah. See here?" The tech pointed to the cement railing. "A small chunk of cement is missing. The whiteness of the cement implies the area hasn't been exposed to air for long. I'll ask Luis to check the back of the deceased's shoes to see if his heel smashed into it before he went over."

"Good work. Let me know what you find out."

***

About time the bitch went out for a run. It was too hot to be hiding behind a tree in the back yard in this damned humidity. Oh, how she missed Utah.

Once Kelly turned onto the access road, Lilly Bladen strutted to the front door and squatted in front of the clay flowerpot. She tipped up the edge and grabbed the key she'd seen Kelly stash there.

The surveillance camera she'd paid a hefty price for better be good, or someone wouldn't be breathing for long. Toting a large shoulder bag, Lilly ducked inside the cool house and looked around.

Eclectic at best. But clean. Good. She didn't have time to dust and vacuum.

Kelly usually ran for thirty minutes, which was enough time to hide a small camera in the bedroom and living room. Lilly wanted to keep track of the snoopy woman.

The girl had brought this on herself. If she hadn't slept with the filthy Indian detective, Lilly might have spared her. Bitches like her always squawked sooner or later. Might as well do her in now.

Lily sighed. Killing brought such a sense of satisfaction.

She shook her head at how today's youth didn't appreciate the art of ridding the country of unclean souls. First Kelly would have to die, and then Derek—in that order. She wanted the filthy half-breed to suffer when she snuffed out his little girlfriend. Lilly lived to see him in pain, the same kind of pain she'd been in when her dear husband had taken his life—all because an Indian received the promotion her husband deserved. Of course, if her husband hadn't gambled their money away, she wouldn't have had to spend her life being a stinking maid. She hated rich people and everything they stood for.

Before she put Derek out of his misery, the big chief and the grandson would need to die too. It was best to erase the whole gene pool. Lilly had already begun the old man's procedure. She'd crushed lily of the valley petals and made him tea. The guy didn't taste a thing.

She laughed at the wonderful irony. A lily by Lilly.

Tee hee. He'd die a slow and painful death, and Derek couldn't do a damn thing about it.

Enough reminiscing. Time for work. Lilly had spent time enough with Carlos to know how and where to plant the cameras. Even though he claimed they were like-minded, he didn't cut her any slack on the price of the surveillance equipment. Carlos was another link that might have to be severed. Stupid immigrant.

Fifteen minutes later, she'd finished installing the devices. Now Lilly would know when Kelly was home and what she was doing with Benally. Between the camera and the homing device in Kelly's purse, the girl wouldn't escape Lilly's ever-watchful eye.

She still couldn't believe her luck when Kelly had left her purse at home one day and Lilly had been able to drop in the tracing device. Dumb bitch never caught on. Kelly never figured out how she was located so quickly in Silverton either. Another reason to rid the world of her kind.

Time to go. Kelly's death would have to wait a little longer. Some psychological torture for the doctor would put the girl in a better and more receptive mood to meet her end.

Gathering her bag and all the hardware, Lilly ducked out the back door and slipped off her hair net and gloves. The sense of accomplishment put a kick in her step.

# CHAPTER TWENTY-SEVEN

As Derek headed back to the station, he punched in Seinkievitz's cell phone number.

"Mac's bar and grill." The noise from the station echoed in the background.

"Funny." Derek told him about the break in the case, specifically about the incriminating letter from Vanderwall's sister. Seinkievitz whistled. "Do me a favor and see about obtaining a warrant for Bladen's house." Derek cranked up the cruiser's AC to high and wiped his sleeve across his brow.

"Because?" Seinkievitz asked.

"If Bladen and Vanderwall fought, blood might have transferred to Justin's clothes."

"Good thinking. You told me you have a picture of Bladen talking to Vanderwall in front of the Waters Edge, right?"

"Yeah."

"Do you remember what he was wearing?"

"The photo is back at the station in evidence if you want to check it out. All I remember is that it was taken at night, so you might not be able to tell exactly what he had on. First, get a warrant. I'll be there soon."

"Will do."

For the first time in weeks, Derek could see the light at the end of the tunnel. Rayne's, Carl's, and Stefanie's killer might be brought to justice. If Justin were the perpetrator, once he was in jail, Kelly would be safe.

The man in the SUV in front of him sat at the green light. It wasn't until Derek honked that the man waved and took off.

He took a deep breath and tried to stay focused, but his mind wandered back to Kelly. Why would Justin call and say his mom wanted to harm her? Was that another way of warning her that he wanted to harm Kelly? Or was he telling the truth for once?

Not having identified Justin as a scum bucket right off the bat made Derek grind his teeth. If only he'd taken more time to get to know the kind of men his sister dated, she might still be alive. And if only she'd told Derek about the baby, or if he'd gone with her to Dad's, she'd still be alive too. If, if, if. He hated that word.

Derek needed to be more proactive. It was time to give Kelly a status report. He pulled into the right lane and dialed her number. After the third ring, his pulse sped up. "Answer, dammit." Five rings, six. He was about to hang up and race to her place when she finally picked up.

"Derek?" She sounded out of breath.

"What's wrong?"

"Wrong? Nothing. I just came in from running. Why are you calling?"

Strictly business. He could take the hint. He took a deep breath, relieved nothing had happened to her. "I have some news about Justin." He told her of the evidence they'd collected at the Waters Edge. "We're hoping not only to place him with Carl the night he died but prove he pushed him to his death."

She let out a croak. "Are you saying that Justin killed this jumper person, as well as Rayne and Stefanie?"

"It looks like it, but we have no proof to tie the cases together. Yet."

"So this whole thing about his mom being the killer was a ruse?" He could hear the relief in her tone.

Derek gripped the wheel. "It could be, but you can't let your guard down. If Justin is our man, he's dangerous. He knows where you live, remember."

"I know, I know." Her voice faded before she added, "And yes, I promise to stay safe."

Her mantra. Let's hope she took care. He hung up just as he pulled into the station. The warrant would take at least another twenty minutes to arrive. He had enough paper work to keep him busy for a good twenty-years, and that was just for this month's cases.

Seinkievitz was standing at the coffee station, drinking his usual sludge when Derek walked up to him. "Shouldn't you be scrapping up some judge to help with the warrant?"

His fellow officer smiled. "Already done, my man. Got hold of Judge Pinkley, who by the way was surprisingly cooperative. I was just waiting for your sorry ass to get here and serve it."

"Well, let's go."

Derek took his truck, while Seinkievitz and the crime techs drove a van to Justin Bladen's place. When they arrived, Derek slapped on his shades and dragged himself out of the car. Seinkievitz stepped out empty-handed.

Derek stopped and faced him. "So where's the warrant?"

"It's cool. It'll be here momentarily."

Sweat beaded on his forehead. "You implied you already had it."

Anger at being duped rushed up his gut. Derek normally didn't let something like this bother him, but the pressure to end the nightmare had eroded any shred of patience he had left.

Before Seinkievitz had a chance to respond, another officer pulled into the drive and waved a piece of paper out the window. How did Seinkievitz do that?

His friend just grinned. "Told ya."

Derek stomped over to the officer and grabbed the warrant. "Thanks."

The two policemen, who'd checked out the residence, stepped outside. "All clear, Detective."

"How did you get in?"

"Jimmied the lock."

Derek nodded. Batting away a host of pesky flies, he donned his sanitation gear before going inside. Once suited up, his team entered the house. The place looked and smelled unlived in. No dishes sat in the sink and the air was either off or too high to do any good. He sneezed from all the dust.

Derek headed straight to the bedroom. He'd visited Justin only a few times but remembered the layout of the place. "Seinkievitz, come in here."

This room was a different story. Clothes were either tossed on the unmade bed or on the floor.

Seinkievitz trotted in. "Boy, someone was in a hurry to get the hell out of here."

"You take the hamper, and I'll search the closet for the shirt."

Derek didn't expect to find it, but sometimes perps didn't realize bloodstains darkened over time. Justin might have stripped the moment he arrived home and not even looked closely at his clothing.

Seinkievitz pulled out the photo Stefanie had taken of Justin. Luckily, he was standing near a streetlight. His short-sleeved T-shirt was light colored, hue indeterminate. Derek tossed the picture on the bed. "Use this as a guide."

Derek studied the photo. Seinkievitz lifted up a pair of jockey shorts and grunted, his face contorted in disgust. "I hate touching a man's used undergarments."

"Get over it. That's why you're wearing gloves."

Derek drew open the sliding closet doors. Half of it contained suits and long sleeved shirts, the other half casual attire. After a quick search, he realized none matched the photo.

He turned to check out the chest of drawers when Seinkievitz swiveled around holding up a yellow T-shirt with faint stains on the front. "Bingo."

Derek stepped over to him, and Seinkievitz pointed to the stains near the shoulder. "You think that's blood?"

"Only one way to find out." Seinkievitz called to Phil Procaro to bring in his crime case.

After a quick spray of luminol, Procaro announced it was blood. Whose it belonged to was anybody's guess.

"Bag it and test it," Derek announced, more relaxed than he'd been in days.

\*\*\*

Kelly had packed and unpacked at least three times already. Part of her wanted to take Derek up on his offer to stay with him, since she'd be safe. However, if she were anywhere near Derek Benally, her traitorous libido would do her in. In the end, she'd get hurt when Derek solved the case and left her.

Still in the process of dealing with her sister's death, she couldn't handle any more turmoil. A little old lady wouldn't get the best of her, even if she had belonged to some hate group in Utah. It was Justin she had to watch out for. If he had killed the man at the Waters Edge Condominium, he was doubly dangerous.

Her gut instinct told her Justin liked her and that he had no grudge against her. If he'd wanted to harm her, he would have done so already. Right? Or was her logic flawed?

She thought back to Justin's phone conversation about his mother-turned-serial-killer, and chills raced down her spine thinking about how she'd run with Justin, gone to the Casino with him, and talked with him on the phone.

If she'd sympathized with his plight when he'd called, would he have asked to come over? And would she have let him? The creep factor escalated at that thought.

The kitchen phone rang, and she jumped. If couldn't be her mom. She never called this late. She wished it was Derek telling her Justin was in jail and all was well.

"Hello?"

Static crackled over the line, and then a soft click was followed by more static. "Kelly. Running away won't do any good. I'll find you."

The voice sounded computer generated, very different from the spooky jerk who'd called her at the Utah motel.

"Who is this? Why are you calling me?"

The voice laughed. Kelly couldn't even tell the gender.

"I want you ready for me when I come."

"Ready for what?" Kelly's voice cracked.

"You need to join your heavenly father."

Did the person mean her dad or God? Not that it mattered either way. She'd be dead. Her hand shook so hard she nearly dropped the phone. "Why are you doing this to me?"

A low growl emanated from the receiver. "Because you can't keep your nose out of other people's business."

"What business?" She could guess, but perhaps this person might slip up and reveal something personal.

"You figure it out. I suggest you run to that Indian man of yours and ask him. Then I can kill both of you at the same time." Mechanical laughter rang through the line.

Goose bumps broke out on her skin. Kelly fought to come up with a retort, but the dial tone ended her chance. "Damn it." She grabbed her stomach, trying to calm the acid burning in her gut.

Stay calm. Think.

Check the caller ID. That's what Derek had told her to do the last time. "Damn." It was another private number. Kelly doubted the caller was Justin though. He would have spoken directly with her and not put some kind of voice altering device on the phone. So who was it? Mrs. Bladen?

Derek would know. She needed to call him. As much as she wanted him here, would that put him in danger too? She couldn't chance her being responsible for his death. It didn't matter he was equipped to deal with a dangerous situation. Things could go wrong at the worst time.

Okay then. If the mountain wouldn't come to Mohammad, Mohammad would have to go to the mountain. In this case, the mountain was the police station. They'd find Derek for her. Surely, no one would attack her there.

Kelly grabbed her purse and keys, mace, and her cell phone. Before she left, she punched a nine and a one into her cell in case she needed to call the police fast.

She sucked in a big breath, her heart racing. If she made it to her car, she'd be fine.

Holding open the front door, Kelly looked right then left. Nobody was on the dead end street. Good.

Her car sat in the middle of her drive, and Kelly sprinted to the driver's side. Though the temperature was in the eighties, the high humidity made sweat form on her chest and legs.

The second her butt hit the car seat, she locked the door and let out a long held breath. Good she'd made it. Before she let down her guard, she spun around to check out the backseat. Phew. Thank God, the seat was empty.

Key in hand, she stabbed it into the lock and turned. The engine growled, but wouldn't catch. Ohmigod! "Come on."

Four tries later, the engine purred. She dropped her head back against the seat as paranoia gripped her.

Once Kelly calmed down enough to drive, she gunned the engine, squealing her tires as she tore down her road, actually hoping the police would stop her for speeding. Then she could get a personal escort to the station.

She turned on the radio to her favorite station, and a familiar song reverberated through the speakers, helping to calm her. Only when she reached the end of her street, did she remember to turn on her headlights. "Stay calm, Kelly. No one's behind you, no one's even on the road." Hearing her own voice seemed to do the trick.

She stabbed a hand into the cookie box she'd forgotten to take inside and stuffed another one in her mouth. She was going to make it.

As she neared the intersection of Dale Mabry and Richmond Avenue, a mile from her home, a large truck roared out from the side street. Kelly slammed on the brakes and twisted the wheel to avoid the collision, but the monster truck drove straight toward her.

*** 

The moment Kelly opened her eyes, she knew something was wrong—actually a lot of things. Pain assaulted her back and legs, and her mouth tasted like she'd swallowed a bucket of sand. Her head throbbed, as though she'd been hit in the head with a crowbar.

The horrible memory intruded. A huge truck had barreled down on her, leaving her no chance to move out of the way. She didn't remember the impact, but clearly the accident had happened or she'd still be driving.

The bastard hadn't tried to swerve or honk his horn. Surely he'd seen her.

He?

Kelly couldn't remember anything other than the big chrome grill that looked like a shark with its mouth open, ready to snap its jaws at her Bug.

Her surroundings finally filtered into her brain. Why was it so black? She strained to see something, anything that would tell her where she might be. The second she tried to push up, she realized her hands were bound together, and her heart raced and her gut soured.

"What the hell?"

A vice like pain took her breath away. She squeezed her eyes closed and panted, waiting for the head pain to subside. A moment later, clear thinking crystallized. This was no accident.

Ohmigod.

Someone had tried to kill her.

The second the realization hit, Kelly expected fear to grip her. Instead, anger nearly strangled her. Whoever wanted her dead wasn't going to get away with it. She'd do whatever it took to free herself.

But how? The moment she moved, nearly every nerve ending fired, paralyzing her again with pain. After taking several deep breaths, rational thought returned.

Her feet were trussed up tighter than a turkey, and anger once more ripped up her body. Her dad had been a cop before cancer ate away at his brain. What had he taught her? That's right—to assess the situation. That's what she'd been trying to do but to no avail.

Okay. Was she still in her car? Probably not. It was darker than hell in here. Sure she'd left the house near midnight, but even the moon would have shed some light through the windshield.

Kelly craned her neck as far as it would go to the right to check if perhaps she was facing the floor mat. Her check brushed against rubber, not carpet. That meant she was no longer in the driver's seat.

But where could she be? And who would have tied her up and left her? She remembered nothing of the impact or being rescued. Hell, she didn't remember being tied up.

She focused on the walls of her prison, hoping her eyes would adjust to the light, but nothing shone.

Was she blind?

Dear God in heaven.

Panic speared her gut. Nauseated, Kelly forced her mind off her pain. Vomiting would only make her plight worse.

Okay, she needed to think logically. Mildew flavored the air, implying she wasn't outside. Her knee rubbed against a bristled pad of some kind. Tentatively, she wiggled her toes, and then her fingers as far as the ropes allowed to determine the physical damage to her body. Everything moved. Good. As Kelly stretched out her legs, her feet came in contact with a wall. She scooted forward and banged her head against the opposite wall.

Though it took most of her reserve, Kelly tried to sit up. Half way to sitting up, she banged her head on the ceiling. Frustration zigzagged through her. This was so not happening to her.

From the size of the compartment, she figured she was in the trunk of a car, a small packing crate or... no. A coffin?

*Don't even think that.* The concept that she might be buried six feet under the ground with each breath eating up valuable oxygen had fear lodge solidly in her throat.

Pushing aside that terrible thought, Kelly raised her bound hands and came in contact with metal, plastic and bulges in the metal. It wasn't a coffin but a car. Good.

If only she could twist around so that her feet were toward the back, she might be able to kick out a light and signal for help—assuming this car was built like that.

She took a deep breath to regain composure, but a cough sent a spasm through her achy body. Shit. She kept coming back to who had done this to her? Justin? Or was the villain his phantom mom?

Uh, oh. Had Kelly stepped on someone else's toes at the lab? She was close to a breakthrough in the cause of breast cancer. Would a jealous coworker have done this? Most likely not, but it was an option.

This was a bad use of her time. Even if she figured out who had trapped her, the knowledge wouldn't get her out of here. An engine fired up and the floor vibrated. The vehicle accelerated fast, smashing the top of her head against a large ridge.

"Ouch. Fuck. Shit. That hurt!"

The car hit a bump and Kelly's hip rose then slammed onto the uneven floor. Dammit. Her eyes watered from the pain.

Her cell phone. Maybe if she could reach it, she could call Derek—or press the elusive number one button. Only where was the damn thing? She reached out her hands as far as they would go, hoping to locate either the mace or the phone, but it wasn't her lucky day.

Before she could formulate a plan, the car stopped. A moment later, the hood to the trunk opened.

"Rise and shine."

# CHAPTER TWENTY-EIGHT

JUSTIN OPENED his eyes from what felt like a really, deep sleep. The problem was that he didn't remember going to sleep. While he loved his soft bed, right now his muscles were on fire. He tried to lower his arms, but they wouldn't budge. What the hell? He gazed upward, confused at what he was seeing. Despite the moonlight shining through the window, he could only tell his arms were above his head.

He tugged, and his wrists complained. Damn it. Somehow he was tied to his metal bedpost. He pulled harder this time, not believing the bindings were real. They held. "Fuck."

The overhead light flashed on, and he squinted against the glare.

"Hello, Justin."

Her voice nearly paralyzed him. He shot his gaze toward his bound feet. "Mom?" His mother stood at the entrance to his room, ten feet from the edge of the bed.

She'd aged. Her hair was now gray, her hips wider, and face more lined. Her beady eyes looked the same however—evil, sick, and quite insane.

He attempted to sit up, but the ropes prevented him. "What the fuck did you do to me?" There was no question who was behind his hostage position.

She waved a Taser at him. "I couldn't chance you fighting me. I had to equalize the playing field." She stated this as a matter of fact, devoid of emotion, as if she tied up people on a daily basis.

He dropped his head against the pillow. "Jesus Christ." When she didn't say anything, he lifted his head up as high as he could. That was when he noticed Kelly kneeling his mom's feet. "Kelly?" His voice cracked.

A surprised shot of anger filled him at her bloodied and bruised face. Her hands and feet were tied, and her hair was matted on one side where a blood clot had formed. His mother stood behind her holding a bloodied knife at her side in one hand, the Taser in the other.

"What are you doing?" he asked. "Are you out of your mind? You kidnapped a doctor?" Not that her status in life should influence whether she was taken or not, but people would be looking for her—Derek Benally being one of them.

"I've come to beg for her life." His psycho mom smiled. "You owe me."

Beg for her life? What the hell did that mean? She had Kelly's life in her hands. Christ. She'd gone further over the edge since he'd last seen her twelve years ago.

"I don't owe you shit." She'd tried to frame her own son for murder for God's sake.

He knew he should go along with whatever she wanted until some form of reason intruded in her pathetic brain, but the years of anger toward her had built to a point where he'd never forgive her.

Her lips went into a full-blown pout. "You ran out on me after your daddy died."

"I had to. I was not only angry that Dad killed himself, I was pissed about being so goddamn poor. It didn't help that you never stopped harping at me."

"That's because you never thought about *me* and how much *I* was hurting. Everything had to be about you. You, you, you."

He refrained from rolling his eyes. Justin wasn't really in the position to piss her off any more than he already had. "I couldn't come back to the house, remember? The police were looking for me." Because of you, you old bitch.

"That's because you went and killed Novaro."

How could his own mother think that? Oh, yeah. Psycho bitch wasn't rational. She hated all Indians—not that he blamed her. "I never touched him. I always figured you did the dirty deed."

She smiled. "You always were a smart boy." The shift from accusatory to prideful came swiftly.

His muscles relaxed for a second, and then stiffened. "You killed him, and then framed me, didn't you?" If he ever got free, he'd kill her —just for the pleasure of seeing her die.

He caught a movement. Kelly held her upper body rigid, but her hands were working to loosen the ropes in front of her. If he kept his mom talking, maybe she'd be able free herself and stop his mother— and get him out of this hell.

His mom shrugged. "You were only eighteen. Besides, you had an alibi, and I figured it would take the focus off me. You were a strong boy. You would have come out unscathed."

Disgust raced through him. "What kind of mother are you?"

Her eyes narrowed into slits and her jaw tightened. "I wouldn't have had to kill him if you'd been a man and atoned for your daddy's death."

His blood froze. "You're insane," he whispered.

"I'm saner than you could ever imagine. How do you think I've gotten away with killing that stock broker man you hung out with or that disgusting foreigner? What was his name? Rafael something?"

"You killed John LaBelle and Rafael Garcia? They weren't even Native Americans for God's sake."

The police had hunted him for weeks, convinced he'd killed those men. Good thing he'd had a rock solid alibi or the evidence would have put him away for good.

"I know, but you liked them. My only regret was not waiting to kill them at a time when you didn't have an excuse." His mother's eyes glazed over.

He couldn't believe she wanted to ruin his life. "My God. You were the one who planted the knife with my hair wrapped around the handle."

She cackled for a second, and then sobered. The right side of her lip curled upward. "It would have worked if those cops hadn't been so incompetent."

He couldn't believe the depth of her hatred. "And you killed Rayne and Stefanie." It was a statement, not a question. The pieces of his life started to fall into place.

Her body jerked rigid. "I had to kill that Indian princess. You got her pregnant. How could you?" she shouted, her yellowed fangs showing. Spittle dripped down her chin. "Didn't I teach you anything?" She yanked Kelly's head back by her hair.

Kelly's eyes widened and her mouth opened, but not a peep came out of her, and his admiration grew for the steely-willed doctor. Kelly was smart not to whimper. His mom hated any show of weakness.

If his bedpost hadn't been metal, he would have ripped his bed apart to escape, and then he would have strangled his mom. "Yeah. You taught me a lot. You taught me to hate, but I'm nothing like you."

"So I can see. You're a weak, pathetic excuse for a man."

He bet she wouldn't believe that if she'd seen how he'd killed Carl Vanderwall. He wasn't stupid. If he told her, she'd run to the police.

He was tired of this game. "What do you want?"

"I want you to turn yourself in for Rayne's murder. I told you that before. They're closing in, and I can't survive in prison."

"You're outta your fuckin' mind if you think I'd take the rap for you."

Her mom lowered the knife to Kelly's throat and drew the tip across her neck. A large welt of blood pooled out, and Kelly gasped.

"Go ahead. Kill her." He put as much distain in his voice as possible.

She pulled back Kelly's head again, and blood gushed down her chest. Kelly's eyes bugged out. Sure, he felt bad for her, but not bad enough to risk his hide.

"This is my last warning. Just so you know, I wore your blue blazer the night I shot Rayne. Her blood is all over it. Once I deliver it to the police, they're going to put you away for life."

Her smugness and audacity infuriated him. His fists clenched, and he debated whether to believe her. His mother's comment about Rayne's pregnancy sunk in. Only he, Rayne and her dad knew she was having a child.

"How did you know she was pregnant?" His mom's uncanny ability to know everything about his life had been driving him crazy.

"Tsk, tsk. You know so little." Her knife hand dangled by her side. "I even had you fooled, didn't I? I was Rayne's maid."

His mother looked down at Kelly before he could respond. "Stand up, girl."

Glaring back to Justin, his mother sneered. "You have twenty-four hours to turn yourself in. If you don't, I'll kill her and leave the jacket where the police can find the damning evidence. I need my freedom."

Before the message registered, she dragged Kelly out the door.

"You can't leave me here," he shouted, struggling against his ropes, cursing when her only response was the gunning of her engine.

✳✳✳

The phone next to Derek's bed rang. He leaned over the nightstand to check the number. "Precinct." He groaned and fell back onto his pillow. He'd followed one lead after another last night trying to locate the elusive Justin Bladen, but by three in the morning his team had decided to wait until morning to continue the search.

Before he arrived home, he left a message for Mariani, the Sheriff at Silverton, to let him know that Bladen was on the loose and to be on the lookout for him. Somehow, he doubted Justin would pick such an obvious spot to hide out, but Mrs. Wolfendon had provided a safe hiding place before.

If the guy did plan to leave town, Tampa's airport security or the bus terminal personnel would detain him. Nothing, however, would prevent him from leaving by car. Even though Derek had notified the Highway Patrol of Justin's flight risk, the chances of them catching him were slim.

The phone continued to ring. "All right, already." He answered. "Benally." He sat up, recognizing the chance to sleep was gone.

"Detective Benally. This is Jodie with dispatch. We received a call about a yellow Volkswagen, belonging to a Kelly Rutland."

Every muscle tensed, his mind focused. "Did something happen?" His heart pounded.

"The vehicle was found on the side of the road. Apparently, it had been involved in a major accident."

Derek froze. "And Ms. Rutland?"

"I'm sorry, sir. I don't have the status of her condition."

He asked more questions, but the dispatcher knew nothing more. Once he hung up, Derek called all the major hospitals in the area, but none knew anything about a Kelly Rutland. Next he tried her cell. Again, no answer. He refused to succumb to the panic that had his gut in a tight hold.

He grabbed his sage packet and squeezed it tightly. "Help me," he prayed, not expecting the guides to answer but hoping they would nonetheless.

Derek was determined to find Kelly. The fact she was missing led him to believe one of the Bladen family members had a hand in her disappearance.

He punched in Seinkievitz's number, but the answering machine clicked on. "It's Benally." He told him about the call from the dispatcher. "Call me." Crap. Seinkievitz slept like the dead.

With his keys in hand, his cell rang again. Caller ID was a private number.

"Benally."

"Thank God I got hold of you. This is Justin Bladen."

# CHAPTER TWENTY-NINE

DEREK WASN'T sure he'd heard the man right. "Justin?" He pressed the button to raise the volume on his phone. A shot of hope tensed every muscle. Was he calling to turn himself in?

"Yes. Hear me out, man. I just spent three hours trying to free myself from my bedposts."

Derek couldn't form an image. "What are you talking about? And why call me? Call 9-1-1."

"You're shitting me, right? Every cop in the county is after my ass. I have something to do first."

"Tell me."

"My mom Tasered me in my sleep, and then tied me to my bed. She has Kelly." His words came out rushed as if he'd run a marathon.

Derek stiffened, his body ready for action. "What do you mean, she has Kelly?"

"My mother brought Kelly to my place with bound hands and feet. Her face was bruised. She looked, well, like hell."

From the distraught delivery, Derek believed him. The pieces began to make sense. "I received a call she was in a car accident."

"That explains a lot. I'm sorry, but I thought Mom had beaten her. Here's the thing," he rushed on without taking a breath. "My mom wants me to cop a plea for killing Rayne and Stefanie only I didn't kill them. She did." His voice escalated to a near shout.

Now was not the time to debate the truth of Justin's claim. "Go on."

"She said if I don't do as she says, she'll kill Kelly. And she only gave me—us—twenty-four hours."

A giant hand snaked up his gut, grabbed his heart, and almost squeezed the life out of him. "Do you believe her?" His heart beat hard in his chest.

"Yes," Justin shouted. "She killed not only your sister and Kelly's sister, but admitted to killing three other people."

Derek's mind whirred with horrible possibilities. The identity of Rayne's murderer gave him some solace, but right now he needed to focus on Kelly. "Where did your mom take her?"

"I wish I knew."

"Where are you now?" He needed a plan. Fast. With his cell pressed against his ear, Derek pulled on a pair of jeans and threw on a button down shirt while he kept Justin on the line.

"At home."

Derek's men had searched Justin's house numerous times. "No you aren't. The truth."

"Not the one in Tampa. I have a safe house. You wouldn't understand. My other place is a small, block home in Odessa. It's a rental. I use it occasionally when I-I need to get away."

That's why his men hadn't found him. Derek needed Justin as a bargaining tool with Lilly Bladen. "Can you meet me?" *Say yes.*

"Anything you want. I just want this nightmare to end before she hurts someone else."

Derek dashed out of his apartment and raced to his truck. He didn't know where he needed to go, but staying home wasn't an option.

He didn't know why the man had suddenly grown a conscience, but now wasn't the time to debate his decision. Derek checked his watch, his heartbeat only now slowing. "You said your mom gave you a twenty-four hour deadline. When was this?"

"Uh, I'm not sure. Two in the morning maybe. My wrists are so bruised and bloody from trying to escape that I lost track of time."

Derek had little sympathy for this jerk. "You sure you don't have any idea where your mom might have taken Kelly?" He jumped in the front seat of his truck and stabbed the key in the ignition.

"No. She's not from around here. Wait. If she was Rayne's maid, maybe—"

Adrenaline spiked his heart. "What did you say?"

"She was Rayne's maid. What difference does it make now?"

A hell of a difference. "Because she's now working for my dad." Fear and anger took hold of him and almost rendered him immobile. A tick stabbed his cheek.

Derek forced the rest of his muscle to move. *Don't think. Do.*

He cranked up the engine and backed out of the parking place, and a hint of burned rubber filtered into the cab.

"What do you want me to do?" Justin asked. "I feel this is partly my fault."

*Try more than a little your fault.* "We'll meet halfway."

They discussed a location on North Dale Mabry before disconnecting.

Derek needed to warn his dad. Now. He knew neither Dad nor Billy would be up this early, but given the emergency, he had to wake them.

The phone rang only once. "Hello?"

"Billy, this is Uncle Derek."

"How did you find out so fast?" he asked. "I was just going to call you."

Now it was Derek's turn to be confused. "About what?"

"The paramedics took Grandpa to the hospital a few minutes ago."

Shit. Fuck. Dammit. His world spun. "What happened?" If Lilly Bladen harmed his dad, he didn't know if he could control himself when he got his hands on her.

"Grandpa said his chest hurt this morning, and he looked real bad too. We learned in school all about the signs of a heart attack. He didn't want to go the hospital, but I called 9-1-1 anyway."

Pride swelled. "You did the right thing."

"Granddad even threw up, but I cleaned up."

"You should be proud of yourself."

"I tried calling you first," Billy rushed on, acting as if he hadn't heard the compliment. "But your line was busy." Strain raised his voice.

"Sorry. I just found out Kelly was missing. She'll die if I don't find her soon." Derek swallowed, trying to suppress his emotions. "But promise me something."

"What?"

"Don't let Mrs. Lupold near you or Dad. She's Justin's mom, and she killed your mother." Billy didn't answer him. Derek waited a beat, praying Billy would understand. "Billy, you okay?"

"It's all my fault then."

He remembered Billy mentioning he suggested Dad hire Mrs. Lupold--AKA Lilly Bladen.

Lupold.

Of course. Now he remembered where he'd heard that name. She was the cook for the leader of the white supremacist group in Utah. Either Lilly was in town during their visit, or she stole the name.

"Listen to me. It's nobody's fault. I want you to call Tom, Grandpa's good friend. His number is on the refrigerator. Tell him what happened, and have him to take you to the hospital. Now." He took a deep breath. "And Billy?"

"Yeah?"

"Don't leave grandpa's side for any reason. Don't go back to the house until I tell you it's safe, okay?"

"Okay." Billy's voice sounded young. Too young. Guilt at not rushing to his father's side warred with saving Kelly. Derek's father was in good hands though, and now Billy would be safe. It was Kelly who needed him.

Anxious to meet up with Justin, Derek put a flashing light on top of his truck and pressed the pedal to the floor.

***

Kelly didn't know which was worse—being shoved in the trunk of a car and threatened by a maniacal woman or being tied down inside a train boxcar that smelled of cattle and bleach. She could barely breathe from the dampness and intense odor. Of course, the stinky bandana Lilly Bladen tied around her mouth didn't help in breathing in quality air. The old rag tasted of mold and some rank chemical.

The woman was totally crazy. She'd tied Kelly's hands behind her back, and then wove the rope through some kind of metal eyelet in the wall. If that wasn't enough to keep her there, Lilly secured her legs together. She'd have more movement in a strait jacket.

Lilly had even bitched the whole time about having to work inside the dirty boxcar. Who told her to go there? She had to have known deserted rail cars weren't designed to be germ free.

Halfway through the take-Kelly-out-of-commission procedure, Lilly had used some kind of air freshener and sprayed the place down. The fumes alone nearly killed Kelly. What kind of woman tried to sanitize a hellhole? With a bleach byproduct, no less.

Kelly knew.

An insane one.

Thank God the woman left shortly after she finished, but Kelly was beginning to wonder what else was in store for her. Surely, Justin's mom wouldn't leave her here to die of thirst. Sick people needed closure, needed to see other people's pain, and they certainly needed the control.

The depression eating away at her was gaining speed at an alarming rate. No one would find her. How could they? She was in one of a hundred cars that were destined to go nowhere. Discarded junk.

For some reason, after they left Justin's house, Lilly had allowed Kelly to ride in the backseat without a blindfold. Yes, she'd been tied up, but a pain in her side made sitting upright difficult. Lilly must have believed Kelly wouldn't live long enough to tell her tale of torture and kidnapping.

Truth was, Kelly didn't really know where she was. The crazy lady must have sensed someone was following her, because she took right turns, then left turns, and drove in circles until Kelly lost track of their location.

Sure, she could identify the Aquarium in Channelside, but once they neared the docks and State Road 60, she became lost. When Lilly finally pulled into some lot, two lone streetlights shone on rusted looking train cars. The place appeared to be some kind of salvage yard she'd never known existed.

Justin's mom had taken the car keys and locked the car doors while she found the right place to stash her hostage. That had been hours ago. Kelly dropped her head back against the metal wall, forcing control. She couldn't give up hope, despite the thirst and hunger that were beginning to take their toll on her body. Her hands and feet had fallen asleep more than an hour ago from the tight ropes cutting off her circulation. Without movement, she might lose an arm or a leg. Right now, the future seemed like a distant hope.

Her thoughts swirled to Stefanie's mantra of thinking positively. If only Stef were here, they'd figure out a way to escape.

Tears oozed out of her eyes, forcing Kelly to blink. Her throat clogged. God, she so didn't need this. Forcing away the bad images, she only allowed the good ones to enter, but that wasn't easy.

Taking as deep a breath as she dared, she begged her muscles to relax. Then Kelly willed herself back to the Utah hotel where she and Derek had made love. She imagined her hands on his wonderfully strong chest and could almost feel his warm lips on hers.

Derek.

Her shoulders finally relaxed as a tear streamed down her face. She'd never get to tell him how stupid she was to think that because he believed in a spiritual guide that he wasn't the man for her. Derek caused her body to sing and her heart to rejoice. Why had she snubbed him?

She must have dozed, because when she opened her eyes, sunlight was sneaking in through a crack in the sliding door. It was dawn already. That meant her death was drawing near. Justin's mom had said she'd kill her in twenty-four hours.

Desperate to find something to help her escape, Kelly looked around the car. Intermittent lumps of dirt, or perhaps feces, lay scattered on the metal floor. Once more bile rose up her throat as reality returned. Kelly squeezed her eyes shut, fearing she'd vomit and choke on it.

When she dropped her head to gain control, a jab of pain pricked her throat where the insane woman had cut her, and another trickle of blood trailed down her chest. She understood the slice was superficial and that her blood had clotted within minutes, but each twist had broken the skin.

She hadn't prayed since her dad had died. Hell, she didn't believe in praying—until now—until she needed Him. But would He listen?

Rustling at the far end of the boxcar dragged her attention away from her self-pity. Whatever it was, it was too small to be a human. A rat, perhaps? Dear God. Kelly stomped her feet, sending numbing aches along her legs. The rat, or whatever disgusting animal it was, stilled. Kelly squinted to find its location, but too many dark shadows filled the car.

She scooted back against the wall. If the animal had found its way in, surely it could find its way out. Kelly tugged again on her wrists, but the rope refuse to give. A flare of agony vibrated up her arms. She could tell the skin on her wrists had long since rubbed off, by the burning sensation that was creeping up her arms.

Why, oh why, had Lilly Bladen targeted her? Had she learned of the trip Derek and she had taken to Utah? Is that what had set her off?

Speculation wouldn't get her any closer to freedom though. Instead, Kelly focused her senses on the outside sounds, praying someone would find her. Birds chirped and cars sounded in the distance, but no voices.

No activity.

No chance for escape.

If there were workers who tended this fleet of rusted trains, they wouldn't be working on a Sunday morning, that's for sure. Damn.

Kelly pounded her feet against the floor once more and waited for a response, hoping her banging would alert a passerby. Nothing. She pounded again. And waited some more.

Who would be sightseeing in a train yard? Kids, looking for trouble? On a Saturday night maybe but not during the day. Not even a homeless man would want to camp out here.

A rustling above her grabbed her attention. It was small scrapping sounds. One pair of feet. Then two.

She dropped her head back. Squirrels. They were just squirrels. Or was Lilly Bladen returning? Oh, God, was her time up already?

# CHAPTER THIRTY

DEREK CHECKED his watch once again. Where the hell was Justin? Was this some kind of ploy to put him on hold while he and his mother harmed Kelly?

What an idiot he was.

Why didn't it occur to him that Justin and his mom might be in on this whole sordid affair together? Justin hated Native Americans. He'd certainly proved it by cheating them. He'd even killed because of them. The man was no saint and couldn't be trusted.

Lilly Bladen was just as bad, if Mariani's reports were correct. Shit.

As Derek started his truck to get the hell out of there, a white Taurus pulled into the lot, but it wasn't Justin's navy blue Mercedes.

On a hunch, Derek waited a beat. As the Taurus neared, Derek spotted Justin in the driver's seat. Was he incognito?

Hand on his Glock, Derek opened the truck door, but he didn't step out in case he needed a fast getaway.

Justin parked ten feet away from him and jumped out. At least he wasn't lying about being tied up. His wrists were wrapped in blood soaked gauze and a hint of sympathy pricked Derek. The guy's hair was messed, his face was dirty, and his clothes looked like he'd grabbed them off a transient.

Justin didn't ask permission as he slid in the passenger side. His gaze shot to Derek's gun hand, and Justin raised his arms in surrender. "I know you think I'm responsible for all this mess, but I'm not. I swear."

Now wasn't the time to bring up the forensic evidence regarding the Vanderwall case. Not wanting Justin to bolt, Derek holstered his Glock.

Stick to the facts. "Can you contact your mother?"

"No, I've tried. She isn't answering her cell."

"What's her number?"

Justin pressed a series of buttons on his phone and spouted it off. "She won't answer, you know."

"Never know when a ringing phone can locate a person. Can I have your number too?"

Justin hesitated, and then rattled it off. Derek stored both numbers.

Time was of the essence. "You know your mother. What would she do with Kelly? Keep her in a hotel or what?"

Justin faced forward, his gaze straight ahead, showing no emotion. "Can you believe yesterday was the first time I'd laid eyes on her since I was eighteen? I had no idea she was so evil. So demented. So sociopathic."

Derek waited to see if Justin would continue, and when he didn't, Derek tried again. "Justin, I need your help. Kelly needs your help." He ground his teeth waiting for this pathetic man to answer. Man did he hate having to rely on Justin to help him find Kelly.

The man ran a hand down his face, and then turned back to Derek with an unfocused gaze. "When I was young, my mother came home after work one day." He glanced upward and shook his head. "My chore was to clean the kitchen, and let me tell you, the woman was a real neat freak. I became sidetracked playing some online game, and she was so upset I'd neglected my duty, she beat me around the face and stomach, and then locked me in my closet for over eight hours."

Justin's lack of expression caused a chill to form in Derek's gut. The man looked dead inside.

"So what are you saying?" Derek asked.

"No hotel. No luxury. We need to find a place that's hidden, dark, and disgusting—but most importantly dark."

An evil, slimy cloud gripped him. "The police found Kelly's car, wrecked and abandoned near her house."

"That explains a lot of why she looked like she did. Kelly's face was bruised, but she didn't look like she'd broken any bones."

"Good." But if she had been more seriously hurt, maybe Lilly Bladen wouldn't have bothered with her.

"Are you thinking my mother wouldn't go far from Kelly's place?"

"I don't know." Derek's mind whirred, mentally examining the side streets where she lived. "I can't think of any area like you described. The closest I can think of is the industrial areas near Channelside."

"There are plenty of ships in dry dock—and old ships are dark. It's Sunday, so no one will be around," Justin said.

Derek pictured the area near downtown. "It's better than nothing. Why don't you follow me? We might have to split up."

Justin nodded and slipped out of the car.

Channelside was an odd mix of expensive high rises, quaint shops, and restaurants that catered to the luxury cruise lines. Because of its shipping capability, it also contained maintenance services. But could someone gain access to the area? Or would Lilly Bladen have stored Kelly in a closed facility nearby?

He didn't have the luxury of analyzing the whole damned town. Gripping the wheel hard, he darted out of the lot. When he arrived, he'd have a better idea where to hide a person. Derek refused to consider Kelly might be dead.

Given the weekend traffic, he made it to the shipyard in less than thirty minutes. Justin pulled in behind him, and they both stepped out of their vehicles.

Derek kept his eye on Justin, not trusting him farther than he could see him. Just because Derek didn't spot a weapon didn't mean the guy wasn't packing.

"Where do you want to start?" Justin asked.

"Find anything small enough your mother could open, yet large enough to hide Kelly." He glanced around. "Since no one appears to be here, shout if you need to. If Kelly is stashed somewhere, maybe she can answer."

Justin pointed to the gate. "The lock's undone on the gate."

Hope raced up Derek's spine.

Justin's gaze shot around the area. "I don't see another car."

"That means nothing. Let's go. I'll search from the tugboat to the right, you take the left side."

Justin saluted and shot off in his appointed direction. Derek headed to the channel, and then edged along the water until he came to a storage shed.

Damn. A huge, shiny padlock held the door closed. The question was whether Lilly had put it there? Derek banged on the door.

"Kelly?" No response. "Kelly?" He placed his ear against the metal but heard nothing.

He turned around and looked up at the large tanker high on its cradle. No way Lilly Bladen could climb up the massive structure without the aid of a crane, and Derek didn't see any hidden nooks or crannies either.

The tangy smell of hot salt air, mixed with paint and oil irritated him. "Kelly?" he shouted.

Only seagulls answered his call. Dividing the area into quadrants, Derek did a thorough search. His legs were tired, but his spirit would not give up. Justin also was performing the same job on the other side of the yard.

Around ten, Justin dragged back to Derek. His face and hands were stained with rust, and grease covered his once blue shirt. "No sign of her. I don't think this is the right place."

Derek didn't respond. He wasn't going to give up. His jaw clenched as he headed off to finish checking the area. Justin followed behind him and grabbed Derek by the arm. "It's no use. We aren't going to find her here."

Bright morning sun streamed into Derek's eyes, causing them to tear. "I can't stop until I find her."

Justin backed off and held up both hands. "Okay, man, but I'm telling you, this doesn't feel right. We lived in Utah. There wasn't much water there. I don't see my mother choosing this place."

"Then where?" Derek wanted to strangle the ideas from Justin's fucking head.

"I don't know." He leaned back against a tall crane. "I need to eat something. We've been at this forever."

"Kelly will die in a little under twelve hours. We can't afford to pamper ourselves."

Justin let out a long breath. His face sagged. "Fine."

***

Kelly's mouth had dried up, and she hadn't been able to close her lips because of the disgusting rag Lilly had stuffed in her mouth. Once the saliva evaporated, the corners of her mouth started to bleed from her numerous attempts to dislodge the offending cloth. Her poor throat remained raw from grunting and shouting.

Dammit. Why her? Why now? Just when she'd found Derek again.

She dropped her head to her chest to build strength, but the intense heat nearly melted her skin off. Would she die from heat stroke and dehydration before Lilly came back? Oh God. She needed help.

One time she foolishly let her elbow touch the side of the hot metal and was burned. The sore still throbbed and ached, as did her cut neck.

She guessed the air inside this oven might be as high as one hundred and ten degrees. Now she knew what lobsters felt like when she used to dump them in boiling water.

It was time again—time to attract attention.

For the hundredth time, she banged her feet against the floor, and her heels protested at the impact. Somebody had to hear her—a passerby, a curiosity seeker, a tourist. Anyone.

Well, anyone but Lilly Bladen.

With the building of the heat, Kelly had lost track of time. Sunlight filtered on and off through the nearly closed door. How many hours did she have left? Eleven or one?

Adding to her misery, she needed to pee, bad, but she refused to go in the boxcar. She wanted to die with dignity.

The sound of an engine along the gravel drive caught her attention, and Kelly stiffened. Was it help? Or was it Lilly? She waited, holding her breath to key into the sound.

The car didn't come close though. Damn it.

She had to find a way to signal she was captive inside.

The rope that tied her hands to the back wall allowed her to rotate her body a few inches so that her hips were at an angle to the wall instead of against it. When she twisted, her raw wrists screamed in protest, but Kelly believed this might be her only hope of escape.

Using the side of her foot, she banged on the metal wall. The sound reverberated, clearly sending out noise. She kicked the wall three times, and then rested. The silence hopefully meant the car must had stopped.

Moaning as loud as she could, Kelly continued to bang and moan.

She paused. The engine started up. Nooo! They were leaving.

"No," she tried to yell, but all that came out was, "Ooooh."

In the distance, cars traveled past, horns occasionally honked, but it was as if the entire yard had been placed in an invisible shield. No one cared. No one came to help.

Kelly twisted back and partly slid down, dejected.

And then she cried.

She was going to die.

# CHAPTER THIRTY-ONE

DEREK AND JUSTIN sat on the tailgate of Derek's truck. He dropped his head into his hands, never more frustrated in his life. What good did his detective skills do when he couldn't find the woman he loved? He'd lost Rayne; he couldn't lose Kelly too.

"Now what?" Justin asked as he wiped his brow with the hem of his shirt.

Derek pressed the button on his watch. "We have, what, less than two hours?"

"Closer to one."

Justin sounded equally as dejected. Derek was tempted to believe he wanted to find Kelly.

"We looked in every storage facility, every warehouse, every conceivable place to hide someone in the entire Channelside area," Derek said. "Unless your mom commandeered a boat and is sailing the high seas, I don't know where else to search."

Justin swatted away the bugs. "Let's discuss this in your cab. The mosquitoes are driving me nuts. Besides, I left the other half of my burger in there, and still I'm starving. You mind?"

And if he did? A big, fat dragonfly buzzed his head. That did it. "Sure."

Derek slid into the driver's side and turned on the overhead light. His stomach already churned with the fear of not finding Kelly, and the smell of the cold hamburger nearly made him gag.

"Do you love her?" Justin asked.

Derek assumed he meant Kelly. He wasn't sure if he wanted Justin to know for fear he might use his feelings for Kelly against him. "Did you love Rayne?" he threw back.

Justin slammed the hamburger down, the paper crinkle sounding like a gun blast. "Of course I did, but that's not what I asked."

Yeah, Derek knew that. "Yes."

"How long?"

He really wasn't in the mood to have this conversation, but Justin was helping him look for her. "Forever."

"Wow." He stuffed the other half of his hamburger in his mouth.

Wow was right. Kelly had been his life in high school, making his life tolerable. No, more than tolerable. She made it wonderful. Even after his mom and dad had divorced, they fought. Living mostly with his mom wasn't always pleasant either.

"What's this?" Justin picked up the cloth wrapped pipe that Derek had placed on the seat next to him. Before Derek could grab it back, Justin unfolded the material. "I didn't think you smoked."

Derek refocused and snatched the Chanupa from him. "I don't." He refused to discuss the meaning of the sacred item with someone like Justin.

"You confiscate it in a drug bust or something?"

"Or something."

Derek rewrapped the pipe and held it on his lap.

Justin's whole demeanor changed from curious to disgusted in a flash. "It's Indian, isn't it?"

Derek didn't answer. Instead, he grabbed the pipe, hopped out of the cab, and stalked away. No way did he want the prejudiced prick to make fun of something so valuable.

His dad's words came to him. *Smoke the pipe. Whatever you wish for will come true.* Right. Only those worthy could reach another level by praying.

Derek glanced over his shoulder. Justin fortunately hadn't followed him out. Good. Derek turned on the flashlight he'd picked up at the store and headed over to a cement wall.

Alone.

Finally.

A small amount of leftover tobacco remained in the bowl. Perhaps he'd give the wish maker a try. What harm could come of it? With less than an hour left of Kelly's sentence, Derek would try anything to save the woman he loved, even if she could barely stand the sight of him. He checked his cell to see if Seinkievitz had called since he too was supposed to be searching for Kelly.

Derek sat cross-legged and took several deep breaths. He had to chance that when he entered his trance state and ceased to be aware of his surroundings, Justin wouldn't sneak up on him.

For Kelly, he'd risk it all.

After lighting the pipe, he inhaled deeply, and the powerful tobacco made him cough.

*Wimp.*

He steeled himself against the sudden loss of control that was sure to come, and he drew in another puff, willing the warm scent down his throat. The smoke swirled into his lungs, and Derek embraced the warmth, embraced the power.

With eyes closed, Derek slowly began to move away from his body. A small figure appeared cowering in a corner of a darkened space. He felt the smoke rattle along his insides, but his hands no longer moved.

It was the light from the bowl that illuminated her red hair.

"Kelly?" he said without opening his mouth.

She didn't answer. Couldn't she see him?

"Kelly?" He willed her to respond.

She was so near, yet Derek was unable to touch her.

He tried to make his feet move and his arms to grab her, but his spirit remained at a distance.

She looked up and seemed anxious, as if she could sense his presence. Derek scoped out the area, trying to get his bearings. The metal walls looked old and rusted. He'd seen many like it during his search today.

Frustration spurred him on. "Where are you, Kelly?"

The heat of his tears ran down on his cheeks, and gurgling water rushed past the container. A train horn hooted.

Then a hand rested on his shoulder. Startled, Derek's eyes flew open. Justin stood above him, a flashlight in his hands.

"You scared the crap out of me," Derek said. He jumped up and stepped back to get away from Justin's grasp.

"What about me? I called you about a hundred times. Where did you go?"

Explaining his vision to Justin would open him to ridicule, not to mention a gazillion questions. "I know where Kelly is."

*∗∗∗*

Kelly had a hard time keeping her eyes open, but what was the use? Total blackness was total blackness. Her senses failed to record her surroundings. Every passing car had raised her hopes, but those hopes were dashed time and time again. Eventually, she stopped listening, stopped smelling the putrid air, and stopped having feeling in her hands or feet.

Her upper arms throbbed from having her arms tied behind her. She didn't try to move her wrists anymore because the rope burn tortured her skin. At least the air inside the car was beginning to cool. The caked sweat and dirt had disgusted her at first, but now she didn't care.

The worst part was that she had to pee—really, really badly. Sitting in hot urine was totally unacceptable however.

A loud clap of thunder aroused her out of her stupor, and then a thin light streamed in the cab. Oh shit. It wasn't thunder, but the big metal door opening. She didn't delude herself into thinking someone had come to rescue her. There hadn't been any shouts. It must be Lilly Bladen.

A strong light blinded her, forcing Kelly to squint, and the insides of her eyes glowed red.

"I'm glad to see you looking so well," Lilly said.

God, she sounded like the wicked witch of the North, or was it the East? Hell, did anyone really care which direction she came from?

"Ca ou ake oo i …" Kelly said. Even she knew she made no sense.

Lilly laughed. "You want me to take off that rag?" She bent down and placed something heavy on the metal floor. A gun, perhaps?

Slightly limping, Lilly stepped behind Kelly and undid the cloth. Freedom—sort of. Her jaw actually ached when she closed her mouth. Slowly, she stuck out her puffy tongue and ran it along her lips, but it didn't do any good. There wasn't a drop of fluid left in her body.

"Did you miss me?" Lilly said, acting as if she'd come home to cook dinner for the family.

Kelly said nothing, not wanting to set her off. Lilly flashed the light at her wrist. "My how time flies. I did so want be able to set you free, but alas, that jackass son of mine never called the police station. And I checked. You couldn't believe how stupid the police are these days. I pretended to be Mrs. Benally and asked if anyone had confessed. Of course, no one had. If only my son had told them he'd killed Stefanie and Rayne, I could have set you free. But no. Justin chickened out. That weakling wouldn't even lie to save me. Is that anyway to treat a mother?"

She hoped her question was rhetorical. Kelly tensed as bile shot up her throat. She pushed back against the metal wall. Her hips and shoulders ached, and the rope rubbing on her ankles and wrists nearly made her pass out from the pain, but she forced herself to remain quiet.

"Well, it's time. Do you have any last words? Not that anyone will be around to hear them. Oh, my goodness, I denied you your last meal, didn't I? The least I can do is listen to your dying wish." She coughed. "Aren't I witty? Your dying wish."

"Why me?" Kelly croaked out, her voice a notch above audible.

"To tell you the truth, I thought my son liked you. I figured he might have a conscience and want to save you, but alas, not."

"I hardly knew Justin. He was Rayne's boyfriend."

Ambient light from the flashlight wasn't enough to see much of the woman's face, but the sudden stillness told her she'd hit a nerve.

"That whore. She got pregnant with my son's blood. The bastard would have been unclean. I had to kill her."

"That's between you and Justin."

"I'm not going to fall for your stall tactics. It's time for you to die." Lilly bent down and picked up what Kelly could only guess was a gun.

Her heart sped up so fast, she thought it would jump out of her skin. Kelly ran through a ton of possible things to say to this crazy woman, but in the end, she understood nothing she said would do a damn thing to stop the inevitable.

Her one regret was not telling Derek that she never stopped loving him. Kelly finally understood how much comfort Derek's spirit guides must have brought him in his time of need. She'd spent her whole life believing in hard facts and science.

Now she could see, she'd been the fool.

∗∗∗

Justin widened his stance and squared his shoulders. He looked like a fucking gun fighter at the OK corral. "How do you know where Kelly is? Have you been stringing me along for some sick reason?"

"Hell no. I just figured it out. Come on," Derek said.

Without giving the explanation Justin apparently wanted, Derek sprinted back to his truck. He trusted Justin would follow, if only to satisfy his curiosity.

The water gurgling, the boxcar, the train horn, all added up to the salvage yard near the Interstate. Why hadn't he thought to look there?

Derek sped as fast as he could. If Justin kept up, fine. If not, who cared. There would be no bargaining with Lilly Bladen tonight.

With no traffic, he made it to the train yard in less than ten minutes. To think they'd been so close, yet so far.

At the entrance to the yard, he slammed on his brakes. A blue Cavalier sat in the lot. That might not mean squat, but it could mean Lilly was here. He bet she never suspected Derek and her son would find her before Kelly's time ran out.

Oh please, make her time not be up.

Justin's headlights came to a halt behind him and his tires crunched on the graveled lot. Derek parked, hopped out, and motioned Justin to stay back.

"Why here?" Justin asked.

"I had a hunch. Let's leave it at that."

"Was there dope in that pipe? Is that you were doing? Smoking some hooch?"

"Sure. Just listen."

Both stood silent. Derek focused his senses, hoping to hear voices, but nothing sounded. He motioned for Justin to take the north side and he the south.

Justin shook his head. "I don't have a gun. If I find my mom, she'll kill me."

"All right," Derek whispered, pissed Justin turned out to be such a wimp. "Follow me, but don't say anything."

They started two-thirds the way down the line of cars, near where the blue car was parked. Derek stopped at each train car, placed his ear on the door, and listened.

Justin broke away and walked toward the car behind the last one Derek checked. Derek raced over to him and grabbed his arm.

Justin pulled away. "I smell bleach."

"Huh?"

"My mom cleaned the world with bleach."

While his logic made no sense to Derek, he was willing to give the train car a try.

Before he got ten feet, a scream burst through the metal walls.

# CHAPTER THIRTY-TWO

DEREK DIDN'T REMEMBER ACTUALLY RUNNING to the train, only grabbing the handle and ripping back the sliding door. A loud, squeaky groan sliced through him. Heart drumming his gun drawn, and the flashlight shining straight ahead, he hopped into the car in one leap.

Lilly Bladen raised an arm to shield her face from the glare but kept her small caliber gun pointed at his chest.

"Drop your weapon," Derek said in his most threatening tone.

"That you Benally?"

Had she expected him? "I said, drop it or I'll shoot."

"Like hell I will. I want you to see her die, you filthy Indian."

He wanted to blast a hole in her chest right there, but he had to try to reason with her. He wanted her to confess and tell him why she killed his sister.

Lilly stepped back, lowered her gun and pointed the weapon at Kelly, her gaze still on him. Derek chanced looking at Kelly for a split second, and his knees almost buckled. Lilly's flashlight shone on Kelly's face. Puffy lips, bruised face, and cut neck. His heart sank. Derek wanted to go to her, but he would have had to go through Lilly Bladen to reach to her.

"You know you won't get away with this?" Derek changed his tone to soft, almost caring, as he edged closer to Kelly. He had to reach he, needed to reach her.

"I don't care. I want you to feel the same pain I did when that Indian killed my husband." Spittle dripped down her chin.

Killed her husband? Try suicide.

"Hi, Mom." Justin stepped from behind Derek. "Put the gun down. Kelly didn't do anything to you."

Her beady eyes squinted and her mouth formed a tight circle. "What are you doing here? How did you get loose?"

Justin held up his hands, and her flashlight swung over to him. "It took a lot of work, but I freed myself."

"You slept with that disgusting woman. How could you?"

"You cleaned her house. How could you do that?"

Her arm shook and the light bounced up and down. "You never should have left me."

Derek had to hand it to Justin for keeping his cool. He slid another foot closer to his destination.

"Mrs. Bladen, for the love of God, put down the gun," Derek said with as much patience as he could muster. "I won't let you kill three people."

"I only need to kill one."

With that, she swung her gun arm and flashlight toward Derek.

He aimed his gun to nail the bitch just as Justin jumped between them. Before Derek could push him to safety, her gun report sounded, and Justin staggered backward, the smell of cordite filling the small chamber. A casing bounced on the metal floor.

Derek then fired two rounds into Lilly Bladen's chest. She dropped to her knees, and the gun clanked to the ground. Her eyes widened. "I wanted you to suffer. I wanted your father to suffer," she huffed out, her words angry, bitter, and spiteful.

At the mention of his father's name, Derek sprung forward and kicked the gun away from her reach. "What did you do to my father?"

He wanted to shake her and beat her senseless, but he needed answers.

She smiled. Blood stained her teeth. "I poisoned him. He's going to die, just like Rayne. You're going to suffer, you filthy Indian."

With that she melted into the floor. She was dead.

Derek couldn't begin to understand the depths of this woman's evil.

"Derek?" Kelly's weak voice shook him out of his trance.

He spun around and dropped down beside Kelly. There was so much to tell her, so much joy to share that he'd found her in time.

First, he had to undo her bindings. With his flashlight in his mouth, he withdrew his knife from the sheath at his leg. In no time, he'd cut her bindings, and then drew her into his lap and wrapped his arms around her. She might have smelled of sweat and blood, but to him, she'd never been sweeter. Kelly was alive and that's all that mattered.

"Justin. What about Justin?" she asked. She appeared more concerned for him than for herself.

Derek had forgotten about the guy in the haste of the moment. He turned. Justin was on the ground, his eyes closed. His chest rose and fell in spasms. "I have to set you down for a moment."

Her lips formed a small smile. "Yes. Help Justin. He saved your life. Go."

Derek replayed the event. Justin had stepped in front of him as Lilly had raised her gun. He couldn't comprehend why Justin had given his life for him—for an Indian.

Derek raced to Justin's side, and then called 9-1-1. He requested two ambulances and one medical examiner. Then he called the hospital to report his father had been poisoned. With what, he didn't know.

"I can help," Kelly said, her voice scratchy and weak.

As much as he wanted Kelly to rest, he could hear the need in her voice. Derek returned to her and helped her over to Justin. Her legs shook, but otherwise, she appeared okay. "I have a med kit in the car. Let me get it," he said.

"Good."

In a flash he was back. "Here you—"

She shook her heard. "He's dead. I couldn't do anything for him. The bullet must have pierced an artery." Justin's flashlight cast enough light to see the tears on her cheeks.

As if the gods pushed them together, Kelly crawled into Derek's arms and sobbed until her body shook no more.

He rubbed her back, careful not to bump her ankles or touch her tender wrists. "It's over, Kelly. No one will harm you again."

"I thought I'd never see you again."

Her words confused him. Because he believed she never wanted to see him again, Derek didn't know how to answer her.

Sirens sounded in the distance, and seconds later, strobe lights from the cruiser and ambulance trailed into the parking lot. Kelly gripped him hard.

"It's time to get you cleaned up," he said.

She nodded as the paramedics helped her out of the car and then into the ambulance.

"Benally."

Derek held up his hands to block the light. "Yeah?"

Medina and Seinkievitz climbed up on the bed of the train car. "When you go after a killer, you go after a killer. What the hell went down?"

He filled them in on the scary night.

Seinkievitz smiled. "You just solved my case. Thanks! And best part is you get to do the paperwork."

Great. He'd be buried for years. "I'm going to let you two dufuses handle this clean up though. I want to check on Kelly."

"You got it."

* * *

Kelly shivered in the emergency room as a nurse cleaned and bandaged her wrists and ankles. She smelled of stale sweat and cow dung. Of all the cars for Lilly Bladen to put her in, why did it have to be one that had carried animals? The bleach she poured on the floor hadn't helped.

Her skin crawled at the thought. She didn't dare count the number of bug bites on her legs. All Kelly wanted to do was go home and take the longest shower known to mankind. Then if it wasn't too late, she'd make amends with Derek.

Hunger pangs sent out a rumble from her stomach. She hadn't

eaten in over a day and a half. It was no wonder her legs had trouble holding her up.

After having her blood pressure measured, which was a tad too low and her temperature taken, which was thankfully normal, they agreed to release her.

"You have to drink a lot of fluids," the pretty nurse told her.

"I promise." Kelly didn't mention that she was a doctor and perfectly capable of taking care of herself.

"Wait here a moment, I'll be right back with a prescription for some pain meds for your cuts and bruises."

Kelly slid off the examination table and attempted to straighten her bloody shirt and pants. Uh oh. How was she to get home? Without a purse, she couldn't even pay a cabdriver. If she hadn't known an administrator in the hospital, she wondered if they would have cared for her.

Good thing she'd stashed a spare key under the flowerpot near the front door or else she wouldn't be able to get into her house. At first, she thought about calling Chip for a ride, but she hated to disturb him. He had to be at work in five hours.

She bet Derek would be working the case for another few hours. Poor man looked beat.

Derek.

He'd showed no reaction when she told him she didn't think she'd see him again. He probably thought she meant she didn't want to see him again, not that she didn't think she'd be rescued.

Her mind was in no shape to be figuring out complicated interpersonal relationships at this hour. She needed food and sleep.

"Need a ride?"

Startled, she turned around. "Derek!"

Kelly wanted to rush into his strong arms, but his stern look made her falter.

His gaze traveled the length of her body. "You good to go?"

She held up both her bandaged wrists. "That's what the doc said."

His whole body relaxed. Tentatively, he raised his arms for a hug, and she rushed into his embrace. Kelly pressed her face against his sweat stained shirt, but she didn't care if he'd rolled in the cow dung. His solid body healed her better than any gauze and salve ever could.

The nurse returned. "Hear ya go." She handed Kelly a prescription. "Take care."

"Thank you." She turned to Derek. "Am I glad to see you," she said, half into his shirt.

"Oh, yeah?" Delight tickled his tone.

Kelly looked up at him. "I could really use some food and a hot shower about now. How about you?"

He smiled and her knees weakened. "I'm right there with you."

Once she finished with the exit paperwork, Derek escorted her to his truck. She looked up at the sky to enjoy the view of the moon. Fast moving clouds skipped in front the orb, tucking them in darkness for a second. The sweet smell of the night blooming jasmine put a renewed bounce in her step. After all she'd gone through she couldn't believe she was alive.

Kelly wove her arm through his. "How did you find me? How did you think to look in a train salvage yard or whatever that place was?"

The streetlamp cast a shadow on his face so she couldn't get a good read on his expression.

He looked down at her with the sweetest smile on his face. "Let's say I had a hunch."

Derek opened the truck door for her and she scooted in, happy to be safe. He climbed in the driver's side.

"What kind of hunch? I know you're good, but no one's that good."

He bit down on his lip and jabbed the key in the ignition. Kelly waited for an explanation but none came. Too tired to dig deeper, she rested her head against the back of the seat.

"Wake up, sleepy head."

Kelly started. The overhead cab light shone in her eyes. She squinted. "What?"

"I thought you wanted a hot shower, some food, and then jump into bed."

"Shower, food, bed, good idea."

Suddenly, she was in Derek's arms—his wonderfully strong arms. Kelly dropped her head against his chest and took a deep breath. "Whew. You smell almost as bad as me."

He laughed and when he placed a big, sloppy kiss on her cheek, joy tumbled in her belly.

When they reached her door, he set her down. "Where's the key?"

"Look under the flowerpot."

Derek retrieved her spare key, opened the door, and then lifted her into his arms again. With his elbow, he flicked on the hall light. Derek strode straight toward the bedroom.

"Where are you going?" she asked.

"To the shower, madam."

Kelly couldn't help but giggle. Only when he let her stand for the second time did it occur to her they were both in the bathroom.

Derek unbuttoned his shirt and slipped out of his shoes and pants before she could move.

"What are you doing?" she asked, not believing he was almost naked.

"I smell. You smell. I need a shower. You need a shower. What's not to understand?" His cheeks dimpled.

Kelly's jaw dropped open. "You're not thinking we're going to shower together are you?"

"Oh, yeah."

# CHAPTER THIRTY-THREE

"TURN AROUND," Derek commanded.

Kelly gave him her back and palmed the shower walls to keep her balance. Derek took one step forward and reached around her to run his soapy hands over her breasts.

"You don't know how good that feels," she said, sinking in against the wonderful contact.

"You should be my hands."

For a moment, Kelly tucked away the horror of the last day or two and thought only of being with Derek, who was ever so naked and very hot.

His jutting erection pressed against the small of her back, and despite the physical and mental trauma of the last thirty hours, her body couldn't help but respond to him. Kelly let the steam fill her nose and relax her aching muscles. "I don't think I'm supposed to get the bandages on my wrists wet."

Derek nuzzled her neck. "Not a problem. You relax and I'll clean you real good."

"Hmmm." She dropped her head back against his chest and let the hot water sluice down her body.

Every muscle throbbed, but Derek's fingers massaged the kinks away. He soaped her neck, and then dragged a finger down her throat. "Are you doing okay? Do you want me to stop?"

Kelly could hear the teasing in his voice. "You better not stop. If you do, I'll fall asleep on my feet. Your hands are the only things keeping me awake."

He nudged his erection against her back. "Oh, yeah."

"In your dreams. As soon as I'm clean, I'm falling asleep."

He said nothing as he methodically worked his way up and over her breasts and down her belly. When he squirted more liquid soap onto his hands, the strong scent of lavender dispersed throughout the hot shower stall. She'd almost relaxed to a point of dozing off, when his slippery fingers slid in between her folds.

Kelly jerked to attention, and her eyes opened wide. Her hips seemed to move in rhythm to his sensual plunging fingers. How could she be turned on after all she'd been through? Like an alien invasion, her emotions took over her mind.

"I think your front's clean," he announced.

She groaned. Soon her back, bottom and legs were soapy, and she let her mind wander to the wonderful ways she'd explore his body.

After he washed and rinsed her hair, she faced him. "Now it's my turn."

He shut off the water. "I washed in between cleaning you up. It's time for you to get some sleep. It'll be dawn soon."

As much as Kelly wanted to experience running her hands down his rippled muscles, fatigue claimed her. "You're right."

Dark circles rimmed his amazing eyes, but before she knew it, Derek had the towel wrapped around her head and body. He swatted her bottom, and then helped her out the door. "March." On his way out the bathroom, he grabbed a towel for himself.

The bed loomed large, and Kelly could barely keep her eyes open. Derek rifled through one drawer after another until he found a rather skimpy black lace nightie. "This will do," he said with a smile.

Too tired to argue, she let him slip it over her head. A second later she was airborne in his arms and then on the cool sheets.

He tucked her in, kissed her gently on the mouth and eyes, and then crawled in next to her. Before she could figure out if that was his hand on her thigh, sleep overtook her.

✳✳✳

Kelly jerked awake, the smell of bacon and coffee teasing her senses. Coffee. Now that was pure Heaven. She sat up and winced, and then fell back against the soft pillows. She felt as if she'd gone ten rounds with a heavyweight.

Closing her eyes again, the fought off a vision of Lilly's hateful face and concentrated on Derek, on how tender he'd been the night before when he washed her and put her to bed.

When Stefanie's smiling face came to mind, Kelly acknowledged her sister would always be with her in times of need. For now, Stef would be safe and always loved in Kelly's mind. Without a doubt, her sister would want her to move on.

Derek carried in a tray, laden with a steaming cup of java and a plateful of eggs and bacon. "Here ya go."

"You are too sweet," she said, tucking thoughts of her sister away for now.

"Wait until you taste the food. A cook I am not."

Kelly didn't care if the eggs tasted like rubber. No one had made her breakfast in bed before. Derek placed the tray next to her, unfolded the linen napkin and placed it on her chest.

She laughed. "You going to feed me too?"

"Depends on whether I can have kisses in between bites."

Kelly dragged the plate to her lap and began to shovel the food into her mouth. She didn't care if her table manners embarrassed her. "This is divine. Aren't you eating?"

"Already did."

A pang of depression stabbed her. She pushed her food around on her plate as she remembered Justin. "I can't believe Justin is dead." She looked up at him. Tears blurred her vision. "Why did he step in front of you like that?"

Derek took her hand in his, and she drew in his strength from his rough palms. "We have fairly strong evidence that Justin killed Carl Vanderwall."

"Justin really did kill someone?" There had been times when she suspected he might have harmed Stefanie and Rayne, but never someone else. "Why?"

"Vanderwall's sister brought in some documentation that claimed Justin was cheating the Seminoles. You remember the photo of Justin by the Waters Edge Condominium that your sister took?"

She nodded. "Yes. It was dark and we couldn't see much."

"Right. But it places him at the scene the night Carl took his dive."

She took a sip of her coffee, letting the hot liquid sear some sense into her. "If he hated Indians, why did he save your life?"

His thumb made small swirls on her palm, distracting her for a moment. "We'll never know, but I spent all day with Justin. Either he wanted to make amends, because he could tell how hate had destroyed his mom, or he couldn't stand the idea of spending the rest of his life in jail."

Poor Justin. His hate had driven him to a place where he couldn't survive. She picked at the rest of her food, trying to put the events that led up to the four deaths—make that five—in order.

Derek sat quietly next to her. She appreciated he understood her need to think. When she finished, he lifted the tray from the bed. "You rest and I'll clean up."

\*\*\*

Derek tiptoed into the bedroom a while later. Kelly's face, though scratched on her cheek, looked peaceful, beautiful, and strong. Her eyelids fluttered open. She smiled and his heart expanded to fill his chest.

"You're awake," he said. He pinched the strap of her purse with two fingers and let it swing in front of him.

"What time is it?" She rolled over to face the alarm clock. "Oh, my, it's late." She looked up at him, and her eyebrows shot skyward. "My purse! How? When?"

"Medina just brought it over. The salvage company found it in the back of your car."

The light on her face disappeared. "And the car?"

He could tell she'd guessed the truth. "Crushed. Totaled. You're lucky to be alive."

"I know."

She plopped back against the pillow and closed her eyes again. A second later she sat up. "I wonder if everything is still in there. Have to get a new license and changing all my credit cards will be a nightmare."

Kelly shoved her hand in her purse and began to pull out her checkbook, make-up, a pack of gum, and a few pens and pencils.

She held up a round object, about a half-inch in diameter. "What's this?" She twirled it around in her fingers.

Derek stilled. He knew what the device was, but how had it found its way into her purse? "It's a tracking device."

Fear flooded her eyes. "Someone knew where I went?" She held up the device. "I never look in that side pocket. No wonder I never noticed it."

"I'm guessing Lilly planted this in your purse. Maybe that's how she knew we were in Utah."

Kelly rubbed her temples. "I feel...violated."

"I'll have my men check out your house. If she was able to track your whereabouts, she might have bugged your place."

"Derek?

"Yeah?"

"Tell me again that horrible woman is really dead."

He sat down on her bed and wrapped his arms around her. Kelly belonged in his arms. She was already deeply in his heart. "She's dead."

Sun streaming in the window made her hair glisten like diamonds. "Derek?"

He leaned back, tilted up her chin ,and searched her eyes. Gone was her fear, and in its place was need, want and... "What?" he whispered.

"Make love to me."

He went rock hard, and his mind couldn't form any words. The baser part of him wanted to pounce and conquer, but Kelly needed all the tenderness he could muster.

She pushed out of his embrace. "Let me do something about all these clothes first." She reached up and grabbed his shirt, and then undid one button. Then the next one. No surprise, she went agonizingly slow. In between each button, she leaned forward and kissed his chest.

"I can't take this anymore," he panted. His fingers itched to tear off his top.

"Be patient." She pulled back his shirt and licked a nipple. "It's Sunday. We don't have to work." Kelly rubbed her hands down his chest and stopped at his pants.

"You're killing me."

She widened her eyes and smiled. "I think you'll live." Her fingers gently squeezed his pulsing shaft, and he nearly came right there.

He drew his hands down to the hem of her gown and began to tug off her nightie, but she shook her head.

His mouth went dry. "Kelly, I don't know how long I can last with you torturing me like this."

She winked, and then with fierce determination managed to unbutton his jeans. Damn woman. "Let me," he said.

He leaned over and shucked off his shoes before stepping out of his pants. His bulging erection sprung from his boxers.

Her eyes widened. "Oh, my."

"Oh, shit," he said.

Her face fell. "What?"

"Condoms." He picked his pants up from the floor, pulled out his wallet, and ripped the condom from its hiding place.

"You carry them all the time now?"

He chuckled. "I was hoping to get lucky." Derek wasn't a fool to think Kelly loved him. She was grateful for saving her life, nothing more. But he wanted her. Always had. Always would. He would never stopped loving her.

As soon as he crawled onto the warm sheets, Kelly pulled off his boxers. In no time, he returned the favor. Naked, he rolled her on top of him, and then ran his hands down her back and over her lovely round butt—smooth, silky, and oh so sexy. He sniffed her hair. "Hmm. Lavender. I like it."

Kelly ran her hands over his stubbly head. "Maybe you should grow your hair."

"You sound like my dad." His heart turned heavy.

"What's wrong?"

"Right when you were kidnapped, Dad was taken to the hospital."

"Is he all right?" Her hands stopped.

"I called the hospital while you were sleeping. Lily claimed she'd poisoned him."

Her eyes widened. "Will he be okay?"

"Yes. Billy's with him now." Billy and his dad made a great pair. They needed each other and could learn from each other. Derek was at peace—at last.

"Who poisoned him?"

"Don't you remember her telling us?" He waved a hand realizing that much of Kelly's short term memory was probably gone. "Lilly Bladen. She was posing as Rayne's maid. After she killed Rayne, she went to work for Dad. It gave her the perfect opportunity to harm him too."

Kelly slowly shook her head. "How long had she worked for your sister? And why would she since she hated Indians?"

"It's only a guess, but I'm thinking she wanted to watch Justin. She'd already tried to frame him twice for murder. If at first you don't succeed, try... Well, you get it. When she learned Rayne was expecting, and that she was part Native American, the woman broke."

Kelly and he remained locked in an embrace, with her heart beating against his. They were one. "Kelly?" He wanted to tell her. Needed to tell her, even if she rejected him.

"Yes?" He leaned her back to see her face. Her dreamy expression made him push on. "I love you."

Without hesitating, she answered, "I love you too, Derek Benally."

He tensed. "But how? You think my visions are a figment of my imagination and that—"

She placed a finger on his lips. "Not anymore. I know that are real. If they hadn't been, you wouldn't have found me."

"True, but are you ready—"

"Shh. Let me finish. While I was sleeping, Stefanie came to me."

Derek leaned forward, forcing his heart to calm. "What do you mean she *came to you?*" He crooked his fingers to punctuate the words.

"I was dreaming, or at least I'm pretty sure I was, when I heard her voice. It was like she was right next to me."

"That's why dreams seem so real." He wanted to offer encouragement, not put words I her mouth.

"I swear Stef was right here. When she smiled, my heart nearly leaped from my chest. I reached to touch her, but couldn't."

He'd had the same experience when he'd dreamt of Kelly in the boxcar. "What did she say?"

Her gaze dropped to her hands. Surely she couldn't be embarrassed, especially after how he'd bared his soul. "It might not have been some out of body experience like you're used to, but it was real to me."

As if he wouldn't think visions were real? "And?"

"She said she was happy and wanted me to be happy too. Stef also said that we were right for each other."

He smiled so hard his cheeks hurt. "I wish I would have known your sister better."

A flash of sadness flitted across her face. "Me too, but I liked her message about being happy. She'd always encouraged me to love myself. I know she'll always be with me."

Derek had enough of talking. He wanted to make love to Kelly, needing to touch her, taste her, and show her how much she meant to him.

He ran his fingertips down her chest, between her breasts and over her flat abdomen. Oh, how he loved the sweet curve of her hips and how her soft triangle hid her mound of joy. Derek leaned her back against the bed and then slipped a finger into her opening. Kelly gasped.

She wiggled her butt, allowing his moist finger better access. He plunged another finger in her and kissed her belly. She moaned, and the sound sent him nearer to the edge.

Kelly tugged on his shoulders. "Come on, Derek. I can't wait any more."

"Patience, my love. Enjoy the moment."

"Kiss me."

He couldn't deny her anything. As he drew near to her delicious lips, she pushed on one shoulder to flip him over. Thinking he'd hurt her, he rolled onto his back. Never did he expect her to straddle him. The joy of seeing Kelly look down at him with love in her eyes nearly took his breath away.

With her hand, she guided his dick right into her. With as much control as he could muster, he clutched her hips and slowly pushed upward to reached the depths of her soul. He closed his eyes and could feel the power of his spirit guides fill him. His lids shot open, fearful they'd whisk him away.

"What's wrong," she asked.

He smiled. "Nothing. Nothing at all."

Massaging her wonderful breasts, she leaned her head back. Blood pounded in his ears, as his heart nearly exploded from joy. Derek eased in and the out, but Kelly seemed to want more. She lifted up and then dropped down. With each pass, her hips moved faster and faster. Time stood still. He thought both of them might have traveled someplace else until Kelly let out a cry of ecstasy. Without warning, he shot his seed into her.

A moment later she collapsed onto his chest, her breathing as fast as his. "I know it sounds clichéd, but did the earth move for you too?" she asked.

He laughed. "Oh, yeah." With Kelly by his side, he realized he could face and conquer any obstacle. "You better watch out. I don't want the spirit guides to come and take you away."

"As long as you come with me, I'll go anywhere."

"Now that's a promise I'm going to hold you to it."

\*\*\*

# EXCERPT—FROM TERROR TO TEMPTATION

*Don't forget to sign up for my newsletter to receive three free books, as well as up-to-date information on my stories. If you prefer to only receive notices regarding my releases, follow me on BookBub.*

✳✳✳

I hope you enjoyed Kelly and Derek's story. Up next is FROM TERROR TO TEMPTATION

**Trust or run? The wrong decision will be deadly.**

After losing three loved ones, Detective Dominic Rossi is an expert at keeping his distance from all things female—that is until he meets Tessa Redman, a woman who seems mighty troubled. She's definitely hiding something from him, but that only brings out his need to protect even more.

When a hot looking detective begins snooping around Tessa's bar, she panics, believing he's there on behalf of her ex-husband—a cop on the take who she turned in—a man who swore he'd kill her.

But Dom's random tenderness awakens something deep inside her, and while he doesn't seem anything like her ex, the guy is a cop—and a rich one at that.

Only after several of her patrons are murdered and her father is killed is she forced to decide: trust Dominic or run for her life?

Keep turning for a sneak peek at *From Terror To Temptation*.

**Here is the first chapter.**

*Charlotte, North Carolina*

About time she got here. Morton Richter ducked down in his seat just as Audrey Mae Thompson and her baby boy, Bobby, rolled to a stop at her duplex. He turned the ignition key to check the dashboard clock for the tenth time in the last hour. What had taken her so long to arrive?

Better not have been another man. His pulse spiked at that thought. *Don't even go the*re. Morton forced a calming breath. Think. She has Bobby with her, which meant she would have been visiting her mama. It was the only explanation.

He unclenched his fists, wiped his slick palms on the nubby seat fabric, and lowered his window halfway, sending in the cold air. He took another deep breath. *Shit*. Did it stink or what? It had been a bad idea to park next to the open dumpster, but he hadn't wanted Audrey Mae to spot him when she got home.

He wrinkled his nose, sat up, and placed the clunky binoculars on the top of the steering wheel, ready for a front row view of Audrey Mae in the flesh.

Damn, it was fucking cold. What'd he expect? He'd been sitting in his truck in the middle of November for three goddamn hours with the engine off.

*Hold on.*

Morton jerked to attention. She was getting out of her car. Just as Audrey Mae hauled little Bobby out of the backseat of her rusty, lime green VW, the front porch light flickered, and then went out. He hoped she'd remembered to pay her utility bill. It wouldn't do to keep a baby in a cold house.

Audrey Mae shifted her kid from one hip to the other as she stabbed her hand in her purse, probably looking for her house key. Good thing the moon was full so he could see her.

Morton started to slip out to give her a hand but then decided it was best to let her settle in first before he surprised her. A moment later, she slipped inside. The lamp in the window came on and cast a yellow-like glow in her postage stamp sized living room.

Through his lens, Morton watched her duck into the baby's room. As he waited for her to return, his foot tapped out a beat.

Sweet Audrey. So vulnerable. So in need of his care. Morton vowed he'd never hurt her child like his old man had hurt him. No. He'd be gentle, no matter if the kid stole his cigarettes or stashed porno mags under the bed. Kids deserved a little fun.

There. She was back with little Bobby now in his pajamas. Morton adjusted the focus ring to get a clearer image of her breastfeeding. Pride swelled. This morning he'd decided he had no choice but to take them away. Far away—where Bobby's no good father couldn't find him and abuse him.

Not wanting to waste any more time, he pushed open the truck door, and the hinge squeaked loud enough to wake the neighbors. *Damn.* If the car noise didn't alert her, the stupid mutt barking across the street would. The dog acted like someone had filleted one of its young.

"Shut up," Morton whispered in a throaty growl.

He hoped to God Audrey didn't question the dog's racket. Of course, around here, she probably didn't even flinch at a gunshot.

He tossed the binoculars behind the seat and closed the door real slow, but it still let out another groan. He needed to fix it, but not until after he took Audrey and the baby away from here.

Morton strode up to her place, wishing he'd brought a flashlight. Just his luck to step in dog shit.

He couldn't wait to see the expression on her face when she saw him in his spiffy new suit. He pretended it was his wedding suit. The flower he'd stabbed in his lapel made it look official too. It shouldn't matter to her the pink carnation was plastic.

Damn. He should have brought her flowers. All women liked flowers. And Audrey Mae was all woman.

He pressed her doorbell a couple of times, liking the sound of the chirping birds. Sweet. Like the woman inside.

"Who's there?"

Her voice came out too shrill, almost as if the sound had frightened her. Had Bobby's father come sniffing around and hurt her again?

"It's me, Morton," he said real slow, wanting to sound non-threatening.

"Go away," Audrey Mae shouted.

She couldn't mean it. The baby began to cry. "Now you've gone and upset Bobby," Morton bit back, trying not to become angry. When she didn't answer, a sharp pain stabbed him behind his eye. "Come on, Audrey Mae. Lemme in," he said with more force than before to make sure she'd hear.

He jiggled the storm door handle. *Shit*. It was locked.

"I told you I don't want nothin' to do with you," Audrey yelled back. "Do I need to get a restrainin' order or somethin'?" Her tone changed to sharp and demanding—real mean-like.

"Don't talk like that, honey. I want to help you and Bobby." He waited a beat, watching his breath frost on the glass.

She wedged open the main door and peered out. Her blondish red hair tangled about her shoulders and her jeans were a little too tight, but to him she looked like a ripe peach ready to be plucked.

"You can't come in. I told you we was finished." Audrey Mae's bottom lip firmed as she clasped Bobby closer to her chest and turned to the side.

"Please?"

*God. I sound pathetic.*

It was just like when he was ten, and he had to grovel in front of his dad to stop him from doing bad things to him.

"Go away!" She slammed the door in his face.

Anger rushed up his gut so fast he had to take a sharp breath to keep from ripping off the door.

"Bitch," he spat out.

Audrey wasn't any better than his no-good mama who'd ignored him when he needed her most. As he stalked back to his truck, Morton knocked the lid off from one of the trashcans. It pinged and rolled half way into the street. He hoped the whole goddamn neighborhood woke up.

Once in his truck, he stabbed the key into the ignition and took off, but he didn't go far. Oh no. Not far at all. He knew women. Audrey Mae would go running back to her mama. And he'd be right there behind her when she did.

From a block away, he pulled over to the curb where he could watch her house. He'd wait for as long as it took. He had no place else to go.

Sure enough, twenty minutes later, Audrey Mae came sneaking out with her bundled up baby and a suitcase. She looked so like his mama, all scared and whimpering, bent over like she was waiting for a beating.

What had he seen in Audrey anyway? Oh yeah. She was a woman with a child who had a bad ex hanging around—a woman who needed protecting.

Her headlights flashed on, and she raced out of her driveway, heading toward Charlotte, where her mama had an apartment. Morton wasn't sure exactly where the older woman lived, but he knew it was somewhere in town.

Keeping a few car lengths behind, he kept an eye on her as she sped up. Audrey took a corner too fast and her VW skidded toward the curb. His heart raced, fearing for Bobby's life. He wanted to yell at her for being so careless, but he knew scared women never listened.

She pulled to a stop at the signal then turned around toward the baby. She obviously had no clue he was two car-lengths behind.

Speckle-like rain drizzled on his windshield, and he wanted to warn Audrey to drive more careful, to tell her the roads would be slick, but before he could get his hand on the door handle to jump out, the signal turned green and Audrey Mae took off, the car's rear end fishtailing through the intersection.

A van, traveling along the cross street going super-fast ran the red light then slammed on its brakes. Tires squealed as the huge vehicle swerved left and then right. Not having enough space to stop, it crashed into the side of Audrey's small car.

Metal crunched, sparks flew. *Oh, shit.*

Audrey's car got squashed.

"Noooo." Morton ripped open his door refusing to believe the two people he'd wanted to protect the most might be dead.

***

*Four years later*

"Ohmigod," Chelsea said. Waiting for the Blue Moon's Bar to open, the waitress hopped up on the barstool and spread the Tampa Tribune on the shiny bar. "Listen to this, Tessa. A woman was shot to death in her car two nights ago on Bayshore Boulevard."

Tessa Redman looked up at the waitress and stopped polishing the counter. Bayshore was less than two miles away. "How horrible." Thinking about a killer on the loose caused a chill to race down her spine. "Maybe I'll ask Judd if I can beef up the lights in the parking lot."

Chelsea's shoulders visibly relaxed. "Great idea. I hate going out by myself at night. It's creepy sometimes."

"Tell me about it." Tessa returned to disinfecting the bar, wrinkling her nose at the strong bleach smell. Her mind reeled with the horror the woman must have experienced in the last few seconds of her life.

Tessa finished cleaning, tossed the rag into a bucket of soapy water, and then stacked the liquor bottles behind her. The crinkling of the flipped page brought Tessa back to the incident, and she stepped in front of Chelsea. "Do the police have any leads?"

The waitress ran a bright red, well-manicured nail farther down the newspaper column. "Not really. All it says is the time of death was around midnight."

"Hmm. Even at that time, I'm surprised no one heard the gunshot."

"Maybe everyone was sleeping."

"Or no one could be bothered."

Chelsea bobbed her head up and down. "I can see that." A hint of regret filled her tone. "Hey, maybe the guy used a silencer."

Before Tessa could speculate on the series of events, the doublewide front doors opened, sending in a shaft of bright sunlight through the dimly lit restaurant, silhouetting a large man. Cool, salt air from the bay filtered in along with him.

"We open at eleven," Tessa announced.

"That's all right," he replied as the doors swung shut behind him. "I just need some information."

As he neared the bar, last night's peanut shells crunched under his commanding steps. He looked down, and then returned his gaze to her face. A narrow cone of light from the overhead lantern illuminated the angle of the man's face. *Whoa.* The sharp plane of his face and powerful shoulders caused her breath to catch, and her heart did an unexpected flip—a sensation she hadn't experienced in...forever.

He held up his police badge, and her heart almost stopped before it raced, and blood rushed from her face. "What do you want?" The panic in her voice made her sound guilty, even to her.

"I'm Detective Dominic Rossi with the Tampa PD. I'd like to ask you a few questions."

The detective's piercing gaze had Tessa grabbing for the edge of the bar. "What about?"

"A woman was killed near here two nights ago. We have reason to believe she might have visited the bar before she was murdered. Were you working Wednesday night?"

Tessa nodded to Chelsea. "Would you mind seeing to the table set ups?" Her heart continued to pound.

"Okay," Chelsea said, pursing her lips, clearing wanting in on the action.

Tessa turned back to the cop, and a lump formed in her throat. "Yes, I was here."

The detective plucked an envelope from his shirt pocket, stepped closer to the bar, and slid a photo toward her. "Do you recognize this woman? I'm sorry it's rather graphic."

Tessa let out a pent up breath. Apparently this cop only wanted a name. She'd be happy to help any way she could and leaned over to get a closer view. The bone-white face of the woman resting against a half open car window grabbed the breath out of her. A trail of blood ran from the woman's blond hair ran down to her neck.

"Ohmigod." Unfortunately, the angle of the photo failed to give Tessa a good look of the woman's face. She tilted the photo toward the light hoping for a better view. "She's kind of familiar, but I can't place her." Her heart thudded at the gruesome scene.

"Her name's Keri Wilkerson. We found a set of matches on her front seat with the Blue Moon's name on it." He pulled out a notepad and flipped to a yellow Post-it tab. "It also had a phone number inside. 813-555-8395."

Her number. Goose bumps raced up Tessa's arms. "I remember her now." She'd told the distressed woman if she needed to talk to call her at home. "She was here Wednesday night."

"Do you remember if she was with anyone?"

Tessa visualized where Keri sat at the bar. "No, she was by herself. I don't remember her talking to anyone but me."

"How did Mrs. Wilkerson seem?"

Tessa pictured the woman—shoulders slumped, mascara blurred under her eyes, but dressed in designer jeans. "Sad, confused, angry."

"Did she say why?"

The larger-than-life cop lifted a lean hip onto the stool and focused on her face as if memorizing it. Tessa didn't like the scrutiny and forced a calm she didn't feel.

"Her eyes were red, and her face was splotchy when she arrived. I could tell she'd been crying. The woman, Keri, came in and ordered a double scotch on the rocks. She downed her drink in a few chugs and ordered another. I couldn't forget her. For quite a while Keri just stared, not saying a word. After about an hour, I asked her if anything was wrong, and she blurted out she'd caught her husband in bed with a man."

His brows arched. "You sure she said a man?"

"Yes. Keri suffered from overwhelming guilt, as if she was somehow to blame for her husband's deception and change of lifestyle."

The detective neatly printed her information in his pad. "Do you remember what time Mrs. Wilkerson left?"

"Not exactly, but I think it was a little before midnight, right before we close."

His face remained unreadable as he continued to jot notes. "May I have your name?"

"My name?" Her heart stuttered.

"Yes."

Did she dare tell him? "Why?"

"For the record."

"Oh. Ah, Tessa." His hand stilled in midair, obviously waiting for her last name. "Redman. Tessa Redman."

His pen went to work again, and she prayed her name wouldn't ring a bell.

"Are you the owner?" He glanced up, his piercing blue eyes locking onto her face.

"No, my half-brother, Judd Redman, owns the Blue Moon."

"Was he around Wednesday night?"

Her stomach turned queasy thinking about Judd's condition. "I'm afraid he's been in and out of the hospital for the last few weeks."

"I'm sorry." His sincere tone surprised her. "What time did you leave here that night?"

"It was after one. I stayed to work on the books since Wednesday is my bookkeeping day, or rather night."

"Can anyone vouch for your presence?"

"No." She tried not to show her annoyance. "What are you implying?"

"I'm not implying anything, ma'am, just doing my job."

As if she'd have anything to do with a murder. *Please.* Tessa glanced over to Chelsea cleaning a tabletop a few feet away, no doubt listening to every word.

The detective looked down at his hands for a split second. "I know you're not open for business yet, but could I have a drink?"

His abrupt shortening of the interview threw her. What was he up to? Was he just another cop needing to take the edge off the horrors of his job? Or was he here for another purpose?

"I'm sorry. I don't serve on-duty policemen."

He lifted his head and seemed to fight a smile. "I meant a Coke. I'll pay."

Heat rose to her cheeks. "Sure. Sorry."

Some psychologist she was going to be. She needed to be more careful about jumping to unwarranted conclusions.

Tessa drew the drink from the tap and handed Detective Rossi the glass. Their fingers touched for a brief moment causing a shock of electricity to bolt up her arm. She jumped back so fast, she felt like a fool.

The cop's long, broad fingers had unsettled her, reminding her of someone else. Tessa choked back her anxiety, picked up a clean rag, and began to polish the spotless, wooden bar again, hoping the detective wouldn't notice her discomfort. The last thing she needed was the exposure of a criminal investigation.

The detective took a large gulp of soda and eyed her above the lip of the glass. "Is there something you're not telling me?"

"N-no."

Chelsea sauntered up to the detective, slid onto the stool next to him and leaned close. "Do you have any other cases you need help with?" She ran a nail down the Pledge can, slow and easy.

Tessa made a silent promise to give the girl a bonus for distracting the policeman.

The detective scanned Chelsea from head to toe before turning back toward the bar. "No."

"Tessa," one of her cooks called, sauntering out of the kitchen, the swinging double doors clacking close behind him.

"Excuse me," she said to the detective, relieved to get away from him. "And Chelsea? Work awaits." She turned and strode toward Roger. "What is it?" She failed to keep the exasperation from her voice.

Roger shuffled his feet from side to side and stuck his hands in his pockets. "We're out of chicken," he announced in the slowest southern drawl she'd ever heard.

"You're kidding. That's like a bar being out of beer. How could this have happened?" she whispered, not wanting the cop to overhear their conversation. She didn't need this aggravation.

"I dunno. Walt does the ordering."

She checked her watch. "And where is Walt?"

His lips firmed for a split second before shooting his gaze shot to the floor. "He's not here."

Obviously. "So what would Judd do in this case?" she asked, praying Roger would offer a quick solution.

"Get some more?"

*Duh.* "Look, we open in forty-five minutes. Can you run down to the store and buy whatever we need?"

Roger let out a long breath and rolled his eyes. "I suppose so."

The kitchen help around here sucked. What had her brother been thinking when he hired these guys? She made a mental note to speak with Judd. On second thought, maybe not. He didn't need the added stress when he was so ill right now. She'd have to handle the crisis herself.

As soon as Roger disappeared into the kitchen, she looked up Walt's number and called him. She kept her back rigid and turned away from Detective Rossi.

"Uh-huh?" Walt answered.

Oh God, she'd either woken him up or he had a hangover. "Walt, where are you? It's after ten already."

"Who's this?"

"Tessa. Your new boss. Remember?" She didn't wait for him to answer. "You're supposed to be at work."

"I quit yesterday." He yawned loudly into the phone. "Charley was supposed to tell you."

Charley, her taciturn bartender, wouldn't bother telling her if the restaurant was on fire. "Why didn't you tell me? Did something happen?" If she could understand his dilemma, she might be able to help.

"I'm moving back to Alabama. Sorry. Didn't my friend show up? He needs a job, and I told him to stop by."

"No."

"He's a good guy and really needs the work. Just don't judge him by his past. Listen, I gotta go."

"I don't—"

He hung up on her. Damn it. Tessa dropped the receiver back onto the cradle and swiveled on her heels. She was half way back to the cash register to check on the change drawer when the phone rang again. She threw up her hands. "What is this? I-4 in rush hour?" she mumbled as she marched back. "Hello?" This time she didn't sound so nice.

"Ms. Redman, please."

Tessa glanced toward the detective, wondering what was going through his mind and why he was still here. His elbows were planted on the counter, his gaze solidly fixed on her. Not a hint of expression laced his face.

"This is she." She kept her voice low. Maybe it was Walt's friend telling her he'd found another job. Wouldn't that suck?

"Ms. Redman. This is Grady Jankowski from the Jankowski Development Company."

Her body tensed, ready for battle. She'd needed the caller to be the cook, not the jerk who kept bugging her every few days about selling the place. She had to believe her brother would recover soon. He loved the Blue Moon, and he didn't need some sleazy developer to come in and liquidate his pride and joy.

"Mr. Jankowski, as I've told you before, the restaurant's not for sale. Please don't call here again."

"Thanks for the Coke, Ms. Redman," the detective called out as she pressed the disconnect button. She whipped around to face him. He smiled and her heart sped up. "Seeing you at work has been an enlightening experience."

Before she could question him what he meant, he tossed a few dollars on the counter and walked away.

✳✳✳

"Rossi," Dom's partner, Phil Orloff, sang out as he walked into his office and tapped him on the shoulder.

"What?" Dom swiveled in his desk chair to face Phil.

"We have a homicide to solve or don't you remember?"

Dom remembered all right. He wished he could forget the way the black gunpowder stippled the Wilkerson woman's temple or the angle at which her head slumped against the steering wheel. Her vacant eyes kept haunting him. They were so much like his mom's eyes after the burglar killed her and Dad. The memory of the bullet hole in each of their heads made his stomach sick.

"Yeah, what about it?" Dom said between clenched teeth.

"Did anything at the restaurant pan out?" Phil leaned against the gray metal desk and crossed his arms, reminding Dom of a damned commando—tough and ornery.

Dom relaxed. "We were right about the victim visiting the Blue Moon the night she was murdered. Ms. Redman, the bar's manager, told me the Wilkerson woman said she found dear hubby in bed with another man the night she died."

Phil whistled. "Now there's something we didn't suspect."

"No kidding." Dom drew the keyboard closer to him, ready to work on the report.

Phil leaned closer. "I know the look on your face. What aren't you telling me?"

Dom sat up. He knew Phil's bulldog tone meant he'd never leave him alone until he gave up the info. "Ms. Redman isn't coming clean. I can feel it. I tell you, Phil, the woman looked downright scared the moment I walked into the bar. I've never seen such wide eyes. Talk about being fidgety. She couldn't wait to get rid of me."

"Well, that's because of your ugly mug," Phil answered without a trace of humor in his eyes.

"I'm serious."

"So am I." He flashed a smile then sobered. "Did you run her name?"

"Of course, but nothing popped up." Dom leaned back in his chair. "Did you check to see when the autopsy would be back on Keri Wilkerson?"

"I did. You should have the results by the end of next week."

"Next week?"

"The woman's only been in the morgue two days," Phil said. "You know how overloaded they are."

"I know, but just this once—" Dom waved a dismissive hand. "Never mind. Did you get anything on the victim's relatives?"

Phil straightened, pulled out a notepad and riffled through the tattered pages. Dom shook his head. The guy needed to get some kind of PDA.

"It's here somewhere," Phil said then smiled. "Yup. Here it is. Only living relative in the area was her husband, Taylor Wilkerson, aged forty-five. I checked out his alibi. He was at the Tampa Art Museum fund raiser until 10:30 p.m. before heading to a party on Davis Island until 2 a.m."

Dom whistled. "On a Wednesday night? Even I'm too old to be partying that late on a work night, and I'm ten years younger."

Phil chuckled. "You? Party? When was the last time you had fun? As in F-U-N?"

Ever since Lisa died, Phil was always worried about him, but he wouldn't confide in his partner if he ever did go out. The whole precinct would have a memo detailing his actions by morning. "None of your business. What else you do you have?" Dom kept his tone even.

"I can take a hint," Phil said. His grin did nothing to calm Dom's stomach. "Let's see." He ran a finger down the pad. "Jimmy finished canvassing the neighbors, but as you might expect, nobody saw anything." Phil looked up.

"No surprise. See what dirt you can dig up on Wilkerson's love interest."

"I'm on it." Phil shoved off Dom's desk and strode back to his own.

Dom studied Keri Wilkerson's file again. There wasn't much he could do until the reports came in. As his palm brushed his short-cropped hair, he contemplated his next move.

The smell of burnt coffee wafted over to him. What he wouldn't give for a cup of his specially mixed Kenyan blend right now, but he'd have to settle for the crap Sergeant Cantori was brewing—that or toothpicks to keep his eyelids open.

As he picked up his blue coffee mug, the exact color of Tessa's eyes, he could almost see her glaring at him. Pretty eyes, but one that held a well of guilt. Her knee-jerk reaction to his simple questions implied she was troubled. Now all he had to do was find out why.

The End

# ABOUT THE AUTHOR

Love it HOT and STEAMY? Sign up for my newsletter and receive MONTANA DESIRE for FREE. Click here

OR Are you a fan of quirky PARANORMAL COZY MYSTER-IES? Sign up for this newsletter. Click Here

Not only do I love to read, write, and dream, I'm an extrovert. I enjoy being around people and am always trying to understand what makes them tick. Not only must my romance books have a happily ever after, I need characters I can relate to. My men are wonderful, dynamic, smart, strong, and the best lovers in the world (of course).

My Paranormal Cozy Mysteries are where I let my imagination run wild with witches and a talking pink iguana who believes he's a real sleuth.

I believe I am the luckiest woman. I do what I love and I have a wonderful, supportive husband, who happens to be hot!

**Fun facts about me**
(1) I'm a math nerd who loves spreadsheets. Give me numbers and I'll find a pattern.
(2) I live on a Costa Rica beach!
(3) I also like to exercise. Yes, I know I'm odd.

I love hearing from readers either on FB or via email (hint, hint).

## Social Media Sites

**Website**: www.velladay.com
**FB**: www.facebook.com/vella.day.90
**Twitter**: velladay4
**Gmail**: velladayauthor@gmail.com
**Tiktok**: Velladayauthor1

# ALSO BY VELLA DAY

## SILVER LAKE SERIES (3 OF THEM)

### (1). <u>HIDDEN REALMS OF SILVER LAKE</u> (Paranormal Romance)

Awakened By Flames (book 1)

Seduced By Flames (book 2)

Kissed By Flames (book 3)

Destiny In Flames (book 4)

Box Set (books 1-4)

Passionate Flames (book 5)

Ignited By Flames (book 6)

Touched By Flames (book 7)

Box Set (books 5-7)

Bound By Flames (book 8)

Fueled By Flames (book 9)

Scorched By Flames (book 10)

### (2). <u>GODDESSES OF DESTINY</u> Paranormal Romance)

Slade (book 1)

Rafe (book 2)

Will (book 3)

Josh (book 4)

Box Set (books 1-4)

Jace (book 5)

Tanner (book 6)

### (3). <u>WERES AND WITCHES OF SILVER LAKE</u> (Paranormal Romance)

A Magical Shift (book 1)

Catching Her Bear (book 2)

Surge of Magic (book 3)

The Bear's Forbidden Wolf (book 4)

Her Reluctant Bear (book 5)

Freeing His Tiger (book 6)

Protecting His Wolf (book 7)

Waking His Bear (book 8)

Melting Her Wolf's Heart (book 9)

Her Wolf's Guarded Heart (book 10)

His Rogue Bear (book 11)

Box Set (books 1-4)

Box Set (books 5-8)

Reawakening Their Bears (book 12)

## OTHER PARANORMAL SERIES

### PACK WARS (Paranormal Romance)

Training Their Mate (book 1)

Claiming Their Mate (book 2)

Rescuing Their Virgin Mate (book 3)

Box Set (books 1-3)

Loving Their Vixen Mate (book 4)

Fighting For Their Mate (book 5)

Enticing Their Mate (book 6)

Box Set (books 1-4)

Their Huntress Mate (book 7)

Craving Their Mate (book 8)

## PACK WARS-THE GRANGERS

Meant for them (book 1)

Meant for wolves (book 2)

Meant for forever (book 3)

Meant for her (book 4)

## HIDDEN HILLS SHIFTERS (Paranormal Romance)

An Unexpected Diversion (book 1)

Bare Instincts (book 2)

Shifting Destinies (book 3)

Embracing Fate (book 4)

Promises Unbroken (book 5)

Bare 'N Dirty (book 6)

Hidden Hills Shifters Complete Box Set (books 1-6)

## CONTEMPORARY SERIES

## MONTANA PROMISES (Full length contemporary Romance)

Promises of Mercy (book 1)

Foundations For Three (book 2)

Montana Fire (book 3)

Montana Promises Box Set (books 1-3)

Hart To Hart (Book 4)

Burning Seduction (Book 5)

Montana Promises Complete Box Set (books 1-5)

Novellas:

Montana Desire (book 1)

Awakening Passions (book 2)

## PLEDGED TO PROTECT (contemporary romantic suspense)

From Panic To Passion (book 1)

From Danger To Desire (book 2)

From Terror To Temptation (book 3)

## BURIED SERIES (contemporary romantic suspense)

Buried Alive (book 1)

Buried Secrets (book 2)

Buried Deep (book 3)

The Buried Series Complete Box Set (books 1-3)

**A NASH MYSTERY** (Contemporary Romance)

Sidearms and Silk(book 1)

Black Ops and Lingerie(book 2)

A Nash Mystery Box Set (books 1-2)

**STARTER SETS (Romance)**

Contemporary

Paranormal